SEDUCING THE HEIRESS

If the Slipper Fits

OLIVIA DRAKE

St. Martin's Paperbacks

This is a work of fiction. All of the characters, organizations, and events portrayed in this novel are either products of the author's imagination or are used fictitiously.

IF THE SLIPPER FITS

Copyright © 2012 by Barbara Dawson Smith.

All rights reserved.

For information address St. Martin's Press, 175 Fifth Avenue, New York, NY 10010.

ISBN: 978-1-250-00177-1

Printed in the United States of America

St. Martin's Paperbacks edition / June 2012

St. Martin's Paperbacks are published by St. Martin's Press, 175 Fifth Avenue, New York, NY 10010.

10 9 8 7 6 5 4 3 2 1

Chapter 1

1836

It all began with a letter.

While the rest of the teaching staff sat down to dinner, Annabelle Quinn hurried along the gloomy corridor at Mrs. Baxter's Academy for Young Ladies. The loud knocking echoed again through the entrance hall, and in her haste, Annabelle nearly tripped on one of the cracked tiles in the foyer. She steadied herself with a hand on the newel post before proceeding to the door.

It was highly unusual to receive a visitor in the evening. The pupils were already settled in their dormitory, and she and the other teachers would soon retire for the night. Few people ever came to this remote country school in the moors of Yorkshire, only the vicar and the occasional tinker or deliveryman.

The massive front door creaked as she opened it. Framed by the purple dusk, a stoop-shouldered stranger in the garb of a workman stood on the porch. "Ye took yer sweet time," he grumbled while shoving a letter at her. "I was paid to put this straight into yer hand."

Orphaned at birth, Annabelle had never received a letter. "*My* hand? But who—?"

The man ignored her questions. He clomped down the steps and climbed onto a sway-backed nag. With a flick of the reins, he went trotting off down the drive.

She turned over the sealed note with great interest. Her mind resurrected a buried dream from her childhood: a long-lost relative arriving to declare that Annabelle had been stolen at birth, and offering to whisk her away into the arms of a warm and loving family . . .

The last light of dusk fell upon the front of the envelope. She blinked at the elegant spidery script. It was addressed to the headmistress.

Annabelle felt instantly foolish. Of course the letter wasn't meant for *her*. The man had been instructed to give the note to someone—anyone—at the school rather than drop it into the postbox by the door where it would not be noticed until the morrow.

In all her twenty-four years at the boarding school, first as a charity student and then as a teacher, Annabelle could not recall a single other instance in which Mrs. Baxter had received a letter by special delivery. If this message couldn't wait until the midday post, it must be extremely important.

The thought gave wings to her feet as she hurried back along the murky corridor to the dining chamber at the rear of the ancient converted manor house. There, she paused in the doorway.

Candles in pewter holders cast a meager illumination over the long table laid with crockery and tin flatware. The aroma of roast beef and potatoes drifted from the covered dishes on the sideboard. The dozen teachers sat listening while Mrs. Baxter read aloud in a gravelly monotone from her well-worn Bible.

Annabelle debated whether or not to interrupt. Did she dare to break the rule of silence during these nightly readings? But what if the letter conveyed urgent news? Wouldn't she then be scolded for not speaking up at once?

She cleared her throat. "I beg your pardon."

Mrs. Baxter stopped in mid-verse and scowled over a pair of rimless reading glasses. A skeletal woman with a bony bosom, she had gray hair scraped back into a bun and covered by a lace widow's cap. "Have you so little regard for the holy Scripture, Miss Quinn?"

"Forgive me," Annabelle murmured, deeming it wise to lower her chin in humility. "But you've received a letter by special messenger."

"No earthly correspondence could be more important than the heavenly Word." The headmistress clapped the Bible shut. "However, since you've been so bold as to interrupt, don't stand there like a dolt. Bring the letter to me at once."

A muffled giggle emanated from one of the teachers, followed by the murmur of whispered conversation. Annabelle knew without looking who they were, razor-tongued Mavis Yates and her dull-witted disciple, Prudence Easterbrook. They were two peas in a rotten pod.

The other women avoided Annabelle's gaze as she walked toward the head of the table. Almost too late, she spied Mr. Tibbles lying beneath the headmistress's chair. The orange tabby cat was Mrs. Baxter's pride and joy—and a bane to everyone else.

As Annabelle handed over the letter, Mr. Tibbles hissed a warning. His green eyes looked demonic in the candlelight and his long tail flicked back and forth on the carpet. Having been scratched in the past, Annabelle wisely backed away and slipped into the single empty chair at the long table.

Mrs. Baxter broke the seal and unfolded the paper. As she scanned the message, her pinched features took on an unusual animation. Twin spots of pink appeared in her waxen cheeks. "Why, this is extraordinary. Most extraordinary, indeed!"

"Is something wrong, ma'am?" asked Mavis in the toadying manner she always used with the headmistress. "I should be happy to lend assistance in any way you wish."

"As would I," Prudence chimed in. "Unless of course it is a private matter."

Removing the glasses from the bridge of her nose, Mrs. Baxter gave her favored two teachers a distracted smile. "How very kind, but your concern is misplaced. It seems I am to have the honor of a visitor from London on the morrow, a fine lady from the royal court. She will wish to meet the staff, so you must all wear your very best."

The news set the dining room aflutter. "The royal court?" chimed several teachers. "Who is she?" "Is she bringing her daughter to study here?"

"Her name is Lady Milford and she is seeking a governess for the young Duke of Kevern in Cornwall. She will be interviewing a select number of you for the post."

Annabelle sat riveted. Cornwall! It seemed as distant and exotic as China or India. For many years, she had yearned to see the sights beyond the insular world of the school. On the rare free day, she would hike the moors and imagine what lay beyond the barren, windswept hills. Hungering for knowledge, she'd read every geography book in the library. She'd pored over maps of England and foreign countries, places with fascinating names like Egypt and Constantinople and Shanghai. She had studied and dreamed and saved when the other teachers had spent their wages on new gowns and ribbons and other frivolities.

Now this was her chance to escape the tedium of teaching manners to giggly young girls concerned only with fashion and gossip. She would have to carefully consider what to say in the interview, how to present herself as the ideal tutor for a young aristocrat . . .

As Mrs. Baxter glanced around the table, her gaze stopped on Annabelle. Those pale eyes took on a distinct chill. "Miss Quinn, you must instruct the maids to clean my parlor from top to bottom. And since you will not be participating tomorrow, you'll have ample time to assist the other teachers in any needlework they might require. Run along now, and close the door on your way out."

The joy drained from Annabelle. She was being banished. She would not be granted a coveted interview. The colossal injustice of it overruled all caution.

She stood up from the table, the chair legs scraping the wood floor. "Please, I should very much like the opportunity to meet Lady Milford."

"Do you dare to gainsay me?" Mrs. Baxter said in tight-lipped astonishment. "I have issued an order and you will obey it."

"But I'm as well prepared as anyone else here to be governess to a duke, perhaps more so. I've studied Latin and Greek, I'm adept at mathematics, well versed in science and literature—"

"Your qualifications are of no consequence. My lady visitor will wish to hire someone from a respectable family. She would never consent to employ a bastard who cannot even put a name to her own parents."

The scornful words echoed in the cavernous dining

chamber. Mavis and Prudence had the audacity to smirk. The other teachers regarded Annabelle with pity or discomfiture. Although most of them were pleasant enough, they would not align themselves with her for fear of being ridiculed, too.

Her cheeks burned with humiliation. It took an effort to harness the impulse to lash out in anger. Protesting further would only invite the headmistress's wrath— typically in the form of docking Annabelle's already paltry wages. She couldn't afford to lose a single ha'penny of her nest egg.

She curtsied to Mrs. Baxter, then walked out of the dining room and shut the door. Annabelle paused there in the dim corridor with her head cocked, trying to discern meaning in the muffled drone of Mrs. Baxter's voice. What was the headmistress telling everyone? Was she giving them instructions on how to act and what to say? Was she announcing the order in which they were to meet Lady Milford?

Realizing her fists were clenched, Annabelle gulped several deep breaths. Wild emotions must not goad her into another impassioned outburst. Better to have a clear mind so that she might determine rationally how to proceed.

One thing was certain, she would not relinquish this golden opportunity. A chance like this might not come along again—ever. By hook or by crook, she *must* finagle her way into an interview.

Shortly after luncheon the following afternoon, the rattle of carriage wheels outside disrupted the discipline in Annabelle's classroom. One minute, the group of fifteen-year-olds paraded in a dignified circle, each girl balancing a book on her head to learn proper posture. The next minute, several students broke rank and rushed to the windows overlooking the front of the school.

"Why, will you look at that!" exclaimed Cora, a redhead with a dusting of freckles over her elfin face. "Have you ever seen such a splendid coach?"

Beside her, a plumpish brunette pressed her nose to the glass and peered downward at the drive. "Who could it be?" Dorothy asked. "Do you suppose it's a new girl? But why would anyone so rich be coming here—and after the term has already begun?"

Annabelle clapped her hands. "Ladies, it isn't polite to stare. Come back here at once."

"Oh, *please,* Miss Quinn, do spare us just a moment," Cora said, casting an imploring glance over her shoulder. "Don't *you* want to find out who's come to call?"

They could have had no inkling that Annabelle already knew, or that her insides were twisted into a knot. The visitor had to be Lady Milford.

For the umpteenth time, Annabelle fretted over how best to present her credentials to the lady. It was a quandary she'd pondered into the wee hours, sewing by the light of a single tallow candle, repairing rips in hems and attaching new lace to the gowns worn by the other teachers today. While she'd labored, she had considered and rejected numerous plans. The fly in the ointment, of course, was Mrs. Baxter. The headmistress would be keeping a sharp eye on the proceedings. But if all went well, there might just be a way—

The thump of falling books yanked Annabelle's attention back to the classroom. The rest of the pupils had seized upon her silence as an invitation. They made haste to crowd around Cora and Dorothy at the windows.

The buzz of their excitement infused Annabelle, too. As a former charity student, she knew the ennui of endless classes in deportment, art, music, and other skills necessary to become a lady. How could she scold the girls when she herself felt an irresistible curiosity?

Maintaining a semblance of dignity, she strolled to join them. For once her tall stature proved a boon. Peering over the heads of the students, she studied the vehicle that rolled up the graveled drive.

The girls were right to ooh and aah.

A team of four white horses drew the cream-colored coach with its fancy gold scrollwork decorating the door. Large gilded wheels glinted in the dappled sunlight. A coachman in leaf-green livery drove the equipage, while a pair of white-wigged footmen perched at the rear.

Annabelle forgot herself and stared openly. Never before had she seen a sight so magnificent. The girls here were mostly commoners, the daughters of local landowners, and they tended to arrive for the term in pony carts or sturdy carriages suitable to the country.

This coach, however, had sprung straight out of a fairy tale.

The fine vehicle drew to a halt in front of the portico. One of the footmen leaped down to lower the step and open the door. A moment later, a woman emerged from the vehicle. Petite and slim, she wore a waist-length black mantelet over a turquoise gown with a fashionably full skirt. A black-veiled bonnet embellished with peacock feathers hid her features from view.

All at once, she cast an upward glance. For one piercing moment, she seemed to stare through the dark tulle straight at Annabelle. Then the woman lowered her head and started up the steps to the porch.

The incident unnerved Annabelle. The skin prickled at the nape of her neck and she stood frozen, her gaze locked on the figure below. How ridiculous to think that keen look had been directed at her. More likely, Lady Milford had merely been inspecting the façade of the school.

Mrs. Baxter appeared on the porch. The headmistress sank a deep curtsy and exchanged a few words with her guest. Then the two women vanished into the ivy-covered stone building.

A collective sigh rippled from the girls. They turned away from the window to chatter among themselves.

"Do you suppose she might be Princess Victoria?" Dorothy asked in a reverent tone.

"At this backwater school?" Cora said with a toss of her reddish ringlets. "Hardly. Besides, Princess Victoria is only seventeen and *I* think this lady looks quite a bit older."

Annabelle said nothing, though she privately agreed. There was a mature dignity in the way Lady Milford had moved, a graceful self-assurance that made Annabelle feel gauche and countrified in her much-mended gown of drab gray worsted wool. How did she dare hope such a vision of elegance would hire her?

She shook off the question. Misgivings would win her nothing. Her credentials were all that mattered. That, and her determination to present herself as the best possible candidate for the post.

Dorothy clasped her pudgy hands beneath a dimpled chin. "Miss Quinn, you simply *must* find out her name. Please, we shall die of curiosity if you do not."

A clamor arose as the other girls chimed their agreement.

"All in due time," Annabelle said. "In the meanwhile, you must practice your posture so you'll know how to comport yourselves someday in the presence of such fine ladies."

Grumbling, the pupils resumed parading around the room while balancing a book on their heads. But an atmosphere of liveliness lingered, affecting everyone's concentration. More than once, a girl squealed as her tome thumped to the floor. The others giggled and whispered among themselves.

Annabelle was too distracted to scold them. The impatience to put her plan into motion gnawed at her composure. But it was too soon, she told herself. Better to wait a while and give Lady Milford an opportunity to chat with the headmistress and to enjoy refreshment from the tea tray.

Annabelle bade the class return to their desks where they took turns reading aloud from a book of manners. Scarcely listening, she eyed the wall clock as it ticked away the sluggish minutes. It seemed an eternity— although no more than three-quarters of an hour had passed—when finally the bell rang and the girls left in a chattering horde, some for drawing classes and pianoforte lessons, others to a choir rehearsal.

Annabelle followed them into the passageway. Her heart kicking up a few beats, she opened a door hidden in the dark paneling and started up the steep wooden staircase used by the servants. While Mrs. Baxter and Lady Milford were interviewing the other teachers, Annabelle had time to set her trap.

With any luck the plan would work. It *had* to work.

The tapping of her footsteps echoed in the narrow utilitarian shaft. The other teachers used the main staircase, but she often took this shortcut to avoid encountering the headmistress, who was wont to pile on extra tasks if she suspected Annabelle had a bit of free time.

Now, she reached the third-floor corridor. Here lay the dormitories for the pupils and bedchambers for the teachers. Annabelle hurried along the passageway, stopping only at a linen closet to fetch a pillowcase. Then she went straight to Mrs. Baxter's quarters.

The door was ajar as usual. The headmistress liked to allow Mr. Tibbles the freedom to come and go as he pleased. Jittery at the notion of being caught, Annabelle glanced up and down the passageway again, then slipped into the bedchamber.

Brocaded green curtains and dark mahogany furniture created a rich, cavelike décor. The scent of stale roses hung in the air. At any other time, she might have been tempted to explore the forbidden place, but not today. Today, she had to find Mr. Tibbles.

"Here, kitty, kitty," she crooned.

The tomcat usually napped up here during the day; she had seen him saunter down the stairs in late afternoon. But now he was nowhere to be found. What if the tabby had changed his habit? That was the one circumstance that worried her. He could be anywhere in the house—or even outdoors.

Annabelle peeked under the bed, in the dressing room, and inside the cabinetry. The ticking clock on the mantelpiece served as a reminder that time was growing short. She was about to give up and seek him elsewhere when the tip of an orange tail moved between the window curtains.

Drawing back the drapes, she found the cat curled up in a patch of sunlight on the sill. He glared balefully at her and bared his teeth in a hiss. "Nice Mr. Tibbles," she murmured, leaning closer, the pillowcase at the ready. "I do need you to be a good boy—"

The cat's paw lashed out, leaving four stinging red lines on the back of her hand.

Annabelle sucked in a breath through her teeth. Then she threw the pillowcase around the little devil and scooped him up. Immediately he transformed into a wriggling, spitting ball of fury. She grimly held on to the cat, the bleached white linen protecting her from the full force of his indignation.

"I *did* try to do this nicely," she told the tabby, while carrying him into the dressing room. "It was *you* who declared war."

Without further ado, she opened a clothes press at random and dropped the bundled cat onto a pile of petticoats. She yanked off the pillowcase and shut the lid quickly.

He howled and scratched inside the chest. But there was no way he could escape. He'd be safe enough for a few minutes, she reasoned, until Mrs. Baxter came charging to his aid.

Annabelle retreated down the stairs, this time going all the way to the ground floor where she peeked out into the corridor. Her gaze swept past the landscape paintings darkened by age and the straight-backed chairs set against the paneled walls, to the closed door at the end of the passage. To her surprise, no queue of hopeful teachers waited outside the parlor.

Alarm niggled at her. What if she had trapped Mr. Tibbles for nothing? What if Lady Milford had hired the very first applicant? What if Mrs. Baxter had recommended Mavis Yates for the post and the matter was already settled?

No, surely the lady would wish to view all the prospects. Deciding upon a duke's governess had to be serious business. Not that Annabelle knew much of the ways of the aristocracy. She'd never had occasion to meet any nobleman beyond a stuffy old viscount who had once delivered his daughter to school here.

The thought rattled her confidence—but only for a moment. She adjusted the spinster's cap that covered her dark hair and then used her fingertip to rub away the traces of blood left by Mr. Tibbles's claws. Nothing could be gained by dithering. It was time to seize her future.

Her arms swinging, she strode boldly down the corridor. She would knock on the door, send Mrs. Baxter off on the rescue mission, and then use the opportunity to beg an interview.

The ploy would work. It *would*.

She had nearly reached the parlor when the rustle of fabric caught her attention. From out of a nearby chamber stepped Mavis Yates.

Chapter 2

Mavis sprang forward to block the door. The long brown ringlets that framed her dark eyes and narrow face brought to mind a floppy-eared hound. A russet gown sheathed her stocky figure, and her nostrils flared as if she were sniffing for vermin.

"You were ordered not to come here," she said, her chin tilted high. "I was correct to assume you would disobey."

Annabelle fabricated a pleasant smile. The last thing she needed was a guard dog standing in her way. "Lying in wait for me, were you? Are you so doubtful of your own ability to earn the post of governess?"

"Certainly not! Lady Milford *will* choose me, she made that quite clear by her praise for my many superior qualities."

So Mavis had had her meeting already. Annabelle glanced at the polished oak door. Who was in there now? "Yet the lady is presently interviewing another contender, is she not?"

Mavis curled her lip. "That is merely a formality. Mrs. Baxter has promised me a glowing recommendation."

"How wonderful for you."

"Indeed, her ladyship was most impressed by my impeccable lineage." Mavis cast a superior look at Annabelle. "My father was a vicar, and we can trace our ancestry back to the finest families in England. Of course, one must pity those poor souls who were born on the wrong side of the blanket and know nothing of their heritage."

"Mmm." Annabelle knew better than to react to the slur. "Well, perhaps I should point out that all your hopes will be for naught if the door opens and Lady Milford catches sight of you lurking out here."

"Lurking—"

"You will appear to be a snoop, and that would hardly speak well for your character, would it? The position of duke's governess requires someone who is exceptionally discreet."

Swallowing the bait, Mavis edged away from the door. "Hush! Do keep your voice down."

"It might be wise for you to leave here at once. That will solve the problem altogether."

Annabelle shooed the other teacher down the corridor. Her brow furrowed in worry, Mavis complied, but only for a few steps. Then she stopped dead and planted her fists on her wide hips.

"Hussy!" she snapped. "You want me out of the way so that you can lie to her ladyship and steal my new position. Well! Your plan will fail, Mrs. Baxter will see to that."

"I'm sure you're right. Which is why you may safely depart from here without a care in the world."

Annabelle reached for the door handle, but Mavis dashed to stop her. "No! You can't go in there. You mustn't—"

The door opened abruptly. On the threshold stood Prudence Easterbrook, her dumpy form squashed into an olive-green gown with too many ruffles. Her squinty brown eyes moved to Mavis—who had flattened herself to the wall beside the door—and then to Annabelle.

"What's this?" Prudence said stupidly. "No one else is supposed to interview. I am the last one."

"I've an urgent message for Mrs. Baxter." To Mavis, Annabelle whispered under her breath, "Do stay out of sight. May I remind you, eavesdroppers do not make trustworthy employees."

With that, Annabelle brushed past them and stepped into the parlor. The cloying odor of beeswax and wood smoke stirred an echo of dread in her. As a girl she had endured many a scolding here and an occasional whipping with the willow switch that was stored in a tall vase beside the door. The punishments had been her own fault for being cursed with a tart tongue. Eventually she had learned to control her headstrong temper, swallow her pride, and behave with humility.

She did so now, assuming an expression of modesty as she approached the two women sitting by the fireplace. In contrast to the spartan furnishings accorded to the teachers and pupils, Mrs. Baxter's private parlor was decorated as richly as her upstairs quarters. Red velvet hangings framed the tall windows. A rosewood desk sat against the wall. Every table and shelf bore china shepherdesses and porcelain cats and other bric-a-brac. A grouping of chairs and chaises stood before the marble mantelpiece, where a wood fire crackled merrily.

Annabelle's gaze settled on Lady Milford, who occupied an ornate chair rather like a throne. Her posture was perfect, her gloved hands resting on the gilded arms. The peacock-feathered hat still sat at a jaunty angle atop her head, but the black veil was drawn back to reveal a face of arresting beauty. She had dark hair and violet eyes, and her skin bore fine lines of age that gave her features a look of distinction.

When she turned her head toward Annabelle, one slender brow quirked upward. It was an expression not of haughtiness, but of keen interest. The scrutiny made Annabelle feel as if she were being assessed and evaluated. Discomfited, she saw herself through Lady Milford's eyes, a too-tall woman in a much-mended dress of unflattering gray.

In an effort to redeem herself with good manners, she sank into a deep curtsy. "My lady," she murmured.

"Miss Quinn! Whatever is the meaning of this?"

Mrs. Baxter's strident voice pierced the air. Her skull-like features were drawn with displeasure. It would take just the right words to avoid making her suspicious.

Annabelle rose to her feet and schooled her face into a look of concern. "I beg your pardon, ma'am. Something has happened that requires your immediate attention."

"Whatever it is can wait until my guest departs. Now run along." With a dismissing wave, she turned to Lady Milford and her voice took on a syrupy sweetness. "My lady, pray forgive the rude interruption. It's such a trial to have insolent servants who do not obey orders."

Annabelle gripped her fingers into fists at her sides. Servant! How demeaning to be placed beneath the rest of the teaching staff. The slight made her all the more determined to succeed in her scheme.

She took a firm step forward. "I'm afraid this is terribly important. It's about your cat, Mr. Tibbles. He's trapped."

Mrs. Baxter's face went pale. She lurched to her feet, a lace handkerchief pressed to her thin lips. "Trapped? What do you mean?"

"He somehow climbed into one of your clothes-presses. Perhaps one of the maids left it open and then he knocked the lid shut. I heard him yowling when I passed by your chamber a moment ago."

Mrs. Baxter hastened forward. "He isn't injured, is he?"

Annabelle pictured the fat old tabby sulking on a soft bed of petticoats. "I can't say, but he was mewling most pitifully."

"Useless girl, why didn't you let him loose?"

Annabelle displayed the scratches on her hand. "I did try, ma'am, but you know how he snarls and lashes at everyone but you." She paused, then added the coup de grâce. "With the way he's carrying on, I fear he could cause himself a great harm."

"Oh!" Gasping, Mrs. Baxter turned to her guest. "Pray excuse me, my lady. This should take only a few moments."

A bubble of elation made Annabelle giddy. Praise God, her plan had worked. But her triumph was short-lived.

As the headmistress started toward the door, she seized Annabelle by the arm. "Come along. You're not needed here."

The glint in her eyes revealed mistrust. Even in a dither about her cat, Mrs. Baxter had the wits to keep Annabelle firmly in her place.

"Oughtn't I stay?" Annabelle said. "My next class doesn't begin for another half an hour. Perhaps her lady-ship wishes for me to bring her refreshment."

"She needs naught from a lowborn chit like you." With a firm grip, Mrs. Baxter yanked Annabelle forward. "Now, silence that impertinent tongue of yours. It's time you learned to speak only when spoken to."

Annabelle wanted to dig in her heels. Yet creating a scene would only serve to discredit her in Lady Milford's eyes. Bitterly, she acknowledged that Mrs. Baxter had already besmirched Annabelle's character. Now she might never have a chance to present her credentials and win her escape from the school.

"Let her stay." Lady Milford's dulcet voice held an unmistakable ring of command.

Looking dumbfounded, Mrs. Baxter turned, still clutching Annabelle. "My lady?"

"You said that I had interviewed all the teachers. But apparently you have forgotten this one."

"Because she's eminently unsuitable. Surely you cannot wish to hire a governess of questionable birth—"

"Nevertheless, I will have a word with Miss Quinn. You may go now."

Mrs. Baxter reluctantly retracted her claws from Annabelle's arm. She skewered Annabelle with a warning glare before scurrying out of the room.

"Pray close the door so that we may converse in private," Lady Milford said.

Annabelle hastily obeyed. In the doing, she caught a glimpse of Mavis and Prudence dashing after Mrs. Baxter, no doubt to complain about the unfairness of Annabelle being allowed an interview. Let the biddies squawk. For once, Annabelle had the upper hand and she intended to use it to her best advantage.

Fortified by the thought, she rehearsed her qualifications as she approached Lady Milford. She halted in front of the noblewoman and stood with her hands clasped in a respectful pose. It was vital that she accomplish her purpose before Mrs. Baxter returned.

"My lady, I—"

Lady Milford held up a silencing hand. "One moment. You will have ample time to speak."

She sat gazing up at Annabelle, assessing her critically, and Annabelle tried not to stare back for fear of being rude. By what criteria did Lady Milford judge the applicants? If it was fashion sense or pedigree, then Annabelle was doomed.

Her confidence faltered. Never before had she met anyone so elegantly lovely. In the turquoise gown and black hat with its peacock feathers, Lady Milford brought to mind an exotic creature from a foreign land. What had attracted such a refined noblewoman to this remote country school when she might have hired someone from London? Was she perhaps visiting friends or family in the area? The answer didn't signify. All that mattered to Annabelle was securing the post for herself.

"Miss Quinn, I've a suspicion you devised that excuse to come in here," Lady Milford said. "May I presume you are interested in the position of governess for the Duke of Kevern?"

"Yes, my lady. If it isn't too forward of me, I'd hoped you might consider my application."

Lady Milford inclined her head in a slight nod. "It is essential that I interview every teacher on staff so that I might make the best choice. Serving a duke is a great honor, no matter how young he might be."

"How old is His Grace, if I may ask?"

"Nicholas is eight and the great-grandson of a very dear departed friend of mine. The child will be going off to boarding school in a year or so, and I worry about his readiness to leave home. You see, he lost both his parents last year in a tragic accident."

Annabelle had surmised his father was deceased, else the boy wouldn't have succeeded to the title. But she hadn't realized he was an orphan. Her heart ached to imagine his loneliness. Perhaps she herself was lucky never to have known her parents at all. "I'm so sorry to hear it," she murmured. "That must have been a dreadful time for His Grace."

"Quite so." Lady Milford glanced over at the dancing flames on the hearth. "Nicholas was always a rather quiet boy, and now he has withdrawn even more. That is why I believe he needs more than just tutors and nursemaids." She looked straight up at Annabelle. "I believe he needs the affection of a mother."

A mother? Annabelle's mouth went dry. What did she know about mothering? Of all the requirements that could have been named, that was the one in which she lacked even a smidgen of experience. The one in which the other teachers held the advantage over her, for they all had come from families in the area.

"Surely the duke has aunts or cousins who might fill that role."

"I'm afraid there's only an uncle, his guardian, Lord Simon Westbury. He is a rather . . . difficult gentleman." Lady Milford smiled enigmatically, then waved a hand at the chaise. "Now do sit down, Miss Quinn. You are quite tall and I've no wish to strain my neck."

"Oh! Of course." Annabelle quickly lowered herself to the edge of the cushions and folded her hands in her lap. Truly, the interview was not going as she'd envisioned. Her ladyship might very well believe one of the other teachers more suited to the task of *mothering* an orphaned boy. It would be wise to emphasize her strengths before

Mrs. Baxter returned to malign Annabelle's character even further.

She took a deep breath. "My lady, please know that I'm prepared to devote myself to watching after the duke. Let me assure you I'm more than capable of guiding his education, too. I'm knowledgeable in the subjects he will be studying: mathematics, botany, literature, geography, and much more. Whatever it is you wish for him to learn, I should be more than happy to work diligently with him until he masters the—"

Lady Milford held up her gloved hand. "I'm sure that is all quite true. I am an excellent judge of character, and you strike me as an intelligent woman, someone who is eminently qualified to teach the boy. That is why I would rather spend this time learning more about you."

Annabelle hardly knew whether to be jubilant at the praise or worried at the prospect of any probing into her background. Cautiously, she said, "What do you wish to know?"

"First, what is your Christian name?"

"Annabelle, my lady."

That slight, inscrutable smile returned to Lady Milford's lips. "How very pretty. Is it a family name?"

"I . . . I have never been told so," Annabelle hedged.

"I see." Lady Milford tilted her head to the side. "I find myself curious about your connections. From where do you hail?"

Annabelle kept her fingers laced tightly in her lap. The last topic she wanted to dwell upon was her pedigree—or lack thereof. Her only hope was to skirt the issue. "I've always lived right here in Yorkshire, my lady. Perhaps that's the source of my desire to seek another position. I should very much like to experience life in another part of England. I would be very content to devote myself to the care of His Grace."

"How did you come to be an instructor at this school?"

Clearly, her ladyship would not be distracted. All manner of fibs and tall tales raced through Annabelle's mind. She had prayed that a miracle would happen and she would not be asked about her past. But perhaps there was no escaping the truth. If she didn't confess, then Mrs. Baxter surely would do so upon her return.

She lifted her chin, prepared to be rejected for her misbegotten birth. "I've been told, ma'am, that I was left here on the doorstep of this school as a babe in swaddling clothes. I do not know by whom."

There, she had spoken it aloud. Would her ladyship assume her to be of the same low moral fiber as her nameless parents? Most people did. Her mother must have been a fallen woman. As to her father, for all Annabelle knew, she might be the daughter of a plowman or a blacksmith or even a highwayman. And as such, she would be unacceptable as companion to a duke.

Lady Milford leaned forward slightly. "Did Mrs. Baxter ever attempt to find out who had abandoned you?"

Abandoned. The word stirred a faint bitterness in Annabelle as she shook her head. "She wasn't the headmistress at the time. The school had a previous owner who died when I was not quite five."

Annabelle glanced down at her entwined fingers. She hadn't thought about that in years. From out of the past came vague memories of a soft voice crooning a lullaby, of gentle hands brushing her hair . . .

"A pity," Lady Milford mused. "I don't suppose you will ever know, then."

Annabelle wished desperately that she could read the woman's inscrutable features. Although Lady Milford didn't look aghast at the story, perhaps she was too well-bred to show her distaste.

"Pray consider the advantage of my having no family," Annabelle said, determined to turn the situation to her benefit. "I shan't ever be called away to nurse a sick relation or beg leave to attend a wedding or a funeral. If you employ me, I shall be always at the service of His Grace, utterly devoted to his care. You can be certain he will never want for my attention."

"You make quite the persuasive case, Miss Quinn." Her violet eyes watchful, Lady Milford lowered her voice. "However, there remains one final test."

Test? Annabelle wondered what it would entail. Perhaps she would be required to write an essay on why she was the superior choice for the position. Or maybe she'd be quizzed on her knowledge of geography or literature. The prospect actually calmed her misgivings. Whatever the examination might be, she felt confident in her ability to perform better than any other teacher on staff.

Then Lady Milford did something odd. Rising from her chair, she came forward to sit beside Annabelle on the chaise. "If you would be so kind as to slip off your shoes."

"Pardon?"

The lady gestured at Annabelle's feet. "Take them off, please. I know it sounds peculiar, but do bear with me. You'll understand in a moment."

She had brought a long velvet reticule, and now she opened the drawstrings and reached inside to produce a pair of fine slippers, which she placed on the floor. Annabelle blinked in surprise. The high-heeled shoes were made of satin the rich color of garnets and covered in exquisite crystal beadwork that sparkled in the light of the fire.

"Ohh," she said on a sigh. "I've never seen anything so beautiful."

"It's merely an old pair given to me by a friend a long time ago," Lady Milford said. "It seemed a shame to let them molder in my dressing chamber. Would you mind trying them on?"

"But . . . you're so dainty," Annabelle said, unable to tear her gaze away from the dazzling sight of the slippers long enough to think clearly. "Surely it's impossible that we'd wear the same size."

"You'll never know until you try."

Feeling caught in a strange spell, Annabelle unhooked her sturdy shoes and tugged them off, one by one. Brown and ugly, they thumped onto the carpet, a sacrilege beside the fine offering from Lady Milford.

Reverently, she slid her toes into one until, miracle of miracles, the elegant slipper perfectly enveloped her foot. It didn't pinch or rub like her cheap shoes, either. The satin felt as soft and supple as wearing a cloud. Quickly, she donned its match and then rose from the chaise, holding up her skirts to admire the slippers. This must be how a princess felt, she thought giddily. Beautiful in every way.

On impulse, she whirled around on tiptoe, imagining herself dancing in the arms of a handsome prince. "Oh, my lady, they *do* fit. How can it be?"

"It appears they were meant for you," Lady Milford said. "You will do me a great favor to take them off my hands."

Annabelle stopped short as reality doused her dreams.

Her fingers tightened around the bunched skirt of her gown. "Surely you're jesting. You cannot *truly* mean to give me such an expensive gift."

"Well, if it will pacify your conscience, you may consider them a loan. That is my only concession. You must humor me, for I am an old woman known for my eccentricities."

Wisdom shone in those violet eyes. How old *was* she?

The question vanished as Annabelle gazed down wistfully at the slippers. They were so very tempting, and yet so impractical. "But where on earth would I wear such lovely shoes?"

"There may be a ball or party at Castle Kevern. In the country, a governess is often expected to attend such events if there are not enough ladies to balance the guest list." She gave Annabelle a critical look up and down. "In addition to traveling expenses, it appears you will need a clothing allowance to improve your wardrobe. One cannot appear a beggar when serving in the household of a duke."

From out of Annabelle's swirling thoughts came one crystal-clear realization. "Does that mean . . . you're hiring me?"

A secretive smile touched Lady Milford's mouth. "Indeed I am. I can think of no one more perfect for the post than you."

Chapter 3

As the mail coach drove away, Annabelle stood beside her battered trunk and glanced around the deserted inn yard at the edge of the village of Kevernstow. Chickens pecked at the bare earth and a few horses grazed in a stone-fenced meadow behind the stables. The inn was little more than a two-story cottage with a thatched roof. A faded sign depicting its name, the Copper Shovel, creaked in the breeze.

Where was the cart that was supposed to convey her to the castle? Before departing the academy on the day Annabelle had been hired, Lady Milford had promised to send a letter ahead making all the arrangements. But there was not a soul in sight.

Grabbing hold of the leather handle, Annabelle dragged the trunk toward the inn. The action kicked up dust and soiled the hem of her gown. She felt stiff and weary after journeying for two and a half days, crammed inside a mail coach with an ever-changing array of travelers. More than anything, she longed to reach Castle Kevern. She certainly didn't want to be forced to wait here for transportation.

The inn door stood open. Pausing on the threshold, she rapped on the wooden panel while peering into the dim interior. A peat fire smoldered on the hearth, but no one sat at the scattered tables. Was the innkeeper napping upstairs? Had he gone on an errand in the nearby village? The arrival of the daily mail coach was surely an important event in such a remote area. So why wasn't he present?

"Hullo?" she called out. "Is anyone here?"

Silence answered her. Leaving the trunk outside by the door, she went across the yard and peeked into the stables. The cool shadows held no sign of life, the horses having been turned out into the fenced pasture. Annabelle ventured behind the inn and found a yard bordered by the great dome of a hill. A patch of straggly vegetables grew in the sunlight, while laundry flapped from a rope strung between two large oaks.

At the rear of the property, the door to the privy creaked open and a stooped old man stepped out. In the process of hitching up his breeches, he caught sight of her and came forward at a trot.

"Missed the mail, did I?"

"Yes, sir." Annabelle pretended not to notice him tucking the homespun shirt into his waistband. Since this region was to be her new home, she deemed it sensible to make acquaintants. "Good afternoon, I'm Miss Quinn. And you are?"

"Pengilly, miss." Bobbing his head, the aging innkeeper gave a toothless grin. "Otis Pengilly."

He thrust out his hand and she shook it, thankful for her gloves. "It's a pleasure to meet you, Mr. Pengilly. Would you happen to have seen a cart from Castle Kevern today? It should have been sent for me."

He scratched a thinning patch of gray hair. "Blaamed if I have."

Pursing her lips, Annabelle glanced up at the afternoon sun. If she tarried too long, she'd be forced to spend a few precious coins on a room at the inn. Hadn't Lady Milford mentioned the castle was located only two miles from the village? "I'll walk, then," she said. "Can you show me the way to the castle?"

Stabbing a knobby finger at a point beyond her shoulder, he said, "Take the path beyond the paddock. Cross the brudge and up the nip."

Brudge? Nip?

Before she could ask for a translation, he nodded at the dark clouds on the distant horizon. "Best be a-goin', miss. There be a bank-up fer a good blaw."

A storm, she interpreted. He believed a rainstorm was imminent. Yet the sky was a hazy blue overhead and any squall looked to be hours away. Accustomed to invigorating hikes over the moors, Annabelle felt certain she could reach her destination long before the rain struck.

She made arrangements for him to watch her trunk until someone from the castle could be sent for it. Then she set off in the direction he'd indicated. As she passed a jagged boulder at the edge of the property, Mr. Pengilly called out after her.

"Come the gloaming, mind the piskies."

She turned back. "Pardon?"

His hands cupped to his mouth, he shouted, "If 'ee spy any wee folk in the wood, take a care not to look lest'n they bewitch 'ee."

Pixies! The realization of his meaning tickled her fancy. Surely he had to be teasing. But Mr. Pengilly looked quite serious about the warning.

Waving a cheery good-bye, Annabelle headed along the trail that meandered over a series of small hillocks. It was a lovely late summer afternoon, warm and mild. Birds twittered in the trees, and the musical trickling of a stream drifted from somewhere up ahead. The sound grew louder until she came upon a stone bridge that spanned a brook.

Ah, the *brudge*.

Annabelle laughed aloud. It seemed she would have to learn the local dialect. *Up the nip* must refer to the steep path on the other side of the water. There, the trail led up a hill shrouded in trees and shrubbery.

She tramped over the quaint bridge. Minnows flitted through the water, playing tag among the rocks. Were she not on a mission critical to her future, Annabelle might have stopped to enjoy the peacefulness of the setting.

But now was no time for dreaming. She wanted to assume her responsibilities as soon as possible, to meet the young duke and settle into her new life. The thought made her smile. How wonderful it would be to care for one small child rather than to teach endless classes in deportment.

Gripping her skirts, she hiked up the hill. This surely could not be the main road to Castle Kevern. Mr. Pengilly must have sent her on a shortcut, for the path was too narrow to allow passage of a vehicle. Besides, there were no ruts to show that any wheels had ever traveled here.

Annabelle reached the top of the rise and stopped to catch her breath. Before her lay a panorama of wooded hills and green valleys where tiny white dots of sheep grazed amid a patchwork of farms. The pastoral setting made a sharp contrast to the approaching storm.

Inky black clouds filled the entire horizon. In the distance, the sea churned with white-capped waves. Annabelle stared in awe. Although she'd read about the ocean in books, nothing could have prepared her for its vast grandeur. Against that dramatic backdrop, the gray stone towers of a medieval fortress brooded atop a cliff.

Castle Kevern.

A thrill coursed through her. The magnificent sight brought to mind stories of King Arthur and his knights of the Round Table, the scandals of the Tudor royalty, the ill-fated romance of Tristan and Isolde . . .

Lightning cut a jagged line through the dark sky, followed several seconds later by the ominous rumble of thunder. A cold gust tugged at her straw bonnet and knocked it off her head. The ribbons remained tied, however, so she let the hat dangle at the nape of her neck.

Not even the impending shower could dampen her high spirits.

As she made her way down the sloping path, Annabelle marveled again at the lucky happenstance that had brought her here. One of the other teachers might have been chosen for the post of governess. Indeed, all of them had been green with envy, Mavis and Prudence in particular. Mrs. Baxter had been miffed, too, though she had not dared to gainsay Lady Milford. But after the lady departed, the headmistress had vented her spleen, accusing Annabelle of being everything from a conniving usurper to a disobedient hussy who would come to a bad end.

Annabelle had been too pleased with her good fortune to pay much heed. She felt no regret at leaving her old life behind—except for her students, who had given her a fine gray silk shawl as a farewell gift. Although the school was the only home she'd ever known, and she'd miss the girls and her few friends among the staff, it was all a part of her past now. The future lay before her, filled with glorious possibilities.

As if to refute her, the wind tossed a fistful of raindrops ahead of the storm. The afternoon grew steadily darker as the black clouds scudded closer to blot out the sun. Brambles tugged at the hem of her gown, but she pulled herself free and forged onward. This vast acreage had to be the ducal lands. Crofters and tenant farmers would be needed to work the squares of cultivated fields. Yet she saw no one on her trek. Maybe they were all tucked inside their cottages to wait out the tempest.

Nearing the final ascent, she noticed a muted rhythmic noise and realized it was the crashing of the waves on the shore. The battlements loomed high above her on the cliff. To reach there, she must ascend a steep path that vanished into a thick patch of forest.

The dense canopy of trees created an eerie twilight. Other than the sea, the only sounds were the scuffing of her shoes and the occasional growl of thunder. Even the birds had taken refuge ahead of the squall. The preternatural hush made it seem as if a wicked spell had been cast over the castle and its surrounding lands.

Come the gloaming, mind the piskies.

The fine hairs prickled at the back of her neck. Annabelle shook off a vague uneasiness. How ridiculous to feel as if she were being watched. Holding up her skirts, she concentrated on navigating the rocky trail. She was stepping over a fallen tree limb when something moved out of the corner of her eye.

Annabelle pivoted sharply. Bracing her hand on the rough bark of a tree trunk, she scanned the area. Her gaze locked on one spot where something stirred in the bushes. The leaves quivered low to the ground. Her heart pounding, she waited to see an elfin figure step out . . .

A fat hedgehog waddled into view. Oblivious to Annabelle's presence, the little animal vanished again into the underbrush.

She laughed out loud. Pixies and faerie folk, indeed! Such mythical creatures roamed only in the pages of storybooks. She mustn't succumb to flights of fancy or she'd scare herself silly.

A bolt of lightning lit the sky and thunder crashed. Annabelle needed no further incentive to resume her climb. Urgency dogged her steps, and she kept her gaze on the path to keep from stumbling. At last she neared the top of the hill. Ahead loomed a grassy sward and then the castle wall, although she could not yet see the entry gate—

A man stepped out from behind a huge granite boulder. Tall and menacing, he blocked her path. "What are you doing here?"

"Sir!" She stopped dead to avoid bumping into him. "You frightened me."

Swift as lightning, he clamped his fingers around her upper arm. "I'll do more than that if you don't answer me."

Annabelle yelped, the sound lost to a crack of thunder. She yanked in vain against his iron grip. "Stop! Let me go!"

"Not until you tell me why you're here."

His aggressive stance intimidated her. He was strongly muscled, a man in his prime. Was he a castle guard? Surely not, for he wore the rough homespun shirt and breeches of a common worker.

Though her heart pounded, Annabelle fixed him with the cold stare she used on disobedient students. "I shall answer nothing when treated so roughly. Remove your hand from me at once."

He glowered down at her. His eyes were a metallic

gray against the browned skin of a man accustomed to laboring outdoors. The wind whipped his black hair into unkempt disarray.

A strange and unsettling tension stirred inside Annabelle. Never in her life had she stood so close to any man, let alone one so hostile. He could overpower her if he chose, so she let her glare convey the message that she would not go down without a fight.

He abruptly loosened his grip and withdrew his hand. "I will have your name. You're trespassing on my land."

She blinked. *His* land? How could that be? The duke was only eight years old. "Doesn't this property belong to His Grace of Kevern?"

The stranger gave a curt nod. "He's my nephew."

Realization flooded Annabelle with chagrin. This rude, scruffy man was none other than Lord Simon Westbury. He was the young duke's guardian—and her employer. Although it galled her, she had to ignore his discourtesy or risk losing her position here before she'd even begun.

"I'm Miss Annabelle Quinn," she said, extending her gloved hand. "You must be Lord Simon. I'm pleased to make your acquaintance."

His harshly handsome features radiated suspicion. He frowned at her fingers until she drew them back. "So you know who I am," he said on a note of irony. "Whatever it is you're peddling, I'm not interested. Now, get along with you."

Turning on his heel, he strode away toward the castle.

Peddling? Why would he think her a traveling peddler when she carried no goods?

Baffled, Annabelle hastened after him. "Did you not receive a letter from Lady Milford? It should have arrived a few days ago."

He stopped, his scornful gaze raking her from head to toe. "Why would Clarissa send you here? If she's match-making again, she ought to have had the good grace to choose a more likely prospect."

What an utter boor! He would benefit from a lesson in manners. Not, of course, that she dared to tell him so.

Annabelle gritted her teeth and forced a smile. "It appears you don't know, my lord. I'm to be the duke's new governess."

Lord Simon's scowl deepened. "The devil you say! The boy already has a tutor . . . Blast it all!"

As if in reprimand for his cursing, the heavens opened and the storm unleashed its full fury. Cold sheets of water drenched them. Annabelle raised her arms in a futile at-tempt to shield herself. The hard driving rain instantly blurred her vision and chilled her to the bone.

"Damned beast of a gust," he muttered. His brawny arm clamped around her back as he propelled her toward the castle. Hampered by her sodden skirts and buffeted by the wind, Annabelle struggled to keep up. All of a sudden, Lord Simon grabbed her like a sack of flour and pinned her close to his side while plowing swiftly through the storm.

The radiant heat of his body enveloped her. Of their own volition, her arms latched onto him. She instinctively turned her face to the protection of his shoulder in an effort to avoid the buckets pouring down from the sky.

His strides long and effortless, Lord Simon carried her through the torrent. She let herself be borne along by the immutable force of his strength. A part of her was scandalized by the way she was plastered against his muscled body. But the need to reach shelter prevailed over maidenly modesty.

He followed close to the castle perimeter, rounded

the corner, and bypassed a massive iron gate. Blinking away the droplets, she noticed he was heading toward the cliff. The rush of waves on the rocks below penetrated the drumming of the rain. For one horrifying instant she feared he meant to toss her over the precipice and into the sea.

She struggled against him. "No—"

Water sluicing down his face, he grimaced at her. His lips moved, but whatever he said was lost to the banshee cry of the wind. He shouldered open a small wooden door in the gray stone wall and stepped inside out of the downpour. At once, he unceremoniously released her.

Annabelle stood dripping in the tunnellike passageway. Rubbing her arms, she shivered from the loss of his body heat. She prayed the gloom hid her blush. How foolish of her to imagine, even for a moment, that he'd intended to commit murder. The wildness of the storm must have addled her senses.

That, and the novel sensation of being held by a man.

Combing his fingers through his wet hair, Lord Simon cast an irritated glance at her. He clearly viewed her as a nuisance. She could only imagine how utterly unlike a proper governess she must appear in her bedraggled garb. Would he send her packing as soon as the rain died down?

"M-my lord," she said, her teeth chattering, "if—if you'd permit me to explain m-my presence here—"

"Come," he snapped.

His boot heels rang on the flagstone floor as he strode away down the corridor. Resentment locked her in place. Did he think her a dog to obey his command?

Then prudence asserted itself, and she made haste to follow him. He had every right to issue orders, Annabelle reminded herself. Who was she but a lowly servant? Worse, she was a mere *applicant* for the post of governess since the position she had believed to be hers now appeared in grave jeopardy.

Her wet shoes squelched on the stone floor. All of her earlier optimism had vanished, leaving her confused and uncertain. Oh, *why* hadn't he been expecting her arrival? Lady Milford's letter must have gone astray. Yet the problem was more than just that. He appeared to have no knowledge whatsoever of any governess being engaged. It begged the question as to why her ladyship had neglected to obtain the approval of the duke's guardian.

Lord Simon started up a narrow winding staircase with Annabelle close at his heels. Rain blew through a window slit. In spite of her anxiety, she looked around with interest. By the rounded walls, this must be one of the towers. The stone steps were worn in the middle from centuries of usage. She felt a keen desire to learn the history of the castle. Would she have that opportunity?

Her stomach twisted. The prospect of being sent away hung over her like a guillotine. She couldn't return to Mrs. Baxter's Academy. She had burned her bridges there. Anyway, to resume her former life would mean giving up her dreams of adventure. She shuddered to think of withering away as an old maid, confined to the prison of the school, never to experience anything of the outside world . . .

The man who held her fate in his hands walked ahead of her. He led the way down a long corridor decorated by dusty old tapestries and shields hanging on the stone walls. With his lord-of-the-manor arrogance, he fit the gloomy ambiance to perfection. She imagined him in knightly armor and helm, crushing his opponents in a tournament, and afterward, striding triumphantly to join his lady . . .

Annabelle stared at his broad back. *Did* Lord Simon have a wife? Surely not. Lady Milford had said the young duke had no female relatives to take the place of his mother. Given his boorish manners, Lord Simon probably frightened off all decent women.

He was grumpier than Mr. Tibbles.

Annabelle clapped a hand to her mouth to stop an untimely giggle. She mustn't compare her potential employer to a spiteful tomcat. And truly, her situation was too dire for humor. Though perhaps if she didn't laugh, she might weep.

He halted by an open doorway. His critical gaze flicked to her bosom, then returned to her face. "You'll need dry clothing. I don't suppose you've brought any."

Does it look like I have? She squelched the sarcastic retort. "My trunk is at the inn. I had no means to transport it here."

His scowl deepened. "I'll have the housekeeper find you something. The moment you've changed, you're to come straight to my study."

As surly as ever, Lord Simon turned his back on her and stalked down the corridor. Annabelle parted her lips to remind him that she didn't know her way around the castle. But perhaps it would be best to keep her own counsel. Asking him for anything, even directions, would only encourage him to view her as weak and dull-witted, unfit to be governess to a duke.

Annabelle shivered. The chill she felt had more to do with the precarious state of her future than her saturated gown. She would not—could not—allow his misogyny to daunt her. Somehow, she had to make herself indispensible to Lord Simon Westbury.

Chapter 4

Seated at his desk, Simon focused his eyes on the accounts book that lay open before him. Or at least he attempted to focus. Twice already he had begun adding a long column of numbers in his head, only to lose his place and have to start all over. The first time, he had been distracted by a crash of thunder outside; the second by the loud pop of a log settling in the fireplace.

He jammed the quill back into the silver inkpot. The damned chamber was too dim, anyway. Although the casement clock showed only half past five, the overcast sky had brought on an early twilight.

Pushing back his chair, Simon grabbed a branch of candles and prowled to the hearth. He held one taper to the flames and then used it to light the others. Yet even with the added illumination on his desk, he felt no inclination to resume his tedious task.

His moody gaze flicked to the letter half tucked beneath the blotter. He picked it up, reread the message, and then threw down the paper in disgust. Blast it all! Clarissa had gone too far this time. She had presumed upon a long-ago friendship with his late grandmother in order to undermine his authority.

Why had she done it? Did she truly believe he was doing such a wretchedly poor job of raising Nicholas?

The sword of guilt stabbed at Simon, but he deflected it. He had sacrificed his own plans and ambitions in order to safeguard his orphaned nephew. He had canceled an extended trip abroad to seek antiquities in Egypt and Greece. He had settled down to a dull life as a farmer—at least until the child was old enough to go to boarding school.

What more was a man supposed to do?

Stewing over the matter, he paced to the tall window and peered out into the murk. The rain had slowed to a steady drizzle. Every now and then, a gust of wind rattled the glass panes. White-capped waves churned against the rocky shoreline, shooting frothy plumes high into the air. As a boy he'd often stolen down there to find whatever debris the latest storm had washed ashore. Bottles, seaweed, a waterlogged shoe—they had all been treasures to him.

At present, however, the wild beauty of the coast failed to interest him. He had too many other matters weighing on his mind. With a grimace, Simon acknowledged the true source of his inner agitation.

It was that woman. Miss Annabelle Quinn.

Her unexpected arrival had brought out the worst in him. Already irritated from a battle-scarred leg that ached in damp weather, he had been too swift to brand her a conniving female out to entrap a wealthy nobleman. There were plenty like that in the neighborhood; he'd even turned one away earlier in the day. But none of them had ever been so devious as to hike up the steep rise of the cliff. They generally came to the castle by carriage along the main drive or lay in wait for him when he went down to the village of Kevernstow.

Besides, the simplicity of Miss Quinn's garb should have told him she was no husband hunter. Her gown was fine, but it lacked the frills and ruffles favored by ladies of the local gentry. She didn't simper or flirt like them, either. So why had he so badly misread her purpose? Why had he been robbed of rational thought by the sight of her emerging from the forest like a wood nymph?

Though no classic beauty, she had pleasing features with chestnut brown hair and a curvaceous figure. He had watched her climb the hill with a purposeful confidence. The sparkle in her blue eyes revealed a zest for life. Maybe he'd been momentarily bewitched by the innocence she exuded—an innocence he'd quickly found suspect.

He tightened his jaw. No young lady was truly innocent, at least not when it came to securing her future. They were all cunning opportunists who deceived and misled a man.

So he had seized hold of Miss Quinn's arm and accused her of trickery. It had not been his finest moment. His actions were especially galling now that the letter had proven the veracity of her claim. She wasn't an idle, highborn lady with marriage on her mind; she was merely a commoner who had come here for employment.

Simon disliked making mistakes. He preferred things to be tidy and organized, everything in its proper place. He had learned that discipline in the military. Meticulous care of one's weaponry could mean the difference between life and death on the battlefield.

Now, the presence of Miss Annabelle Quinn in the castle irritated him like a burr under the saddle of a cavalry horse. She was sand thrown into the well-oiled

machinery of the household. He felt impatient to inform
her that her services were not needed here.

He glanced over his shoulder at the empty doorway.
What was keeping the woman? He himself had changed
out of his wet clothes in a matter of minutes. She shouldn't
be lost since he'd instructed one of the maids to escort
her here. Maybe like all females, Miss Quinn liked to
dally at her toilette.

His mind produced a vivid image of her standing
naked in the firelight while leisurely toweling herself
dry. He knew she had fine breasts; they had been pressed
against him when he'd carried her through the deluge.
Memory added the womanly shape of her hips and waist,
all arranged in a temptingly perfect hourglass figure.

He pressed his overheated forehead to the coolness
of the glass pane. Devil take it, he would not be acting
upon his base instincts. His behavior toward her had
been reprehensible enough already.

A tapping sounded on the open door to his study. He
pivoted as swiftly as a boy caught with his hand in the
sweets dish. On the threshold stood the object of his
erotic fantasies.

Drab was his first thought. *Thank God* was his
second.

The wet nymph was gone. Miss Annabelle Quinn now
wore a baggy gray gown that was buttoned to her throat.
An old-maid's white cap hid most of her rich brown hair.
The transformation added at least a decade onto her age.
She now looked every inch the dowdy, no-nonsense gov-
erness.

She cast a surreptitious glance around the study, her
gaze taking in the walls of books, the elephant's foot
stool, the small statues and trinkets he'd collected on his

travels. Then she waited patiently, her chin lowered slightly, the picture of modesty.

Simon found satisfaction in her docility. A humble servant would be easier to handle then a headstrong termagant. "Come in," he said, seating himself on the edge of the desk.

Miss Quinn walked toward him. The borrowed gown had been made for a shorter woman, and the high hem revealed a pair of sturdy shoes and a glimpse of trim ankle. Stopping in the middle of the rug, she dipped a graceful curtsy.

"Good evening, my lord." Her voice was soft and modulated, utterly unlike that of the indignant maiden of the forest. "I do hope I haven't inconvenienced you. The housekeeper had some trouble in finding the proper attire for me."

"Never mind." Simon picked up the letter from the desk and tapped it against his palm. "It gave me the opportunity to locate Lady Milford's note."

Miss Quinn's eyes glowed like stars, lending an unwelcome beauty to her face. "Oh, thank heavens! Where was it?"

"I'd mistaken it for a social invitation and tossed it into a drawer."

"Then you'll know that what I told you is true. Her ladyship engaged my services as governess to His Grace."

Simon gave a cool nod. "Indeed. Which means I owe you an apology. I should not have mistreated you."

"You believed me to be a trespasser."

"Be that as it may, it's no excuse for my ungentlemanly behavior. I trust you will accept my expression of remorse."

"Certainly, my lord. I shan't give it a second thought."

The earnestness of her expression, the warmth in her blue eyes, disturbed him on a visceral level. She would not feel so happy in a moment.

Simon rose from the desk and strolled to the hearth, his hands clasped behind his back. "In regard to the position offered to you, I find myself in a quandary. Lady Milford failed to consult me in the matter. I never granted her permission to hire anyone."

"I don't understand."

"I'm afraid you've journeyed here on a false promise, Miss Quinn. My nephew has no need of a governess. My staff handles his care quite competently."

The light faded from her eyes. Clasping her fingers together, she took a few steps toward him. "Are you *quite* certain Lady Milford never spoke to you about finding a governess? Perhaps she suggested it to you in passing, and you've merely forgotten."

"Absolutely not . . ."

Yet a dim memory gave Simon pause. The last time Clarissa had come to visit, a few months ago, they *had* spoken briefly of Nicholas. She had suggested the boy needed love as much as an education. Unwilling to coddle him, Simon had dismissed the matter. But now Clarissa had taken it upon herself to meddle with the household staff.

"I understand that her ladyship was a dear friend of the young duke's great-grandmother," Miss Quinn went on. "She spoke with great fondness of the boy, as if he were her own great-grandchild. Indeed, I'm certain she must have his best interests at heart."

Simon clenched his jaw. So much for docile and submissive. The woman was supposed to accept his verdict and depart the study, never to be seen again. Instead, she was actually trying to change his mind. How had he let himself be drawn into discussing his decisions with a mere servant?

He stalked to the window, then turned back around. "*I* am the boy's guardian. *I* make the decisions regarding his care. And *I* say he is too old for a governess."

"I'm sure you're a most excellent guardian," she said, her chin lowered in a deceptively meek pose. "However, women have a strong instinct for the care of children. Lady Milford believes His Grace is in need of a woman's supervision." Before Simon could object, she hit him with a question. "Pray tell, what sort of boy is he?"

"Quiet and well behaved. Which is why I won't have him pampered and spoiled."

Though perhaps Nicholas was *too* quiet, Simon reflected grudgingly. Most days he didn't even know there was a child on the premises, except for Fridays when the boy was brought to Simon's study for an audience. Even then, Nicholas was painfully shy and had to be coaxed into speaking.

"His situation is different from that of other little boys," Miss Quinn observed. "Considering the tragic death of his parents, I doubt he would be *spoiled* by having someone who is steady and dependable in his life. Rather, he would benefit from having a bit of . . . mothering."

That was precisely the same argument Clarissa had used with Simon. At times he wondered if Clarissa had guessed his resentment toward the boy, although Simon took great pains to hide it. Nothing could be more shameful than to blame a child for the sins of his parents.

Yet every time he looked at Nicholas, he saw Diana. Beautiful, fickle, deceitful Diana. Even after all these years, Simon could not rid himself of a cold kernel of hatred for his late sister-in-law.

Miss Quinn was gazing at him expectantly. As if she trusted him to make the right choice for Nicholas. Damn it, why had he allowed himself to be drawn into this absurd debate?

"You overstep your bounds, Miss Quinn. I see no reason to continue this conversation."

"It was never my intention to cause offense," she said, bowing her head slightly and gazing up at him through the screen of her lashes. "I was only thinking of His Grace. Lady Milford gave me reason to believe that I could be of great comfort and guidance to him."

"Lady Milford was wrong. It's a pity you were misled, but that is none of my concern."

She stared at him. "You're sending me away, then?"

Those eyes. They were wide and blue, beseeching him.

"Yes," he stated. "Although considering the bad weather and the lateness of the hour, you may tell the housekeeper to provide you with a room for the night. Now go on, you may leave."

Miss Quinn made no move to depart. She clasped her hands beneath her bosom and took a tiny step forward. "My lord, if I may please be allowed to speak on one more point. You see . . . I've a proposition for you."

All the blood in his head rushed to his loins. His gaze locked to hers, and he leaned forward slightly as if she'd pulled him by a string. "A proposition," he repeated.

She nodded. "In spite of our misunderstanding, I remain convinced that I can be of service to you. If you'll just hear me out."

"Go on." His fevered mind was already picturing her naked in his bed. He wanted to see all that glorious hair spread out on the pillow. He wanted to watch her eyes darken with passion . . .

"Thank you." She hesitated as if gathering her courage. "My lord, I would like to suggest a trial period, perhaps a fortnight—or longer if you desire. During that time I would accept no payment for my services until you are completely satisfied with my performance."

A trial period to be his mistress? He stared at her in befuddlement. "Without payment."

"Precisely," she said with a nod. "That way, you've nothing to lose in allowing me to stay because you won't be paying my wages. At least not until you can see for yourself that His Grace has benefited from my guidance."

Nicholas. She was speaking of his nephew. Simon had never felt more brainless—or more frustrated. He crossed his arms and hoped she had no notion of what had been going through his mind. "I thought I'd made it clear that you'd disrupt his schedule."

"I won't, I give you my solemn vow. I'll be most accommodating to his tutor and the other servants. Please, he's just a little boy who needs a mother. And I—I would very much like to have this chance to prove my worth."

The hint of desperation in her eyes grabbed at him. He knew nothing of her background except what Clarissa had mentioned in the letter, that Miss Quinn had been employed as a teacher in Yorkshire. Now he found himself inordinately curious. Was she just another impoverished woman like thousands of others? Or had something else happened in her past to make her look so desperate?

Too bad. It wasn't his responsibility to save every lost soul in the world.

Nevertheless, Simon found himself abandoning his better judgment and saying, "Fine, I accept your proposal. Just stay out of my way. Both you and the boy."

Chapter 5

Following the housekeeper through a maze of dark corridors, Annabelle quelled the urge to skip and dance. She had done it. She had convinced Lord Simon to hire her as governess—at least temporarily. The bargain would cost her a bit of income, but the sacrifice of half a month's wages was preferable to being summarily dismissed from the castle with no prospects. At least now she'd have a roof over her head and the opportunity to prove her worth.

And by the heavens she *would* prove herself. That disagreeable, arrogant, condescending nobleman would soon wonder how he'd ever managed without her on staff.

Mrs. Wickett, a dour woman with salt-and-pepper hair and a ring of jangling keys at her waist, stopped outside a closed door. The oil lamp in her hand cast monstrous shadows over her plain features. "'Tis the nursery," she said. "'Ee must be quiet lest we disturb His Grace."

"Is he already asleep, then?"

"At six sharp he takes his dinner, then at six-thirty he reads fer a bit. At seven, 'tis lights out."

"That seems rather early for an eight-year-old."

"'Tis the master's wishes." Mrs. Wickett pruned her lips. "'Ee must heed his lordship's timetable. The schedule be on the wall right inside here."

The housekeeper opened the door and led the way into the nursery suite. The wavering light of the lamp revealed a spacious schoolroom with pint-sized tables and chairs, a globe on the teacher's desk, and numerous low bookshelves filled with volumes. Rain pattered against the nearly dark windows.

"His Grace's chamber be through there," Mrs. Wickett murmured, pointing toward a doorway where a faint light could be seen at the end of a long corridor. "Ah, there be the nursemaid."

A rotund woman in a homespun gown and apron came waddling out of the room across from His Grace's. She was smothering a yawn behind her hand. Upon entering the schoolroom, she made a servile bob of her head to Mrs. Wickett.

"Miss Quinn," the housekeeper said, "this be Elowen. She helps His Grace in bathin' and dressin' as well as cleanin' the nursery. Elowen, Miss Quinn be the duke's new governess. Henceforth, 'ee'll be answerin' up t' her orders."

Elowen flicked a rather dull, bovine glance at Annabelle. "Aye, mum. The cheel is abed."

Her accent was even thicker than Mrs. Wickett's, but Annabelle gathered that *the cheel* meant "the child."

"Go and fetch a denner tray fer Miss Quinn," the housekeeper said. "Be quick about it now."

Elowen trudged out the door.

Mrs. Wickett clucked her tongue. "Never in a hurry, that one, but she's good and loyal t' His Grace. Come, 'ee'll stay in the other wing."

She proceeded through a doorway on the side of the schoolroom opposite the duke's quarters. Annabelle trailed the woman down a short passage and then into a small bedchamber with a narrow iron bedstead, a chest of drawers, and a single straight-backed chair. The stone walls were barren of decoration, but Annabelle knew the gloominess would be rectified once her belongings were delivered. Already she wondered where to hang her embroidered samplers and the small wooden cross she'd owned since childhood.

Muttering, the housekeeper took a corner of her apron and wiped the crockery bowl atop a washstand. "Cobweb," she grumbled. "If I'd known t' expect 'ee, the place woulda been spit-spot."

"I'll be happy to tidy the room myself. I don't wish to cause any trouble for anyone."

"'Tis the maid's duty t' clean," Mrs. Wickett said with a look of disapproving shock. "What manner of house dost 'ee hail from?"

Annabelle realized her blunder. At the academy, she'd been expected to assist the staff in everything from delivering the mail to washing dishes in addition to her duties as a teacher of etiquette. But now, as governess, she occupied one of the highest positions in the household. Menial work would be considered beneath her.

"In Yorkshire, I taught at a school rather than a house," she said in an effort to smooth the woman's ruffled feathers. "I'm sure I'll learn your customs here soon enough."

"Hmph." Lifting the glass globe of the lamp, Mrs. Wickett used the flame to light a candle on the bedside table. Then she whisked the dustcover off the bed and tucked it beneath her arm. "Elowen will make 'ee a fire after she brings dinner. Now, mind 'ee be ready at dawn. His lordship don't like slouches. Night t'ee."

The housekeeper bustled out of the chamber, taking the lamp with her. "Good night to you, too," Annabelle called after her.

As the sound of the woman's brisk footsteps faded away, she sank onto the straight-backed chair and looked around with interest. A sense of happy anticipation simmered inside her. She was a governess at last. This stone-walled room would be her new home for the coming year until the young duke went off to boarding school.

Unless, of course, Lord Simon sent her away before then.

The thought dampened her high spirits. From a distance came the rhythmic crashing of the waves. The tapping of the rain on the single high window made Annabelle aware of how alone she was. Things had not turned out in quite so sunny a manner as she'd imagined on the long mail coach ride here.

Lord Simon did not want her here. And he ruled the household with an iron fist. He had made his views crystal clear. *I am the boy's guardian. I make the decisions regarding his care. And I say he is too old for a governess.*

Yet he had engaged her services nonetheless. Could it be he was not so unyielding as he wanted people to believe? Or was he merely a spendthrift who sought to take advantage of her free labor? Whatever the case, Annabelle intended to heed his parting words.

Just stay out of my way. Both you and the boy.

She shivered, as much from the harshness of his words as the chill in the air. What a dreadful thing for him to say about his own nephew! She could only imagine how the young duke must feel to be shunned by his closest relative. If he hadn't already been put to bed, she would have enjoyed meeting the boy tonight.

The bedchamber had no clock, but surely it couldn't be much later than seven. Despite the long and arduous day, she felt too full of energy to sleep. It would have been a pleasure to unpack her books or to pass the time with needlework. Lady Milford had been kind enough to provide a generous clothing allowance, which Annabelle had used to purchase fabric and thread for several gowns. Unfortunately, though, all of her belongings were packed in the trunk she'd left at the Copper Shovel.

The notion of continuing to sit here, gazing into the semidarkness, held little appeal. She felt impatient to take up her duties and cement her position in the household. Perhaps it might be wise to familiarize herself with the duke's daily schedule.

Taking the pewter candlestick, Annabelle ventured out into the darkened schoolroom. She made a slow circuit of the chamber, holding up the candle to see better. She looked through the teacher's desk to find pens and paper, a chart of multiplication tables, along with slates and chalk. There were no toys anywhere, not even a rocking horse or a set of marbles. Didn't wealthy children have lots of games and toys? She'd gathered as much from the chatter of the girls at Mrs. Baxter's Academy. Perhaps the duke's playthings were kept elsewhere.

Annabelle walked to the schedule that was tacked to the wall beside the door. By the flickering light of the candle, she perused the long list written in a man's heavy black script. *7:00 wake & dress, 7:30 morning prayers, 8:00 breakfast, 8:30–11:30 lessons, 12:00 luncheon, 12:30–1:30 silent study* . . . The list continued on with notations as to which subjects were to be taught on specific days. Lessons were taught until four-thirty each afternoon, and afterward, reading was recommended for the duke to keep up with his studies.

Did His Grace never have the chance to run outdoors and explore nature like a normal child? Apparently not.

A flurry of raindrops struck the windows, an accompaniment to her troubled reflections. At least the schedule explained the lack of toys. Nicholas was allotted no time to play. How sad to think of him living such a regimented life. It reminded Annabelle of her girlhood when she'd been required to help the maids with the cleaning. Often, she'd gazed outside, longing for the chance to use a skipping rope or to climb a tree.

Nicholas was a duke, yet he had no leisure to be a child, either. Did he at least have the opportunity to have other children as friends? Or did Lord Simon keep his ward confined here, cut off from the rest of the world?

Just stay out of my way. Both you and the boy.

Annabelle found that callous statement more disturbing than ever. Her fingers itched to tear down the schedule and toss it into the nearest rubbish bin. But perhaps it was too soon to make judgments. Better she should observe for a few days before rushing headlong into changes.

Nicholas had a tutor, and how she would fit into the daily program remained unclear. Perhaps she could discern his academic progress by examining his textbooks.

Heading across the schoolroom, she glanced down the corridor and noticed a faint glimmer underneath the boy's door. Was he still awake? Or had a lamp been left burning because he was afraid of the dark?

Annabelle had to know. Leaving her candle on a table, she walked quietly down the passageway. His door stood slightly ajar. She knocked softly, and when there was no response, she peeked inside to find a large, well-appointed bedchamber.

The light came from a wood fire burning low on the grate. A pair of wing chairs and a table created a cozy arrangement by the hearth. Her gaze swept over the shadowy lumps of furniture to the four-poster bed with its rich blue-and-gold hangings. The brocaded coverlet revealed the outline of a small form.

The duke must be asleep.

Annabelle told herself to leave. She had no business here when she'd been warned by the housekeeper not to disturb Nicholas. Yet she found herself tiptoeing to the bed. Surely it could do no harm to have a look at him. She wouldn't wake him, of course; he might panic at seeing a stranger in his bedchamber. But after traveling halfway across England, she craved to put a face with his name.

On the bedside table sat a framed miniature of a distinguished-looking young man in ceremonial robes. Beside him stood a beautiful blond lady. They must be the boy's parents, Annabelle realized with a pang. How tragic to think that he had lost them. Surely they had showered him with the love denied to him now by his coldhearted uncle.

Bending over the bed, she saw that Nicholas had burrowed deeply beneath the quilts. Could he breathe under there? Afraid he might grow uncomfortable during the night, she carefully drew back the quilt.

A grouping of feather pillows lay beneath the blankets. The bed was empty.

Sucking in a breath, Annabelle straightened up at once. Her heart thumped in shock. Where was the duke? Had he wandered off in his sleep? Should she raise an alarm?

How horrible if he came to harm on her very first night here . . .

No sooner had she taken two steps toward the door when a slight movement by the fireplace caught her attention. Half-hidden by one of the wing chairs, a small figure huddled on the rug. A pair of eyes peered out from between the furniture.

Nicholas.

Relief made her sway on her feet. From his furtive manner, he clearly hoped to remain unseen.

The poor lad must be wondering who she was. And no doubt he wished to avoid being punished for sneaking out of bed.

Annabelle cast about for a way to alleviate his concerns. Tapping a finger on her chin, she said aloud, "Dear me, I wonder what could have happened to His Grace. I am to be his new governess, and I was very much looking forward to meeting him."

Nicholas remained very still.

"Whatever am I to do now?" she went on, pacing in a show of worry. "His Grace is supposed to be in his bed at this hour. If he's gone missing, I shall be obliged to inform Lord Simon. That is certainly *not* something I wish to do. Indeed, if it could be avoided, I would *never* cause trouble for His Grace over such a small matter."

No response.

She heaved a loud sigh. "Oh, well, there is naught to be done here. I must make haste to find his uncle at once . . ."

As she started toward the door, something rustled by the fire. A boy with rumpled flaxen hair popped up to stare at her over the arm of the chair. His voice low and urgent, he said, "*Please* . . . you mustn't . . ."

A voluminous nightshirt swallowed his slight form. He had delicate features reminiscent of the woman in the miniature. The anxiety on his pale face reached out to Annabelle.

She feigned surprise by placing her hand on her

cheek. "My word, you gave me quite a fright! I didn't
see you over there. Are you perchance Nicholas, the Duke
of Kevern?"

A tiny bob of his head was her only answer. Both
Lady Milford and Lord Simon had mentioned the duke's
shy nature. Who could blame him for being timid when
he'd lost his parents and had been left to the care of servants? When his own uncle viewed him as a burden?

Annabelle curtsied. "It's a pleasure to make your
acquaintance, Your Grace. I am Miss Annabelle Quinn,
lately of Yorkshire."

He made a credible half bow from the waist. Someone had taught him manners. Regarding her with wary
green eyes, he whispered, "Are you . . . are you truly my
governess?"

"Indeed I am. And may I add, I've traveled quite a
long distance to meet you. I do hope you can forgive me
for being too impatient to wait until morning."

He nodded slowly. Just then, she noticed that he was
clutching something in his hand.

Curious, she took a few steps closer, careful not to
alarm him. She spied a small army of toy soldiers arranged on the rug before the fire. The sight touched her
heart. Was this the only time he had to play? In secret,
after he'd been put to bed?

It would seem so. It also seemed likely the canny little rascal had arranged the pillows in his bed so that it
would appear as though he were asleep to anyone who
came to check on him.

Annabelle knelt down, as much to examine the battlefield as to place herself on his level. The array of
figurines were a sight to behold. He had made two armies
facing each other, one of soldiers and the other of cavalry.
The uniforms appeared somewhat old-fashioned, and the

paint was chipped on a few as if they'd enjoyed frequent use.

"What a fearsome battle. May I take a look at one?"

Nicholas lifted his small shoulders in a shrug.

Annabelle decided to take that as an assent. Careful not to disturb the formation, she picked up a red-coated soldier holding a musket. Although the piece fit perfectly into the palm of her hand, it was surprisingly heavy. She glanced up to see that Nicholas held a miniature cavalryman on horseback. Keeping a furtive eye on her, he ran his fingertip over the figurine as if it were precious to him.

"Is that one special?" she asked.

Another shrug. His reluctance to speak could not be more clear.

Poor lad, she couldn't blame him for being wary. No one had warned him that a new governess was to arrive. He had no way of knowing if she'd tattle on him or snatch his toys away.

Annabelle ached for him to realize that he was safe with her. Perhaps the toy soldiers gave her a chance to do so.

"Have you had these for a long time?" she asked gently.

He hung his head, rather guiltily, she thought.

"I shan't scold you for being out of bed, at least not this once." She placed her hand over her heart. "On my honor, I do solemnly swear that anything you confess to me will not go beyond these four walls."

Nicholas stared down at his small bare toes. After a moment he glanced up and whispered, "I found them."

"Found them where?"

He pointed toward a chest in the corner. "In there."

"Then they are yours."

His chin tilted down, he shook his head. "They belonged to Papa . . . and Uncle Simon. I'm not to touch them without permission."

Annabelle couldn't imagine why Nicholas should be denied the use of his father's old toys. Everything in the castle belonged to him by birthright. Except, of course, that as the boy's guardian, Lord Simon held the reins of power. "Then we must obtain your uncle's consent."

His face going pale, Nicholas lifted his chin to gaze beseechingly at her. "Please don't tell . . . he'll be angry."

Annabelle's heart squeezed painfully. How appalling that he should be terrified to ask his uncle a simple question. The man must have treated Nicholas harshly to have inspired such fear in him.

A hearty dislike for Lord Simon solidified in her. Family members should love each other, especially when one was a lonely orphaned boy in desperate need of affection.

A sound out in the corridor caught her attention. Rising to her feet, she placed a finger over her lips to warn Nicholas to be quiet. He watched, wide-eyed, as she went to the door to peek out.

In the schoolroom, a plump woman set down a tray on the desk and then disappeared into the corridor that led to Annabelle's bedchamber. Elowen was back and she'd gone to lay the fire.

Annabelle returned to Nicholas. "The maid has brought my dinner. I'll tell her that I've checked on you already, so there's no need for her to disturb you."

The boy said nothing. He stood clutching his tiny cavalry horse, looking so withdrawn and guarded that she yearned to draw him close in a hug. But given his reserve, it was too soon for that.

"I'll come back in half an hour," she said. "You may play for a bit longer, Your Grace, but I'll expect you to

pick up your army and be in bed when I return. I hope
I can count on you to do so."

Nicholas continued to regard her warily. He made no
rush to return to his game, as he would have if he trusted
her. Like a cautious creature of the forest, he remained
unmoving as she walked out of the bedchamber.

Chapter 6

The following morning, Annabelle started her first day as governess by committing a serious blunder. She overslept.

Her eyelids fluttered open to the bright sunlight streaming through a crack in the curtains. For an instant, she didn't recognize her surroundings: the stone walls, the single high window, the porcelain bowl on a washstand across from her narrow cot.

Then she sat up straight as the events of the previous day washed over her. Lord Simon Westbury had half dragged her out of the violent rainstorm and into Castle Kevern. His rude, hostile treatment of her had come as a shock. It had taken considerable persuasion to convince him to hire her, albeit temporarily. Today she needed to give him no reason to regret his decision.

How late *was* it?

Throwing off the covers, Annabelle hopped out of bed. The stone floor chilled her bare feet. Heedless, she raced to the door, cracked it open, and peered out. A man's muffled tone came from the schoolroom. It was not a voice she recognized.

Nicholas's tutor must be here already.

Aghast at her own tardiness, she hurried through her ablutions. Since her trunk hadn't been delivered yet, she'd had to sleep in a borrowed shift. Her soaked garments had been borne away by a maid. Annabelle had meant to arise at dawn and fetch them back, for surely they were dry by now. Instead, she'd have to don the same ill-fitting dress she'd worn the previous afternoon.

Drat it all! Back at the academy, she'd always been awakened by the bonging of the casement clock outside her tiny chamber. But here, the thick stone walls had blocked out all household noise. The only sound was the lulling whisper of the sea against the rocky shore.

Heaven help her, she simply *must* appear the capable, efficient governess. If Lord Simon learned of her tardiness, she might very well be dismissed on the spot.

Bending down, she peered into the little mirror over the washstand while hastily pinning her hair. Then she jammed a white spinster's cap over the slapdash bun. There was no time for breakfast. Longing for a hot cup of tea and a piece of toast, she hurried down the gloomy corridor to the schoolroom.

In the doorway, she came to an abrupt halt.

Nicholas sat at a pint-sized table directly in front of the teacher's desk. Beside him towered a middle-aged man clad in the dark robes of a professor. The tutor's back was turned, showing the wisps of graying brown hair that fringed his balding pate. In the next instant, she spied the ruler he lifted high in the air.

"Your uncle will hear about this!" The man brought the stick down and whacked the boy's knuckles.

It happened so swiftly she had no time to react.

Nicholas cowered in his chair. A small whimper escaped his pinched lips.

As the tutor raised the ruler again, Annabelle sprang forward. She rushed across the schoolroom and seized hold of his forearm. With her other hand, she knocked the wooden stick out of his fingers. It went clattering to the floor and slid underneath the desk.

The man staggered sideways, then pivoted to face her. Anger twisted his narrow, foxlike features. "Wha—" he sputtered. "Who are you? How dare you interfere!"

"I'm Miss Annabelle Quinn, His Grace's new governess. And you will *not* strike him like that ever again."

He glowered, his brown eyes raking her up and down. "Governess? Lord Simon never informed me there was a new member of the staff."

She should have guessed, Annabelle thought. Lord Simon had exhibited little interest in the education of his nephew. Why would he consider the hiring of a governess to be important enough to mention? The answer was, he wouldn't.

She glanced down at Nicholas who sat very still. His small shoulders were hunched, his head lowered, as if he hoped to shrink from sight. Using a corner of his sleeve, he furtively rubbed at the slate in his lap. A fierce sense of protectiveness gripped her. She would not allow him to be mistreated, not by this man and not by Lord Simon, either.

"His lordship engaged my services only yesterday," she told the tutor. "Henceforth, I shall be overseeing His Grace's studies."

"I beg your pardon? If Lord Simon was displeased with my lessons, he would have told me so. Why, he knows I'm an exemplary tutor."

You're a bully, that's what.

Annabelle swallowed the retort. Her tenuous position here required a conciliatory manner, no matter how much she detested this man. Anyway, it wouldn't do to fling insults in front of Nicholas.

"I'm here to ensure that His Grace receives a well-rounded education," she said. "I'm also to watch out for his safety in any manner necessary. Now tell me, what has he done to merit such a harsh reprimand from you?"

"He was scribbling nonsense instead of heeding my history lecture." The tutor snatched up the slate from the boy's lap and thrust it at her. "There! See how well he listens?"

She found herself gazing down at the chalk sketch of a horse. Nicholas had tried to rub it away, but enough remained for her to see that he had an uncommon flair for drawing. The fine rendering brought to mind the miniature cavalryman that he'd clutched the previous evening. When she'd returned to his bedchamber after eating dinner, the army of toy soldiers had been cleared away and he lay in bed, fast asleep—or at least pretending to be. She'd been pleased that he'd obeyed her instructions without a fuss.

Now, however, it seemed he'd acted out of fear of punishment. She suspected that he seldom—if ever—received kindness from this man or from Lord Simon. Why would Nicholas expect anything better from her? For all he knew, she'd report his every transgression to that despicable uncle of his.

"What I *see* is that His Grace has a wonderful artistic talent." She handed the slate back to Nicholas. "Such a gift should be encouraged rather than punished. Now, if you would be so kind as to tell me your name."

"The Reverend Percival Bunting." The tutor spoke with a note of grating superiority. "I am vicar of St. Geren's Church in the village."

Vicar? Startled, Annabelle noticed for the first time

the stiff white collar that rimmed the neckline of his robe. She would never have taken him for a cleric. The only one she'd ever known in Yorkshire had been a plump, happy fellow who'd loved children—the exact opposite of this curmudgeon.

"Is His Grace's tutor ill, then?" she asked in confusion. "Are you filling in for him?"

"Quite the contrary. I am in sole charge of educating His Grace." His mouth twisted in a sour line. "Or at least I was given to believe that I was."

"But what of your duties in the parish? Visiting the sick, writing sermons, conducting services . . ."

"The assistant curate is capable of handling day-to-day matters in my absence. Everything else can be dealt with upon my return to the vicarage each evening."

Annabelle seized upon the chance to prove her usefulness. "Then my presence here will allow you more time to attend to those tasks."

He drew himself up with self-importance. "Nothing can be more imperative than training the Duke of Kevern to take his righteous place as a peer of the realm. You cannot possibly surpass my qualifications for the role. After all, *I* was once a lecturer at Oxford."

Oxford! The news dismayed Annabelle. She'd expected a tutor of modest background, someone easily replaceable. But Mr. Bunting had a lofty résumé—which made her own situation all the more shaky.

As if privy to her thoughts, he stepped closer, a smirk on his narrow face. "And what, pray tell, are *your* credentials?"

"I taught at a fine academy in Yorkshire," she said glibly. "I'm well versed in all subjects from mathematics to science to literature. Lord Simon would never have hired me otherwise."

Annabelle held his gaze, refusing to look away. She buried any qualms at embellishing the truth. If ever Mr. Bunting found out she'd merely taught etiquette at a school for girls, he'd whine to Lord Simon and she'd be tossed out at once.

Then Nicholas would be left without an advocate. He would be subject to the cruel whims of this man.

"Yorkshire," Mr. Bunting muttered with a shake of his head. "What is there in such a provincial place but sheep and barren moors?"

"It is no more provincial than Cornwall," Annabelle countered. She bent down to pick up the ruler from beneath the desk. "Now I'm sure you'll agree there's no point to wasting any more valuable classroom time." Without seeking his permission, she seated herself on a nearby chair and kept the ruler in her lap.

"What do you think you're doing?" he said huffily.

"I intend to observe your lessons. It will be very useful for me to know the progress of His Grace in his studies."

The vicar glowered for a moment as if debating the wisdom of trying to oust her from the schoolroom. Then in a swirl of black robes he stalked to the desk. "Do as you please," he muttered. "But this is an affront, and I fully intend to take up the matter with Lord Simon."

Annabelle strove for a serene expression. Now was not the time for another rejoinder. He would only use it as ammunition when he lodged his complaint against her. And he *would* complain, she had no doubt about that. She could only hope to deprive him of any further offenses to report.

Mr. Bunting cleared his throat. He launched into a monologue about the British colonies that included reciting lists of names and dates from a textbook that lay open on the desk. Within minutes, Annabelle was struck by the mind-numbing quality of his presentation. The vicar rattled on about obscure political and historical facts that could be of little interest to a boy of eight.

Indeed, Nicholas appeared to be gazing out the bank of windows behind the vicar, where the sky had been washed clean of yesterday's rainclouds and gulls soared against a palette of blue. Annabelle struggled to keep her own mind focused on the lecture. As the morning progressed, she found herself growing increasingly distressed.

Mr. Bunting was clearly unsuited to teaching a young child. He failed miserably at engaging the duke's attention. His dull delivery would have bored even a classroom of university students. What had Lord Simon been thinking to hire such a stuffy, self-important man?

She pursed her lips. Lord Simon was indifferent to his nephew's well-being, that's what. To him, Nicholas was merely an annoyance to be kept out of sight in the nursery.

Just stay out of my way. Both you and the boy.

No wonder Lady Milford believed Nicholas desperately needed a governess. Her ladyship wished to shelter the young duke from both Lord Simon and Mr. Bunting. That must have been why she'd rejected the other teachers at the academy; she'd been searching for someone who could commiserate with the orphaned little boy. Someone who had once been lonely and vulnerable herself. Someone who knew exactly how he felt.

Someone willing to fight his battles for him.

Tightening her fingers around the ruler in her lap, Annabelle prayed she wouldn't disappoint her ladyship. It would require tact and diplomacy to secure her position here at the castle. She'd have to keep a firm rein on her temper. Already, she had caused trouble, and the vicar would not take kindly to any more interference. If she was sacked, then Nicholas would be left on his own again.

His Grace of Kevern sat like a statue with his hands folded in his lap. Poor lad, he didn't trust anyone, and who could blame him? He had been betrayed by all the adults in his life: inadvertently by his parents when they had died, by Lord Simon, who barely acknowledged his presence, and by Mr. Bunting, who had a taste for harsh discipline.

But now Nicholas had *her* as his advocate.

The thought imbued Annabelle with strength. For the first time in her life, she felt as if she'd found her true calling. It was a sense of purpose that she'd never felt while teaching the pampered girls at Mrs. Baxter's Academy.

The opportunity must not be allowed to slip away. She had a fortnight to convince Lord Simon to keep her on staff. A fortnight in which to prove herself indispensible. A fortnight in which to find a way to eject Mr. Bunting from the castle once and for all.

After tending to an errand in the village, Simon was riding back to Castle Kevern when he spied a familiar dog-cart trundling toward him on the muddy road. The driver lifted his hand and waved imperiously.

Simon cursed under his breath. So much for his hope to return home without further delay. His already belated midday meal would have to wait even longer. He was also testy from a cramp in his thigh from an old war wound.

He'd been in the saddle since dawn, traversing the estate and assessing the damage done by the storm. Fields of ripening corn and barley had been flattened. A crofter's roof had caved in from the heavy rain and a thatching crew had to be arranged. An entire flock of sheep had escaped through a breached fence and had to be shepherded back onto Kevern land.

Now he was faced with mollifying a peevish employee.

Beneath a wide-brimmed black hat, Percival Bunting's face bore a pinched expression. That came as no surprise. This morning, the vicar would have met the inimitable Miss Annabelle Quinn.

Simon drew his mount to a halt beside the dogcart and pony. His gray gelding danced back and forth, requiring a firm hand on the reins. "Vicar," he said with a cool nod. "A bit early for you to have left the schoolroom."

"Through no fault of my own, I assure you." Bunting aimed an indignant look up from the low, two-wheeled vehicle. "It is most providential to have encountered you, my lord. We must have a word at once, if you'll be so kind as to attend me to the vicarage."

"I'm busy today. Speak your mind here and be done with it."

Bunting glanced back and forth at the surrounding forest as if he expected an army of eavesdroppers to pop out from behind the tree trunks. "It is regarding Miss Annabelle Quinn," he said, pronouncing her name as if it were a concoction of vinegar and pepper. "Imagine my astonishment when she marched into the schoolroom this morning. I had no notion the woman had even been hired."

"Do forgive the oversight," Simon said unrepentantly. "I presume you took the matter in stride."

"Naturally! I pride myself on being a most accommodating man. However, I confess to being unable to fathom your purpose in adding her to the staff. If you are displeased with my services, then pray tell me how I might improve myself."

You could try not being a pompous ass. "Don't make too much of it. I'm merely doing what's best for my nephew. Miss Quinn can supervise his studies and provide him with any mothering he might need."

"Mothering? I thought we'd agreed His Grace is too old for a governess."

"Quite so. But Lady Milford believes otherwise and I've decided to defer to her better judgment."

Simon was still annoyed that Clarissa had acted without his express permission. Months ago, she'd striven to convince him that Nicholas needed someone to replace his mother. Simon had bluntly pointed out the folly in her reasoning. When had the boy ever known love and affection from Diana? It wasn't as if he had anything to miss. The late Duchess of Kevern had been too dedicated to her own frivolities to pay heed to her only child.

A pity he himself had been blind to Diana's self-seeking nature when they'd first met all those years ago. He'd found out the hard way, when she'd scorned his marriage proposal and shifted her sights to George and the title.

Bunting continued to whine. "My lord, pray do not think it unseemly of me to question your decisions. However, I must point out that having a woman in the schoolroom is a disruptive influence. She will distract His Grace from his studies."

"What exactly has she done?"

"For one, she attempted to prevent me from rebuking His Grace for daydreaming. As you know, the boy must not be coddled if he is to be prepared for Eton next year. I cannot maintain discipline in the classroom so long as that female continues to interfere."

Simon wanted nothing to do with their petty squabbles. "I expect you'll find a way to compromise. Is that all?"

"Unfortunately not! The woman also had the temerity to inform me that she was canceling this afternoon's classes so the duke could take her on a tour of the castle. She is wasting precious study time. You must speak to her on the matter at once!"

"I can't imagine it'll do him any harm to enjoy a half-holiday. In the meantime, you should take advantage of her help and find a way to divide the classroom duties."

"I beg your pardon?" The vicar's lips flattened together. "She cannot possibly be a suitable teacher. She lacks an Oxford education. How can we know she is even qualified in the slightest?"

"Lady Milford selected Miss Quinn. That is recommendation enough for me. Good day, Vicar."

Simon urged his mount to a trot up the winding road to the castle. He hoped to God that would be the end of it. Continuing to referee quarrels between those two was not a prospect he relished. He expected his employees to perform their duties unobtrusively, just as the cavalrymen under his command had obeyed his orders without question.

Overseeing a large household and estate had never figured into Simon's plan for his life. At this very moment, he should have been in Turkey or Greece or some other exotic locale, exploring ancient ruins in search of lost treasures. The previous autumn he'd been waiting to board a ship in Dover when the letter had arrived with the tragic news about George and Diana.

A few more hours and he'd have set sail for Athens . . .

Simon thrust his bitterness and regret back into the lockbox of memory. Returning to Cornwall had not been so terrible a hardship. Castle Kevern had been his boyhood home, after all. He knew every inch of these woods, every cave along the rocky shoreline, every hill and meadow and cove. Besides, honor would not permit him to shirk his obligation to watch over the estate for Nicholas.

His brooding thoughts settled on his nephew. The vicar brought Nicholas to the study at teatime every Friday afternoon for a report on his studies. But the boy's timidity always stymied Simon. As a child, he himself had been a boisterous lad, talkative and unafraid of any adult. *Precocious,* his late grandmother used to say with a wink.

Nicholas, however, seemed afraid of his own shadow. He seldom offered more than a few halting, mumbled words. Maybe Miss Annabelle Quinn would have better luck in coaxing the boy to talk.

Simon hoped so. She certainly had a skill for persuasion. Only consider the ease with which she had convinced him to grant her a trial period of employment. One look from those expressive blue eyes had scrambled his brain. *I've a proposition for you,* she'd said. He'd immediately assumed that she wanted to be his mistress.

He grimaced. What a fool he was to keep remembering how her womanly body had felt clasped against him—or the way her rain-drenched gown had clung to her bosom. Miss Annabelle Quinn was a servant in his employ. A liaison was out of the question. Besides, what had lust ever gained him but trouble?

The stone turrets of Castle Kevern appeared through the lacework of green leaves and tree branches. From a distance came the sound of the waves against the cliffs, and the air carried the brackish scent of the sea. A sense of homecoming soothed his irritability. After being on horseback since dawn, he looked forward to dismounting. He'd order a tray sent to his study, shut the door, and claim a little peace.

Riding up the drive, he spied a fine carriage parked just outside the castle wall. He recognized the gold crest on the door and groaned through clenched teeth. Visitors. Damn it, he'd be required to play the gentleman. Unless he could sneak in without being seen . . .

But any hope of escape swiftly vanished as two ladies stepped out of the vehicle.

Chapter 7

"How very magnificent!" Annabelle said as she and Nicholas entered a long room with an arched stone ceiling. Groupings of chairs provided a place in which to view the paintings on the wood-paneled walls. "What is this chamber called?"

The boy uttered an inaudible reply.

After the noontime meal in the schoolroom, she had convinced Mr. Bunting to take the afternoon off. Then she'd asked Nicholas to escort her on a tour. Her purpose was as much to learn her way around the castle as to nurture a friendship between them. For the past hour, they had been wandering through a maze of rooms both upstairs and downstairs: the buttery, the chapel, the great hall, and various towers.

The trouble was, Nicholas had offered little commentary. He'd trudged silently at her side, never speaking except in response to a direct question. Annabelle had been obliged to make most of the conversation. Not that she minded. Only time and patience would convince him to become more comfortable in her presence.

Or at least she hoped that would be the case.

"I'm sorry, I didn't quite hear you," she prompted gently. "Would you mind speaking a bit louder?"

"The portrait gallery."

"Ah, of course," she said as they strolled over the fine Turkish carpet. "Silly me, I should have guessed from all the paintings here. Can you tell me who any of these people are?"

He lifted his small shoulders in a shrug.

"They must be Kevern ancestors," she replied for him. A wistful pang crept into her heart as Annabelle tried to pretend she was viewing an unbroken chain of her own forebears. But her relatives had not been aristocrats garbed in finery; they likely had been servants or tradesmen—commoners who lacked the funds to have themselves immortalized on canvas. "You're quite lucky, you know. *I've* never seen a single portrait of any of my family members."

Nicholas slanted a cautious glance up at her. Though he said nothing, Annabelle thought she saw a glimmer of curiosity in his somber green eyes.

"May I share a secret, Your Grace?" she confided to encourage his interest. "It's something very important. But you will have to give me your solemn promise not to betray my confidence. Can you do that?"

After a moment of consideration, he gave a wary nod.

She guided him to a brocaded chair and then perched on a nearby hassock so they sat at eye level. She lowered her voice to a conspiratorial whisper. "No one here knows it, but I was orphaned as a newborn baby. I've never met my parents, let alone any uncles or aunts or cousins or grandparents."

Nicholas blinked as if startled by the notion of her as a child, and an orphaned one at that. By some miracle, he voiced an unprompted question. "But . . . who took care of you?"

"I was left at a school for young ladies. It was lonely at times, but I did have friends to keep me company."

Mostly among the staff, for the girls at the academy had wanted nothing to do with a charity student—especially not one who was scorned by the headmistress. Annabelle kept that part to herself. It was best not to burden Nicholas with certain wretched aspects of her youth. She only wanted him to understand that she too had experienced the hollow ache of having no parents. "Eventually I grew up and became a teacher. And so here I am."

Nicholas stared at her. With his hands resting on the gilded arms of the chair, he brought to mind a young prince on his throne. "Papa said that when I grow up, I shall be obliged to sit in Parliament and listen to dull speeches."

She laughed, pleased that he'd lowered his guard. It was the longest string of words he'd ever spoken to her. "Yes, I suppose you will. Thankfully, that's still quite a few years into the future."

He fell silent again, his gaze lowered, and Annabelle wondered if he was thinking about his father. According to Lady Milford, the duke and duchess had died in a tragic accident the previous autumn. Annabelle wished she knew more about the circumstances. Had Nicholas gone to sleep one night only to awaken in the morning to find out they were gone? How bitterly unfair that a little boy should lose the two people he loved most in the world.

"You must miss your papa very much," she murmured. "Did he often give you advice?"

"He and Mama were away in London a lot." Clearly

reluctant to say any more, he picked at a thread in the seam of his short trousers. His action made her notice the faint redness across his knuckles.

The sight stirred sympathy and anger in her. That dreadful vicar! The last thing a boy like Nicholas needed was to be bullied from sunrise to sunset. Every child deserved to feel safe in his own home, surrounded by people who loved and protected him.

Annabelle yearned to give him that comfort. The first step was to gain his trust. But prudence told her she wouldn't succeed if she pressed him too much about his past. Better to take things slowly than to upset him with too many questions.

Deciding to change the subject, she rose from the hassock and went to one of the portraits on the paneled wall. "This fine gentleman must have lived in the time of Queen Elizabeth. See the starched ruff around his neck? Only imagine if you had to wear such an itchy collar all day."

The comment tweaked a shy half-smile from Nicholas. As they walked through the gallery, she kept up a one-sided dialogue, pointing out interesting details about the portraits and adding tidbits of English history. Perhaps it was her imagination, but he seemed more relaxed in her presence now.

"You like to draw," she observed. "Perhaps one day, you'll paint a picture that will hang here in the gallery."

His eyebrows quirked in a thoughtful frown as if he'd never considered such an event was even possible. Then he cast a sideways glance up at her. In a doubtful tone, he said, "I'm not very good at drawing people."

"No? Then perhaps you could paint a portrait of one of the horses in the stables. How about it? Is that a worthy ambition?"

"But . . . dukes can't be painters."

"Surely even peers of the realm are allowed to have pastimes. And you've a natural talent for sketching. Have you ever taken lessons from a drawing master?"

He shook his head rather dejectedly. "Art is for ladies. Vicar said so."

Annabelle had yet another reason to dislike Mr. Bunting. "Nonsense. Many famous artists have been men—Rembrandt, Reynolds, Gainsborough."

Nicholas seemed to like the idea. While he paused to gaze up at a landscape painting of horses in a meadow, Annabelle decided to give him a moment alone to think. She stepped to the bank of tall windows that ran the length of the gallery.

Castle Kevern was not quite like the sketches of fortresses that she'd seen in books. Certainly, there were Gothic arches, battlements, and carvings of fearsome gargoyles. But a previous Duke of Kevern had expanded the central keep so that now it resembled a large country manor house nestled within the massive stone ring of the walls.

From her vantage point on the upper-floor gallery, she looked down on a courtyard where a dolphin fountain merrily burbled. The fairy-tale setting sparked her imagination. For an instant, she fancied herself a medieval maiden flirting by the fountain with a knight in shining armor . . .

The vision evaporated as a trio of people walked into view.

The one in the middle was Lord Simon. Two ladies flanked him, each clinging to one of his arms.

Intensely curious, Annabelle pressed her nose to the wavy window glass. Were the ladies neighbors? Or guests who had come to stay overnight? Whatever the case, they were both garbed in the height of fashion, the younger one in a peach-colored gown with a feathered bonnet on her blond hair, the older woman in stately marine blue.

Lord Simon bore no resemblance to the fearsome ogre of the previous afternoon. As the party strolled across the cobblestones, he was the epitome of the charming gentleman, smiling and talking to the ladies, seemingly entranced by their company.

At least until he looked up at the gallery.

Annabelle's heart lurched into her throat. Warmth spread upward from her core, bringing a flush to her cheeks. She swiftly stepped back and out of sight. Had he spied her? Maybe he'd just been glancing at one of the birds that sailed through the courtyard.

She willed her pulse beat to slow. It was ridiculous to feel so breathless. Even if Lord Simon *had* seen her, it wasn't as if she'd done anything wrong.

Nicholas appeared at her side. Raising himself on tiptoes, he attempted to peer over the high windowsill. "Please, Miss Quinn, what are you looking at?"

"Nothing of consequence." Unwilling to distress him with any mention of his uncle, she took his arm and drew him away. "Only a seagull. You'll have to excuse my gawking because I never saw one before yesterday."

"Never?"

"Never. I grew up far inland. There was no ocean for a hundred miles or more. The biggest body of water was the pond by the village green." She deliberately kept her voice light and cheerful. "Now, we must complete our tour of the castle before teatime. Are there any more rooms that we've missed?"

He cocked his head in consideration. "We haven't been to the library."

"Wonderful! I adore libraries." Annabelle dipped a

curtsy while motioning for him to proceed. "Lead on, Your Grace."

Nicholas obliged by taking her through a maze of tun-nellike corridors. It would be a miracle if ever she learned her way around the castle, Annabelle decided. They passed through several arched doorways and went down a flight of winding stairs, their footsteps echoing loudly against the stone walls. She couldn't help but marvel at the ancientness of the fortress. How mind-boggling it was to imagine all the people who had lived here for hundreds upon hundreds of years. What secrets did these walls hold?

She glanced down at Nicholas as they walked along yet another passageway. The better question might be, what secrets did *he* hold?

He'd lapsed into silence again, but at least he'd spoken freely to her in the gallery. It was a start, anyway. She wanted him to be tranquil and untroubled as all children should be. Judging by the slight frown on his brow, he looked far too solemn for a boy of eight.

If only she had a window into his soul. What occu-pied his mind?

All of a sudden, he told her. "Miss Quinn," he said in a hesitant tone, "do you really think I could learn how to draw?"

"Most certainly. As a matter of fact, I could teach you the basics myself." At the academy, she'd been re-quired to master each subject in the event the instructor was ill and needed a substitute. Posture and etiquette had been her assigned specialty, but she also knew art, music, diction, and other topics.

The dejected look lingered on Nicholas's face. "Uncle Simon won't allow it."

Annabelle pursed her lips. That curmudgeon mustn't

be permitted to kill the boy's dreams. Nicholas had a God-given talent that ought to be nurtured and encouraged. Somehow she had to find a way to help that didn't result in him having his knuckles whacked with a ruler.

Perhaps she could give him art instruction after his regular lessons were finished for the day and the vicar was gone. She resolved to take another look at the schedule that Lord Simon had devised for Nicholas. If she had her way, she'd rip up that wretched timetable and toss it into the nearest dustbin.

For a moment she toyed with the notion of ignoring Lord Simon's rules altogether. But she couldn't afford trouble. If the opportunity presented itself, she must attempt to somehow convince the man to grant his permission for art lessons.

She turned a bright smile on Nicholas. "Just leave the matter to me. Now, you'll need better materials than chalk on slate. Have you any proper supplies for drawing? A sketchbook and a set of pencils? Or some paints?"

He mutely shook his head, though his eyes shone with longing. The sight touched her in a visceral way. It was heartbreakingly clear that he hungered for someone to fight his battles for him.

"Well," she said, gazing down at Nicholas as they walked around a bend in the corridor, "I daresay we shall have to do something about that—oh!"

She stopped short to avoid colliding with a stout maidservant who was heading through a doorway. The girl gasped and quickly stepped sideways. Porcelain cups and plates rattled on the large silver tea tray in her hands.

"Do pardon me!" Annabelle exclaimed. "I didn't see you—"

At that moment, a small bowl slid across the highly polished surface of the tray. Annabelle lunged and caught it just in time. But she couldn't prevent the contents from spilling. Lumps of sugar went bouncing all over the floor.

She immediately sank to her knees to retrieve the pieces. Some of them had broken into bits, leaving grainy debris scattered everywhere. Annabelle swallowed a groan. What an unfortunate way to introduce herself to the household staff. No doubt everyone belowstairs would hear about the clumsy new governess.

"I'm ever so sorry," she said over her shoulder to the maid. "This is entirely my fault."

Collecting fragments as she spoke, Annabelle crawled around the stone floor at the entrance to a finely appointed drawing room. Several more pieces of sugar had landed on the large Axminster rug. Scooting forward, she reached for a lump that had come to rest against a polished black boot.

A man's boot. Two of them.

Disbelief iced her veins. Slowly she tilted her head back. Her gaze followed a pair of trouser-clad legs upward over a midnight-blue waistcoat to find Lord Simon staring down at her.

One black brow was cocked in his unsmiling face. His slate gray eyes revealed nothing of his thoughts. Inconsequentially, she noticed how dark his sun-browned skin looked in contrast to his elegant white cravat. Then he cut his gaze toward the fireplace.

Two women sat side by side on a chaise near the hearth. The same two ladies he'd escorted through the courtyard. One old and one young. Judging by their matching fair hair and blue eyes, they must be mother and daughter. From this close vantage point, they were even more stylish than Annabelle had perceived from the gallery window.

She felt instantly dowdy in her borrowed, ill-fitting gown. Her cheeks burned, though her limbs were frozen. She could only imagine how ridiculous she'd looked while scrambling around on the floor.

With a fatalistic perception of her blunder, she returned her gaze to Lord Simon. Words deserted her. Crouched on her knees, she could only stare up at him in mortified shock.

He stood with one hand on his hip, his deep blue coat pushed back to reveal a trim waist. "Miss Quinn," he said on a note of droll irony. "May I ask why you are not in the schoolroom?"

Moistening her dry lips, she murmured, "His Grace . . . was taking me on a tour of the castle."

Lord Simon looked beyond her. "Where is he, then?"

Annabelle glanced around. The maid was setting the tea tray on a table in front of the ladies. Nicholas was nowhere to be seen. "I . . . he was with me only a moment ago."

"Indeed."

That single word conveyed a host of meaning. Rebuke and scorn and something else. Something that made her feel like the object of a jest—as if her mishap had amused him. The sensation intensified when the younger lady leaned close to her mother and murmured an inaudible comment. Then they both laughed.

The two of them reminded Annabelle of the snootier teachers at the academy. The ones who had delighted in humiliating her at every turn.

She attempted to rise to her feet. But her skirts were tangled and her hands were full of sugar crumbs. To make matters worse, she could feel the lace spinster's cap coming loose from her slipshod bun.

A steadying hand gripped her elbow. Lord Simon was helping her up. She didn't want his assistance; she wanted nothing to do with any of these snobs.

Nevertheless, she could hardly refuse. As she stood, his scent of spice and leather wafted over her. Their gazes met and his faint, wry smile knocked the edge off her anger. She had the sudden impression that he sympathized with her discomfiture. Was she wrong to think he'd been mocking her?

The younger lady arose from the chaise and glided to Lord Simon's side. Taking hold of his arm, she looked straight past Annabelle as if she didn't exist. "Is His Grace nearby, Simon? Oh, I should very much like to see the dear boy."

"Louisa simply adores children," the older lady said, gracing her daughter with an indulgent smile as she picked up the pot to pour the tea into cups. "She will be an excellent mother someday."

Annabelle saw straight through the woman's attempt to push Louisa at Lord Simon. Goodness, could anyone be more transparent?

If Lord Simon noticed, he must not have minded, for he smiled at the woman beside him. They made an exceptionally handsome couple, dainty, fair-haired Louisa so ladylike beside his tall, dark form. By comparison, Annabelle was a blot of ink on a pristine sheet of vellum.

She was also a trespasser at this high-society gathering. The sooner she escaped, the better. Her cupped hands full of sugar, she bobbed an awkward curtsy and then edged toward the door.

"Miss Quinn," Lord Simon called after her. "See if the boy is waiting out in the passage."

Annabelle disliked the notion of ushering Nicholas into the drawing room. He would find it an agony to be cooed over by these ladies. Didn't his uncle realize the difficulties of being shy? Maybe he simply didn't care.

Much to her relief, the corridor was empty. She glanced up and down to be certain. Nicholas must have gone back to the nursery. "He isn't here, my lord."

Lord Simon flashed an apologetic smile at the ladies. "I'm afraid you'll have to see my nephew another time. Whenever he vanishes, it's quite impossible to find the lad."

While his guests clucked and commiserated, Annabelle stood frozen just outside the chamber. *Whenever he vanishes?* Did Nicholas make a habit of running away because he was afraid of his uncle? She couldn't believe how blasé Lord Simon sounded about the matter.

His lack of concern irked her. Nicholas was a defenseless child, not a stray dog or cat. It was time the man recognized that.

She stepped back into the doorway. "My lord, might I beg a word with you?"

He paused in the act of accepting a teacup from the older lady. His dark gaze skewered Annabelle, causing an involuntary rush of gooseflesh over her skin. Apparently he wasn't accustomed to being summoned by the help.

He set down the cup, excused himself from his guests, and strode into the corridor to join her. "What is it?" he snapped.

Up close, he looked far too intimidating, and Annabelle half regretted the impulse that had goaded her to speak. But Nicholas longed for art lessons, and if *she* didn't fight for him, who would? "I'd like to discuss His Grace's schedule with you."

"Now is neither the time nor the place."

Despite his brusqueness, she kept her own voice even. "Then I must ask for an appointment with you at a more convenient time."

Her show of cool self-assurance faltered when a loose strand of hair tickled her cheek. Since her hands were sticky with sugar, she attempted to swipe the piece away with the side of her wrist. But the action only caused it to shift across her mouth. Without thinking, she pursed her lips and blew it aside.

Lord Simon stared at her mouth. If anything, his scowl darkened. He yanked a folded handkerchief out of an inner pocket of his coat, shook it open, and held it out to her. "Clean off your hands," he growled.

Startled, Annabelle glanced at the pristine white linen, then at him. "That won't be necessary. I can wash up in the kitchen in a moment."

"For pity's sake, just do it."

His voice brooked no nonsense, and after a moment's hesitation, she dumped the crumbled bits of sugar into his handkerchief and dusted off her palms. He wrapped up the cloth and thrust it at her.

"There will be no appointment," he stated, his face cold. "I see no need to meet with you."

The hard edge to his voice rattled Annabelle. Dear God, had she overstepped her bounds? Did he intend to send her packing?

The very real possibility clutched at her. Why, oh why, had she committed so many blunders in front of him today? Having taught etiquette, she of all people knew proper behavior. He must think her inept and ill-mannered, an utter dunce unsuited to being governess to a duke.

"My lord, I ask only that you to hear me out."

"I already know what it is you wish to say." His

mouth twisted disapprovingly. "I met Bunting on the road and he told me about the difficulties the two of you are having."

"He did . . . ?"

"I don't intend to be subjected to another litany of complaints. Nor do I wish to arbitrate any squabbles in the schoolroom. Settle your own disputes with Bunting—or leave the castle. The choice is yours."

Turning on his heel, Lord Simon strode back into the drawing room to rejoin his guests. Annabelle was left clutching the small bundle of his handkerchief. It was too late to explain that she'd merely wanted to ask him about art lessons for Nicholas.

Now, circumstances left her little choice. At the risk of losing her position, she would have to find a way to rearrange that wretched schedule herself.

Chapter 8

Descending the steep steps to the cellar, Annabelle breathed in the scents of baking bread and damp stone. It was just after dawn, and Nicholas would sleep for another hour. Hopefully, that would give her ample time to glean a little information from the staff.

On this subterranean floor, the servants performed many of their daily tasks out of sight of the gentry. Here lay the kitchen, the laundry, the wine cellar, the butler's pantry, and various storerooms. She headed down a narrow corridor toward the soft glow of light that spilled from a doorway. As she'd surmised, it was the kitchen.

The cavernous chamber was much larger than the one at Mrs. Baxter's Academy. Gleaming copper pots hung from hooks, and open hutches held stacks of dishes and glassware. Along one stone wall stood a hearth massive enough to accommodate a suckling pig.

A gray-haired woman with a white apron cinching her plump waist bent over the fire to stir the contents of an iron cauldron. In the center of the room, a pair of young kitchen maids in mobcaps chattered at a long worktable while they peeled a mountain of potatoes.

One of the maidservants glanced over at Annabelle in the doorway. The girl leaned forward to whisper to her companion; then they both fell silent and stared. Wooden spoon in hand, the cook turned around as if to chastise them.

The woman's eyes widened at Annabelle, and she motioned to one of the maids. "Livvy, stop gawkin' and come stir the kittle."

The smaller of the two girls jumped up to take over the task. Wiping her knobby hands on her apron, the cook hurried forward. Her plain but pleasant features were flushed from the fire. "Mrs. Hodge, I am," she said. "'Ee must be the new governess. Might I fetch 'ee some bruck-fast?"

"A cup of tea with toast would be marvelous."

Mrs. Hodge clucked her tongue. "A body needs more'n that t' start the day. And 'ee shoulda rung the bell. Or sent Elowen t' bring a tray."

Annabelle had deliberately slipped out while the nursemaid was busy scrubbing the floor in the schoolroom. "I don't mind coming down myself. Might I sit at the table here?"

The cook looked aghast. "In the kitchen? A lady like 'ee?"

Annabelle wanted to correct the woman. She might *look* the lady in the stylish bronze silk gown given to her by Lady Milford. She might speak and behave according to the posh manners she'd been obliged to teach at the academy. But she'd always felt most comfortable among the servants, for at least they did not look down their noses at her for having been born on the wrong side of the blanket. "I'm perfectly content staying right here, truly I am."

"As 'ee wishes. These two hen wits are Livvy and Moira. They'll fetch 'ee some fare."

In short order, Annabelle sat sipping a hot cup of tea at one end of the worktable. Mrs. Hodge bustled around the kitchen, disappearing into the pantry for a sack of raisins and coming back out to prepare a tray of buns for baking.

With a shy smile, Livvy brought over a rasher of toast along with a dish of steaming porridge from the kettle and a small jug of cream. She bobbed a curtsy before hastening back to her potato peeling at the other end of the table.

Except for the girls at the academy who'd been practicing for their court debut, no one had ever genuflected to Annabelle before. The novel occurrence was a stark reminder of the gulf between her and the other servants. As governess, she occupied a place at the pinnacle of the hired staff. Her mission today, however, would be much easier if they viewed her as one of them.

While pouring a dollop of cream into her porridge, she noticed the two maidservants stealing curious glances at her. They had ceased their chatter and it was clear they felt constrained by the presence of a stranger. If ever she was to learn anything useful, Annabelle would have to extend the hand of friendship.

She caught the eye of the huskier of the two girls. "You're Moira, aren't you?" she said with a warm smile. "You delivered the tea tray yesterday to Lord Simon and his guests."

A dull flush came over the girl's broad features. "Beg pardon, miss, fer bumpin' inta 'ee."

"Nonsense, it was my fault, including the misfortune with the sugar. I'm afraid I was speaking to His Grace instead of watching where I was walking."

Livvy clutched a half-peeled potato to the bib of her apron. "Oh, miss, I been thinkin' ever since Moira told me wot happened. I'm wonderin' if mayhap 'twas a pisky that tangled thy skirts."

Annabelle held back a laugh just in time. The girl wasn't jesting; she appeared utterly earnest, her eyes big and brown in her freckled face. Across from her, Moira bobbed her head in agreement. The innkeeper at the Copper Shovel also had warned about watching for piskies in the woods. A belief in such fanciful beings must be prevalent among the country folk in the area.

"That's kind of you to say so," Annabelle said. "But it wouldn't be fair of me to blame my own misstep on anyone other than myself. Besides, I can assure you I didn't see any piskies."

Livvy leaned forward, her bony elbows braced on the table. "'Ee wouldna see them, miss. Such wee creatures are invisible t' us. Oft times they play tricks and do mischief."

Moira chimed in, "They be known t' hide things, too. They like t' curdle the milk and cause the bread t' burn."

"Just the other evenin'," Livvy confided, "I saw their tiny lights on the hillside below the castle. 'Tis said they dance at night and leave a ring o' toadstools."

"Bosh," said Mrs. Hodge as she pulled out a loaf of bread from the oven and then slid in the tray of raisin buns. "All this talk o' lights an' milk curdlin'! 'Tis what comes of idle minds."

Annabelle shared the cook's skepticism. All the incidents the maids had mentioned could be attributed to human causes.

Not wanting to scoff, she opted for diplomacy. "I suppose we'll never know if it was piskies or my own clumsiness. I'm only thankful that Lord Simon didn't sack me on the spot."

"Oh, not his lordship," the cook said while rolling out another sheet of dough. "He's a hard man, t' be sure, but a fair one."

Fair? What about the coldhearted way he treated his nephew? Annabelle burned to ask, but she had to be careful. The staff would be very loyal to the master.

"That's good to know," she said. "By the by, he was kind enough to lend me his handkerchief to hold the sugar that I spilled." Annabelle reached into her pocket and placed the sadly crumpled scrap of linen on the table. "I was wondering, Mrs. Hodge, if it could be washed and returned to him."

"I'll take it t' the laundry myself," Mrs. Hodge said, dusting the flour off her hands. "I be needin' t' have a word wid the footman about his lordship's bruckfast."

She took the handkerchief and trotted out of the kitchen.

The ploy had worked better than Annabelle had hoped. She'd wanted a chance to speak to the maidservants without being under the cook's watchful eye. If she could coax them into her confidence, she might convince them to share their knowledge of the family.

Swirling her spoon in the bowl of porridge, she remarked, "I must say, I feel blessed to have found a position in such a fine house. Do you both like working here at the castle?"

The maids bobbed their heads in unison.

"'Tis better'n plowin' the fields an' milkin' the cows," Moira said, paring a potato and then passing it to Livvy for slicing.

"Or shovelin' muck fer me dad," Livvy added.

Moira wrinkled her nose. "Ew, 'tis a nasty chore, t' be sure. Did I ever tell 'ee about the time I slipped an' fell in a big steamin' pile? Stunk fer a week, I did. No one would sit aside me in church."

That sent the girls into a fit of giggles.

Annabelle steered them back on topic. "His Grace is such a dear little boy. It's a pity he lost his parents at so young an age. If you don't mind my asking, I never heard what happened to them."

Moira's face sobered. "'Twas a terrible wreck of their carriage. The duke was drivin' the duchess when they was run off the road."

"Happened in London," Livvy said solemnly, "not long after Samhain."

"Samhain?"

"The last day in October month," Livvy said. "There's bonfires an' feastin' an' dancin' t' mark the start o' the dark time o' year."

All Hallows' Eve. Though curious to hear more about the local customs, Annabelle had too many other questions and too little time in which to ask them. "Do you suppose the accident caused His Grace to become so quiet and shy? Or has he always been rather timid?"

The two girls stared blankly at her. "Timid?" Moira said, pausing in the act of reaching for an unpeeled potato. "His Grace is some fine, weel-behaved lad."

"He's most polite and mannerly," Livvy added in his defense. "We're proud t' serve him, we are."

Their allegiance to the duke apparently prohibited even the slightest whiff of criticism. "Oh, I meant no complaint," Annabelle said hastily. "I merely wondered if perhaps he might still be grieving for his parents. So that I can better assist him, you see."

"Ah," Livvy said with a sage nod. "Well, Elowen says he's the very best o' lads. She'd be sure t' tell us if he was forlorn."

Elowen, the nursemaid, seemed a rather dull-witted woman who wouldn't notice a fly if it sat on her bulbous nose. Not that Annabelle intended to voice that opinion.

"Thank you," she said, "that's good to know. Any information you can give me about the duke and his family is a tremendous help."

The maids smiled. They looked more relaxed now, their hands busy at peeling and slicing potatoes. "We're most always in the kitchen," Moira said. "But we do hear things from time t' time."

Not wanting to appear a rumormonger, Annabelle paused to savor a spoonful of creamy porridge. "I understand that Lord Simon became His Grace's guardian last autumn. It must have been a comfort to the child to have someone familiar in the house during his time of grief."

"Oh, but his lordship din't know His Grace a'tall," Livvy said. "They'd ne'er before met."

Annabelle dropped her spoon. "Never?"

"Aye," Maura confirmed. "His lordship was a captain in the cavalry. For many years, he was away fightin' in foreign lands."

Annabelle hadn't thought Lord Simon the heroic sort. Now she saw him in uniform on horseback, barking orders to his men and leading a charge into battle. Perhaps the news explained his brusque manner, for he must be accustomed to strict obedience. Then another picture entered her mind: Nicholas clutching the toy cavalryman in his hand. Was it possible that he admired his uncle as much as he feared him?

She would have to find out. The notion made her all the more determined to see if the rift between nephew and uncle could be bridged.

"Why does no one address him as Captain Lord Simon?" she said.

"The master thinks it too formal, seein' how he resigned his commission," Livvy said. "Mrs. Wickett told us so."

"She's the housekeeper," Moira added, then blushed. "But I'm sure 'ee's already met her."

"It's difficult to believe he didn't return home on leave from time to time," Annabelle said. "Nicholas is eight and that's quite a lot of years to be absent from the family."

The two maids exchanged a look. A silent communication passed between them as if they were debating how to respond to her comment.

"His lordship had good reason fer stayin' away," Moira said while glancing at the door. "But 'ee mustn't think me a gossip fer sayin' so."

Too intrigued to finish eating, Annabelle pushed her bowl aside. "Please, do tell me. It's important that I understand everything going on in His Grace's life. I shan't betray your confidence."

"Well," Moira said, "I know some that say his lordship was sweet on the duchess afore she was wed. They say the duke stole her away."

"Lord Simon couldn't bear t' see his true love married t' his older brother," Livvy added. "'Tis said he enlisted in the cavalry and left England so he wouldn't have t' go t' the weddin'."

Annabelle sat back in her chair and tried to absorb
the revelation. Lord Simon had once been madly in love
with Nicholas's mother. Was *that* why he wanted nothing to do with Nicholas? Because he couldn't bear to look
on the child who reminded him of his lost love?

Just stay out of my way. You and the boy.

The memory of his harsh words crushed the budding
sympathy in her. She wouldn't allow herself to make any
sentimental excuses for his behavior. Lord Simon was a
cold, aloof aristocrat with a shriveled knob in place of his
heart. She would do everything in her power to keep him
from mistreating Nicholas.

She realized the maids were still gossiping about Lord
Simon.

Livvy was saying to Moira, "Lady Louisa's always
visitin' here. Do 'ee think his lordship be keepin' company wid her?"

"Blaamed if I know, but he did look sweet on her
yesterday, smilin' and such," Moira said. "Mayhap we'll
see a weddin' come spring."

Livvy propped her chin on her work-chapped hands
and sighed dreamily. "I surely hope so. Lady Louisa is so
fine and pretty. No' like that uppish Miss Griswold."

"Or that oogly Lady Joan. What a cadge-o-bones
she is!"

"If his lordship weds that one, he'd have t' feed her
a cartload o' cream t' fatten her up. Else he'd ne'er find
her in the marriage bed."

The maids burst out giggling. Annabelle smiled politely, though she didn't join in their laughter. She was
too busy considering what they'd said. Apparently, Lord
Simon was being pursued by all the marriage-minded
ladies in the neighborhood.

The notion caused a disturbing tension in the pit of

her stomach. If indeed he married, what effect would it have on her place here? Perhaps his bride would embrace the role of mother to Nicholas. Would Lord Simon have no further use for Annabelle? After all, mothering the child had been the primary reason Lady Milford had sought out a governess for the duke.

Annabelle felt an even greater urgency to oust the vicar and take over His Grace's schooling. Only then would she be indispensible.

Chapter 9

At teatime on Friday afternoon, when Nicholas was scheduled to have his weekly audience with Lord Simon, Annabelle couldn't find the boy. One minute he'd been curled up on the window seat in his bedchamber reading a book, and the next he'd vanished.

His disappearance had happened at least in part due to her own vanity. She'd slipped into her chamber for a moment to check her appearance. The last time she'd encountered Lord Simon, in that dreadful incident with the sugar, she had looked slovenly in borrowed clothing. Suspecting he was shallow enough to judge her competence as a teacher on outward appearances, Annabelle was determined to look her best today. Accordingly, she'd worn the finest of her three new gowns, a blue silk that enhanced the color of her eyes. A lace spinster's cap covered her neat bun. In the little mirror over the washstand, she looked sober and proficient, equal to the task of tutoring a duke.

But all her preparations would be for naught if she couldn't find Nicholas. Where had he gone?

She searched his bedchamber, looking under the bed,

behind the draperies, and inside the mahogany wardrobe. His copy of *Robinson Crusoe* lay abandoned on the window seat. Surely if he'd left the nursery, she would have heard his footsteps out in the schoolroom. Her door had been open during the few minutes of her absence.

"Your Grace?" she called. "Are you here? Your uncle is expecting us very soon."

No answer.

She stepped out into the passage and peeked into Elowen's chamber. The spartan furnishings gave the boy nowhere to conceal himself. She couldn't ask the nursemaid for help because the woman had gone down to the servants' hall to have her tea.

After fruitlessly combing through several other empty chambers, Annabelle could only conclude he must have slipped out in order to avoid the conference with his uncle. He'd disappeared the same way on their tour of the castle when they had encountered Lord Simon and his lady visitors in the drawing room.

But she'd hoped that Nicholas was beginning to trust her to protect him. After three days here, she had seen encouraging signs that he was warming to her. He'd diligently applied himself to art lessons after the vicar was gone for the day. They'd enjoyed several excursions downstairs to the library to choose books. Each evening, they had set up the toy soldiers in his chamber to fight mock battles. Today, though, he had been more reserved than usual and Annabelle flayed herself for not realizing he must have been dreading this meeting.

She glanced at the casement clock. Less than ten minutes remained before the appointment. "Your Grace!" she called once again. "Do come out. We haven't the leisure to play hide-and-seek."

Only the distant murmur of the sea answered her.

Nicholas knew every nook and cranny of the castle. There were a hundred places where he might conceal himself.

Annabelle hurried out of the schoolroom and down the winding stone steps. At the bottom, a housemaid was on her hands and knees washing the floor with a rag and bucket. She stoutly professed not to have seen the duke. The news mystified Annabelle since there was no way out of the nursery other than down that particular flight of stairs.

Of course, Nicholas knew how to be quiet and stealthy. Perhaps he'd stolen by while the woman's back was turned.

The other time he'd vanished, he hadn't returned to the nursery straightaway. It had been an hour later that he'd reappeared in his bedchamber. He'd been stubbornly reticent on where he'd been, and Annabelle had been reluctant to press him.

Now she wished she'd done so. He must have a safe place that he retreated to whenever he felt threatened.

Spurred by urgency, she hastened on a search of the castle. Nicholas wasn't in the great hall, the drawing room, or the chapel. Nor had he gone down to the cellars. She even raced back up to the nursery to check for him again.

All to no avail.

Breathless, she paused in a drafty stone corridor and tried to think of where else to look. Accompanying him to this weekly meeting was one of the tasks she'd wrested from Mr. Bunting's control. She had a sinking suspicion that Nicholas had never dared to run away from the vicar. The poor child would have obeyed out of fear of being thrashed.

By comparison, Annabelle would appear weak and

ineffectual. Nevertheless, she felt obliged to inform Lord Simon that his nephew had gone missing. It was a safe guess that the master of the castle would be less than pleased.

She trudged toward his study in the north wing, but her steps faltered when she spied his open door. It wasn't too late to turn back. She could retreat to the schoolroom and ask a footman to deliver a note saying that Nicholas was unwell and the meeting must be postponed.

No. She mustn't turn coward now. Better she should view this as an opportunity to discuss Nicholas's schooling. Today, Lord Simon couldn't claim he was too busy since he'd already set aside the meeting time in his schedule.

She took a deep breath for courage. Then she rapped lightly on the open door and stepped into the study. Having braced herself for a confrontation, Annabelle was disconcerted to find herself alone.

Lord Simon wasn't even here.

The chair behind the mahogany desk was positioned at an angle as if he'd just arisen from it. A quill lay atop a stack of papers on the polished surface. By the fireplace, an untouched tea tray sat waiting on a table. The air held the faint tang of leather and spice, a heady masculine scent that she associated with him.

Had he gone in search of Nicholas? Surely not. By the mantel clock, she was only a few minutes late. Even a stickler for punctuality wouldn't have given up already.

Deciding to wait, she ventured a few more steps into the room. The only other time she'd visited here had been on the day of her arrival. It had been dusk then, the chamber gloomy. Now, the bright sunshine gave the place a far more inviting aura. The windows looked out on the pearly blue expanse of the sea and the waves crashing onto the rocky base of the cliff.

On any other day, she would have been content to spend hours drinking in the wild beauty of the view. It was so very different from the landlocked hills of Yorkshire. But an edgy tension constricted her insides. She desperately wanted to get this interview over with and done.

To steady her nerves, Annabelle made a slow circuit of the room. A wall of oak shelves held rows of accounts books, some looking very old, the leather bindings cracked and faded. The rest of the study was decorated by an assortment of interesting oddities, and she distracted herself by examining some of the items on display.

There was an alabaster statue of a woman in Grecian robes minus her head. A pear-shaped stringed instrument rather like a lute. A primitive tribal mask carved out of wood.

Lord Simon had been stationed overseas in the military. Were these relics that he'd collected on his journeys? They must be. A wistful envy took root inside her. How exciting it would be to travel the world and observe the way foreigners went about their daily lives. Back at the girls' academy, she had fed her interest in different cultures by poring over every geography and history book in the library. She had prided herself on her knowledge of distant countries. But seeing these artifacts in real life illustrated how very little she really knew.

An unusual object on a table in the corner caught her eye. It resembled an intricately decorated silver vase—except for the snakelike hose dangling from the center. Curious, she leaned closer and sniffed. The device exuded a faint smoky aroma that reminded her of the pipe tobacco used by the village blacksmith back in York-shire.

She picked up the hose and tried to discern how the apparatus worked. If indeed this was a device for smoking, where did one put the tobacco and how was it lit? And why would anyone prefer such a complicated contraption when a pipe was smaller and easier to use?

"Looking for something?"

Lord Simon's voice made her jump. Annabelle dropped the hose with a loud clang. She spun around to see him lounging against the doorframe. He was not wearing his coat or cravat, and his shirtsleeves were rolled up to reveal muscled forearms. In his black knee boots and casual garb, he looked more like a pirate than a nobleman. The sight of him caused a dark lurch of pleasure deep inside her.

No, it wasn't pleasure she felt. It was relief that finally she had the chance to air her grievances on Nicholas's behalf.

Remembering her manners, she curtsied. "Lord Simon, you startled me."

"Oh? This *is* my study. Why are you here instead of Bunting?"

"The vicar has departed for the day." Convincing the reverend to make that one concession had been about as easy as taking a cat out for a walk on a leash. "Henceforth, I shall be responsible for bringing His Grace to these weekly meetings."

"Then kindly explain why my nephew didn't accompany you."

As Lord Simon spoke, his gaze made a slow sweep of her from head to toe. If he noticed the improvement in her appearance, he showed no sign of it. His face remained cool and expressionless.

She laced her fingers together to keep from checking that her hair remained neatly tucked into its spinster's cap. "I was hoping you'd agree to just the two of us speaking today. It's important that we discuss His Grace's schooling—"

"I presume Nicholas has run off again."

So much for her attempt to prevaricate. A dozen excuses flashed through her mind. But denial would be futile since he could easily find out the truth. "Unfortunately so," she admitted. "However, I'm certain he's in the castle somewhere. As soon as we finish here, I intend to find him."

"Since he isn't here, we *are* finished. Good day, Miss Quinn."

He walked to the tea tray and leaned down to pour himself a cup from the silver pot.

Nonplussed, she stood unmoving. How could he dismiss her just like that? She wanted to lash out at him for his appalling lack of interest in his nephew's education. But she had to remember Nicholas. He was all that mattered. For his sake, she would swallow her pride and pacify this beast.

"Please, my lord. This is very important."

He turned to scowl at her. "I thought I'd made it clear that you and Bunting were to work out the details of the boy's lessons between the two of you."

"Yes, you did." Annabelle knew she stood on shaky ground. She needed to sound proficient rather than shrewish. "However, I'm not certain that you realize the dire situation in the schoolroom. His Grace is a very bright child, yet he appears to be lagging somewhat in his studies. I believe his disinterest is due to the poor quality of the vicar's lectures. The man speaks too far above the comprehension level of a young boy."

Lord Simon gave an impatient shake of his head. "Nonsense. As to my nephew's progress, it's perfectly adequate. Each week he recites to me what he's learned."

"His Grace is quite adept at memorization. However, he spends much of his time in class staring out the window when he should be listening and learning."

"You're becoming something of a troublemaker, Miss Quinn." His expression disapproving, Lord Simon stirred sugar into his cup. "I must say, at least Bunting has never had any difficulty in bringing the boy here on time."

"Of course he hasn't," Annabelle said, unable to keep an edge of frustration from her voice. "He uses intimidation and corporal punishment to frighten your nephew into obedience."

"Being soft will hardly prepare Nicholas for the rigors of attending Eton next year."

"Nor will beating him into submission."

Laying down the spoon, Lord Simon turned around sharply to frown at her. "Beating him?"

"He smacked Nicholas on the knuckles with a ruler. And all for the sin of drawing a picture on his slate during class."

His hard expression relaxed a bit. "Bunting told me about the incident on the day it happened."

"Then you agree with what he did?"

Lord Simon walked over and handed the cup to her. "Spare the rod and spoil the child. Isn't that how the saying goes, Miss Quinn?"

Annabelle glanced down in surprise at the steaming cup of tea. It seemed too civilized a gesture in the midst of their quarrel. Yet at least it indicated he was willing to let her stay for a few minutes. "But . . . the duke is your ward. Surely you want to protect him from undue harm."

"Boys need discipline or they'll misbehave. It's a fact of life."

"I'm perfectly aware that brute force can induce a child to behave. But isn't it better for Nicholas to do what's right because he's been taught good morals and a sense of responsibility?"

Lord Simon glanced over his shoulder as he poured a cup of tea for himself. "He has to learn to obey authority. Frankly, it matters little to me how you accomplish it."

His indifference toward the duke grated on her. Blowing on her tea, she recalled what the kitchen maids had said—that Lord Simon had been in love with Nicholas's mother and that his elder brother had stolen her away. Afterward, Lord Simon had renounced his family and left England for many years. Had hurt and anger hardened his heart toward the duchess's son?

Annabelle took a sip from her cup. There was another possibility—that Lord Simon had always been cold and uncaring. That he'd driven Nicholas's mother away with his callous nature. She might have been a pretty possession to him, nothing more, and his overweening pride had not been able to tolerate her rejection of him.

Whatever the case, it didn't excuse his apathy now. An innocent child should never suffer for the sins of his parents.

Common sense told her that she ought to abandon the futile argument, yet she couldn't remain silent, not when Nicholas's welfare was at stake. She looked at Lord Simon, who was walking toward her with a plate of tea sandwiches.

"Perhaps you should try to understand why the duke behaves as he does," she said, waving away the plate.

"It's my observation that he hides because he's frightened of you."

"What? I've never laid a hand on him."

"Can he know for certain that you won't do so in the future? You're a stranger to him, my lord. He never even met you until after the death of his parents."

Fixing her with an icy stare, Lord Simon placed the dish on his desk. "Gossiping with the staff, Miss Quinn?"

That look gave her a chill. But she couldn't give up without doing her best to convince him. Using her most persuasive tone, she said, "It's important for me to know all the circumstances that affect His Grace. How else am I to help him?"

"You can make certain he doesn't run away from you again."

"It's *you* he runs away from, *you* he fears. If you showed him a measure of love and kindness, perhaps he'd be more eager to visit you."

His face darkened. "Enough," he snapped. "I've long outgrown the need for lectures from a governess."

The reminder of her place made Annabelle aware that she'd pushed him too far. She was only here on a fortnight's probation. It would be a miracle if he didn't toss her out of the castle for insubordination. And then what good would she be to Nicholas?

She set down her tea on the nearest table, the cup rattling in the saucer. "Pray forgive me, my lord," she said, lowering her gaze. "I spoke out of turn. If you'll excuse me now, I must go search for His Grace."

Annabelle curtsied and started toward the door. She hadn't taken more than two steps when Lord Simon wrapped his hand around her arm and brought her to an enforced halt. "Wait," he growled.

The firm pressure of his fingers sent heat through the

thin silk of her sleeve. The sensation was so unexpected that she uttered a strangled gasp. Half afraid she'd driven him to violence, Annabelle jerked her eyes up to his.

But though his expression held irritation, he appeared far from ready to strike her. Rather, he gazed down at her with an intensity that compelled her to stare back at him. She couldn't help but notice his gorgeous gray eyes and thick black lashes. Not since the rainstorm on the day of her arrival, when he'd hauled her inside the castle, had she stood so close to a man. The novelty of it had a curious effect on her, weakening her limbs and quickening her heartbeat.

Then he glanced down at her mouth, and the look in his eyes altered subtly to warmth. Tilting his head slightly, he brought his face closer to hers. In a low gravelly tone, he said, "Miss Quinn, if only you would—"

Whatever he'd intended to say ended abruptly as footsteps sounded behind Annabelle. Startled, she glanced over her shoulder to see a wiry, middle-aged woman in servant's garb enter the open doorway.

Mrs. Wickett, the housekeeper.

Annabelle knew instantly how compromising the scene must appear. Before she could move, however, Lord Simon loosened his hold on her arm and stepped away. He cocked a cool eyebrow at the woman and waited for her to speak.

"Do pardon me, Lord Simon," the woman said, bobbing a curtsy. "I stopped to see if your tea tray was adequate."

"Quite. If that's all . . ."

Under his unrelenting gaze, the housekeeper slid a cryptic glance at Annabelle before retreating from the study.

The incident left Annabelle shaken. Good heavens,

what would Mrs. Wickett think to find the two of them standing so close? The last thing Annabelle needed was for salacious gossip to spread among the staff—not to mention to suffer another threat of dismissal. Perhaps if she hurried, the housekeeper would see her depart and realize that nothing untoward had happened.

"I really must leave now," she murmured, starting for the door.

"Stop," Lord Simon commanded. "I'm going with you."

"With me—"

"I've a suspicion where the boy is. We'll need a lamp." He strode across the study and lit the wick of an oil lamp at the fireplace. Then he brushed past her and went out into the corridor.

"Follow me," he said.

Intrigued, she made haste to obey. Unfortunately, Mrs. Wickett had already vanished from the passageway, but Annabelle had more important matters on her mind now. Lord Simon's sudden act of cooperation had left her off balance. If he'd known the duke's location all along, why hadn't he said so at once? And why in heaven's name did he need light?

He tramped down the passageway, his footsteps ringing sharply on the stone floor. He didn't turn even once to see if she walked behind him. It was as if he'd forgotten her presence. *Miss Quinn, if only you would—*

What had he been about to say to her?

If only you would cease irritating me?

If only you would learn to obey me?

If only you would allow me to make mad, passionate love to you?

No! Not that. Never that. For heaven's sake, he had made it quite clear that he could scarcely tolerate her company. He must have been about to chide her for pestering him, that was all.

Trailing in his wake, she found herself watching Lord Simon with a strange fascination. He moved with a smooth efficiency and an energetic masculine grace, forcing her to scurry in order to keep up. Maybe it wasn't so strange, this compulsion to study him. Having grown up in an academy for girls, she had been around very few men in her life—and certainly never one as strikingly handsome as Lord Simon.

Nor one as arrogant and overbearing.

According to the household gossip, many eligible ladies in the district had set their caps for him. Either they didn't know of his cold nature or they didn't care. In his exalted world, wealth and noble blood were all that mattered.

If *she* ever married, it would only be for love.

The thought nestled in a secret chamber of her heart. Annabelle tried not to dwell upon it, for women in her reduced circumstances often remained spinsters. She was too educated to draw the interest of a workman, yet too impoverished to entice one of the gentry. The fact of her base birth added another blow against her chances of attracting a decent husband. For that reason, she had resolved to spend her life loving the children entrusted to her care. She certainly didn't need a man to make her happy . . .

Abruptly, Lord Simon turned through an arched doorway with Annabelle right behind him. She was startled to realize that he'd brought her to the chapel. Three short pews on either side led to a finely carved stone altar on a dais. Behind it hung a cross flanked by window slits. The sun shining through the stained glass cast shards of jeweled light over the room.

"The duke isn't here," she murmured, reluctant to disturb the hushed aura. "I checked before I came to your study."

"You didn't know where to look."

Carrying the lamp, Lord Simon walked confidently up the aisle with Annabelle in pursuit. Instead of going to the altar, he veered over to the right, where a large medieval tapestry hung on the stone wall. It depicted a countryside scene with prayerful peasants giving thanks for the harvest.

He drew back the tapestry. "Hold this," he ordered, handing her the lamp.

Annabelle obliged, her nose tickling from the dust that rose from the old cloth. The fine stitchery caught her attention, and for a moment she paid no heed to Lord Simon. Then she realized he was pressing on the wall.

"Whatever are you doing?" she asked.

"Seeing if I can find the right stone. It's been quite a long time . . . ah, here it is."

With a grating noise, one of the stones moved. Much to her amazement, an entire portion of the wall shifted inward to reveal a small entry into a gloomy passage.

The doorway was situated a few feet above the floor, and now Lord Simon leaped lithely up into the space. He reached out to take the lamp from Annabelle.

Then he extended his hand to her.

Chapter 10

Annabelle hesitated. "What's in there?"

"This is a priest-hole. It was used during the Dissolution when the family cleric needed a quick escape from Cromwell's men. There are tunnels that would lead him—and the family—to safety."

Or it could be a trick. Annabelle had a mad vision of Lord Simon locking her away in a place where no one would ever find her again. A hundred years from now, someone would find a pile of bones and a few scraps of blue silk . . .

He seemed to read her mind, for his lips quirked into a compelling grin. "Come," he said, crooking his forefinger at her. "You know you're curious."

That smile revealed why he was so successful at charming the ladies. But Annabelle knew better than to succumb to it; she had seen him without the mask of civility and she knew his callous nature. Only Nicholas mattered to her. To find him, she would take any risk.

Grasping his strong fingers, she let Lord Simon pull her effortlessly up into the priest-hole. He placed his hand on her waist to steady her until she had secure footing, and in spite of her sense of caution, his touch made her heart thud faster. It made no sense, for she didn't admire or even *like* the man.

Especially not when he looked as if he ought to have a patch over one eye and a cutlass clenched in his teeth.

"This way," he said.

Hunching his broad shoulders, he started down the narrow tunnel. Like him, Annabelle had to duck her head to avoid the low ceiling. The tapestry had flapped shut behind them, and if not for the lamp, they would have been plunged into total darkness.

The flame cast quivery shadows on the stone walls. Cobwebs hung overhead in places, and the air smelled dank and stale and faintly salty. She concentrated on keeping her skirts from brushing the grimy floor and walls. The gloomy setting played with her imagination and she wondered again how much she could trust Lord Simon. This seemed like a peculiar way to go looking for Nicholas.

"Where is the duke?" she called.

Lord Simon glanced over his shoulder at her. "I believe we'll find out in a moment. I used these tunnels, too, as a child."

His words took a moment to sink in. "You can't mean that Nicholas comes through here. It's far too frightening."

They had reached a cross point where three tunnels veered off in different directions. Here, the walls appeared to have been hewn from solid rock. The ceiling was a bit higher, and Lord Simon paused to stare at her in the light of the lamp. "All boys like to explore. I actually find it encouraging to think he isn't a pansy."

Annabelle found it nothing of the sort. She was still

trying to envision such a timid child voluntarily entering this dark maze. Rubbing her arms against the chill in the air, she decided not to belabor the point. "Aren't you worried he'll hurt himself?"

"If he didn't show up for days, I'd know where to look for him. Does that satisfy your maidenly fears?"

She ignored his mockery and focused on his lack of concern. "He could lose his way."

"The tunnels are laid out in a simple, straightforward fashion." Lord Simon pointed to one that made a gradual descent. "That one goes down to the cellar. The one straight ahead leads to the library. And the steep steps over there take you up to the family living quarters, including the nursemaid's chamber—in case she had to smuggle the heir out when the castle was under attack."

Annabelle caught her breath. "And you think that's how Nicholas eluded me today?"

"I'd wager my life on it. Come, we'd best hurry if we're to catch the little scamp in the act." Lamp in hand, Lord Simon started up the staircase leading to the upper floors of the castle.

Annabelle clutched her skirts and valiantly mounted the steep steps. There was no banister to hold, and she didn't want to even think of the consequences if her foot slipped. What madness! She still couldn't quite believe Nicholas would brave these cobwebby shadows in order to avoid facing his uncle. "What makes you think he's gone this way? Perhaps he went down a different tunnel."

"He didn't. Not if he found the secret room."

"Secret room? What do you mean?"

"You'll see. Have a care now, or he'll hear us."

Annabelle lowered her voice. "I do hope this isn't a wild goose chase."

Lord Simon glanced over his shoulder. In the shadows cast by the lamp, he glared as fiercely as any pirate. "For pity's sake, will you for once just obey me?"

Pursing her lips, she concentrated on climbing the steps. He was right, she should be more subservient. But there was something about the aggravating man that brought out the worst in her. At least he seemed certain about their destination. Lacking a better alternative, she had no choice but to follow his lead.

The tunnellike staircase reached a narrow landing where it split in two. Leaning close to her, Lord Simon pointed to the left, where a door could be seen in the shadows above. "The nursery," he said, his voice a mere breath of sound against her ear. "He'll be this way."

With a jerk of his head, he indicated they would be going up the opposite branch. A short flight of steps took them to another small door made of sturdy wood.

Lord Simon handed her the lamp and then crouched down to peer through the keyhole. He glanced up at her and gave a terse nod. Annabelle wanted to take a look for herself, but to her consternation, he sprang to his feet and reached for the door handle. The stern look on his face alarmed her. Did he intend to browbeat the child?

She caught hold of his muscled forearm. "Please," she whispered, "let me be the one to speak to him."

"No, you'll keep silent."

With that, he swung open the door, ducked his head to avoid the low lintel, and stepped inside.

Annabelle hastened forward to enter a snug little room. The rounded walls told her they were standing in one of the towers. The window slits cast bars of sunlight over the meager furnishings and the threadbare rug on the floor.

The light also illuminated Nicholas.

He sat cross-legged on a large tasseled cushion with a number of toy soldiers arrayed around him on the rug. He clutched his favorite cavalryman to his thin chest. In palpable shock, he stared up at his uncle. His lips were parted, his green eyes large and panic-stricken in his pale face.

Lord Simon stepped forward, his hands on his hips. "You were told to be in my study," he said sternly. "I'd like to know why you disobeyed my command."

Nicholas lifted his shoulders in a tiny shrug. He looked too terrified to speak.

Annabelle hurried to Lord Simon. "I'm sure he meant no harm—"

"Say one more word, Miss Quinn, and I shall send you packing."

Did he mean that literally? He would make her pack her trunk and leave the castle?

He did. His ice gray eyes revealed a gravity of purpose. She compressed her lips to hold back a retort. She didn't dare challenge his authority when he was in such an ill humor.

He stepped closer to the boy and towered over him. "You gave Miss Quinn a terrible fright when she couldn't find you. That is a craven act unworthy of the Duke of Kevern. Do you understand me?"

His eyes big and fearful, the boy gave a small nod.

"You will apologize to her at once."

Nicholas hung his head and mumbled something inaudible.

"Speak louder," Lord Simon prodded.

"S-sorry, Miss Quinn."

Her heart aching, Annabelle gave Nicholas a brief smile of commiseration. The poor lad looked so wretched that she yearned to gather him in her arms and protect him from harm. But she daren't show him any affection in the presence of Lord Simon.

"You used the tunnels to shirk your duties," he told the boy. "I will have your word of honor that you will never do so again."

"Yes, sir," Nicholas whispered.

"I'm sure you realize that your act of disobedience cannot go unpunished."

Lord Simon paused, gazing down at his nephew with an inscrutable expression. Did he see in Nicholas the woman he'd once coveted? The beauty who had rejected him in favor of his elder brother?

Annabelle hoped he wouldn't take his revenge here and now. His dislike of the boy could not be clearer. She curled her fingers into fists and waited for a draconian sentence. What would it be, bread and water for the next month? Several nights locked in the dungeon? Fifty lashes with a willow switch?

She would *not* stay silent if he did anything so cruel. The anticipation of injustice was so strong in her that she was left speechless when he rendered his judgment.

"You shall write an essay on the importance of obedience. Miss Quinn will determine if it adequately covers the topic." Lord Simon flicked a cool glance at Annabelle. "I will expect it to be on my desk in the morning."

On Sunday, Annabelle took Nicholas to St. Geren's Church in the village of Kevernstow. Although the vicar's sermon likely would be tedious, she believed the duke needed to develop a firm religious foundation in his life. It wasn't enough that the schedule had Nicholas devoting every Sunday morning to reading passages from the Scriptures. A child should also experience the fellowship of worshipping in the company of friends and neighbors.

She had been surprised to learn that no one in the castle had been escorting Nicholas to weekly services. The vicar surely would have urged Lord Simon to do so. Or perhaps Mr. Bunting *had* done so but to no avail. According to the housekeeper, the master attended church only on special occasions like Christmas and Easter.

The coachman let them off in front of the quaint little stone chapel that was nestled beneath a canopy of oaks in the middle of the village. Lush banks of rhododendron and hydrangea bushes dotted the old cemetery alongside the church. A number of villagers and members of the local gentry milled in separate groups outside the open door. Many of them turned to stare as Annabelle and Nicholas disembarked.

Their interest in the young duke was understandable. Nicholas had been kept so sequestered at the castle that they likely hadn't seen much of him over the years. Determined to make friends for his sake, Annabelle smiled graciously at those who caught her eye.

Her good humor died when she spotted Lady Louisa and her mother standing with a portly gentleman at the edge of the throng. The petite debutante resembled a porcelain doll in her straw bonnet and pink ruffled gown. The two women started toward Annabelle, no doubt intending to coo over the duke. Luckily, the bells clanged in the tower and everyone began to flock into the church.

Holding the duke's hand, Annabelle walked down the aisle to the Kevern family pew directly in front of the altar. Nicholas took his place beside her. Looking quite smart in his miniature brown coat and knee breeches, he swung his feet and glanced around with interest at the statuary and candles. It pleased her to see him as relaxed as any normal little boy, for he was too often solemn.

The pipe organist began playing as Mr. Bunting emerged from the vestry and walked to the altar, accompanied by a younger man also garbed in clerical robes. It was then that Annabelle noticed a rise in the whispers behind them. She thought it strange, for one would expect the parishioners to hush at the commencement of the service.

Then the cause of the buzz slid into the pew. Lord Simon took the seat on the other side of his nephew.

Annabelle stiffened, her heart thumping and her gloved fingers clenching in her lap. Whatever was he doing here? She stole a glance at him, enough to see that he looked extremely handsome in a charcoal gray coat that matched his eyes. Nicholas instantly ceased his fidgeting and sat perfectly still. His anxiety was palpable as he stole a wary look at his uncle.

The congregation began to sing a familiar hymn. Annabelle opened her prayer book and sang by rote, though her mind made no sense of the words. She was too aware of Lord Simon's deep baritone blending with the other voices.

His abrupt appearance in church couldn't be a coincidence. He must have heard from Mrs. Wickett that Annabelle had brought Nicholas here. Had she done something wrong? Did he mean to chastise her for failing to ask his permission to deviate from that odious schedule?

Surely not. She might be making too much of the matter. Perhaps the man had merely felt the need to cleanse his soul.

She hadn't seen Lord Simon in the two days since they'd found Nicholas hiding in the tower room. His study had been empty when she had delivered the essay. Nicholas had labored over the composition for hours.

He'd wanted the piece to be perfect, and his desire to please his uncle touched her heart.

Had Lord Simon read the essay? Or had he cast it straight into the rubbish bin?

Whatever the case, she had to admit the assignment had been a fitting punishment. It had made Nicholas reflect upon the importance of fulfilling one's duties—a vital lesson for a boy who needed to learn the responsibilities of his high rank. The worthy endeavor also had forced her to reassess her opinion of Lord Simon. Maybe he wasn't such an ogre, after all.

Just stay out of my way. Both you and the boy.

Was his gruff manner merely a façade? She couldn't say for certain, though it was obvious he was a reluctant guardian. Except for that once-a-week meeting, he left the child to the care of servants. Twice already she had attempted to discuss the duke's schooling with him and he had fobbed her off.

Well, perhaps Lord Simon's presence in church today would prove to be a boon. At least he would have a taste of the vicar's dreary oratory.

Mr. Bunting began the service with prayers and a reading from the Scriptures. Then he mounted the few steps to the pulpit and launched into a sermon about the virtues of being charitable toward one's neighbors. To her consternation, the homily proved to be better than his tedious classroom lectures. In parts, it was even inspirational. The vicar was clearly more suited to preaching than teaching.

While that was good for his parishioners, it wreaked havoc with her hope of expelling him from the schoolroom. And little wonder Lord Simon had brushed off her complaints. He would have no reason to believe the vicar tutored any differently than he sermonized.

At the close of the service, the congregation stood respectfully in their pews. Annabelle realized they were waiting for the duke to leave first. She took his small hand and they followed the vicar and his associate down the aisle with Lord Simon close behind them.

As they emerged into the sunshine, she glanced at Lord Simon and curiosity prodded her to speak. "I didn't expect to see you here," she murmured. "Mrs. Wickett said you don't often go to church."

He arched an eyebrow. "Am I in for a scold, Miss Quinn? Be forewarned, that's hardly the best way to encourage my attendance."

The glint in his dark gray eyes brought a blush to her cheeks. She couldn't quite tell if he was laughing at her or just resorting to his usual acerbic style of conversation. How foolish of her to feel breathless in his company. Better she should bide her tongue and avoid his mockery.

Mr. Bunting greeted the people as they filed out of the church. Ignoring Annabelle, he awarded Lord Simon an ingratiating smile. "I'm most honored to have you and the duke present today. I must say it is excellent timing, for I've had to replace my assistant curate just this week. May I introduce you and His Grace to Mr. Harold Tremayne?"

He indicated a young man in clerical robes who stood nearby. Annabelle's first impression was that Mr. Tremayne looked more like a dashing gentleman of society than a humble, purse-poor curate. He had an abundance of wavy brown hair, and one lock fell artfully onto his brow. With his perfect white teeth and his refined features, he emanated a worldly sophistication that transcended his sober black garb.

Mr. Tremayne shook hands with Lord Simon, then bent down with his hands on his knees to address Nicholas. "It is indeed a great privilege to serve you, Your Grace."

The boy cast a cautious look at him before ducking his chin and taking great interest in his shoes. Annabelle hoped that in time she could help him overcome his shyness. It was too much to expect on his first outing, though. Eventually he would need to learn to converse with the people he would one day rule—

"And who might this lovely young lady be?"

Annabelle realized Mr. Tremayne was addressing her. She had been standing back, conscious that she was only the hired help and thus not entitled to an introduction.

"Miss Quinn is my nephew's governess," said Lord Simon.

"Ah," Mr. Tremayne said, fixing his appreciative blue eyes on her. He reached for her gloved hand and squeezed it lightly. "Mr. Bunting mentioned that he shares his classroom duties with you. However, he neglected to say how very pretty you are."

Smiling, Annabelle extracted her hand from his. The smooth compliment made her uncomfortable, for she'd always considered her looks to be rather ordinary. Still, it was pleasant to be noticed by a handsome man. "Thank you," she said on a laugh, "but I'd rather be praised for my teaching abilities than anything superficial."

"A bluestocking, are you? Do you like to read? I've a passion for history myself. Perhaps we might talk sometime."

"That sounds delightful—"

"I'm afraid the duke's schedule allows her very little free time," Lord Simon broke in. "As a matter of fact, she and the boy were just now returning to Castle Kevern."

He placed his hand at the small of her back and propelled her toward the ducal coach, which was parked beneath the shade of an oak. Nicholas trotted alongside them, clearly happy to escape all the people.

Nonplussed, Annabelle glanced up at Lord Simon. The warmth of his hand through her gown threatened to turn her legs to jelly, an unwelcome reaction that only served to irritate her. "Why did you hurry us away like that? I was in the midst of a conversation."

His cool gaze slid over her. "I didn't engage your services for you to be flirting with the locals."

"Flirting? I most certainly was not—"

"Lord Simon!" trilled a feminine voice. "Surely you aren't leaving so soon."

Annabelle glanced over her shoulder to see Lady Louisa and a group of her genteel acquaintances strolling after them. The fair-haired beauty raised her dainty gloved hand in a wave.

"Go on now." Lord Simon gave Annabelle one final push toward the coach and then turned back to meet Lady Louisa halfway.

Annabelle was tempted to linger just to spite him. But she dared not disobey his order. Besides, she didn't want to subject Nicholas to the fawning of these aristocratic ladies.

As the boy clambered into the coach, she stole another glance at Lord Simon, who now stood beside Lady Louisa. His head was bent close to hers as he listened intently to whatever she was saying. Then he smiled, offering her his arm as they strolled back toward the chapel.

The sight stirred an unpleasant reaction in Annabelle. She attributed it to disappointment in his character. At least now the mystery of why he'd come to church had been solved.

He must have known Lady Louisa would be present.

Chapter 11

Monday was Grievances Day.

It was the one morning of the week that Simon abhorred, for he was required to resolve every mundane dispute presented to him by the tenants of the estate. Nothing irritated him more than having to sit through hours of testimony about laundry snitched from clotheslines or cows cursed into giving sour milk.

By custom, the audiences were held in the library, which was part of the original keep of the castle. Simon occupied the thronelike chair that all the Kevern ancestors had used. It had the same lumpy cushions and peeling gilt on the arms as it had had in his father's day.

The traditional retainer stood at his side, ready to assist in any manner Simon required. Not that Ludlow could do much; the white-haired old man was hunched from arthritis. If not for the long-handled gold mace that he leaned on during these ceremonies, he might have toppled over like the gnarled oak he resembled.

At the moment, Simon was mediating a quarrel between a middle-aged housewife and her neighbor, whose goats had wandered into the woman's garden and eaten all the plants.

Mrs. Maddiver stood face-to-face with her adversary, a hardworking young farmer by the name of Jenkins. Her hands jammed on her ample hips, she railed, "Only stubs left in me garden. All me roses and asters gone—all gone!"

"'Ee left the gate unlatched," Jenkins growled. "'Twas thy own fault."

She poked a finger at his chest. "'Ee let thy goats run free. Now 'ee must pay for the damages. Ten shillin's, no' a pence less."

"Ten—" Jenkins exploded. "That's robbery! 'Ee can take it out o' me dead hide."

"A fine notion, that. Mayhap I weel!"

"Enough," Simon snapped.

When the two continued to argue, Ludlow thumped the base of his staff against the floor. That caught their attention, and they both turned toward Simon, while continuing to squabble.

"All me herbs is eaten, m'lord," Mrs. Maddiver complained. "An' the parsnips an' squashes, too."

"Bosh, they'll grow back," Jenkins said. "'Tis called *nature*."

"Winter's a-comin'. Dost 'ee think me capable of miracles?"

"'Tis only September month. Some sad poor gardener 'ee must be t' fail at winter crops."

She bristled, and before the pair could go at each other again, Simon deemed a swift resolution was in order. "Mrs. Maddiver, you may take some seedlings from the castle gardens to replace what you've lost. Jenkins, you'll give her a round of cheese from your goats—your largest and best."

Both of them protested, Jenkins saying that the fine was too stiff, and Mrs. Maddiver that she wanted silver in her pocket lest he poison the cheese. Simon threatened to levy an additional fine on each of them if they failed to comply with the ruling.

As the two walked grumbling out of the library, Simon blew a sigh of relief. "I'm hoping that's the last one for the day," he told Ludlow.

"Allow me to check, my lord."

Leaning heavily on the mace, the stooped old retainer shuffled at a snail's pace toward the doorway. Simon had attempted to convince the man to retire months ago, but Ludlow refused and Simon had been reluctant to press the issue. He knew he himself would hate to be put out to pasture someday. A man needed to feel useful, not be coddled in a rocking chair with a rug over his knees.

He stood up, stretching his legs and wincing at the cramp in his left thigh. What a pair of old gimps he and Ludlow were. Damp weather and too much sitting tended to aggravate the old wound, while vigorous physical activity had proved the best remedy. For that reason, he was impatient to conclude today's session and head outdoors. Many tasks on the estate awaited his inspection. A crew of workmen were digging a drainage ditch along the eastern edge of the property, and there had been a report of poachers to the south.

In an effort to alleviate the muscle spasm in his leg, Simon limped around the library. He had always liked this chamber with its tall shelves of books and the rich scent of leather bindings. Apparently his nephew did, too. He'd heard from the housekeeper that Annabelle often brought Nicholas here after his afternoon classes were finished.

Annabelle. When had he begun to think of her in so familiar a fashion? Not the previous day when he'd gone to church for the sole purpose of being in her company. No, his awareness of her had grown from superficial attraction to genuine interest several days before that. If he had to pinpoint a moment, it had been when he'd shown her the secret passages. The spark of adventure in her eyes had entranced him. Few ladies of his acquaintance would willingly explore a maze of dark, dirty tunnels.

Actually, he couldn't think of *any* woman as bold and audacious as Annabelle. It made him wonder if she would be a firebrand in his bed.

Bracing one hand on the back of a wing chair, Simon bent down to brutally massage his thigh. He had no business spinning erotic fantasies about an employee. He'd always scorned gentlemen who sought out their pleasures among the maids and governesses. A servant had little choice but to submit—or risk losing her position in the house. He couldn't do that to Annabelle, especially when he'd seen for himself that she genuinely cared for his nephew's welfare.

No matter how overly protective her methods might be.

In regard to *that,* he had no intention of allowing her to voice any more complaints about the vicar. The man had been remarkably successful in making Nicholas behave. Rather than the cosseting she advocated, the boy required a firm hand. Annabelle herself needed to learn obedience to duty, too.

"Have you hurt yourself, Lord Simon?"

For an instant he thought his imagination had conjured her voice. Then he straightened up fast as Annabelle came hurrying from the doorway, with Ludlow trudging behind, inch by slow inch.

Her sudden appearance here knocked Simon off kilter. So did the look of concern on her face. Her typical expression toward him was defiant or mulish or disapproving—never *worried*.

Reaching his side, she glanced down at his leg. "You looked as if you were in pain a moment ago."

"It's nothing, just an old scar," he said tersely. "My leg becomes stiff when I sit for too long."

That wasn't the only part of his anatomy that was stiff. Her closeness stirred his blood. It made no sense since she was dressed primly in a high-buttoned gray gown with a spinster's cap over her scraped-up bun. Yet he found himself wondering how her hair would look loose on his pillow. *No.* He didn't want her there—or here. "You're supposed to be upstairs, helping with the lessons."

"I'm perfectly aware of that. However . . ."

She fell silent in deference to Ludlow, who hobbled up to Simon and thumped the base of his staff on the floor according to the ancient ritual. "Miss Quinn, my lord. She has come to present her grievance."

"What?" Simon glared at her. "You aren't allowed to do so. Grievances Day is for the tenants only."

"I work for you," she said in a reasonable tone, "and I'm certainly a tenant of sorts, living as I do under your roof. Besides, I've a problem that must be resolved. A very important one."

"If it involves my nephew's schooling, we've been through all that already."

"It doesn't matter if you've heard it a thousand times. In accordance with custom, you are required to listen to all sides of the issue before you render judgment. I heard the other servants talking about it in the kitchen this morning."

"Those *are* the rules, my lord," Ludlow intoned in his quivery old voice, "passed down through the generations."

Good God. Simon had no appetite for rehashing their previous quarrel. She already had made her case to him, and it had been a weak one based on her own high-handed opinions. He had to give her credit for persistence, though. Perhaps it would be wise to put an end to her nagging once and for all.

"As you wish, then," he said with an impatient sweep of his hand. "But my judgment today will be firm. Once it is rendered, you must never again bring up the subject."

"Agreed—although one would hope you'd always show an interest in the duke's education."

Simon clenched his jaw. How was it that this outspoken female had the power to stir guilt in him? Hadn't he set aside his plans for his life in order to take care of Nicholas? What more did she expect of him?

A pound of flesh, no doubt.

Ludlow cleared his throat. "The Judgment Throne, my lord."

Reminded of the outmoded tradition, Simon grudgingly took his seat on the tall chair and resigned himself to another episode of discomfort from the lumpy cushions. "Speak your piece quickly, Miss Quinn. It's nearly time for my luncheon."

Annabelle appeared unmoved by his hunger. Quite a difference from that look of concern when she'd entered the library. Standing there with her fingers laced together at her waist, she embodied every strict governess he'd ever encountered as a boy.

"As you know," she said, "I'm deeply concerned that His Grace is not learning as he should. I believe it is due to the quality of his lessons. What's more, the rigid schedule you've required him to follow each day is hardly conducive to developing his skills and interests."

"Balderdash. The only skills he should be developing are in mathematics, literature, and the like."

Annabelle eyed him in that no-nonsense way of hers. "I'm not referring to book lessons but to his special, God-given talents. The duke has a remarkable aptitude for drawing. Were you aware of that?"

From out of the lockbox of memory came the image of Nicholas's mother laughing while she sketched Simon's portrait. He slowly shook his head. "No."

The downward slant of Annabelle's mouth conveyed disapproval. "Well, then, I should tell you that I've taken the liberty of replacing some of his afternoon study time with art instruction."

"Fine. If that's all—"

"It isn't," she said crisply. "You should know that I was forced to modify His Grace's schedule because every moment of his day has been regimented. He has been allotted no time whatsoever for play. Perhaps you don't realize it, but every child needs the freedom to run outdoors. It's necessary to his health and well-being."

"I've no objection to a bit of leisure so long as he keeps up with his lessons."

Frowning, she tilted her head. "Then why did you devise the schedule this way? It dictates nothing but constant, unrelenting study."

Was that true? Her certainty lobbed a hole in his confidence. "I recall seeing a schedule months ago, but it must have come from Bunting. *I* didn't compose it."

"Yet you *did* approve it."

Simon felt as if he were being grilled in a courtroom. "I suppose so," he admitted tersely. "But you must be exaggerating. If it's as rigorous as you claim, I doubt I would have sanctioned it."

"Then allow me to refresh your memory." Reaching into a pocket of her gown, Annabelle drew out a paper and stepped closer to hand it to him. "Is this the schedule that you saw?"

Simon unfolded the paper and scanned it. To his chagrin, the program was indeed meticulous, with the boy's every moment strictly controlled from dawn until dusk.

He had a sinking suspicion he might very well have approved the schedule without paying it much attention. The weeks after George and Diana's sudden deaths had been gut-wrenching and extremely busy. To bury his grief, Simon had thrown himself into the task of learning all the myriad details of running the estate. He'd been satisfied that the castle staff along with the vicar as tutor were looking after his nephew.

"This *is* Bunting's penmanship," he confirmed. "But I'm afraid I can't determine whether the schedule has been changed since I reviewed it last winter."

Annabelle's one uplifted eyebrow spoke volumes. She thought less of him for being so unfamiliar with Nicholas's daily activities. What was it she'd said to him that day in his study?

It's you he runs away from, you he fears. If you showed him a measure of love and kindness, perhaps he'd be more eager to visit you.

Simon resisted the urge to shift in his chair. He shouldn't feel guilty for doing his best, given the circumstances. He refolded the paper and tucked it into an inner pocket of his coat. "I'll instruct Bunting to revise the schedule. Is that all?"

"No. There is also the matter of the vicar's teaching methods." Her skirts swishing, she paced back and forth in front of his throne. "Mr. Bunting doesn't seem to know how to engage the attention of a child. His lectures are extremely dull. Have you ever actually listened to any of them?"

Simon shook his head. "I see no reason to do so. Now, enough of this interview. Your time is up."

"You aren't allowed to pass judgment without hearing *all* the evidence." Her gaze shifted past him. "Isn't that true, Ludlow?"

Simon had forgotten the old retainer was standing a step behind the throne.

The man made a creaky bow. "Indeed, miss."

Annabelle returned her attention to Simon. "There, you are obliged to do this one thing. I would like for you to come upstairs to the nursery and listen to the vicar for yourself."

"That would be a colossal waste of my time." Wondering at her persistence, Simon scowled. "I know what this is all about. You're trying to get rid of Bunting so you can take over the schoolroom. Tell me, why should I believe you'd be any better at instruction than him?"

"Because I understand children. And I remember well what it's like to grow up alone as an orphan."

On that unexpected statement, Annabelle turned on her heel and walked away. He hadn't known anything about her background other than that she had taught at a school in Yorkshire. Did she have no family at all? The answer didn't signify. She was merely the governess and a cheeky one at that.

Instead of heading to the arched doorway, she made a slow circuit of the library, peering closely at the shelves. Moodily he wondered at her purpose. It was hardly the moment to seek out a book to read. He was about to say so when the sway of her hips distracted him. He felt beset by the desire to press her down on one of the library tables and sweeten her vinegary lips with a kiss . . .

Then he noticed that she'd stopped alongside the fireplace and was running her fingertips over the stones.

Irked with both her and himself, he barked, "What the devil are you doing?"

"I'm looking for the entry. You said there was one here in the library."

Her meaning hit him like buckshot. *The tunnels.* Hadn't he warned her that was a family secret? Apparently not.

Rising hastily from the throne, Simon strode straight to her side. He caught her eye and frowned a warning to keep silent. Being Annabelle, she parted her lips to speak, anyway. So he reached surreptitiously for her wrist and lightly pressed it in admonition.

As he'd hoped, his action startled her into obedience.

He turned his head to address Ludlow. "That will be all. You may go now."

The myriad wrinkles on the man's face settled into an obstinate expression. "The judgment has not yet been rendered."

"It will have to be postponed until after I've gathered all the evidence. Now kindly leave us. That is an order."

"Yes, Lord Simon." Leaning on his staff and muttering under his breath, the ancient retainer walked at a slow shuffle toward the door.

The wait for his departure seemed interminable. Beneath Simon's fingers, the pulse in Annabelle's wrist beat swiftly. Her skin felt warm and smooth, and he was sorely tempted to run his thumb over the tender palm of her hand. The faint, enticing fragrance of her made him wonder if the scent originated in the valley between her breasts.

Not that he would ever find out.

As Ludlow vanished into the outer corridor, she pulled her hand free and stepped back. "Did I say something wrong just then?"

"Only the family knows about the tunnels. I'd like to keep it that way or God knows the servants will be having trysts in there."

"You showed *me*."

That he'd trusted her was a fact Simon still couldn't fathom. "You were distraught about Nicholas. Besides, you needed to know where to look for him if ever he disappeared again."

Annabelle seemed to accept the explanation, though she still looked puzzled. "How did His Grace learn about the tunnels? It wasn't from you."

"George—his father—must have showed him."

The faint furrowing of her brow vanished. "Well, then. I shan't give away your family secrets. You have my word." Pivoting back to the wall, she glided her fingers over the stones again. "So where is the entry door?"

"There's no need for secrecy. We'll take the main stairs."

She glanced over her shoulder, her expression exasperated. "That won't work. We need to use the tunnel so that we can enter the nursery wing without being seen."

So that was her plan. "You expect me to *spy* on Bunting?" Simon shook his head in disgust. "I'm sorry, that seems rather unsporting."

"Pish-posh. This isn't a game. This is Nicholas's *life*. Besides, how else are you to witness the vicar as he really is?"

She picked up a candle from a table and gracefully

stooped down to light it at the fireplace. Captivated in spite of himself, he stared at the swanlike curve of her neck and the delicate shape of her ears. Then she stood up again, standing so close he could have caressed her cheek if it wouldn't have been an act of supreme stupidity.

She ducked her chin in a pose of earnest modesty. "Please, Lord Simon. Will you show me the entry?"

Those eyes. They were so big and blue . . . He couldn't find a coherent reason why he should refuse anything she asked.

"You're looking in the wrong place," he said gruffly.

Striding across the library to a wall of shelves, he shifted several old books and felt around for a tiny latch concealed in the ancient wood. When he compressed it and gave a push, a section of shelves moved outward with a loud creaking sound.

"How very clever," she exclaimed. "I would never have guessed the door was hidden there."

"I'm surprised the hinges haven't rusted. It probably hasn't been used in years."

Annabelle stepped past him and into the tunnel. "We'd best hurry or Mr. Bunting will be finished with his history lesson."

Simon followed, pausing long enough to pull the heavy door shut behind them. When he turned again, Annabelle was already several yards ahead. She had her hand cupped around the candle flame to keep it from blowing out. The faint glow penetrated the stygian darkness.

Walking at a crouch through the low tunnel, Simon fixed his gaze on her womanly figure. A cobweb caught at her cap, and she brushed it away without any squeamish female histrionics. How like her to have taken the lead. She showed only a cursory deference to his position as master of the house. Any man who wed such a bossy woman would be a fool, indeed.

Then again, the fellow would be compensated by the pleasurable prospect of taming her to be ridden.

Simon pushed the distracting thought from his mind. More important things required his attention—such as keeping up with her swift pace. Upon reaching the junction where the tunnels split off, Annabelle headed straight for the one that led to the nursery. She cast a quick glance over her shoulder at him before starting up the steep steps.

He found it significant that she made no further attempt to persuade him to her cause. Apparently she believed that what he was about to witness would speak for itself. Simon still harbored strong doubts, though. Percival Bunting might be stodgy, but the man was hardly a tyrant. Even if he *had* devised that onerous schedule.

On the stairs above him, Annabelle had reached a door concealed in the stone wall. It led into the nursery. Simon took the remaining steps two at a time so that he was right at her heels when she entered a tiny, unoccupied bedchamber. The nursemaid slept here, he recalled. Being on this floor was like stepping back in time. The air held the same odors of chalk dust and beeswax that he associated with his childhood.

The muted drone of the vicar's voice drifted from the schoolroom.

Annabelle blew out the candle and quietly placed it on a table. Catching his eye, she put her finger to her lips. Then she tiptoed out the door.

What clandestine nonsense. It reminded him of the highwayman games he'd once played with George when they would attempt to sneak up on a servant with their toy pistols in hand.

Nevertheless, Simon took care to be silent as he entered the narrow passageway. Annabelle had stopped just short of the open doorway and pressed herself to the wall. From this vantage point, only a portion of the schoolroom was visible. Both Nicholas and the vicar were out of sight.

At least now, Bunting's words could be discerned. He was lecturing about the dynastic civil wars between the houses of Lancaster and York that had resulted in the Tudors taking the throne of England. Simon remembered being fascinated by all the court intrigue and the bloody battles of that medieval period. His governess had woven the Kevern family history into the story to make it even more colorful. But all Bunting offered was a dry recitation of dates, a mind-numbing list of Henrys and Richards with little to distinguish one from another.

Even worse, the vicar had abandoned the soaring oratory of the pulpit. He spoke in a monotone guaranteed to drive an eight-year-old boy to a case of the fidgets.

Her arms folded, Annabelle rolled her eyes and shook her head as if to say *I told you so.* Simon allowed her a wry look. Though it pained him to admit it, she'd been correct in her assessment. He should have been paying more heed to his nephew's education all these months. He shouldn't have buried himself in estate matters. Not even if it was damnably difficult to look at Nicholas without remembering Diana's deceit . . .

A shout came from the schoolroom. Bunting had raised his voice in wrath. "Naughty child! Give that to me at once."

Simon stiffened, his gaze fixed on the empty doorway. At the sound of a slap and then a child's smothered cry, he felt Annabelle's fingers clutch convulsively at his arm.

She started forward, but Simon sprang past her. He

entered the schoolroom to see Percival Bunting leaning over the boy's desk and saying nastily, "Your uncle will whip you when he hears about this."

Simon caught a fistful of the cleric's robes and yanked him back. "No, it's you I'll whip if ever you abuse my nephew again."

Bunting's foxlike face drained of color. A small object fell from his hand and went bouncing across the polished wood floor. "Lord Simon! I—I didn't see you come in."

"Thank God for that or I might never have known what a scoundrel you are." Simon thrust the man away so that he went staggering into the teacher's desk. "Collect your belongings and get out. You'll not be returning."

"But my lord—"

"Do it now lest I see you removed from the vicarage as well."

Scowling, Bunting emptied a few things from the desk and slammed the drawer. He made a wide berth around Simon, but glared daggers at Annabelle. She crouched beside Nicholas's chair, her arm around the boy.

As the vicar stalked out of the schoolroom, Nicholas slipped from his seat and scooped up what the man had dropped. It appeared to be a miniature cavalryman, one of the set Simon had once played with as a boy. Nicholas scuttled back to the safety of Annabelle's arms. Wiping the tears from his face, she murmured soothing words.

She sent a keen stare up at Simon. "His Grace was forbidden to use these toy soldiers. Did that order come from you—or from Mr. Bunting?"

"Good God, it certainly wasn't me."

Frowning, Simon watched her fuss. Why would she think he'd object to a child playing with old toys? The answer came swiftly. Because he'd never given her cause to believe otherwise. Because he'd been a hard taskmaster toward his nephew.

It's you he runs away from, you he fears. If you showed him a measure of love and kindness, perhaps he'd be more eager to visit you.

His white-hot anger having dissipated, Simon felt the impulse to ruffle the boy's hair or perhaps crouch down to speak to him. But the force of long habit held him rooted in place. It wouldn't be fair to build an expectation of affection in the child. Nothing had changed. He still felt a strong aversion to Nicholas. Perhaps if the boy didn't have fair hair and green eyes, the same refined bone structure as Diana, things would have been different. But reality could not be altered.

He shifted his gaze to Annabelle. "Well, Miss Quinn. It appears you are now my nephew's sole teacher."

She looked up at him. Her expression showed no gloating, only a profound gratitude. "Thank you."

Her appreciation made him uncomfortable, given the way he'd neglected his guardianship. "Thank yourself. I'm indebted to you for your intervention. Good day." Before he could be tempted to linger, Simon turned on his heel and strode out of the schoolroom.

Chapter 12

Three weeks later, Annabelle knelt on the stone floor in her bedchamber and opened her traveling trunk. Although most of her belongings had been unpacked shortly after her arrival at Castle Kevern, she'd kept a few spare items in storage. She quickly rummaged through a pile of fabric remnants, searching for a long strip of blue silk left over from one of her gowns. If she hurried, she could sew the piece into a makeshift ribbon.

In an hour's time, she was expected downstairs to join a party of guests. The invitation had been delivered by a footman only ten minutes ago. No, it was not precisely an invitation, but rather a terse command from Lord Simon. The brief message had been scrawled in black ink on a sheet of folded paper, followed by his initials.

You are requested to attend dinner tonight at seven o'clock. S.W.

The note had caught Annabelle completely off guard. How could the man expect her to ready herself on such short notice? There was no time to stitch a fine gown suitable for high society. One of her everyday dresses would have to suffice.

She'd already known from the bustling preparations belowstairs that a large number of guests were expected. Some of them would be staying here at Castle Kevern for several nights. When Annabelle had been hired, Lady Milford had mentioned that a governess sometimes was included in social gatherings. But Annabelle had never imagined such a circumstance would actually occur. Lord Simon seldom entertained visitors beyond a few brief afternoon callers. And ever since Mr. Bunting had been dismissed, Lord Simon had ignored her as if she didn't exist.

Inside the trunk, her fingers brushed against the fringe of the gray silk shawl that her students had given her as a farewell gift. It might be the perfect touch to complement her dark blue gown.

A small bundle lay beneath the shawl. Sitting back on her heels, she opened the soft leather pouch and found herself gazing down at a pair of high-heeled slippers.

Lady Milford had bequeathed these elegant shoes to her. Strange, Annabelle had forgotten their existence until this very moment.

She reverently glided her fingertips over the deep garnet satin of one shoe. The crystal beadwork glittered in the last rays of sunlight from the high window. It seemed impossible that such fine footwear belonged to her. Never in her life had she owned anything so exquisite.

The desire to put them on swept through her. But practicality asserted itself. These slippers were more suited to a grand ball than a dinner party in the country. Besides, she lacked the proper gown to do them justice.

With great regret, Annabelle tucked the slippers back into the trunk. It seemed unlikely that she'd ever have the opportunity to wear them. Still, it was a pleasure to know they were hidden there, waiting like a lovely secret.

She found the long scrap of fabric and set to work trimming and sewing the edges. Then there was barely enough time to ready herself. At last she wore her best blue silk gown with the newly made ribbon threaded through her upswept hair. Filled with jittery anticipation, she peered into the tiny mirror over the washstand and wondered if she'd been too daring to leave off her spinster's cap.

Would Lady Louisa and her mother attend tonight's dinner? The prospect of being near those two fashion plates daunted Annabelle. No matter how much she fussed over her appearance, she would look hopelessly provincial by comparison . . .

Oh, botheration, what did it matter? No one would pay heed to the governess except out of politeness. Lord Simon would be too busy fawning over the highborn ladies. Not, of course, that she cared a fig for his company, anyway.

Barring him from her thoughts, she picked up the gray shawl and headed through the shadowy schoolroom to the ducal bedchamber. Elowen sat dozing in the rocking chair, her chin sunk to the broad expanse of her bosom. Nicholas lay on his stomach in front of the fireplace, playing with his toy soldiers.

He glanced up, his green eyes alight. "Miss Quinn! I've made the Battle of Waterloo."

"Oh, my. Let me take a look." Annabelle crouched down to examine the battlefield, where an array of miniature soldiers lay in a tumbled heap. "I see Napoleon's men have suffered quite the rout."

"The King's cavalry will kill all the frogs. Pow!" Nicholas swooped his favorite cavalryman into the pile and scattered the pieces.

Annabelle smiled to see him behave like a typical

boy. In the weeks since the vicar had been tossed out of
Castle Kevern, Nicholas had blossomed. He was learning
his schoolwork by leaps and bounds now that she had
tailored the lessons to his age. He was still reserved much
of the time but at least his aura of anxiety had eased. For
too long, his fearfulness had been honed by Mr. Bunting.
Although Lord Simon had never struck Nicholas, the
vicar had planted the seed of dread in the boy and wa-
tered it with dire threats and false warnings.

Much of what she'd attributed to Lord Simon had
actually been perpetrated by the vicar, from the onerous
schedule to the lack of toys in the nursery.

For as long as she lived, Annabelle would never forget
the thrill of seeing Lord Simon take charge that day in the
schoolroom. His wrath had been a sight to behold. He had
seized Mr. Bunting and given him a verbal thrashing. He
had come to the defense of his nephew in no uncertain
terms. He had cast out the vicar even though it meant ad-
mitting he himself had made a mistake in hiring the man.

At the time, she'd believed the incident had softened
Lord Simon's heart. She'd hoped he finally would unbend
and begin to show affection for Nicholas. She hadn't been
daunted even when he'd walked out the door with nary a
word to the boy.

But as the days had progressed, the truth became
disappointingly clear. Lord Simon had not altered his
habits one iota. Just as before, he exhibited little interest
in Nicholas. The aggravating man avoided the nursery,
and Annabelle had caught only an occasional glimpse
of him in the corridors of the castle. She *did* give him
credit for joining them in church on Sundays, though
afterward he always escorted them straight to the coach,
then went to chat with Lady Louisa and her friends. It

was as if the young duke didn't exist outside the regimented weekly meetings.

Just stay out of my way. Both you and the boy.

Annabelle told herself to be satisfied. Nicholas was much happier now. Like all children, he deserved to be safe from harm. Yet he also needed love from a family member, not merely from the hired governess—no matter how fond she'd grown of him.

On the rug, he galloped his toy horseman through the ranks of the infantry. Smiling, she combed her fingers through his flaxen hair. "You may play for another half an hour, Your Grace. Don't forget to put away your soldiers before you go to bed."

For the first time, he glanced over at her dress. "You look pretty. Are you going to a party?"

"Just downstairs for dinner. Can you say good night to me now?"

He scrambled up to throw his thin arms around her neck. That in itself was a sign that he'd changed from the timid boy she'd first met. Feeling blessed to have earned his trust, she returned his hug, silently vowing to give him all the affection his uncle had denied him.

But Annabelle knew she couldn't give up. Somehow, there had to be a way to make Lord Simon realize that his duty to the child required more than merely providing an education. It was past time the man became a loving father to Nicholas.

Several minutes later, she paused in the corridor outside the dining chamber. The murmur of voices and the clink of dishes drifted from the arched doorway. A sudden qualm gripped Annabelle. Although she'd taught etiquette and deportment, never in her life had she attended a society event. She'd almost prefer to be wearing a maid's uniform and toting a tray of champagne glasses.

Nonsense, she scolded herself. These aristocrats were no better than her merely because of an accident of birth. Character mattered far more than bloodline. She would simply act as if she belonged among them.

Her chin held high, she stepped into the doorway—and paused in dismay.

Several footmen were chatting to one another as they laid out the silverware and crystal on the long, linen-draped table. Another servant lit the candles in the silver candelabra. At the far end of the room, the housekeeper fussed over one of the lush flower arrangements.

Where were all the guests?

Mrs. Wickett glanced at Annabelle standing in the doorway. Her lips thinned, and she came bustling forward, the ring of keys jangling at her waist. "Miss Quinn! 'Ee don't belong here."

"But . . . Lord Simon invited me to dinner. Am I too early?"

"Indeed so," the housekeeper said, her plain features drawn in a disapproving look. "His lordship's guests have gathered in the drawin' room. They shan't come to the table until the gong has been rung."

The middle-aged woman eyed her as if she were a bumpkin just fallen off the turnip cart. Annabelle strove for a pleasant expression. Her mistake in coming to the dining chamber was especially galling since Mrs. Wickett had never warmed to her like the rest of the staff. She seemed to carry a grudge for some unknown reason, and Annabelle only hoped that in time, the woman would cease to view her as an outsider.

"Thank you," she said with a gracious smile. "I do beg your pardon for the interruption."

As she turned to go, Mrs. Wickett muttered in a rather nasty tone, "'Ee needn't have such airs, missy."

"Airs?"

The housekeeper stepped into the corridor, out of earshot of the other servants. Knobby fingers clutching the white apron cinching her waist, she thrust her face close to Annabelle's. "'Ee might have cajoled Lord Simon into oustin' the vicar from the schoolroom. But don't 'ee think, because o' one dinner invitation, to work thy wiles on the master. I won't tolerate such wickedness from my staff."

A flush seared Annabelle's cheeks. So that was the source of the woman's rancor. She believed Annabelle had designs on Lord Simon. How had Mrs. Wickett formed such a wildly mistaken assumption?

Then Annabelle remembered the day Nicholas had vanished. The housekeeper had walked into the study at the very moment Lord Simon had taken hold of Annabelle's arm. Mrs. Wickett had seen them standing close together and erroneously concluded they were flirting, not quarreling. In the subsequent excitement of traversing the secret tunnels to find Nicholas, Annabelle had forgotten the incident.

"I'm afraid you've misconstrued my character," she told the woman. "What you've implied is utterly untrue."

Mrs. Wickett gave Annabelle's gown and hair a scornful scrutiny. "Well! Time will tell, won't it? One false move, an' I'll see 'ee gone from this castle—and the good reverend back in his rightful place as tutor."

Turning on her heel, the housekeeper marched back into the dining chamber. Her quick steps and rigid posture made it clear that her ill opinion hadn't altered one iota.

Feeling somewhat rattled, Annabelle headed down

the corridor. The notion that anyone could harbor such vitriol toward her cast a pall over the evening. A disturbing thought entered her mind. That day in the study, when they'd stood so close, she had felt an undeniable attraction to Lord Simon. Had Mrs. Wickett's sharp eyes seen what Annabelle had been afraid to admit to herself?

The buzz of conversation and a burst of laughter emanated from the drawing room just ahead. Annabelle paused in the corridor to adjust the shawl around her shoulders. A part of her wanted to retreat to the safety of the nursery. But that would be an act of cowardice when she had sworn to enjoy this rare evening.

Her head held high, she stepped into the arched doorway. Some three dozen elegantly clad gentlemen and ladies stood in small groups, while a few older women sat gossiping by the fireplace. Her gaze went straight to Lord Simon, for he was the tallest man in the room. His back to her, he was surrounded by several young women, including dainty blond Lady Louisa. They all seemed to be vying for his attention.

The sight of him caused a lurch deep inside Annabelle, and she attributed it to disgust for his neglect of his nephew. The man could spare no time for Nicholas yet he had ample leisure for flirting. How she would love to point that out to him—if it wouldn't endanger her position in the household. She had to learn to bide her tongue with him, as she'd once done with Mrs. Baxter and the other teachers.

Accepting a glass of champagne from a passing footman, she scanned the party. There appeared to be a few more women than men present. Odd that, for she'd assumed her invitation had been tendered in order to balance out the couples. Perhaps there were additional gentlemen who had not yet arrived.

No one paid heed to her other than a pair of gray-haired biddies with raised eyebrows who whispered between themselves. Deciding to be amused rather than offended, Annabelle seated herself in a chair by a bank of ferns. The governess wouldn't be expected to mingle, she reasoned. Here, she could sip her first ever glass of champagne and observe the habits of the haut ton from a discreet distance.

The bubbly taste proved a refreshing delight. But she was immediately distracted when a young gentleman separated himself from the throng and strolled toward her.

She nearly didn't recognize him without his clerical robes. Garbed in a forest green coat and tan breeches, his wavy brown hair neatly combed, Mr. Harold Tremayne looked more like a stylish man-about-town than a lowly assistant curate.

He bent low and kissed the back of her hand. "My dear Miss Quinn. Have you come to rescue me?"

Glad to see at least one friendly face, she set down her glass on a nearby table and smiled up at him. "Why, Mr. Tremayne, rescue you from what? I cannot imagine how you could be in any danger here."

"Until you walked in, I was in peril of dying of utter boredom." On that absurd statement, Tremayne indicated the chair beside hers. "Do you mind if I join you?"

"Please do. I would enjoy the company."

He seated himself, taking care not to wrinkle the tails of his coat. "Thank you. As you're new to the district, too, I suspect you know as few people here as I do."

"Have you not met all the better families in the parish, then?"

"Being in possession of a person's name is vastly different from being able to chat with the familiarity of a friend. I vow, within five minutes of my arrival, I'd exhausted my repertoire of comments on the weather and the splendor of the room."

He seemed to have no trouble conversing with *her,* and Annabelle suspected he was denigrating himself on purpose to make her feel more at ease. Then another thought distracted her. Since the assistant curate had been invited, did that mean the vicar was lurking somewhere as well?

Annabelle peered at the gathering, but many of the guests were standing in groups and they blocked the others from view. "Did you come alone?" she asked.

"Yes, I'm afraid poor Percival was denied an invitation."

She tried to hide her relief. It would have been awkward indeed to encounter Mr. Bunting, especially since he'd looked coldly past her in church the past few Sundays. "I see."

"You needn't be polite," Mr. Tremayne said, chuckling. "One can hardly blame you for not wishing him to be present. I understand there was quite the brouhaha in the schoolroom several weeks ago."

Annabelle blushed to imagine how Mr. Bunting must have railed against her in the privacy of the vicarage. "I'm very sorry you had to hear of it."

Mr. Tremayne placed his hand over hers. "Rest assured, I don't think ill of you, Miss Quinn. Quite the contrary. I've only one complaint to lay at your doorstep."

His familiar manner discomfited Annabelle, so she pulled her hand free and laced her fingers tightly in her lap. "What is that?"

"Bunting is no longer absent most of the day. Must you have sent the snarly fellow back to the vicarage to plague me?"

She stifled an indelicate laugh. "Really, Mr. Tremayne. You oughtn't be making such impertinent remarks. But do tell me, will he disapprove of you for coming here tonight?"

Mr. Tremayne shrugged. "I reminded him that my invitation was due to my connections. You see, my late grandfather was Viscount Merriman—though I am only the second son of a second son. That is why I've been forced to earn my bread as a man of the cloth."

So she'd been right to identify him as a member of the gentry. "You've chosen an admirable vocation. Will you take holy orders soon?"

"Next year, if all goes well. Until then, I'm condemned to share quarters with your archnemesis."

His vilification of the vicar, while gratifying, seemed inappropriate for the setting. "We shouldn't speak of this here. And please know that I bear no grudge against Mr. Bunting. I would as soon everyone forgets our disagreement."

"As you wish." With a genial smile, Mr. Tremayne changed the subject. "It would be proper for us to speak sedately of books, I think. Then anyone rude enough to eavesdrop will be most impressed by our intellects."

"Now you're teasing me."

"What else is a man to do at such an event than tease the prettiest girl in the hopes of making her laugh?"

Annabelle *did* laugh at his silliness. "I'm too old and sensible to heed such flattery, Mr. Tremayne. Now, perhaps I should not be keeping you from the other ladies. There may be one who is more deserving of your attention."

"Ah, modesty becomes you. As to the other ladies, I'm afraid they seem far more interested in our host."

The reference to Lord Simon tempted Annabelle to

glance in his direction. As before, a bevy of beauties clustered around him. She had to concede he looked arrestingly handsome tonight in a midnight blue coat, his white cravat a complement to his sun-burnished face and thick dark hair. The other gentlemen in the drawing room paled by comparison to his broad-shouldered strength and cool confidence.

He abruptly turned his head and looked straight at her. Annabelle experienced the burn of those dark gray eyes in the form of a mad pulsation deep within her. She felt overheated and sorely in need of a fan. He didn't appear pleased to see her here . . . or did he object to her sitting with Mr. Tremayne?

On her first visit to St. Geren's Church, Lord Simon had rudely ended her conversation with the assistant curate by rushing her and the duke away to the coach. *I didn't engage your services for you to be flirting with the locals,* he'd said.

How ludicrous. If Lord Simon disapproved of her speaking to any one of his guests, he shouldn't have commanded her to attend this dinner party in the first place.

She aimed a deliberately flirtatious smile at Mr. Tremayne. "It does appear that you're stuck here in the corner with me. We shall have to find a way to keep ourselves entertained until dinner."

"My dear Miss Quinn, whatever words leave your pretty lips are bound to fascinate me." He leaned closer, his voice full of fervent emotion. "I can absolutely assure you of that."

The ardent look on his face disturbed her. Mr. Tremayne seemed a trifle forward in his manners, especially for someone who had dedicated his life to the church. Perhaps his upper-class background had given him a sense of entitlement. If he was one of those gentlemen who viewed the governess as fair game, she would have to take care not to encourage his attentions.

She was casting about for an excuse to escape him when Lord Simon's voice cut through the buzz of conversation in the drawing room.

"I see our guest of honor has arrived at last," he said.

Leaving his flock of admirers, Lord Simon made his way to the door as a slim, stately lady in claret-colored silk glided into the chamber. He placed his hands on her shoulders and leaned down to kiss her cheek. The dark-haired woman smiled up at him, speaking words that could not be discerned over the murmurs of the guests.

Annabelle caught her breath in pleasure. "It's Lady Milford!"

A thought jumped to the forefront of her mind. Could *that* be why she had been included in the dinner party tonight? Because Lady Milford had requested her presence? Yes, it all made sense now. The invitation had not come from Lord Simon by some magnanimous decree, but because he'd been honoring the wishes of a venerated family friend.

"Do you know her, then?" Mr. Tremayne asked.

The assistant curate was looking rather intently at her, so Annabelle explained, "Lady Milford recruited me for the position of governess here at Castle Kevern. I owe her a debt of gratitude."

"Ah, I see."

"Is there something wrong?"

Mr. Tremayne pursed his lips as if he were considering a tactful way to put his thoughts into words. "I'm merely surprised. Her ladyship is hardly the sort to seek out governesses. You see . . ."

Knowing little about the mysterious woman, Annabelle was intrigued by the prospect of learning more. "Pray go on."

"It isn't for the ears of a virtuous young lady like yourself. Perhaps I've already said too much."

"Don't be coy, Mr. Tremayne. I am hardly ignorant in the ways of the world."

"As you wish, then. Once upon a time, Lady Milford was mistress to one of Mad King George's sons, although I don't recall which one. It stirred up a frightful scandal."

Lady Milford, a royal concubine? Annabelle was shocked and fascinated in equal measures. Never had she suspected that the kind, graceful woman could harbor such a notorious background.

Across the drawing room, Lady Milford was greeting the other guests. She possessed a rare beauty that was untouched by the ravages of time. Yet her allure transcended the physical. Even in her advanced years, she had an unusual magnetism that had the gentlemen crowding around her and the other ladies staring in envy.

Annabelle glanced at Mr. Tremayne. "How do you know this? Were you a member of the court?"

"My parents moved in high circles. One overhears things as a child." He paused, his gaze slightly narrowed. "I do recall that she was bastard-born, so I suppose one would expect such a female to carry on illicit affairs."

Stung, Annabelle compressed her lips. Not a soul here at Castle Kevern knew of her own lack of parentage, so Mr. Tremayne couldn't possibly guess that he'd insulted her as much as Lady Milford. "Yet she does bear the title of lady."

"The prince arranged a marriage for her, I believe. To a doddering old lord who didn't mind if his young and beautiful wife took a lover . . ." Mr. Tremayne flashed Annabelle a shamefaced look. "I do beg your pardon. I can see that I'm embarrassing you. It's crude of me to be speaking of such matters."

Annabelle nodded coolly. Better he should think her afflicted by maidenly modesty than to guess at the true nature of her disgust. He could have no inkling that the gossip he'd imparted had made her all the more loyal to Lady Milford, for they both had suffered criticism because of an accident of birth.

She found herself eager to renew an acquaintance with the woman. Scandal or no scandal, she owed Lady Milford a great deal. Perhaps during the course of the evening an opportunity would present itself for them to exchange a few brief words.

Then the decision was taken out of her hands.

Lady Milford leaned close to speak to Lord Simon. He offered her his arm and they came strolling across the drawing room.

They were heading straight toward Annabelle.

Chapter 13

She rose swiftly from her chair and adjusted the shawl around her shoulders. The last thing she wanted was for a gossipmonger like Mr. Tremayne to be privy to their conversation. "If you'll excuse me," she said, "I'd like a word in private with her ladyship."

The assistant curate leaped to his feet, too. "Of course. Though I'd hoped that later we might . . ."

Annabelle stepped away, pretending not to hear him. It was best not to encourage a man who held such snobbish views. At least she'd found out quickly about his contempt for those born out of wedlock. That alone had revealed everything about him that she needed to know.

Lord Simon and Lady Milford met Annabelle halfway across the drawing room. She made her curtsy with pleasure. "My lady, I'm so very happy to see you here."

Lady Milford greeted her with a warm smile and a kiss on the cheek. She exuded the delicate fragrance of lilacs. "It is indeed wonderful to meet again, Miss Quinn. You look especially lovely tonight. Don't you agree, Simon?"

His cool gaze flitted over Annabelle. "Quite. Which

is why she oughtn't have been hiding behind the ferns with the assistant curate."

"Mr. Tremayne was kind enough to keep me company," she said, matching the hint of mockery in his tone. "I trust that was permissible."

He frowned slightly. "I meant no criticism, only that it's customary to mingle with all the guests."

Meant no criticism—what bosh! Lord Simon clearly did not want his female employees to be associating with any gentlemen. "Alas, Mr. Tremayne was the only person I knew here," she said. "Apart from you, of course, and you were otherwise occupied with your . . . admirers."

Harem was the word Annabelle would rather have used if it wouldn't have been extremely impolite. Lord Simon already looked annoyed and she could only think it was because he'd been forced to invite her to this party. Just to provoke him, she held his gaze and refused to cower like a servant.

With a faint smile, Lady Milford had been observing the exchange. Now, she slipped her hand through Annabelle's arm. "Come, the three of us must sit and enjoy a chat. I'm sure Miss Quinn has much to relate about the duke's progress in his lessons."

"I'm afraid that will be impossible," said Lord Simon. "I've given instructions to the head footman. Dinner will be served in a moment."

On cue, the gong sounded out in the corridor. The guests began to line up according to rank for the procession into the dining chamber.

Lady Milford quickly took Annabelle's hand and placed it on Lord Simon's arm; then she moved to his other side and tucked her own hand into the crook of his elbow. "There, Simon, it will do your reputation well to be seen escorting *two* ladies in to dinner."

The unconventional move put Annabelle in a quandary. The aristocratic guests would be offended if a governess led the way. Should she excuse herself and move to the rear of the line as custom demanded? But she had no wish to offend Lady Milford, who was only being kind.

Lord Simon cocked an eyebrow. "We cannot ignore precedent, as well you know."

"Oh, la!" Lady Milford said with a flutter of her fingers. "This is merely an informal dinner in the country. The standards are not so strict as in town. Unless, of course, you have become too tediously dull to dare flout the rules."

He glowered at her another moment, then broke into a laugh. "You always did know how to maneuver a man, Clarissa."

With that, Lord Simon walked them to the head of the line. Annabelle could feel the stares of the other guests and heard their whispers, but she held her chin high. Their opinion held little weight since she didn't belong to their exclusive circle, anyway. Why not enjoy the moment? Never had she imagined herself being escorted by the handsome—if infuriating—son of a duke.

How envious the teachers at the academy would be to see her now. Perhaps she would do well to remember that this venture into the upper crust was merely temporary. At the end of the evening, she would return to her little chamber in the nursery and her ordinary life as governess.

The party proceeded down the corridor and into the dining chamber. Mrs. Wickett had vanished, thank goodness. Annabelle didn't think she'd be able to enjoy dinner with the housekeeper glaring crossly from the corner. Lord Simon showed Lady Milford to a place of honor at one end of the long table. Then he guided Annabelle to a seat nearby, where a small white placard displayed her name.

He held the chair for her, and as she sat down, she glanced, up to voice a polite thanks. Much to her shock, he was staring down at her—or rather, at her bosom. His brooding gaze shifted to hers, and their eyes held for a long heated moment. She glimpsed something dark and powerful and raw in him, something that stirred her deeply. Then he strode away to take his place at the opposite end of the table.

Afraid she might be blushing, Annabelle lowered her gaze to the table to avoid catching the eye of any guests filing into the dining chamber. She felt utterly shaken and unable to put a name to the firestorm that Lord Simon had ignited inside her. What had that look meant? Was he *attracted* to her?

It didn't seem possible. The man was hardly even civil! He had never before given her cause to believe he might harbor a romantic interest in her. Except, of course, for that moment in his study a few weeks ago, when Mrs. Wickett had walked in to find them standing close together.

And then there'd been that day in the library when Annabelle had almost blurted out to Ludlow the secret of the tunnels. Lord Simon had caught hold of her hand to caution her to keep silent. His nearness had rendered her weak-kneed, though she'd convinced herself the reaction was one-sided.

But what if he too felt this wretched tug of desire?

The possibility thrilled her, even as common sense warned against drawing conclusions based on a burning look or a brief touch. A man in his exalted position would never marry a governess, let alone one of dubious lineage. If Lord Simon felt anything at all for her, it could only be lust—and she had no intention of ever engaging in an illicit liaison.

A footman brought a tureen of soup, and she ladled a clear beef consommé into her bowl. Her gaze strayed to Lord Simon, who sat at the far end of the table. He smiled and conversed with the young ladies seated on either side of him, one a scrawny brunette and the other, the beauteous Louisa.

Now there was the sort of lady he would choose as his wife.

Annabelle acknowledged a knot of envy inside herself. The cold, hard truth was that the son of a duke would never court a woman like herself. He could want her for only one purpose—and she should count herself lucky that he seemed disinclined to charm her into his bed.

Nevertheless, she couldn't deny a buoyant happiness inside herself. The dining room took on a brilliant glow as she gazed down the linen-draped table at the flickering candles in the silver candelabra, the bouquets of red roses and white asters, the sparkling china plates and the engraved silverware. The footmen in their formal wigs moved among the guests, helping to serve the guests while the butler poured burgundy wine into crystal glasses.

She spotted Mr. Tremayne sitting midway down the long table, thankfully too far away to embroil her in conversation. Lord Simon had objected to her speaking to the man. Could his criticism have arisen from jealousy?

How foolish of her to want to believe that! But even more foolish was this desire she felt for Lord Simon. Perhaps her weakness for him arose from the fact that she'd known so few men in her life. Maybe it was only natural that upon leaving the girls' academy she would feel drawn to the first handsome gentleman she met . . .

"You look rather familiar," said the balding man beside her. He was Lady Louisa's father, Lord Danville, an affable man with ginger side whiskers and a reddened nose. "Have we met?"

She manufactured a polite smile. "I'm Miss Quinn, and perhaps you remember me from St. Geren's. I've been bringing the Duke of Kevern to services each Sunday."

"Oh-ho!" Lord Danville said with a big smile. "Why, that's the very thing. But I still think your eyes remind me of someone . . . why, it might be Princess Victoria, I believe. Very pretty blue eyes, indeed!"

Seated across from them, Lady Danville was as elegantly slender as her husband was comfortably stout. "She's merely the governess, Nigel."

Lord Danville glanced dumbly at his wife. "What—oh, very good," he said, looking a bit confused. "Very good, indeed."

As he returned his attention to his soup, Lady Danville flashed him a disdainful look that made Annabelle dislike the woman all the more. She could not forget the humiliation of that day when Lady Danville and her daughter, Lady Louisa, had laughed at Annabelle for spilling the sugar onto the floor.

Lady Danville aimed a speculative gaze at Annabelle. "There *is* something familiar about you, Miss Quinn. From where do you hail?"

"Yorkshire, my lady."

"And who are your people, your family?"

Hiding her alarm, Annabelle took a sip of her wine. "Alas, I'm an orphan. I lost my parents long ago."

She looked down at her plate, striving for a sad expression in the hopes that the woman would show compassion and pry no further.

But Lady Danville persisted. "Don't be coy. You must be privy to their names. Do tell me at once."

Lady Milford spoke from the foot of the table. "Miss Quinn is not subject to your inquiries, Harriet. It should be enough for you to know that she came highly recommended. I am happy to report that His Grace is flourishing under her care."

"With all due respect, Mr. Bunting might disagree," Lady Danville said. "He told me that it was *her* interference that caused him to be barred from the schoolroom here."

Lady Milford glanced at Annabelle in such a way that it was apparent she hadn't known about the vicar's dismissal. Then she laid down her spoon and aimed a steely stare at Lady Danville. "Miss Quinn is my protégée. The next time you spread rumors about her, kindly remember that."

Lady Danville's gaze faltered. She compressed her lips and uttered no retort, much to Annabelle's amazement. How was it that Lady Milford wielded such power over the shrew?

Lady Milford went on in a milder tone. "Nigel, why don't you tell us about the hunt? It is to be the day after tomorrow, is it not?"

A smile creased Lord Danville's robust features. "Indeed, we will make quite a large party. Since my dear Louisa has made her debut, she will be joining us this year. She has become quite the crack shot, I must say. She will put all of us gentlemen to shame!"

"The gentlemen will be more interested in her beauty,"

Lady Danville corrected, glancing down the table at her daughter. "Or shall I say, one man in particular."

Lord Simon.

The soup went tasteless in Annabelle's mouth, but she forced herself to finish it. It was no concern of hers which blue-blooded girl he chose to court. She and Lord Simon lived in different worlds. She didn't even like the rude, arrogant, insufferable man.

Except when he had defended Nicholas against the vicar's cruelty. Oh, *then* Lord Simon had been like the hero in a storybook. What a shame he had failed ever since to show his nephew even the smallest sign of affection.

As the footman bore the soup dishes away and Lady Milford deftly guided the conversation onto the latest news from London, Annabelle strove to be quiet and unobtrusive. It was a relief to have the attention turned away from her. And she refused to allow any further thoughts of Lord Simon spoil this rare evening of luxury.

Instead, she concentrated on savoring the sumptuous courses of fish and quail and cheeses, followed by an apricot cream cake that she'd watched Mrs. Hodge prepare in the kitchen that morning. At the time, Annabelle had never imagined that she'd be upstairs enjoying a slice herself in the company of the best families. How very different it was from sharing a tray with Nicholas in the nursery.

After dinner, the ladies retired to the drawing room for tea and gossip while the gentlemen remained in the dining chamber to drink their port. Annabelle hoped to use the opportunity to slip away, but Lady Milford insisted they sit together on a chaise out of earshot of the other women.

"I have been on pins and needles," her ladyship confided, patting the back of Annabelle's hand. "You cannot imagine my delight upon hearing that you'd ousted that dreadful man from the schoolroom. Pray tell me how you accomplished the matter so swiftly."

Annabelle related everything from her initial assessment of the vicar's poor teaching skills to her attempts to convince Lord Simon to look into the boy's rigorous schedule, and finally the moment when they'd caught Bunting in the act of striking Nicholas.

Distress on her fine features, Lady Milford shook her head. "I could see the child was unhappy the last time I came to visit, and I suspected it was due to the vicar. But Simon would hear nothing of it."

"He was skeptical," Annabelle admitted. "It took me three attempts before I was able to convince him."

"He can be quite obstinate at times. I am suitably impressed by your persistence in standing up to him."

"I had to keep trying for the sake of His Grace. Nicholas is such a darling boy. I've grown very fond of him."

A misty quality entered Lady Milford's beautiful violet eyes. "There, I knew you would be the perfect governess. You have accomplished even more than I'd hoped."

Feeling undeserving of the woman's praise, Annabelle glanced down at her lap. "I've done my best for him, yet he needs love from—" She stopped, not wanting to sound critical of Lord Simon.

"From his uncle," Lady Milford said with an astute nod. "We must speak frankly, my dear. Simon does indeed shun the child for reasons you've probably learned from gossip belowstairs."

"I've heard that he courted the late duchess," Annabelle admitted.

"He seldom speaks of Diana, though I'm certain he has never forgotten her treachery. A man who loves so deeply suffers greatly when his heart is broken." Lady Milford squeezed Annabelle's hands. "You must help him heal, my dear."

"Heal?"

"Why, yes, by convincing him to accept Diana's son, Nicholas. I am depending upon you to bring them together."

Annabelle released the breath she'd been holding. What a relief to know that the woman wasn't suggesting Annabelle take a romantic interest in him. "I wish I knew how."

Lady Milford's lips curved in a mysterious smile. "You seem a resourceful woman. I'm sure you'll find a way."

Annabelle felt daunted by the assignment. Did Lady Milford realize what she was asking? It was one thing to reorganize the schoolroom and quite another to confront the master about his private affairs. Besides, she'd already asked him to pay more attention to Nicholas, only to be rebuffed in no uncertain terms.

She was about to tell Lady Milford so when the gentlemen returned to the drawing room. The young ladies crowded around Lord Simon and begged him to allow dancing. On his order, the furniture was moved aside and the rugs rolled back. A pair of footmen carried in a pianoforte and placed it in a corner. Mindful of her position on the lowest rung of the social ladder, Annabelle offered to play.

It was somewhat of a relief to select the appropriate music sheets and then sit down to let her fingers flow over the keys. She was no great musician, but the guests were too busy dancing and laughing to notice the occasional small mistake. From her vantage point in the corner, she took pleasure in watching the graceful movements of the gentlemen and ladies.

Too often, her gaze strayed to Lord Simon as he squired various ladies, both young and old. The man was a study in contrasts. He could be cold and cantankerous at times, yet charming and witty to his guests. He could ignore his nephew, yet pay close attention to the ladies. He could snap and snarl at Annabelle, yet subject her to a stare so hot it made her bones melt.

A man who loves so deeply suffers greatly when his heart is broken.

Those words disturbed her. She would rather believe him shallow than capable of feeling a deep, abiding love. Perhaps Lady Milford didn't know him as well as she thought. The woman might have been making conjectures about Lord Simon based on her own experiences with men. If he was really such an admirable person, he would show a little love for Nicholas. It shouldn't matter to him who had mothered the boy.

Mr. Tremayne came to turn the pages for her. "What a pity you have to sit here," he said. "I should have liked to have danced with you."

Preferring to be alone with her thoughts, Annabelle pretended to be concentrating on the music. "I don't mind. I enjoy playing."

To her consternation, he remained beside the pianoforte, making small talk and blocking her view of the dancers. She soon found herself gritting her teeth behind a fixed smile. What had been a pleasant task became a chore when she could no longer see the other guests.

Mr. Tremayne seemed oblivious to her irritation. "We never did finish our conversation. Perhaps you'll take a walk with me on the morrow."

"I'm afraid that's impossible. I shall be busy with His Grace."

"Can you not ask a nursemaid to watch him for a while?"

"I take my role as governess very seriously, Mr. Tremayne. I've no spare time whatsoever."

She hoped that statement would be strong enough to discourage his attentions. Yet he continued to chat as if her words meant nothing to him. As she finished playing the song, Lord Simon strolled into view, carrying a glass of champagne.

"Miss Quinn needs a rest," he told the assistant curate. "Perhaps you'd be kind enough to seek another lady to take her place."

A scowl flitted over Mr. Tremayne's face. The two men exchanged a long glance as if gauging each other. Then Mr. Tremayne nodded to Annabelle and stalked away into the milling crowd.

Annabelle hardly dared to look into Lord Simon's eyes. The lifting of her spirits couldn't possibly have anything to do with the man who had come to her rescue. She simply wouldn't allow it.

He offered his hand to her, and it would have been impolite to refuse his help. As she rose from the bench, the brief grasp of his fingers made her keenly aware of his strength.

She quickly withdrew her hand. "Thank you. It *is* rather nice to stand after sitting for so long."

He gave her the flute of champagne. "You've had no refreshment or respite for nearly two hours. I'm afraid you've allowed us to take advantage of you."

"I'm perfectly happy to do my part."

"Why so meek? For once, you've ample reason to scold me."

"It isn't my place to rebuke the master of the castle."

A half-smile touched his lips. "That fact has never stopped you before. Now drink."

Annabelle took a sip of the refreshing wine, savoring the burst of bubbles on her tongue. It might be imprudent, but she couldn't help returning his smile as all the gaiety of the night came rushing back. The candlelit chamber with its rich appointments seemed like the setting of a fairy tale. And here she stood with the handsome prince.

Or was he really the evil ogre in disguise?

If only she knew.

Lord Simon leaned against the pianoforte. The action brought him closer to Annabelle, so close she could have reached out and traced his lips with her fingertip. "If someone else can be induced to play," he said, "you will dance with me."

Her pulse fluttered. "Is that a request? Or a command?"

He chuckled. "A command tempered by the knowledge that you, Miss Quinn, are prone to disobedience."

The notion of waltzing with him filled Annabelle with keen longing. What would it be like to be held in his arms? Just for a few moments, she wanted to fancy herself a lady being courted by the most eligible gentleman in the room. Yet it would be most unwise to accept his invitation if it meant encouraging his lust . . .

As she hesitated, his smile faded into one of cool charm. "Feel free to refuse," he said. "It was Clarissa's idea, anyway. She thought it unfair that you'd missed all the fun." He glanced back at the guests, where Lady Milford stood chatting with several dowagers.

The light dimmed in Annabelle's reckless heart. By force of willpower, she maintained a pleasant expression while placing her half-empty glass on a nearby table. "If truth be told, I'm rather weary. A governess must keep early hours."

On cue, the casement clock out in the corridor bonged twelve times. The deep intonations underscored her sudden craving to depart.

"Midnight," he murmured, watching her intently. "Time for Cinderella to run off to her garret."

"Indeed it is," she said lightly, picking up her shawl. "I shall endeavor not to lose my slipper on the way. Good night."

Leaving him, she headed toward the arched doorway. How strange that he would utter such a remark when she had been reveling in the fairy-tale atmosphere. Sometimes it seemed as if he could read her thoughts—while she herself had little clue as to his.

She couldn't resist glancing back one last time at the glittering assemblage. Lord Simon had gone straight to Lady Louisa to engage her in conversation. So much for his interest in the governess. It was a surprisingly bitter pill for Annabelle to swallow.

As she watched, he bent his head to whisper in Lady Louisa's ear. Annabelle suddenly realized who the girl resembled with her fair hair and delicate features: the woman in the miniature beside the duke's bed.

Nicholas's mother, Lord Simon's lost love.

Chapter 14

"Look what I found, Miss Quinn!"

Annabelle walked gingerly over the rock-strewn sand to the place on the beach where Nicholas was hunkered down. As she reached his side, he glanced up, his face bright with excitement. The stiff breeze had tousled his flaxen hair and he had smudges of dirt on his hands. He looked exactly as he ought, a little boy intent on exploration.

"Do you see it?" he asked, peering into a shallow rock pool that had been left by the low tide.

She leaned down to look. "I see lots of things."

Strings of reddish seaweed undulated slowly in the water, providing shade for various shells, a starfish, and the brown blob of a sponge. Ever since the vicar had been banished from the castle, she and the duke had embarked upon several expeditions down to the beach for the purpose of a science lesson. Having known only the moors of Yorkshire, she found the seashore as new and fascinating as Nicholas did. In the library she had discovered a book that contained illustrations of the flora and fauna along the coast. Together, they had been learning the names of all the various sea creatures, as well as researching those to avoid touching, such as jellyfish and sea urchins.

"There's a prawn hiding in the rocks," he said, pointing. "He's waving his leg at us."

"That's his antenna, I believe," Annabelle said. "It appears to be attached to his head."

"Can I catch him? I could keep him in a jar and feed him crumbs."

She smiled ruefully. "I'm afraid he would miss his home here, darling. It's best we leave him to find his family."

Nicholas accepted the verdict with a solemn nod. He went scrambling over the rocks to the next pool. Carrying a sack with a few things he'd collected, she strolled behind him, one hand on the ribbons tied beneath her chin. Even on such a balmy day, the brisk wind tugged at her straw bonnet. The air held the briny aromas of fish and seaweed that she had grown to enjoy.

"Could we explore the cave?" Nicholas asked suddenly, pointing back at the cliff. "We might find buried treasure left by pirates."

At low tide, the sea had withdrawn from the massive boulders at the base of the cliff, where the dark opening of a cave could be seen. But Annabelle had been warned by the housekeeper never to allow the duke to play there.

The tide comes in fast betimes, Mrs. Wickett had said. *'Ee could be caught there and drown.*

Annabelle smiled regretfully at him. "Unfortunately, it's dark inside the cave, and we haven't a lamp with us. Besides, I would have to ask your uncle's permission."

"Oh. He'll just say no."

Clearly disappointed, Nicholas returned to his hunt for treasure. He was right about Lord Simon, she thought, her lips pursed. The man took no interest at all in his nephew. But she had resolved not to spoil this lovely day by brooding about that exasperating man.

High above on the cliff loomed Castle Kevern. Tilting her head back, Annabelle admired the turrets and towers outlined against the blue sky. It was a magnificent sight that she never tired of viewing. The ancient stones were silvery gray with bits of crystal that sparkled in the sunlight.

Something else glinted up there, too. Something close to the ground, something like the flash of sunlight on a mirror . . .

Squinting in an effort to see better, she took a few steps forward. The flicker abruptly vanished. Was someone up there watching them with a spyglass? Someone who realized he'd been spotted and had pulled back out of sight?

How absurd. Lord Simon and his houseguests had left early that morning for a shooting party at Lord Danville's estate, several miles distant. Only the servants were present at the castle.

The more Annabelle considered the notion of a mysterious spectator, the more ludicrous it seemed. There could be no rational reason for anyone to observe her and the duke in such a clandestine fashion. She must have seen the glint of sunlight off a metallic rock—or perhaps a shard of broken glass.

Her disquiet subsiding, she turned her back on the castle. Nicholas hadn't noticed anything amiss. A short distance away, he was using a piece of driftwood to dig an embedded shell out of the sand.

While he was occupied, Annabelle strolled closer to the water. The vastness of the ocean filled her with awe, as did the hypnotic rush of the waves. She could gaze at the sea for hours, watching the colors change from a pinkish sheen at dawn to greenish-blue during the day and then to deep black with the approach of night. Yet for all its beauty, treachery lurked beneath the surface. Here and there, sharp rocks poked out of the water. The servants had spoken of ships that had gone aground during storms along this coast.

A gull swooped low, making its raucous cry. Annabelle watched the bird for a moment as it rode the air currents. Then she saw that Nicholas had finished excavating his trophy. Now he was attempting to cram the too-large seashell into his pocket.

She hid a smile, for the task was impossible and he'd only succeeded in spilling sand all over his short trousers. "Would you like me to put that in our collection bag, Your Grace?"

"Yes, please."

He handed the conch to her. After their first trip down to the beach, when he'd wanted to gather everything in sight, she had learned to bring a gunnysack in which to deposit his treasures. It could be anything from a dried starfish to a pretty rock or a floating bottle. Then they would take the flotsam back to the classroom for study. Sometimes, if they found something particularly interesting, he would sketch the item for his art lesson.

Annabelle added the shell to the bag and then tightened the drawstrings. "Hmm, it's growing quite heavy," she said. "I'm afraid that means it's time for us to go back to the castle."

He squinted against the sun to look up at her. "Just a little while longer? Please?"

"It will soon be time for your geography lesson. But perhaps tomorrow, depending on the weather and the tides."

Like the good boy that he was, Nicholas didn't argue the point. Instead, he bounded ahead of her to the stairs that had been cut into the side of the cliff. The steep path took them some distance beyond the castle to a place where the cliff descended into a gentler slope.

Nimble as a monkey, he mounted the steps. "Have a care, Your Grace," she called after him.

The wind whipped away her words. But she knew he'd heard her because he turned slightly and waved to her. He continued his ascent, while Annabelle made slower progress, hampered as she was by the gunnysack and her long skirts. He disappeared over the top before she'd even reached the halfway point.

The boy knew not to go on without her. Nevertheless, she made haste, not taking time to enjoy the spectacular view of the sea. She was breathless by the time she reached the top. The stairs gave out onto a forested hill, the same hill she'd climbed on the day she'd first arrived at Castle Kevern.

She stood there a moment and looked around. Nicholas was nowhere to be seen. A chill feathered down her spine. What if someone really *had* been watching them? Someone who had abducted the duke?

A sudden gust dislodged her straw bonnet. Preoccupied, she let it dangle by its ribbons against the back of her neck. Where was Nicholas?

Then she spotted the boy sitting atop a boulder half-hidden in the trees. Instantly she felt silly for letting her imagination run wild.

As she went hurrying toward him, he heaved a big sigh. "What took you so long?" he asked. "I've been waiting *forever*."

Annabelle laughed. "Braggart," she said. "Now, do

climb down, Your Grace. We've still a short walk ahead of us to reach the castle."

Nicholas jumped down. "I'm a captain in the cavalry. I'll protect you from the enemy."

He trotted down the path, venturing to the edge every now and then to shade his eyes with his hand while he peered into the woods. Annabelle smiled to see him playing make-believe like any other child. How amazing to think he was the same frightened little boy she'd met just over a month ago. He'd only needed gentle guidance, a sense of security, and most of all, love. That was something he hadn't received from the vicar—or from his uncle.

Her thoughts strayed reluctantly to Lord Simon. In the two days since the dinner party, she hadn't seen him at all. According to the kitchen staff, he had been busy entertaining his guests. Early this morning, he had escorted the company to a shooting party at the estate owned by Lady Louisa's father. At this very moment Lord Simon might be riding with the dainty blond beauty, perhaps luring her away from the crowd so they could share a stolen kiss . . .

Annabelle gave herself a stern lecture. She had no right to feel a twinge of envious longing. She and Lord Simon lived in different worlds and nothing would ever change that fact. How he spent his time was no concern of hers—except that Lady Milford had charged her with the daunting task of mending the rift between him and his nephew.

A man who loves so deeply suffers greatly when his heart is broken. You must help him heal, my dear . . . I am depending upon you to bring them together.

Annabelle scowled down at the dirt path. Nearly a

decade had passed since Lord Simon had been jilted by Nicholas's mother. The man shouldn't still be carrying a grudge—especially not toward a sweet and innocent child. But she could think of no way to broach such a delicate topic without jeopardizing her position as governess.

Heal him, indeed! Lady Milford might as well have asked Annabelle to scale the walls of the castle without rope or ladder.

To make matters worse, Lady Milford had come up to the nursery for a visit the previous afternoon. Nicholas had joined the two women for tea, and afterward, her ladyship had asked Annabelle to write to her in London. *I shall be hoping to hear of your progress with Simon,* she'd murmured on her way out the door. *Remember your promise.*

Annabelle sorely disliked the prospect of disappointing Lady Milford when she owed the woman such a debt of gratitude. Somehow, there had to be a way to convince Lord Simon to spend more time with his nephew . . .

She suddenly noticed that Nicholas had strayed off the path. He was making his way down the forested slope rather than proceeding up toward the castle.

"Your Grace!" Annabelle called. "Where are you going?"

A rabbit bounded ahead of him into the underbrush, and Nicholas gleefully chased after it. "I need to catch the enemy," he said over his shoulder.

"Don't venture too far, darling."

Annabelle assured herself he couldn't get lost in these woods, at least not for very long. Just beyond this hill, there were meadows and farms in the valley. Above, through a break in the trees, Castle Kevern towered on the cliff.

Nevertheless, she hurried after Nicholas as he tracked his prey downhill. For too long his imagination had been stifled by the vicar. It was good for him to have the freedom to enjoy an adventure like any normal little boy.

In his knee breeches he had the advantage of her, for the abundant undergrowth kept catching at her skirts. As she bent down to unhook her hem from a clump of brambles, Annabelle heard the snap of a twig somewhere behind her.

A footstep?

Her skin crawled at the notion of being followed. Maybe she hadn't been wrong to think someone had trained a spyglass on them from up on the cliff.

She turned to scan the area. Sunlight filtered through the tall firs and beech trees and ancient oaks, dappling the clumps of tiny blue flowers and the dense greenery. She couldn't see a living soul on the hill above her. But the sloping woodland had numerous dips and depressions where a person might be hiding. Additionally, the huge boulders and thick tree trunks could provide cover for someone who didn't wish to be seen.

Or perhaps it was merely a piskie.

The thought injected a bit of humor that served to dilute her unease. Maybe this was how superstitions were born, from a naturally occurring sound or sight that was misconstrued by the local folk. Logic told her that if there was another entity in these woods, it could only be human—perhaps a servant from the castle or a workman taking a shortcut.

In the kitchen, she'd heard mention of a poacher, but that had been an isolated incident at the southernmost edge of the vast estate. Besides, no one on such an illicit mission would dare to venture so close to the castle. The risk of discovery would be too great.

She and the duke were perfectly safe here.

Annabelle turned back to see that Nicholas had stopped partway down the hill. He was gazing at the ground, but she couldn't tell at what. A wry smile tugged at her mouth. She hoped to goodness that he hadn't managed to trap the poor rabbit. He'd want to keep it as a pet, and then she'd have to explain to him the difficulty of stuffing the squirmy, frightened animal into the gunnysack.

Oh, well. Perhaps one of the stablemen could be coaxed into building a hutch. It might be educational for Nicholas to have the responsibility of feeding and caring for a rabbit.

Pondering the matter, she gingerly made her way down the steep forest floor. A tiny stream trickled among the fallen leaves, and as she stepped over the wet rocks, the sole of her shoe slipped. She braced her hand on the nearest tree trunk to steady herself.

An angry bee whizzed past her ear. A fraction of a second later, she heard the deafening crack of a gunshot.

Far ahead of her, Nicholas fell to the ground.

Chapter 15

The shot echoed through the woods and across the valley. She froze for a split second, her mind battling disbelief. *A poacher.* There must be a poacher, after all.

Dropping the gunnysack, Annabelle spun around. "Stop!" she shouted. "Don't shoot! There's a child here."

All lay silent except for her own harsh exhalations. A quick scan of the forested slope revealed no movement among the tall trees, no sign of where the gunman might be hiding.

There was no time to find him.

In a mad panic, she went scrambling down the hill, slipping and sliding on thick layers of leaves. Mud and dirt soiled her hem but she scarcely noticed. Her only thought was for Nicholas. Had he been struck?

Oh, dear God, he must have been. She had seen him go down. He had vanished from sight. Had he been badly injured . . . or killed?

The thought wrenched a sob of terror from her throat. It couldn't be true. It just couldn't. Where was he? She thought knew the place, but he wasn't there . . .

A few yards ahead, Nicholas popped into view. He scrambled to his feet and stood looking down at his hands.

His fair hair was messy, his clothing dirty, but Annabelle had never seen a more welcome sight. Sinking to her knees, she caught hold of his shoulders and gave him a frantic look-over. It was a vast relief not to see blood anywhere on him.

She clutched his small, warm body close to hers. "Oh, darling, I saw you fall. Are you all right?"

He nodded, his look more curious than fearful. "Was somebody shooting?"

Annabelle wrestled her wild emotions under control. Her heart was still pounding madly. It wouldn't do to frighten him, so she forced herself to speak calmly. "Yes, I think so. It . . . must have been a poacher."

He lifted his chin. "Poachers are not allowed here. They must be made to go away so they don't kill my rabbits."

At his imperious frown, she swallowed a hysterical bubble of laughter. It was *he* who needed protection, not the wildlife. Thank goodness, he must not have realized just how close the shot had been. If the bullet had hit him . . .

Annabelle rose shakily to her feet. Though she burned to find out who had fired the gun, her first duty was to Nicholas. He must be taken straight back to the safety of the schoolroom. "You're quite right, I'll speak to your uncle about it as soon as possible. Now come. We must return to the castle at once."

Slipping her arm around him, Annabelle urged him away from the area where she estimated the shooter to be, all the while keeping a sharp eye out. She felt dangerously exposed, having no means to protect the duke except to keep him close to her side as they traversed at a wide angle up the hill. The only sounds were the scuffling of their feet through the underbrush and the distant crash of the waves on the other side of the cliff. Not even the birds twittered in the treetops. It was as if a hush had fallen over the woods.

Where was the gunman? She could see no sign of him anywhere. What if he fired again?

No. No, surely he wouldn't. When she'd shouted, he must have realized his mistake. Now he would be lying low until he could slink away without being caught. Oh, how she would love to give the coward a severe tongue-lashing!

An unwelcome suspicion wormed into her mind. What if she was wrong to think him a poacher? What if chance had had nothing to do with the incident? What if the shooting had been deliberate?

Her mind shunned the possibility. It simply couldn't be. For what wicked purpose would anyone fire a gun at a young boy?

Except that he was no ordinary little boy. He was the wealthy Duke of Kevern, owner of this immense estate, descendant of a noble lineage that included royalty . . .

Nicholas tugged on her arm. "Look what I found," he said, holding up a small object in the grimy palm of his hand.

Annabelle gave it a distracted glance. The piece was a dirt-encrusted bit of metal with some markings on it. Because she didn't want to alarm him, she attempted to speak normally. "How remarkable. Where did you get it?"

"I picked it up back there. You know, where we heard the shot."

Her mind resurrected that terrible moment. Annabelle

realized that Nicholas had vanished from sight because he'd seen the tiny treasure lying on the ground. He must have bent down to grab it at the very instant the bullet had been fired.

She shuddered to think of what might have transpired if not for that chance action.

"I'm *very* glad you picked it up," she said. "Very glad, indeed."

As they emerged from the forest, they found themselves on the main drive that sloped upward to Castle Kevern. Annabelle had never been happier to see the tall gray towers and high battlements looming only a short distance away. Intent on ushering him inside those protective walls, she hurried Nicholas toward the open iron portcullis.

The drum of hoofbeats behind them caught her attention. A rider was fast approaching, though the bend in the road and the thickness of the woods hid him from view. No one was expected, the guests were gone for the day, and for all Annabelle knew it could be the gunman. On instinct, she urged the duke back toward the screen of trees.

"Where are we going?" Nicholas asked in confusion.

"Just over here for a moment."

Before they could take shelter, however, the horseman cantered into sight. It was Lord Simon in his hunting finery: a dark burgundy coat with buckskin breeches and black knee boots. Upon seeing them on the grassy sward at the edge of the forest, he reined his large gray gelding to a halt, the animal dancing and snorting.

A vast sense of relief washed through Annabelle. Never had she been happier to see him. Then abruptly her blood ran cold as her gaze fell on the object lashed to the back of his saddle.

A hunting rifle.

His gaze intent on them, Lord Simon called out, "Why are you out here? Is something amiss?"

"His Grace and I just went for a walk," she said, forcing a smile while keeping Nicholas close to her side. "I—I thought you would be gone all day."

"Lady Louisa took ill so the party broke up early. The others decided to go into the village to look at the shops." He swung down from the saddle and walked toward them, leading the horse by the reins. He was limping slightly, favoring his left leg. His sharp gray eyes studied her, and it was clear that he'd noticed her distress. "Something *is* wrong. Tell me."

Annabelle hesitated. She hardly knew what to say. Was it mere coincidence that he had appeared so soon after the shooting and in possession of a rifle?

Until Nicholas married someday and sired a son, Lord Simon was the heir presumptive. He would become the Duke of Kevern if . . .

No. To think that he might murder his nephew for personal gain was just too hideous to contemplate.

Nicholas gripped her hand. Gazing cautiously at his uncle, he said in a small voice, "There was a poacher, sir. He was shooting in the woods."

Lord Simon's expression darkened as he stared down at the boy. Then his gaze snapped to Annabelle's. "Do you mean to say this happened while you two were out there just now?"

She nodded shakily, deciding to play along with the poacher explanation. "Yes, just a few minutes ago. The bullet passed rather close to where we were standing. Of course we came straight back here."

Lord Simon's face took on an even more thunderous look. She had never seen him so angry, not even the time when the vicar had struck Nicholas. "Who was the man? Describe him to me."

"I can't. I never saw him."

"Where exactly did this occur?"

"That way," Annabelle said, pointing into the forest. "On our return from the beach, Nicholas ventured off the path. He was . . . he was chasing a rabbit when—" Her voice broke and she couldn't trust herself to say more.

Lord Simon placed his hand on her back, urging her toward the castle. "Come," he ordered, not unkindly. "Both of you need to go inside."

Together they hurried into the courtyard where the dolphin fountain splashed water, the merry sound a stark contrast to the darkness inside her. Lord Simon shouted for a groom to take the horse to the stables. She tried not to flinch from the warm pressure of his hand against her back. Could those fingers have held the rifle, aimed it at Nicholas, and pulled the trigger?

Did he despise his nephew that much?

Annabelle ordered herself to cease the wild speculation. All the facts had yet to be gathered. She needed time to think, to assemble the pieces and find logic in the madness. First and foremost, Nicholas must be protected from harm. Only then could she seek answers.

The duke seemed blessedly unaffected by the events, likely because he hadn't realized just how close the bullet had come. He trotted straight to the fountain, where he leaned over the stone edge and proceeded to wash his dirty little treasure in the burbling water.

Before she could follow, Lord Simon caught hold of her wrist. "Take the boy upstairs to his nursemaid," he said in an undertone. "Then I want you back down here at once. In the meantime, I'll have a look around. If I'm not here when you return, wait for me."

He turned on his heel, stalked out the massive gateway, and vanished from sight.

Fifteen minutes later, Annabelle paced the courtyard. It had been wrenching for her to leave Nicholas to play with his toy soldiers with only Elowen to watch over him. Annabelle had extracted a promise from the maidservant not to let him out of her sight, even for an instant.

Despite the balmy weather, she rubbed her arms in an attempt to dispel a bone-deep chill. Even the brightness of the sun couldn't penetrate the darkness of her thoughts. Her mind kept worrying over the course of events. She felt certain someone had been spying on her and Nicholas from the cliff. If that same person had been waiting for them to leave the beach, it meant the shooting hadn't been the act of a careless hunter.

The villain must have concealed himself along the trail that led back to Castle Kevern. But they had strayed off the path, and so the gunman had been forced to reposition himself. That was when she'd heard the twig snap behind her on the hillside. Moments later, the shot had been fired.

By whom? And for what purpose? And worse, was it merely a ghastly happenstance that shortly thereafter, Lord Simon had ridden up the road with a rifle strapped to his saddle?

Reason told her he was the only one who would benefit from the duke's death. Yet her heart resisted believing Lord Simon was a murderer. If he wanted his nephew dead, why shoot him in broad daylight and invite a criminal inquiry? Why risk being seen by a passing farmer or a servant? There were easier ways to make a death appear to be an accident. Poison the boy's food, for instance. Or lure him up to the parapet and push him over onto the rocks below . . .

Annabelle shuddered at the gruesome image. Until the truth came out, she must keep an extremely close watch over Nicholas. She must also be careful not to make assumptions. Without solid proof on her side, she dared not make such a serious accusation against a man as powerful as Lord Simon.

Treading a circuit around the fountain, she tried to think of anyone else who might want Nicholas dead. Lady Louisa wished to wed Lord Simon, and if Nicholas were out of the way, she could aspire to become Duchess of Kevern, rather than merely the wife of a second son. Her father, Lord Danville, had bragged at the dinner table that she was a crack shot. Perhaps Lady Louisa had only claimed to be ill this morning, then had ridden here on the sly.

Yet try as she might, Annabelle couldn't picture the elegant lady hiding in the bushes and stalking her prey. It was ludicrous even to consider such a thing. However, it was always possible that Lady Louisa had hired a ruffian to do the wicked deed.

And at least it proved there were other scenarios to consider—in addition to the possibility that the shooting truly *had* been unintentional, the mistake of a nearsighted local who'd wanted a rabbit for his stewpot.

The crunch of footsteps on gravel made Annabelle whirl around to see Lord Simon striding into the courtyard. He looked no less grim-faced than he'd been earlier.

She darted forward to meet him. "Did you see anyone?"

"No, but I did find this." He was carrying the gunny-sack with their treasures from the beach.

"I forgot all about that!"

"It was helpful that you'd dropped it," he said. "It enabled me to pinpoint exactly where you were stand-ing. But I'm afraid I didn't see evidence of a bullet any-where in the immediate vicinity."

One of his dark brows was raised, giving him a look of faint skepticism. Was he hinting that she must have imagined the incident? So that he could claim it had never happened?

"I heard the bullet fly directly past me," she insisted. "It made a peculiar whining sound. Almost instantly, there was a loud report that echoed across the valley. Nicholas heard it, too."

"If you don't mind, I'd like for you to come out there with me. You may be able to help me determine the route of the bullet."

Her heart skipped a beat at the notion of venturing into the woods with Lord Simon. Tall and intimidating, he loomed over her. He could easily overpower her in the isolation of the forest where no one would witness his attack. But she had to risk it for Nicholas's sake.

Biting her lip, she nodded. "Of course."

He left the gunnysack in the courtyard, then led the way into the trees. Sunlight sifted through the branches of the leafy oaks and tall firs. The brambles and vines helped create the illusion of a primeval forest far from civilization. Annabelle hadn't remembered the hill be-ing quite so steep and difficult to navigate. Of course, at the time, her mind had been focused on getting Nicholas back to the castle as swiftly as possible.

Lord Simon's fingers suddenly closed around her arm.

She drew a sharp, involuntary breath, glancing up to find him regarding her curiously.

"I didn't mean to startle you," he said. "I thought you might need help stepping over this log."

His nearness made her nervous. But she mustn't flinch every time he came close or he might realize her suspicion of him. "I suppose I'm on edge," she said. "Are you absolutely certain the poacher is gone?"

"Without a doubt. Anyone reckless enough to fire a gun so close to the castle wouldn't linger to face the consequences."

His hand firm on her arm, Lord Simon assisted her over the rotted remains of a tree trunk. It was the act of a gentleman, Annabelle told herself, and under normal circumstances she would have appreciated the courtesy. But there was nothing normal about this day.

A short distance later, they reached the spot where the tiny stream trickled through fallen leaves. "This is where I dropped the gunnysack," she said.

"It was lying at the base of that beech tree." Lord Simon stood a few steps away, his gaze steady on her. "I want you to tell me exactly what happened. Don't leave anything out. Will you do that?"

Annabelle nodded. To give an accurate accounting of the events, she must assume he knew nothing, that he hadn't been the one hiding in the bushes. Nevertheless, she felt reluctant to tell him the part about the spy on the cliff. If it had been him . . .

"As I said, Nicholas and I had just come up from the seashore. We took the path that led back to the castle, but he spied a rabbit and went chasing after it. I followed him as he came downhill this way." She indicated the approximate route behind her.

He studied the ground. "There's a heel mark right here. Did you slip?"

"Yes. The stream made the ground damp. My shoe skidded on the fallen leaves and I braced my hand on this tree." Reliving the awful event, she flattened her palm against the smooth bark. "That was when I heard the bullet. It sounded like . . . an angry bee flying past my ear. Then Nicholas fell out of my sight . . . and I thought . . . I feared . . ."

As the horror of that moment swamped Annabelle, an uncontrollable shudder shook her and she uttered a small moan. If the bullet had been fired an instant sooner, Nicholas might have been killed. That sweet little boy . . . dead . . .

At once, she found herself enclosed in Lord Simon's arms. His action was so unexpected that she lacked the will to object. As he pressed her close, his muscled chest provided surprising comfort and his body heat penetrated the coldness in her heart. Never before had she been so near to a man. Never had she known he could make her feel protected in a way that swept away logic and reason.

Surrendering to temptation, she burrowed her face into the crook of his neck and slid her arms around his waist. The steady beating of his heart soothed her distress. She needed this closeness with a keen desperation. Sweet heaven, she could scarcely believe how perfect it felt to be held by him.

His hands stroked in a soothing pattern over her back. "It's over, Annabelle," he murmured. "Nicholas is safe. There's no harm done."

His use of her first name caused a quake inside Annabelle. It startled her to an awareness of the impropriety of their embrace. Lord Simon was her employer and a man far above her in rank. Worse, he might have been the gunman. For all she knew, he might be deliberately charming her for the purpose of allaying her suspicions.

On that sobering thought, she broke free and retreated a few steps. "I—I'm sorry, my lord. I don't know what came over me."

His eyes regarded her with cool intensity. "You've suffered a shock, that's all. There's no need to apologize."

"I didn't feel so paralyzed at the time of the incident."

"You instinctively did what needed to be done. You ran to check on my nephew, to see if he'd been hit."

"Yes." She bit her lip and looked away. "At first I couldn't see him and it terrified me."

"If you think you can manage it, why don't you show me exactly where he was standing?"

The question provided her with a much-needed excuse to escape his compelling presence. "Of course."

Annabelle gingerly picked her way down the forested slope. It was disturbing how easily his embrace had broken through her guard. She must keep a clear head and remember that trusting Lord Simon could be extremely dangerous. No one else had a better reason than he did for wanting Nicholas dead. And for an even more compelling purpose than inheriting the dukedom.

The boy was a constant reminder of the woman who had spurned Lord Simon.

She reached a small flat place that jutted into the hillside. Birds twittered in the ancient oaks that brooded over the miniature plateau. "Nicholas was standing right here," Annabelle said, pointing at the ground. "You can see the depression in the leaves where he knelt down."

Lord Simon stopped beside her, his brow furrowed. "I didn't realize he'd ventured quite so far. I'd assumed he was much closer to you."

"No, he was running to catch the rabbit, you see. I could scarcely keep up."

Lord Simon paced away from her. He seemed to be inspecting the nearby trees. Then he crouched down to gaze more closely at one of the oaks more than a yard distant from where she stood. "We're in luck," he said over his shoulder.

"What do you mean?"

"You'll see in a moment."

He reached into his pocket for a penknife, employing the tip of the implement to dig at the bark. Then he returned to her and displayed a flattened ball nestled in his broad palm. "The bullet."

Her heart tripped over a beat. She felt compelled to touch the misshapen orb with her fingertip. It seemed so tiny for something that could kill a person. "So the poacher fired this with his rifle."

"No." Lord Simon gave a decisive shake of his head. "It's too small for the bore of a rifle. This ball came from a pistol."

Chapter 16

A pistol! A giddy sense of relief washed through Annabelle. Then the rifle that had been lashed to the back of his saddle meant nothing. Nothing at all. Lord Simon had carried the gun with him only for the hunting party at Lord Danville's estate.

Yet the news didn't entirely exonerate him. She had to be careful not to take him at his word, for he might be leading her astray. He had reason to plot the duke's death. And for all she knew, he might have kept a smaller weapon secreted in his saddlebags.

"Do you mean . . . a dueling pistol?" she asked. Didn't many wealthy gentlemen own such a set? Annabelle wasn't certain, though she'd read about men challenging each other to duels over insults to their honor.

Lord Simon deposited the ball in an inner pocket of his coat. "There are many types of pistols. However, what's intriguing is that hunters generally use a rifle. The aim is more accurate when firing at a distant target."

Her heart tripping over a beat, she gazed at him through the veil of her lashes. "Are you suggesting that the gunman wasn't a poacher, after all?"

"I said *generally*. A pistol may have been the only weapon the scoundrel possessed." Lord Simon spoke distractedly, the frown on his sun-darkened features indicating he was intent on his private thoughts. "Wait right here. Now that we have two points of reference, the trajectory will lead me directly to the spot where he was hiding."

Starting at the oak, he marched in a straight line up the slope and past the place where she'd been standing when the shot had been fired. He continued onward several yards, then slowed down to peer closely at the undergrowth as he mounted the hill.

Annabelle anxiously watched him. Had he found something yet? Or were his actions an elaborate scheme designed to deceive her?

Only time would tell. In the meanwhile, she distracted herself by making a circuit of the ancient oaks. Despite being on an incline, the ground in this area was level except for a waist-high mound covered in thick vines, rather like an overgrown altar. With the leafy branches overhead and the trees marking the four corners, Annabelle felt as if she were standing in a cathedral designed by a nature deity.

What an odd fancy!

She glanced up the hill to see Lord Simon moving higher toward the castle. Where was he going? Had he found a trail left by the gunman?

Too restless to stand still, she continued walking around the perimeter of the oaks until she had made a full circle, arriving back at the place where Nicholas had dropped out of her sight. Here, he had stopped chasing the rabbit when he'd spied his little treasure lying on the ground.

On impulse, Annabelle crouched down to view the

scene from his diminutive height. How different the
world looked from a lower vantage point. It brought the
surroundings into sharper focus. Thick piles of leaves and
humus carpeted the earth, perfuming the air with a rich
scent. A short distance away, a spider spun a web between
the dried branches of a fallen limb. Shafts of sunshine
cast a soft buttery light over the gentle mound in the center of the oaks.

Something glinted beneath the tangle of vines. She
scooted closer and gingerly parted the vegetation, peering deep within the foliage.

Then she reached in and pulled out . . . a gardening
trowel.

In great surprise, Annabelle turned the small implement over in her hands. It appeared to be rather new.
Surely it would be pitted with rust if it had been abandoned here for many years. Had someone lost it recently?
Or concealed it on purpose?

But why would anyone hide such a tool? The middle
of a forested slope was hardly the ideal place to garden.

Mystified, she glanced around, looking for evidence
that someone had been digging in the vicinity. Her
gaze sharpened on the spot where Nicholas had been
standing. In several places, crumbs of dirt lay atop the
foliage as if the leaf mold had been shoved aside, and
then manually moved back into place to camouflage
the area.

She used the edge of the trowel to scrape away the
natural debris. Quickly, it became obvious that the earth
beneath the covering had been disturbed, for the hard
surface was broken and powdery. Someone *had* been
digging here quite recently. But for what purpose?

There was one way to find out.

She glanced up to see Lord Simon nearing the top of

the hill. To pass the time until his return, she decided to scoop out soil from the area. Scraggly roots impeded her excavation, and for a few minutes she turned up nothing but pebbles and an occasional black beetle.

Then a dull glimmer caught her attention. Reaching into the hole, she plucked a small object out of the loose dirt. It looked to be a very filthy coin.

Buried treasure?

Intrigued, she rubbed her thumb over the surface to clean off some of the grime. The object appeared to be made of gold, but it didn't resemble any recognizable British coin. When she tilted it to the sunlight, the well-worn markings showed a stylized horse surrounded by leafy foliage. The other side depicted a mighty stag with antlers.

How very odd. If the artifact was indeed currency, there was no numerical value stamped into the metal. Nor were there any words to use for the purpose of identification.

The tramp of footsteps signaled Lord Simon's return. Reminded of his quest, Annabelle scrambled up to greet him. "Did you see any sign of the gunman?"

"There was a place just off the path where he must have been lying in wait. The foliage was crushed there—" Lord Simon broke off, staring down at the shallow hole and the pile of soil beside it. "What the devil have you been doing?"

"Someone hid a trowel beneath the vines over there." She made a vague wave at the mound. "When I looked around, I noticed there were signs of excavation beneath the leaves. And see what I found buried in the dirt?"

She handed him the coin. One eyebrow raised, he turned over the piece while examining it in the light filtering through the trees. "How extraordinary." His voice held a note of excitement that she'd never heard from him before. "It appears to be quite ancient."

"Nicholas found a small bit of metal here, too," she said. "He bent down to pick it up at the very instant the shot was fired."

Lord Simon glanced sharply at her. "And that's why you thought he'd been struck."

"Yes. Do you suppose that's a Roman coin?"

He shook his head while gently rubbing his thumb over the image. "It looks Celtic to me. I've seen similar pieces in museums. The Celts were the native people in Britain at the time of the Roman occupation."

"They were pagans who worshipped nature," Annabelle added with growing enthusiasm. "Their priests were called Druids. Cicero wrote about them, as did Pliny the Elder."

For the first time that day, a smile touched Lord Simon's lips, giving a hint of the attractive man behind the misogynist. "Did you read that in the original Latin? If so, I'm most suitably impressed."

She colored slightly under his scrutiny. "Yes, well . . . do you suppose it's possible this was once a holy place to the Druids? An outdoor church, perhaps? These oaks look quite prehistoric."

"They do, indeed." Lord Simon walked slowly around the quartet of massive trees, pausing to stare up into the gnarled old branches. "The Celts had a particular affinity for oaks. They believed that a nature deity resided in each one. To this day, we Cornish have a superstition about cutting down oaks. It is considered to be bad luck."

"This little clearing looks rather like an outdoor cathedral, don't you think? The trees mark the corners." She placed her hand on the central mound. "And here is the altar."

"Very observant, Miss Quinn." His gray eyes alight, Lord Simon glanced around as if seeing the area for the first time. "As a boy, I roamed all over these woods. Odd how I never took any notice of this particular place."

"Someone else must have noticed, though," she said, taking a step toward him. "Someone who hoped to dig up buried treasure."

His face sobered. "Quite so. Where exactly did you find that trowel?"

She pointed to the base of the altar. "Right there."

Lord Simon circled the mound, pushing the vegetation aside in places. Suddenly, from the other side, he pulled forth a full-sized spade that had been concealed beneath the vines. "It seems our mysterious digger came well prepared. I must say, this explains quite a lot."

"What do you mean?"

He propped the spade against the mound. "Just as I suspected, there was never any poacher. And once I saw where the bullet had struck, I knew that Nicholas could not have been the target, either. He was too far away from the gunman. Therefore, I could only conclude the villain was aiming at *you*."

Annabelle was almost too flabbergasted to speak. Of all the statements he could have made, that was the last one she'd expected. "At *me*? Why?"

"I didn't know the answer until you found it right here. The gunman must be the same person who hid the shovel and spade." His gaze bored into her. "That shot was meant as a warning to frighten you away from this place."

Lord Simon refilled the hole and layered the area with dead leaves until it appeared undisturbed. He also replaced the spade and trowel where they'd been found beneath the vines. After determining that nothing more could be accomplished at the moment, he took Annabelle's arm as they mounted the steep hill to the path.

"I'll station a sentry to watch the site from a distance," he told her. "At no time will it be left unguarded. With any luck, the villain will return and he'll be apprehended."

That reminded Annabelle of something. "A few weeks ago, one of the kitchen maids mentioned seeing a ghostly light here on the slope after dark. She was certain it was piskies."

"Piskies! Alas, I doubt the little creatures carry pistols." Chuckling, he guided her around a patch of brambles. "That tells me something, anyway. Our villain has been doing at least some of his work at night. I may just take a shift myself this evening."

"But you've a houseful of guests to entertain."

"Everyone is leaving on the morrow, so I imagine they'll opt for an early night." His jaw tightened. "If indeed there are ancient artifacts buried on this land, they belong to the Duke of Kevern. As the boy's guardian, I fully intend to prevent them from being stolen."

Seeing his resolute expression, Annabelle felt a seismic shift in her heart. His determination to protect Nicholas's legacy held the unmistakable ring of truth. Dear God, how wrong she'd been to suspect Lord Simon. How could she have ever thought him so dastardly as to hide in the bushes and fire a bullet at his own nephew?

She had wanted to believe the worst of him, that was why. After all, he had shunned Nicholas for reasons she found intolerable. But it was a vast leap from disliking a child to murdering him.

Now she would have to live with the discomfiting

knowledge that Lord Simon deserved an apology that she didn't dare to voice. Her position as governess might very well be in jeopardy if ever he learned of her low regard for his character.

Annabelle averted her eyes so he wouldn't see her guilt. There would be time enough later to flay herself in private. For now, she needed to concentrate on the mystery.

As they crested the hill and started along the path that led to the castle, she asked, "Who in the area has an interest in Celtic history?"

"I've been wondering that myself," he said. "Unfortunately, the answer is—everyone. The locals still celebrate pagan feast days like Beltane and Samhain. And you can't travel half a mile without meeting a farmer or a shepherd who believes in the old superstitions."

"If the people here have such esteem for the Druid ways, it seems they'd hesitate to disturb a holy site."

"Not everyone has scruples when tempted by buried treasure. However, the scoundrel might be an outsider who learned of it from one of the locals. I'll make inquiries to see if there's anyone new in the neighborhood."

The perpetrator had to be someone utterly ruthless. Now that Annabelle had had time to absorb the shock, she could better appreciate her lucky escape. The bullet had passed within inches of her head. What if her foot hadn't slipped? What if she hadn't leaned against the tree trunk? She might have been seriously injured—even killed.

Grateful to be alive, she drew a deep breath of salty air. Her straw bonnet had slipped off earlier, with only the tied ribbons securing it at the nape of her neck. A lady would have donned it again, especially in the presence of a gentleman. But Annabelle wasn't feeling very proper.

The brush with death had shaken her to the core, and now she wanted to savor the simple joys of sunshine on her face and the sea breeze stirring her hair.

If she dared to admit it, the vibrancy inside her also had much to do with the man walking beside her. She was very aware of his hand cupping her arm as if he thought her a fine lady, his social equal.

If only that were true.

A pulse of longing assailed her depths. Against all wisdom, she wanted to experience his embrace again. This time she would slide her arms around his neck and tilt her mouth up for his kiss . . .

The notion was as sinfully irresistible as the man himself. Glancing his way, she caught Lord Simon gazing at her with a hooded expression. The wind had tousled his dark hair and lent him the rakish air of a pirate. Was he thinking about ravishing her?

The raucous cry of a gull broke the silence. Shocked at her own wicked thoughts, Annabelle averted her eyes. Nothing could ever come of such yearnings. Unlike Lady Milford, she could never indulge in a liaison without facing a life of ruin. Annabelle didn't have a doddering noble husband who'd given her carte blanche to carry on an affair with a royal prince. She could depend upon no one but herself.

Lord Simon's voice intruded on her thoughts. "It would be helpful to see the artifact that my nephew found," he said. "I'd like for you to bring it to my study as soon as possible."

In her present frame of mind, Annabelle had little tolerance for his avoidance of Nicholas. "Better yet," she countered, "you could come straight upstairs to the nursery to see it."

"Then you trust me to be near Nicholas?"

"What do you mean?"

He cocked a sardonic eyebrow. "You believed *I* was the gunman. Don't bother to deny it. I saw your horrified expression when you spied my hunting rifle."

So he had known all along. Aghast, Annabelle hardly knew how to respond. She could tell little from his expression except that he had the heartless look of a tomcat toying with his prey.

But she would not play the mouse.

She slowed her steps and turned to face him squarely. "Yes, I do admit that the notion entered my mind. I had to consider all possibilities in order to safeguard the duke. I'm sorry if that offends you, my lord, but my first duty is to protect him. And since I've yet to see you display any affection at all for him . . . well, I could only think the worst."

Lord Simon listened in tight-lipped silence. With a slight tug on her arm, he urged her to continue walking down the path that skirted the east wall of the castle. "You're as blunt as Clarissa," he said. "At least I can bid *her* adieu on the morrow."

"Then you'll not send me packing, too?"

"No, I need you . . . to watch over Nicholas. You've done a fine job with the boy. It's clear he's fond of you."

His praise warmed her more than it ought—perhaps because she'd so seldom had anyone compliment her. And what had that pause meant? Annabelle didn't wish to know. "It isn't difficult to win the affections of a child," she said. "One needs only to be kind and loving, and the sentiment will be returned tenfold."

"Come now, you belittle your abilities."

"No, it really *is* that simple. His Grace would grow fond of you, too, if only you gave him a chance."

"I know nothing about children," he said dismissively.

"Nonsense. You were a boy yourself once."

"Not like Nicholas. I was boisterous, outspoken, and always embroiled in some sort of mischief. Many a time I slipped out of the nursery to avoid doing my lessons."

Annabelle could imagine him sneaking through the secret tunnels as a means of escape. "You must have been a trial to your governess."

"It seems that's a talent I've never lost."

One corner of his mouth curved in the raffish smile he used on all the ladies. Truly, he posed a far greater danger as a charmer than when he was angry. The best cure for her wayward attraction would be to force him back to a serious discussion.

"Just because you engaged in more tomfoolery," she said, "doesn't mean you've nothing in common with His Grace. He enjoys the same things as any boy—playing with toy soldiers, reading adventure stories, searching for flotsam on the beach."

"He's far too shy and quiet. It's impossible to know what he's thinking."

"That's a poor excuse for avoiding his company." Afraid she might never have a better chance to break through to him, she dared to add, "I'm beginning to believe that underneath all that manly bluster, you're something of a coward."

"A coward!" As if burned, he let loose of her arm and took a single step backward. "By God, if you were a man I'd call you out for such an insult."

Annabelle's heart beat faster. But she wouldn't quail under his furious glare. Nor would she retract her statement. By his own actions, Lord Simon had demonstrated that he couldn't face the pain of the past. He had shunned the duke's company because Nicholas resembled the woman who had spurned Lord Simon so long ago.

On impulse, Annabelle placed her hand on his sleeve. His arm felt as hard and rigid as the man himself. Lowering her voice, she said, "I cannot pretend to know how painful it must have been for you to lose the woman you loved. But you're too mired in the past, and it will be an even greater tragedy if you fail to forge a bond with Nicholas. He's a wonderful little boy who deeply admires you."

"Admires me," he repeated in a tone heavy with skepticism.

"Yes. He always plays with a particular cavalryman from the set of soldiers you owned as a boy. It cannot be merely a coincidence that he chose that piece as his favorite."

His face cast in stone, Lord Simon appeared unmoved by her avowal. His silence destroyed any hope she had of convincing him. He had no intention of softening toward Nicholas.

Ever.

Her throat felt thick with unshed tears. It was too much on top of all the other distressful events of the day. Taking back her hand, she gave vent to her frustration. "Oh, how can you be so hard-hearted? If only you could see how blessed you are to have family in your life. I would give my soul to have a nephew like Nicholas to love."

Turning her back on the man, Annabelle marched down the path toward the front of the castle. A servant was supposed to wait to be dismissed, but she'd broken every rule already, so what did one more matter? If her recklessness earned his wrath, then so be it. He took Nicholas for granted and she simply couldn't tolerate the injustice of it any longer.

As she neared the portcullis, Lord Simon caught up

to her. She could see him out of the corner of her eye, though she refused to acknowledge his presence. Talking had accomplished nothing. She might as well go back to pretending he didn't exist.

But he demanded her attention.

"We're about to have company," he said as they entered the courtyard. "My guests are returning from their sojourn in the village."

Annabelle had been too wrapped in turmoil to take much notice of the outside world. Now she detected the distant rattle of carriage wheels coming from far down the drive. As she picked up the gunnysack, she said coolly, "Then I'll leave you here to greet them. Good day."

He caught hold of her arm before she could depart. His gaze locked to hers. The icy wrath had vanished into something stark and raw, something that resurrected a foolish hope in her.

"They can fend for themselves," he said. "I'm going up to the nursery with you."

Chapter 17

As Simon followed Annabelle up the narrow flight of stone steps, he stared broodingly at her flawless hourglass figure. The sway of feminine hips, the glimpse of lush breasts, provided a distraction from the chaos of his emotions. Lust, he understood. It was all the other feelings she'd stirred in him that he could do without.

He was a damn fool for letting the woman get under his skin. The instant she'd started her tirade out there on the path, he should have commanded her to stop.

Not that she would have obeyed. Annabelle didn't seem to grasp the fact that she was merely the governess. She had a reckless disregard for his authority. She was determined to interfere, poking and prodding into his private affairs.

I'm beginning to believe that underneath all that manly bluster, you're something of a coward.

His pride still smarted from that bayonet thrust. He'd been blindsided by her frank appraisal of his actions. She had ripped open old wounds and refused to back down even in the face of his fury.

Most galling of all, she was right. He *had* lacked the

courage to face the pain of the past. Ever since he'd returned to Castle Kevern after an absence of ten years, he had held himself aloof from Nicholas. He'd been too ready to punish an innocent boy for the sins of his parents.

Yet of all the things Annabelle had said, the one that had jolted Simon the most was her last statement before storming off toward the castle.

If only you could see how blessed you are to have family in your life. I would give my soul to have a nephew like Nicholas to love.

Weeks ago, Annabelle had mentioned that she'd been orphaned at a young age. Simon had thought little of it at the time. But today, the eloquent longing in her voice had blunted his rage and caught at his heart. She knew what it was like to grow up alone and lonely—and she didn't want Nicholas to suffer the same fate.

She cared more for the boy than Simon did.

An uneasy shame nudged at him. For the past year, he had deluded himself into believing he was fulfilling his responsibility to his nephew. Out of selfishness, he had robbed Nicholas of the time and attention he deserved. In denying him affection, Simon had abdicated his duty to provide for the needs of his family.

The realization was a bitter pill to swallow. By his own neglect, he had created a situation he didn't know if he could fix.

Reaching the top of the stairs, Annabelle headed down the dim corridor to the nursery. She didn't look back, didn't even acknowledge his presence. Clearly she had her doubts as to his ability to change his ways.

Simon intended to prove her wrong—somehow. Despite the havoc she'd wreaked in his ordered life, he felt a reluctant admiration for her audacity. She had confronted him not out of a shrewish desire to maneuver and manipulate, but because she truly wanted what was best for Nicholas.

For that same reason, she had gone into the forest with Simon even while suspecting him to be the gunman. She'd been ready to risk her own life to protect the boy. Only once had he seen a crack in her strength. While describing the moment of the gunshot, she had been visibly shaken. He had taken her into his arms—and promptly forgotten his resentment of her for misjudging him.

God! Beneath her prickly temperament, she was so warm and soft—and that bullet had come dangerously close to killing her. The need to protect her burned inside Simon. If it took his last breath, he intended to hunt down the gunman and wring his neck.

But first he had to right another wrong.

Feeling like a prisoner on his way to the gallows, he followed Annabelle through a doorway and into the schoolroom where an array of little tables and chairs stood empty. The smell of chalk dust and book bindings brought back memories of his childhood. Through the bank of windows, a gull sailed freely against a slice of blue sky.

How he envied that bird.

"His Grace is waiting in here," Annabelle murmured. She proceeded down the passage that led to the bedchamber he and his brother George had once shared.

Simon's steps slowed of their own volition. Odd that he could lead a charge into battle, yet feel so loath to visit a young child. This wouldn't be like the weekly meetings when Nicholas answered regimented questions

about schoolwork and then recited what he'd learned
that week. Today, Simon somehow had to befriend his
nephew.

He needed to prove to Annabelle that he wasn't the
monster she believed him to be.

His jaw set, he stepped into the bedchamber. It looked
much as he remembered with the canopied bed that had
been his brother's, the pair of chairs flanking the fireplace, the battered trunk in the corner where he'd once
kept his toys. The only thing missing was the cot where
he'd been relegated as the second son instead of the favored heir.

Nicholas knelt on the window seat with his back to
the door. He was marching a toy soldier up the leaded
glass of the window—at least until he looked over his
shoulder at them. Slowly, he sank back onto his heels
to watch them warily.

Annabelle addressed the stout nursemaid who sat in
the rocking chair, her stubby fingers plying a needle and
thread along the hem of a baggy white garment. "Elowen,
you may go down to the kitchen now and prepare the
duke's tray."

Elowen set aside her mending, then bobbed a curtsy
and lumbered out of the bedchamber.

"Darling," Annabelle said to Nicholas, "your uncle is
here to see the little treasure you picked up on the hillside. Now, if you will excuse me, I'll leave you two
alone."

Leave them? Simon had been counting on her to
smooth over any awkward silences in the conversation.

As she turned to go, he blocked the doorway. "I want
you to stay."

"No, my lord." Those gorgeous blue eyes held a sym-
pathetic look at odds with her steely tone. "I won't be

used as a crutch. I'm afraid you'll have to manage this on your own."

She brushed past him, and he clenched his teeth to keep from snapping at her. A crutch! Damn it all, he'd show her he was not so craven as to dodge a simple chat with a child.

How hard could it be, anyway?

Hunched on the window seat, Nicholas had made himself as small as possible. He tilted down his chin as if hoping to avoid notice. Every now and then, he sneaked a glance at Simon.

As always, Simon felt a twist in his gut to look at him. By God, the boy resembled his mother. They shared the same blond hair, the same green eyes and delicate facial structure, though in manner they were vastly different. Where Nicholas was painfully shy, Diana had relished being the center of attention. She had teased and flirted and driven Simon half mad with lust. She had led him on with kisses and caresses and hints of accepting his ardent offers of marriage, only to spurn him the moment his titled brother had arrived in London for the season . . .

The old bitterness threatened to choke Simon. Nicholas should have been his child, not George's. How dared the two of them die and leave Simon to care for their son.

You're too mired in the past . . .

Annabelle's voice echoed in his mind, spurring him to march across the bedchamber to his nephew. "You found something out in the forest. I'd like to take a look at it."

Nicholas eyed him apprehensively, then reached into his pocket and slowly extended his open palm. A bit of metal gleamed there in the sunlight. His head hung low, he whispered, "I—I didn't steal it, sir."

"No one said you did." Simon tried to see matters from the boy's perspective. Realizing how testy he sounded, he made an effort to moderate his tone. "Did you think I meant to punish you?"

Nicholas moved his thin shoulders in a shrug.

"You may lay that worry to rest. I only wanted to examine this." Careful to make no swift movements, Simon took the relic from Nicholas's small hand. "May I join you?"

Nicholas scooted to the farthest edge of the window seat, leaving room for Simon on the cushion. He sat down, grateful to have the artifact on which to focus his attention. The piece was slightly bigger than his thumbnail. Fashioned of gold, it was embossed with wavy lines that were clearly part of a greater design. The one rough edge indicated that it must have broken off of a much larger object.

An object that likely dated back almost two millennia to the time of the Celts.

He burned to know what else lay buried beneath the soil on the hillside. This piece and the coin seemed to indicate that more treasures awaited discovery. He wondered if the mound in the center might not be an altar, as Annabelle had thought, but rather a burial site. The notion invigorated his imagination. How incredible it would be to unearth the tomb of a Celtic king or a Druid priest. And what an ironic twist of fate, too. When he'd received notice of his brother's death, Simon had been in Dover, about to embark upon an expedition to Greece and Turkey to seek out antiquities. He'd never imagined that a cache of artifacts lay hidden right here on Kevern land.

With his forefinger, he absently traced the engraving on the gold. How long had the intruder been digging in that spot? Had he just begun his search? Or had he already extracted the bulk of the treasure? A cold anger gripped Simon. The bastard had been trespassing on the ducal estate, stealing property from right under his nose, even daring to fire a warning shot at Annabelle and his nephew.

If indeed it had been merely a warning.

Simon couldn't shake the gut feeling he'd had out in the woods during his examination of the scene. From his reconstruction of the bullet's trajectory, Annabelle might well have been struck had her foot not slipped.

He tamped down the rise of horror. Better he should figure out what had happened. Why would the villain seek to kill her? A murder would only draw people to the hillside, thereby increasing the possibility that someone might stumble across the holy site. It made no sense.

He could only conclude that the gunman either had been extraordinarily inept with a pistol—or completely deranged. Simon would far rather it be the first. It stood to reason that a bumbler could be caught more easily than a madman. As soon as he was done here, he intended to question the staff, to try to find out if anyone had been seen roaming the woods . . .

"Is it a pirate treasure, sir?"

Nicholas's tentative voice broke into Simon's dark thoughts. It took an effort to drag himself back to the present. His nephew sat watching, a spark of earnest hope in his eyes. For an instant, Simon saw himself in the lad. At the age of eight, he would have believed the same thing on discovering a gold artifact out in the forest.

"So you've heard tales of the pirates who once roamed this coast."

Nicholas gave a small nod. "Papa used to tell me stories of them."

"I see." Simon didn't want to picture his brother as a loving father, so he concentrated on the bit of gold that he placed between them on the window seat. "What you found here is much older than any pirate treasure. It belonged to the Celtic people who populated Britain thousands of years ago."

Nicholas glanced down at the piece. "Oh." He sounded disappointed. "Are you *sure*?"

Simon chuckled. "Yes, I'm afraid so. There are similar pieces in the natural history museum in London. Besides, I've spent the past ten years studying antiquities such as this one."

"But . . . Papa said you were a captain in the cavalry."

George had spoken of him? As swiftly as the question arose, Simon brushed it away. Yet it continued to disturb him on a visceral level. After that final quarrel, when ugly words had been spoken and the two of them had come to blows, he had assumed his brother was as determined as himself to cut off all family ties.

Simon had left England and never looked back. For a decade, there had been no letters, no visits, no communication at all with his brother. Simon had only returned to London upon resigning his commission, and even then, he'd avoided society where the Duke and Duchess of Kevern reigned supreme. He'd paid a visit to the family solicitor in order to collect an inheritance from his late grandmother—which was the sole reason why the lawyer had known where to send word about the deaths of Simon's brother and sister-in-law: to Dover, where Simon had been awaiting passage to the Continent.

Now, he found himself wondering about all those lost years of estrangement. Maybe guilt had eaten away at George. Maybe he'd suffered remorse for stealing the woman Simon had loved. Maybe that was why he'd mentioned Simon to Nicholas. But speculation served no purpose. Simon could never forgive his brother's betrayal.

But that didn't mean he had to shun George's son.

From the corner of the window seat, Nicholas sat watching Simon. How had he ever thought the boy's eyes were like Diana's? She had been sensual and cunning, while her son's gaze reflected the purity of innocence. Nicholas could have no inkling of the love triangle that had turned brother against brother—nor should he.

Yet the past had affected his life nonetheless.

Nicholas glanced down at something he clutched in his hand. It was one of the little cavalrymen from the set of toy soldiers—presumably the special one that Annabelle had said he carried as a talisman.

He's a wonderful little boy who deeply admires you.

The knot of emotion inside Simon squeezed tightly. What the devil had he ever done to earn that admiration? Nicholas had known his uncle only as a gruff stranger who wanted little to do with him.

But all that would change beginning now.

"You're right," he said, "I was a captain in the cavalry. I was stationed in quite a few different spots . . . Istanbul, Kabul, Cairo. That's where I developed an interest in ancient relics. It was a hobby, you see, while the military was my chosen career."

Nicholas seemed to be hanging on his every word, so Simon continued. "Perhaps sometime I could point out those places to you on the globe in the library. And I kept my uniform, too, if you'd like to see it."

Nicholas's face lit up. "Please, sir, right now?"

Chuckling, Simon shook his head. "No, not today. But perhaps in a day or two, once my houseguests depart." That would also give Simon time to conduct his inquiries in the village. Time to track down the gunman and see justice done.

"Do you promise?" Nicholas asked. His doubtful tone indicated he did not trust Simon to keep his word.

"On my honor as a gentleman. Now, if you've any other questions, I'd be happy to answer them."

Relaxed, Simon leaned against the window frame. This conversation hadn't been as difficult as he'd anticipated. Being a boy, Nicholas would wish to hear more about battles and weaponry, fighting skirmishes with tribal factions, living in tents on windswept plains, and riding on patrol in wild mountain terrain. There were a thousand stories Simon could tell Nicholas on whatever topic interested him.

The boy fingered the cavalryman a moment before giving Simon a pensive look. "Did you know my mama?"

The question knocked the breath out of Simon. For a moment he couldn't speak. "Er, yes. As a matter of fact, I did. But it was a very long time ago and I don't remember her much."

The lie was absolutely necessary. God help him, he didn't want to field questions about Diana. Nothing could be more discomfiting than to have to pretend amiability toward the woman who had ripped out his heart.

"Sometimes I forget what she looks like," Nicholas confessed in a worried tone. "Does that make me bad?"

"No! No, of course not." Simon leaned forward to give the boy an awkward pat on the shoulder. "It just . . . happens as time passes."

"Miss Quinn says that whenever I forget Mama and Papa, I should look at their picture." Nicholas hopped off the window seat and trotted to the bedside table, returning with a small silver frame, which he thrust at

Simon. "See? Maybe this will help you remember her better, too."

Flummoxed, Simon found himself staring down at a miniature portrait of the late Duke and Duchess of Kevern. George wore his crimson ceremonial robes and ducal coronet. Beside him, Diana looked exquisite in pale Grecian robes, a diamond tiara nestled in her blond hair. They appeared eternally young and beautiful, caught forever in watercolors.

Expecting to feel a wave of cold bitterness, Simon instead found himself studying the pair with a dispassionate eye. Their images stirred only a trace of melancholy in him. In truth, his gaze lingered longer over his brother's familiar features than those of the woman beside him. Simon had to admit he missed the brother who had been his rival in everything from sculling to hunting to skirt-chasing.

But that didn't mean he forgave George. Some wounds cut too deeply ever to heal.

Nicholas took the miniature and replaced it on the bedside table. He stood there a moment, tracing his fingertip over his mother's face. "Mama was so pretty. Papa always called her his angel." He turned to give Simon a troubled look. "Is that why God called her home to heaven . . . because she was supposed to be an angel?"

The question left Simon utterly stymied. What was he to say to that when he knew Diana had been shallow and frivolous, willing to betray one brother in order to win the other? It didn't seem right to make up a lie just to placate the boy.

Nicholas watched him as if he expected Simon to know all the answers in the universe. The boy looked so small and forlorn that Simon felt compelled to comfort him. He knelt down and pulled his nephew close in a quick hug.

"I don't know, son. I truly don't know."

The boy's arms hesitantly circled Simon's neck. A lump stuck in his throat. He had never imagined himself embracing George's son. Yet it felt strangely like having a part of his brother back.

If only you could see how blessed you are to have family in your life.

Yes, he did see now what Annabelle had meant. He had regarded Nicholas as a burden thrust upon him by a cruel twist of fate. He had not wanted to acknowledge the blood tie that bound them. But perhaps it wasn't too late to undo that mistake.

A movement in the doorway drew his attention. As if his thoughts had summoned her, Annabelle stood there watching the two of them. She had tidied her appearance and looked every inch the strict governess again. Her rich brown hair was drawn into a severe bun and covered by that ugly spinster's cap. He much preferred her windblown and hatless, her face tilted to the sunshine.

Their gazes met, but he couldn't quite read those lovely blue eyes. She addressed Nicholas. "The luncheon tray has arrived, Your Grace. It's waiting for you in the schoolroom."

Nicholas obediently trotted to her side and out of the bedroom. As she turned to follow the boy, Annabelle flashed a mysterious half-smile over her shoulder at Simon. Then she vanished.

That brief curve of her lips ignited his blood. In any other female, he would have thought it a come-hither look. But Annabelle wasn't an accomplished flirt like the ladies who chased after him. She was strong, principled, self-reliant—and she expected those around her to be-have accordingly.

Did she still think him hard-hearted? He hoped not. He did so want to win her esteem . . .

Irked with himself, Simon jumped to his feet. How pitiful for a man of his rank to be craving a word of praise from a servant. He must be stark, raving mad. Indeed, Annabelle had stirred a bedlam of emotions in him, the chief of which was . . .

Lust. It had to be lust.

To hell with propriety. He wanted her in his bed so he could find relief from this burning obsession. He would kiss and caress her until she was moaning with need, begging for the ultimate release. Beneath all that prim garb, Annabelle was a passionate woman, and a torrid affair would bring them mutual pleasure.

Yes.

But first he had to clear up the mystery of the gun-man. He had to mete out justice and make absolutely certain that neither Nicholas nor Annabelle faced dan-ger again. Then and only then could he concentrate on seducing her.

Chapter 18

Nearly a week later, Annabelle and Nicholas headed downstairs to the library. The duke had learned to apply himself diligently to his morning lessons. Today, he had done so well on his mathematics examination that as a special treat, she had ordered their afternoon tea brought to the library so they could spend a few leisurely hours reading together.

He hugged a copy of *Robinson Crusoe* to his chest as they headed down a dim-lit passage. "Are there any other books with pirates in them?"

"I don't know, but we can look." Adjusting the gray silk shawl around her shoulders, she smiled down at him. "You're becoming quite the bibliophile."

"Bib-what?"

She repeated the word more slowly. "A person who loves books. Or more specifically, you could be considered a collector of books since every volume in the library belongs to you."

A pleased expression dawned on Nicholas's face. "I *do* own them all, don't I? There must be hundreds and hundreds."

"Thousands, perhaps. It's a large room with quite a lot of shelves."

"Millions and millions," he embellished. "Billions!"

Annabelle laughed. "Well, I hope not quite so many or it will take me forever to find another history of the Celts—"

As they turned the corner, she came to an abrupt halt. The door to the library was closed. Was someone in there? The servants did their cleaning early since she and Nicholas often came to the library in the afternoon. She could think of no one else who might close the door . . .

Except Lord Simon.

Her heart lurched at the prospect of encountering him. Since the day of the shooting, she had seen him only once, when she'd brought Nicholas to his study for the scheduled Friday meeting. Much to their surprise, Lord Simon had been wearing his full military regalia. He had proceeded to tell them stories about his adventures as a captain in the cavalry. Annabelle had been transfixed by the sight of him in his crimson coat and black trousers, the medals decorating his chest, the sword sheathed at his side. But the fascination she felt was due to more than the outer trappings of the man. She had been deeply touched by his effort to form a bond with Nicholas.

Unfortunately, four days had passed since then. Four days in which Lord Simon had been busy with his investigation, or so she'd heard from the other servants. Everyone had been aghast at the news of the shooting. Apparently he had called each of them into his study for a private interview to ask if anyone had seen a stranger lurking on the hillside. According to gossip in the kitchen, Lord Simon also had ridden down to the village on several occasions to make inquiries there.

Was it possible he was questioning someone in the library right now? Or entertaining a visitor? Curiosity flourished inside her.

"Why is the door closed, Miss Quinn?" Nicholas asked.

"I can't imagine, but we shall find out."

Annabelle hastened forward to rap on the carved oak panel. She waited a moment but no sound emanated from within the room. Turning the brass handle, she cautiously opened the door and peeked inside.

No one occupied the vast chamber with its long walls of oak shelves. Rays of sunlight slanted through the leaded-glass windows and fell on the empty tables and comfortable chairs. Logs had been laid in the hearth, though no fire had been lit.

Disappointment filled Annabelle. Of course, it was only logical to feel let down. She would have liked the chance to ask Lord Simon about the progress of his investigation.

"Much ado about nothing," she said to Nicholas as they went inside. "Perhaps one of the servants closed the door by mistake."

He stayed close to her side. "Or maybe somebody came through the secret tunnels to spy on us. Do you think it could be a pirate?"

She smiled, running her fingers through his flaxen hair. "No, darling, the tunnels are a family secret. Only you and your uncle know about them."

"And you, too, don't forget!" He grinned in obvious pleasure at having caught her in a mistake.

"True," she admitted, "but only because we had to find you that time you ran away. Now, will you put *Robinson Crusoe* back on the shelf where you found it? Then you may choose something else to read."

He headed off to a section by the windows. Annabelle went in the opposite direction, to the east wall where the history texts were shelved. The well-organized collection gave joy to her heart. She had always loved the library at Mrs. Baxter's Academy, but the one at Castle Kevern put it to shame. Surely every book ever printed must be shelved here, and Annabelle looked forward to reading as many of them as possible over the coming months.

A pang touched her heart. In less than a year's time, Nicholas would go off to Eton and she would leave the castle to find a post elsewhere teaching another child or children. She might never again see Nicholas—or Lord Simon. But perhaps today was too soon to fret about what the future might hold . . .

As she walked past a potted plant, something flew out at her. Something large and black.

She gasped and jumped back, the shawl sliding off her shoulders. The rush of flapping wings filled the air. In the next instant, she realized what it was.

A bird!

Her heart pounding, she stared up at the black crow that circled the high ceiling. It flew to a top shelf and perched there, glaring balefully down at her.

Nicholas came running to her side. "How did a bird get in here?"

"I suppose it fell down the chimney."

His eyes as round as saucers, he stared up at the crow. "Can we put him in a cage? I could feed him bits of bread."

"I doubt there's a cage large enough in the castle. And I daresay crows are not like little songbirds, anyway. They're meant to be free outdoors."

Nicholas thought for a moment. "I'll open a window," he said. "Maybe he'll fly out."

"What a clever idea. Thank you."

He went trotting across the library at the same moment that a maid arrived with their tea. It was Livvy, the skinny, freckle-faced girl from the kitchen. "Where do 'ee want this, miss?"

Annabelle gave a distracted wave of her hand. "Anywhere will do."

As the maid toted the tray to a polished oak table in the center of the room, Annabelle watched the crow, still clinging to its high perch. The closed door now made sense—someone must have wanted to keep the bird confined in here.

But who—and why? Perhaps a servant had discovered the crow, shut the door, and had gone to seek help in catching it . . .

The bird abruptly took flight.

Livvy uttered an earsplitting shriek. The tray slipped from her hands and thumped down onto the table with a jarring clink of china.

The girl sank into a crouch on the floor, throwing her apron up over her mobcapped head. She cried out, "Oh, no . . . sweet Jesus save me!"

Annabelle shifted her gaze from the wheeling bird to frown at the panic-stricken maid. Nicholas had opened the casement window, and now he turned to stare at Livvy, too. The last thing Annabelle needed was for him to become alarmed by the maid's hysteria.

"Do be quiet, Livvy. I can scarcely hear myself think."

"But . . . but, miss. 'Tis a *crow*!" She launched into a fresh torrent of caterwauling.

"Crow or sparrow, it makes no difference," Annabelle said firmly. "Better we should concentrate on removing it from here."

The bird sailed to the tall casement clock, settled atop it, and let out a single raucous cry.

Peeking out from the shelter of her apron, Livvy wailed, "'Tis an omen . . . an omen o' death!"

"Nonsense. I'll hear no more of your superstitions. I'll wager it is more frightened of us than you are of it." As she spoke, Annabelle picked up her shawl from where it had fallen on the floor. "Nicholas, kindly move aside and I will shoo it toward the window."

The boy nodded, his eyes large as he backed away.

Annabelle cautiously approached the bird. Stealth mattered little since it watched her with beady black eyes. Odd, the creature *did* have a malevolent look about it . . .

Squelching the irrational fear, she took aim and flicked her shawl at the high perch. The bird squawked and flew away, though not toward the window. It soared to the ceiling, then alighted on the top rung of the ladder used for access to the highest shelves.

Livvy cowered and sobbed.

Nicholas trotted forward, his eyes bright with excitement. "I can climb up there and scare him, Miss Quinn."

Thank goodness he seemed to view this as an adventure. "I appreciate the offer, but that won't be necessary. I'm sure I can induce the bird to move."

Annabelle went to the ladder and pushed it along the shelves. As she'd intended, the bird took flight with black wings flapping. It swooped down and this time came to rest on the tall back of a chair.

The chair occupied a dais in an alcove of the room. At once, she recognized the peeling gilt of the arms, the threadbare scarlet upholstery and lumpy seat. It was the chair Lord Simon had occupied on Grievances Day when she had come to convince him to dismiss Mr. Bunting. What had Ludlow, the old retainer, called it? The Judgment Throne.

How appropriate, for the pesky crow was about to meet its judgment.

"I've an idea," she murmured to Nicholas. "Stay right here while I try to get closer."

She crept toward the crow, tiptoeing to keep from startling it. Across the library, Livvy was still snuffling loudly and Annabelle hoped the sound would cover any slight noise that she might make. She edged around behind the bird. Once she was within arm's length, she slowly readied her shawl. Then she tossed it over the crow.

The large square of fringed gray silk landed dead center on the bird. Instantly, she dove forward to keep the crow from escaping.

A muffled squawking emanated from within the fabric. She scooped up the bundle and attempted to control the bird's frantic fluttering.

Nicholas clapped his hands. "You caught him, you caught him! Hurrah!"

"Hurrah, indeed," said Lord Simon from the doorway. "That was quite the impressive feat."

Annabelle almost dropped the shawl and its contents.

Walking into the room, he addressed the maid. "Livvy, I could hear you halfway across the castle. Stop your sniveling at once and go back to your duties."

The freckle-faced maid pulled the apron from her head, scrambled to her feet, and made a mad dash for the door.

Lord Simon continued toward Annabelle, and one corner of his mouth quirked in the charming half-smile that always turned her legs to melted butter. His black hair was windblown as if he'd just come in from outdoors, and he was dressed in a coffee-brown coat over an open-neck shirt, tan breeches with knee-high boots. Even in common garb, he exuded the confidence and authority of a nobleman in his prime.

As he reached her side, he cocked an eyebrow and glanced down. "Have you decided to keep the bird, then?"

In her momentary absorption, she'd forgotten the ensnared crow. "Of course not! I'm intending to let it outside."

"Allow me." He took the wriggling bundle from her, walked across the library to the open window, and leaned forward on the stone sill.

Annabelle hurried after him, as did Nicholas. They were just in time to see Lord Simon unwrap the shawl. The crow tumbled out, then spread its wings and soared into the blue sky.

"Look!" Nicholas shouted. "It's free!"

"What a relief," Annabelle said, meaning every word. "I don't know what I'd have done if my method hadn't worked."

"It was unorthodox but effective," Lord Simon remarked.

As he handed the shawl back to her, she made a sound of dismay. The bird's claws and beak had pulled some threads and left a number of small holes in the gray silk. "Oh, drat. It's ruined."

He inspected the damage. "Can you not mend it?"

"Possibly, though it will never look the same. It was a farewell gift to me from the students at the academy." Burying her dismay, Annabelle summoned a smile. "Never mind, it can be replaced. I've been wanting an excuse to visit the village shops."

As she folded the shawl, a black feather floated to the

floor. Lord Simon gave it to Nicholas. "A souvenir, Your Grace."

Nicholas happily stuck it in the buttonhole of his coat. "Miss Quinn said the crow fell down the chimney. I never knew that could happen."

"It shouldn't have. Up on the roof, there's netting across the opening. It must have come loose."

Or had it? Annabelle couldn't shake a suspicion that someone had deliberately put the crow in the library, knowing that she and Nicholas often came here in the afternoon. But why? To frighten them?

"What a pity the fire wasn't lit," Lord Simon went on as he shut the window. "You could have had roasted crow with your tea."

The boy giggled, and Lord Simon grinned at him.

"Now, there's a gruesome thought," Annabelle chided, though it was a pleasure to see how much more comfortable they were with each other now. "I don't believe I would enjoy that dish very much."

"Well," Lord Simon said, "I daresay it wouldn't be as unpalatable as eating humble pie."

His dark gray eyes studied her with a disconcerting directness. She found it impossible to look away. What did he mean by that statement? He had to be referring to the way she'd scolded him about his treatment of Nicholas, shamed him into visiting his nephew, then tricked him by leaving him alone with the boy.

Did Lord Simon resent her for humbling him? A man of his high stature surely had taken umbrage at being lectured by a servant. Although she didn't regret her actions, Annabelle also felt discomfited to think that he might regard her as a shrew.

How foolish to yearn for his admiration. Such sentiments were better left to noblewomen like Lady Louisa and her friends.

A confused frown wrinkled Nicholas's brow. "How do you make a humble pie?"

"It's just a silly old saying," Lord Simon said, giving him a pat on the head. "Now, I see there's quite an array of cakes on that tea tray. You'd better be quick if you want first choice."

Nicholas dashed over to the table to eye the dish of sweets.

"No more than one piece," Annabelle called.

"You may have two," Lord Simon contradicted her.

"With all due respect, my lord, he'll make himself ill."

"Nonsense, I used to sneak more than that when the nanny's back was turned. Now come," he said, lowering his voice to a murmur, "I need a word with you. Alone."

He placed his hand at the small of her back and nudged her toward a private corner of the library. That peculiar melting sensation assailed Annabelle again so that she forgot her momentary pique. She caught a tantalizing whiff of his scent, a blend of leather and spice. The warm pressure of his touch seemed as intimate as a kiss . . .

No, she must *not* imagine his lips on hers. Nothing could be more scandalous. Not only was Lord Simon her employer, he had been born with a sterling ancestry, while she could not even put a name to her parents. Rather than spin reckless dreams, she would do well to remember her proper place in the household.

She stepped away and set the folded shawl on the nearest table. Keeping a circumspect distance from him, she murmured, "Dare I hope you've news to relate about the gunman, my lord? Has he been apprehended?"

Lord Simon grimaced. "Unfortunately not. The fellow is as much a mystery as ever. I've interviewed all the servants and tenants, and none of them have seen anyone suspicious lurking on the hillside."

"In the kitchen, they said you'd gone into town to ask questions, too."

"I spent a good deal of time tracking down the various ne'er-do-wells who often drink ale at the Copper Shovel. But I'm convinced none of them have the brains or guts to commit a heist right underneath my nose." Looking disgruntled, he leaned against a bookshelf and crossed his arms. "I've also kept a watchman stationed near the site each night, but to no avail. The villain seems to have gone into hiding."

"Maybe he's given up. Maybe he realized he went too far in firing that shot. And now that he knows there will never be a chance to dig for treasure, he's left the area."

"I hope not," Lord Simon said grimly. "That would rob me of the chance to wring his neck for nearly killing you."

He looked so fierce that Annabelle's heart constricted. She mustn't let herself think he cared for her. It was only that he wanted to see justice served.

"What will you do next?" she asked.

"I intend to begin excavating the site. I expect it shouldn't take more than a fortnight."

Excited, she took a step toward him. "Do you really think there's treasure buried there?"

"Why else would the gunman have shot at you? Judging by the coin you discovered, along with what Nicholas picked up, there may be a cache of buried artifacts—or even a tomb."

"A tomb! With a mummy like the ones in Egypt?"

"One can always hope." He eyed her with keen interest. "After I resigned my commission last year, I'd intended to travel throughout the Mediterranean countries in search of antiquities. That had long been my passion, to study ancient civilizations. So you see, it would be quite the peculiar twist of fate for me to find such artifacts right here at home."

Hearing the enthusiasm in his voice, Annabelle realized with a pang just how much he had sacrificed. "You gave up that journey because your brother and sister-in-law had died. And you had become guardian to Nicholas."

"Yes." His mouth slanted wryly. "Quite reluctantly, I'll admit. It was not the plan I'd envisioned for my future."

Annabelle imagined him on the brink of departure, about to fulfill a lifelong dream, only to be called back to care for the child of the man and woman who had betrayed him. Put in that light, his actions at least became more understandable.

She glanced across the library at Nicholas. Having eaten his cake, he had gone in search of something to read. He knelt on the floor in front of one of the shelves, his head tilted to read the spines of the books.

What a blessing that Lord Simon had overcome his aversion to the boy. For as long as she lived, Annabelle knew she would never forget the joy of seeing him embrace his nephew that day in the nursery. It had made her want to weep with happiness.

"Things do have an odd way of turning out for the best, though, don't they?" she mused.

"Indeed so."

The husky note in his voice lured her gaze back to Lord Simon. He stood watching her intently. His black

lashes were lowered slightly, his eyes a deep and fath-
omless gray. Annabelle felt a deep-seated throb of desire. Though she knew little of men and their ways, she
felt certain in that moment that he wanted to kiss her.
And her imprudent heart reveled in the knowledge.

She reached for her shawl. "I should return to Nicholas now," she murmured.

Lord Simon's hand settled warmly over hers, stopping her from leaving. "Not yet. There's another reason
I called you over here. You know about the Samhain
ball, don't you?"

For days, the kitchen had been abuzz with chatter
about the upcoming annual event. The castle would be
cleaned from top to bottom, the ballroom floor polished
for dancing. By long tradition, the aristocratic guests
would each bring a contingent of their servants. That way,
the staff could take turns attending their own Samhain
festivities outside the castle.

"Of late, there has been talk of little else," she said.

"I would like to invite you to the ball."

A lurch of longing assailed her. How she would love
to be a part of his world, to don an exquisite gown, to
know the exhilaration of dancing with him. "I appreciate your kindness, my lord. However, it would be more
appropriate for me to attend the servants' party."

He smiled as if he'd expected her refusal. His thumb
rubbed over her palm, heating her skin and eroding her
defenses. "Do come, Annabelle," he said, her name a caress on his lips. "You know you'd enjoy it. Please, I want
you there."

When he looked at her like that, she could not draw a
deep breath, for the swift beating of her heart constricted
her lungs. How was it that he had the power to stir her
desires against her will? She ached to accept his invita-

tion, yet feared that what he truly wanted was a forbidden liaison. Nothing could be more dangerous to a woman in her position than to succumb to the master's seduction . . .

Quick footsteps tapped in the corridor. An instant later, Mrs. Wickett walked into the library. The housekeeper stopped short, her gaze riveted to Annabelle and Lord Simon. The slight narrowing of her dark eyes indicated censure.

Annabelle swallowed a groan. Of all times for Mrs. Wickett to appear! The woman already believed Annabelle wanted to lure Lord Simon into an illicit relationship. How very damning the scene must look with them standing so close together, Lord Simon's hand on hers.

Mrs. Wickett bobbed a curtsy. "Do pardon me, m' lord. One of the servants reported hearing a commotion in here."

Lord Simon straightened up, cool hauteur shuttering his face. "There was a crow flying loose," he said. "Thankfully, Miss Quinn caught it, and I released it out the window."

"A crow . . . inside the house!" The housekeeper looked aghast. "Why, 'tis a portent of death to someone here—"

"Enough," Lord Simon said rather forcefully, with a glance at Nicholas, who sat cross-legged on the floor with a book in his lap. Lord Simon strode toward the housekeeper, with Annabelle close behind him. Then he addressed Mrs. Wickett in an undertone, "There'll be no talk of such foolish superstitions. Is that clear?"

A mask of subservience came over the woman's plain features. "Of course, m'lord."

"Mrs. Wickett," Annabelle said, "would you happen to know who shut the door to the library earlier?"

Lord Simon aimed a quizzical frown at her. "Shut the door?"

"When Nicholas and I arrived, the door was closed. I thought perhaps one of the servants had discovered the crow and went to fetch help. But no one ever came."

"I heard naught of it," Mrs. Wickett said doubtfully.

"Then find out," Lord Simon ordered.

"Aye, m'lord. And I did come to seek 'ee for another reason. There be visitors in the drawin' room." The woman slid a chilly look at Annabelle. "'Tis Lady Danville and her daughter, Lady Louisa."

Chapter 19

Holding Nicholas's hand, Annabelle paused outside the old cemetery beside St. Geren's Church. Vines climbed over the low stone fence that enclosed the graveyard, and brilliant colors painted the oak and beech trees. A gust of wind sent a shower of red and gold leaves over the gravestones. Autumn here in Cornwall was much milder than in Yorkshire, yet she was glad to have worn the gray mantlet over her gown.

She glanced down at Nicholas. Carrying a little bouquet hastily gathered in the castle garden, he looked far too sober for a boy of eight. "Dearest," she said, "it's quite all right if you wish to change your mind. You don't have to do this."

Nicholas lifted his chin with a trace of ducal pride. "I want to leave roses for Mama. They were her favorite."

Annabelle gave him a commiserating smile. "Then do lead on, Your Grace."

Unlatching the iron gate, she allowed the boy to precede her into the cemetery. This visit had not been in her plan for the day. She had made arrangements for Nicholas to remain at the castle while she went to shop in Kevernstow on her afternoon off. But he had begged to accompany her, asking if he might visit the gravesite of his parents. The request had tugged at her heartstrings. Apparently no one had brought him here since the day of their funerals nearly a year ago.

Why had she never thought to stop after Sunday services? Perhaps because she'd been too absorbed in watching Lord Simon flirt with Lady Louisa.

Scolding herself for even thinking of the man, Annabelle followed Nicholas down the gravel path. On either side of them stretched rows of tombstones, some mossy with age, others overgrown with brambles. Then there were those that had regular visitors, for the plots were well tended with manicured grass and fresh flowers.

Nicholas headed toward a mausoleum made of pale marble. The grand square building stood in a prominent location shaded by a stand of oaks. Scarlet and gold leaves dusted the large stone angels that flanked the entry with its iron gate.

The boy stopped, glancing up at her. "I don't want to go inside. Do you think Mama will mind if I put her flowers right here?"

"I'm sure she'd think it the perfect spot."

As he laid the posy of roses at the foot of one angel, Annabelle found herself blinking away tears. It didn't seem fair that a child should have to mourn the loss of his mother and father at such a young age. Maybe in a way it had been a blessing that she'd never known her own parents. At least she had no memories to cause her grief.

Kneeling beside the boy, she guided him in saying a few prayers. Then they retraced their path and went out the gate. In an effort to cheer him, she said, "Would you like to stroll along the high street, Your Grace? Perhaps we might find a bakery and buy you a sweet."

His face brightened. "A chocolate tart?"

She laughed. "I can't promise, but we'll see."

Annabelle also hoped to find a shop that sold dry goods. She needed to purchase fabric suitable for a fine gown, for she had decided to accept Lord Simon's invitation to the Samhain ball. The thought buoyed her spirits. It would be a shame to avoid the glittering assemblage just because she feared to encourage his attentions.

After all, it wasn't as if the man would be pursuing *her*. He would be busy dancing with his harem of ladies from the neighborhood. Annabelle could enjoy the festivities from her place with the older women, and perhaps even dance a time or two with an elderly gentleman who was kind enough to partner the governess. Heaven knew, it might be the only chance in her life to attend such a splendid event.

As she and Nicholas walked past the old stone church with its ancient bell tower, she spied a pair of men talking in the garden outside the rectory. Mr. Bunting and Mr. Tremayne.

Annabelle's steps faltered, and she regretted her lack of foresight. Had she not been so lost in thought, she could have crossed the cobbled street with Nicholas in an effort to avoid encountering those two. But it was too late now.

Mr. Tremayne lifted his hand in a quick wave. He said something to the vicar. Mr. Bunting swiveled around to glower at Annabelle, his eyes dark in his foxlike face. Then he turned on his heel, his black clerical robes flapping as he disappeared into the rectory.

Not so the assistant curate.

Mr. Tremayne came hurrying down the path, obliging Annabelle to stop. In a blue coat with a maroon waistcoat, his wavy brown hair neatly combed, he looked far too stylish to be an underling cleric in a rural church. "Why, Miss Quinn! And Your Grace! What a rare surprise to see you here in the village."

Bowing, he caught her gloved hand and brought it to his lips.

His effusive manner made Annabelle uncomfortable, and she smiled politely while withdrawing her fingers. "We were visiting the cemetery. Our coachman is waiting at the Copper Shovel to take us back to the castle."

Nicholas tugged on her arm. "But Miss Quinn, aren't we stopping at the bakery?"

Annabelle groaned inwardly. She had hoped to give the impression that they had no time to talk. "Of course, darling."

"Then I shall accompany you," Mr. Tremayne declared. "It is only proper that such a pretty lady have a gentleman to escort her."

Nicholas looked askance at the man. The boy made no comment, however, as he started ahead of them down the narrow lane with its charming collection of houses and shops. A few villagers stopped to smile at him for it was unusual to see the Duke of Kevern in their midst.

Annabelle reluctantly tucked her fingers in the crook of Mr. Tremayne's proffered arm. Although she'd seen him at church, it was the first time they'd been alone since the party at the castle when Lady Milford had come to visit. On that occasion he had spoken disdainfully of Lady Milford's bastard birth, and his intolerance had told Annabelle much about his character.

But perhaps she ought not judge him so harshly. Many people held the same prejudice. It would be charitable to give him a second chance. Besides, she didn't want enmity to spoil such a beautiful autumn afternoon.

"I'm glad for your company," she said. "It's been quite a while since we've had a chat."

"Indeed! And so much has happened in the interim." He placed his hand over hers. "Words cannot express how worried I have been about you, Miss Quinn."

As they strolled down the street, she frowned at him. "Worried?"

"Everyone in the district has heard about the shooting last week. To think that a scoundrel has been roaming the estate, armed with a weapon, firing at you and the duke! Why, it is not to be borne."

Annabelle looked ahead at Nicholas, who had stopped to peer into a shop window. That dreadful incident still had the power to make her tremble, though she took care to hide her feelings. "I greatly appreciate your concern. However, I'm sure the fellow is long gone. He wouldn't linger here for fear of suffering the wrath of the duke's guardian."

Mr. Tremayne still looked troubled. "I do hope you are right. Mr. Bunting heard from Lord Simon that there may be buried treasure near the place of the shooting— ancient Celtic artifacts. Is that true?"

Annabelle thought it best to reveal as little as possible. "I wouldn't know. You'll have to pose your questions to his lordship."

"Well! If there is, then the villain may return to steal such rare and costly items. I trust Lord Simon has posted guards at the site?"

"Day and night, so you may relax your mind on that matter."

As they continued to stroll, Mr. Tremayne cast a sidelong glance at her. His blue eyes were narrowed as if to hide his thoughts—or perhaps it was just a defense against the brightness of the sunlight. "I would venture to say, Miss Quinn, that *you* are more precious than any cache of old relics. If there is the slightest possibility that the villain is still lurking about, I wonder that Lord Simon would allow you and the duke to come into town unaccompanied."

Annabelle felt reluctant to admit that she hadn't asked Lord Simon's permission. It simply hadn't seemed necessary.

Nevertheless, she kept her watchful gaze trained on Nicholas, who had stopped to observe two young boys tossing a ball back and forth in the street. "We're perfectly safe with the coachman," she said. "And I'm sure we can depend upon *you* to protect us here in Kevernstow."

"Absolutely!" Mr. Tremayne placed his hand over his heart in a rather theatrical gesture. "I am always at your service. Indeed, the moment I heard of the shooting, I came straight to the castle to offer my support to you. But alas, his lordship turned me away."

Annabelle slowed her steps. "Lord Simon did?"

"Why, yes." The assistant curate's smooth features took on a rather hangdog look. "It's happened on several other occasions, as well. Just yesterday afternoon, in fact. He said you were much too busy with His Grace to entertain a caller."

Annabelle was dumbstruck. That must have been right after Lord Simon had left them in the library. As to the other times, she spent most days up in the schoolroom with Nicholas, isolated from the rest of the castle. "I'm sorry. I didn't know."

"I rather thought that might be the case," Mr. Tremayne said, patting her gloved hand. "I'm afraid the fellow seems to have taken something of a dislike to me. Perhaps you haven't noticed, but on Sundays he always hurries you and the duke into your coach after church before I can speak more than a word or two to you."

She *had* noticed. Since Lord Simon rode his horse to services, he didn't need to depart straightaway; he stayed to mingle with Lady Louisa and her friends. "I hardly think that's a reflection on you, Mr. Tremayne. He's merely a protective guardian to the duke."

"Ah, but I must respectfully disagree. His antagonism toward me is quite palpable. I can't imagine what I've done to offend him." The assistant curate paused to give her a rather intent stare. "Or perhaps I can. He is very possessive of you, Miss Quinn. And I believe he views me as . . . a rival for your affections."

Annabelle had had that very thought herself on the night of the dinner party. Now, against her will, she felt a secret thrill at the notion that Lord Simon could be jealous. Certainly he seemed drawn to her. She had felt the full force of his charm the previous day in the library when he'd asked her to attend the Samhain ball.

She realized that Mr. Tremayne stood watching her. He had a forwardness about him that made her ill at ease. Though on the surface his manner was genteel, she had the impression that he didn't quite regard her as a lady.

"Lord Simon is my employer," she said coolly. "I will not gossip about him. Good day."

A scowl crossed his aristocratic features, but Annabelle paid no heed. She walked away to join Nicholas, who still stood watching the boys with the ball. She felt guilty for neglecting him even for a few moments. He needed friends, she thought with a pang. Perhaps some of the noble families in the area had children who could be invited to the castle to play.

She placed her hand on his shoulder, intending to suggest they do their shopping, when Mr. Tremayne stepped to her side again.

His hands clasped, he spoke fervently. "My dear Miss Quinn, I have offended you. Pray don't go without accepting my sincerest apology."

Annabelle could see no way to refuse without creating a scene on the street in full view of any watching villagers. "As you wish. You may consider the matter forgotten."

His chin lowered in a remorseful pose, Mr. Tremayne made no move to depart. Instead, he entreated, "I promise to be on my very best behavior if only you'll allow me the pleasure of your company."

"I hardly think—"

"Please? Should I utter the slightest word of offense, you may silence me at once. Thenceforth, I won't speak again. My lips shall be sealed."

He pretended to lock his mouth with an imaginary key. The action was so absurdly unexpected that Annabelle laughed aloud. He chuckled, too, and she felt an easing of her earlier qualms. He was an attractive man, if a bit too chatty for her taste. But surely there could be little harm in tolerating his company for half an hour or so until it was time to return to the castle.

At the very moment they were laughing together, an open carriage drawn by a fine pair of bay horses rumbled down the cobbled street. She stared in surprise to see Lord Simon on the high perch.

Her heart performed a cartwheel within the confines of her corset. Why was he not on the gelding he usually rode? Whatever the reason, he looked meltingly handsome in a charcoal gray coat and tan breeches, the brisk breeze ruffling his black hair.

He had spied them, too, for he guided the team to the side of the road and jumped lithely to the ground.

"Well, well," Mr. Tremayne murmured. "Something tells me that trouble lies in store."

Flipping a coin to one of the boys playing ball, Lord Simon bade the lad watch the vehicle. Then he strode toward them.

His expression of cool politeness offered no clue to his thoughts. He looked every inch the haughty lord of the manor as he acknowledged them with a nod. "Miss Quinn. Mr. Tremayne. What an unexpected pleasure."

From the tightness in his voice, Annabelle knew he was angry. The assistant curate had said that Lord Simon had been keeping them apart on purpose. Her initial delight in seeing him altered suddenly to mulish irritation. Did he intend to dictate who she chose to be her friends?

She slipped her fingers around Mr. Tremayne's arm. "The pleasure is entirely ours, my lord. It's a fine day to shop—or to take a drive, don't you agree?"

Nicholas had been eyeing the carriage and horses with great interest. Now, as if on cue, he tugged on Lord Simon's sleeve. "Please, sir, will you take me for a ride?"

As he glanced down at his nephew, Lord Simon's stern expression softened briefly. He reached out and ruffled the boy's flaxen hair. "In a few moments, yes, I shall."

"Hooray!" Nicholas said as he darted off to examine the carriage and horses from a safe distance.

The two men assessed one another, and tension radiated in the air. Lord Simon wore that arrogant look again. "It's been good seeing you, Tremayne. But now I'm sure you've sermons to copy or pews to polish."

Mr. Tremayne matched his stare. "As it so happens,

I'm free at the moment to escort Miss Quinn to the shops."

"Perhaps you don't understand me," Lord Simon said, taking a step closer, his tone deceptively quiet. "I intend to take her—and my nephew—back to the castle now."

Unwilling to be the center of their juvenile fight, Annabelle decided to wash her hands of the two of them. "I'm going nowhere until I do my shopping," she announced. "My lord, if you'd be so kind as to keep a watch on Nicholas for a short while. Mr. Tremayne, perhaps we will have an opportunity to talk another time. Good-bye."

With that, Annabelle marched away down the street. She refused to look back. Instead, she peered in shop windows until she spied one that had ladies' hats and other sundries on display.

The bell over the door tinkled as she entered the shop. It was not a large place, but a vast variety of sewing supplies crammed the shelves and counters. A stout woman with merry blue eyes and faded brown hair emerged from a back room to voice a cheery greeting. She showed Annabelle the area where the long bolts of fabric were stored.

"The new governess, are 'ee? His Grace is a right fine cheel, he is. Don't 'ee worry, we all look out t' protect him."

"Thank you, that's very kind." Annabelle listened with half an ear as the woman expressed her indignation over the recent incident with the mysterious gunman. Annabelle needed only to murmur and nod every now and then while she looked through the rolls of cloth.

An azure blue silk caught her eye. Removing one glove, she ran her bare fingertips over the soft, supple material. It would be perfect with a deep cream underskirt. The garnet slippers that Lady Milford had given her would add a pretty, if unconventional, touch to the gown.

The shopkeeper helped her select buttons and thread, lace and ribbons. By the time Annabelle was done, she'd made a sizable dent in her savings. It seemed shockingly extravagant to squander so much on a gown that she would likely wear only once. And yet she did so want to dress as beautifully as the other ladies at the ball. She wanted Lord Simon to notice her . . .

She put a firm stop to that dangerous thought. While the shopkeeper wrapped the purchases, Annabelle wandered around to examine the other goods. A display of shawls caught her attention, one in particular that was made of a cream-colored merino so fine it was almost sheer. She let the airy fabric sift through her fingers. If only it weren't so wildly impractical, it would look perfect with her ball gown . . .

The bell over the door jangled. At the sound of male footsteps, she felt a little catch in her chest and dropped the shawl back onto the table. Without even looking, she knew who stood behind her. Nevertheless, she glanced over her shoulder to see Lord Simon looming in the doorway, Nicholas at his side.

The shopkeeper beamed at them. "M'lord, 'tis an honor. Dost 'ee like a chair t' sit?"

"That won't be necessary, Mrs. Littlejohn. How are the grandsons?"

"Growin' too fast," she said on a laugh. "Much like our young duke here. Such a right handsome fellow he is."

The shopkeeper handed Annabelle the string-tied parcel, which Lord Simon took from her without a word. As he held the door and she preceded him out into the street, she knew by his stiff manner that he was still irked.

Let him stew. She had every right to come into town on her afternoon off—and to speak to whomever she liked. Their disagreement might even have a beneficial effect. Maybe it would keep him at arm's length so he'd lose interest in her.

"Miss Quinn, wait until you hear." Nicholas tugged on her hand. "Uncle Simon bought me *two* tarts."

She smiled down at his dear face in the bright sunshine. "Let me guess what kind. Chocolate with powdered sugar."

"How did you know?"

"The evidence is around your mouth." She gave him her folded handkerchief. "There now, clean yourself, please."

While he was busy, she noticed that Lord Simon had led them to his carriage. "Our coachman is waiting at the Copper Shovel," she said.

"Not any longer."

So he had ordered the vehicle to return to the castle. In his present ill humor, she couldn't imagine why he would insist upon driving them himself. He offered no explanation as he helped her up into the high perch. Nor did she intend to ask for one.

Like a monkey, Nicholas scrambled up the other side of the carriage and plopped down at the far end. "May I ride right here?" he begged. "I won't see anything if I'm squashed in between."

"Suit yourself," Lord Simon said, as he secured the parcel to the back of the carriage.

He bounded up, and much to her chagrin, Annabelle found herself seated in the middle, much too close to him. Their legs and arms brushed even though she made every effort to avoid contact. She couldn't imagine the arrangement was to his liking, for a glower hardened his features. He snapped the reins and the pair of sleek bays set off on the meandering road that led out of the village.

Annabelle kept an eye on Nicholas, though she had a keen awareness of the man beside her. The cool breeze and the sunshine should have lifted her spirits—if not for Lord Simon's testy manner.

"Why did you go out in the carriage today?" she asked him.

"I had a call to pay."

An unpleasant understanding struck her. "Ah. You took Lady Louisa for a drive?"

He cast an enigmatic glance at her. "Yes."

The news was a bitter pill to swallow. She was *glad,* Annabelle told herself firmly. Glad because it provided a necessary reminder that he was far beyond her reach. If he still harbored any interest in her at all, it could be for only one purpose—a purpose that had nothing to do with marriage.

His wedding vows would be reserved for a lady of his own class.

Though a knot formed in her throat, she kept her expression serene. Now was not the time to sort through her tangled emotions. If he insisted upon being reticent, then she would be as well.

After all, there was a lovely day to enjoy, with the leaves changing to red and gold in the patches of woods. They passed picturesque farms and green pastures nestled in the hills. Around every bend in the road lay a new sight for Nicholas to exclaim over, from a hawk wheeling against the blue sky to a dog chasing a fat sheep back into its herd.

While the boy was busy watching the countryside,

Lord Simon spoke in a low, grating tone meant for her ears alone. "I want you to stay away from Tremayne."

She tilted her head sharply to look at him. He was gazing at her, his lips thinned, his eyes piercing. The chaotic swirl of feelings inside her coalesced into anger. "Am I allowed no friendships, my lord?"

He set his jaw and glanced back at the road. "I never said that. Just not—him."

"Without explanation?"

"Are you truly so naïve?" he muttered under his breath. "The scoundrel has designs on you."

Naïve! Lord Simon might have much more experience of the world, but that didn't mean she was dense. "And you do not have designs?" she whispered icily. "Or am I naïvely misreading *your* intentions toward me?"

He gave her a quick, sharp look, and Annabelle half wished she could call back her words. Dear heaven. She should have bided her tongue. What if she was horribly wrong to think that he desired her? What if he had only meant to be kind when he'd invited her to the ball?

No, she wasn't mistaken. The previous day in the library, he had radiated lust, from the heated look in his eyes to the caress of his hand on hers. He had given her a crooked smile that promised something wicked and wonderful if only she would succumb to him.

Now, however, his face appeared set in granite. He glared at the road ahead, his hands tight on the reins as he guided the horses down a hill. The lump in her throat thickened. The miserable truth was, she didn't want to believe he had no interest in her as a woman. She wanted to dream that he might—just *might*—suffer from the same emotional tangle as she did. That by some miracle he was falling madly in love with her and his feelings were strong enough to transcend the barriers of class. Why, oh why, was she so foolish?

Oblivious to the tension between them, Nicholas pointed at a small, rocky waterfall half-hidden in the woods alongside the road. "Look, Miss Quinn. May we stop and go see it?"

Grateful for the distraction, she smoothed her hand over his wind-tousled hair. "It's quite lovely. Perhaps we can—"

"Not today," Lord Simon snapped. "I've work to do."

Nicholas glanced cautiously at him. Then he ducked his chin before turning away to look quietly out at the countryside. Seeing his small shoulders hunched brought a poignant reminder to Annabelle of the fearful boy he'd been on her arrival.

She compressed her lips. Blast Lord Simon! It was best to avoid conversation or she might say something else she'd regret. Nicholas didn't deserve to witness a quarrel.

Placing her arm around the boy, she spent the remainder of the trip talking with him about the various sights. She ignored Lord Simon altogether. Yet her senses remained stubbornly aware of him. Whenever the wheels hit a bump in the dirt road, his body brushed hers. The breeze carried an alluring whiff of his spicy scent. His expert handling of the reins made her wonder how those hands would feel caressing her.

By the time they drove through the open gate of the castle, she was more than ready to be rid of him. Lord Simon jumped down while a groom ran out to hold the horses. Nicholas hopped to the ground by himself. Because of her skirts, Annabelle had to make the descent more cautiously. She had only started down when a pair of strong male hands caught her by the waist and lifted her the rest of the way.

She turned around swiftly, only to find herself trapped between the large carriage wheel and Lord Simon. He made no move to step aside. He was still holding her, and the warmth of his fingers caused that curious melting sensation she both craved and despised.

His moody gaze flicked to her lips. She thought for an instant that he meant to kiss her right out here in the courtyard—and that she would lack the willpower to refuse him.

But he merely issued a harsh command. "You're not to leave the castle grounds again without my permission. Is that clear?"

Her spine stiffened. "Perfectly, my lord."

He looked as if he wanted to say something more. But with a haughty bow, he turned on his boot heel and strode away.

Chapter 20

Simon knew he'd made a muddle of things. He had thought of little else in the three days since he'd caught Annabelle with Tremayne. The memory of them laughing together was imprinted on his brain.

Sitting in a copper tub of warm water in his dressing room, he groped around the bottom for the cake of sandalwood soap. Finding it, he scrubbed the grime from his body. What he really needed was an icy plunge in the ocean so he could purge himself of this wretched fever for her. A day spent at hard labor, shoveling dirt at the Celtic site, had provided only a temporary distraction. The moment he'd trekked back up the hill to the castle, thoughts of Annabelle had returned to plague him.

Despite her sharp intellect, she was too innocent to understand a man like Tremayne. But Simon understood. He had taken the man's measure from the start and had seen that the assistant curate was ill-suited to a pious life. Born a gentleman of privilege, Tremayne harbored a sense of entitlement toward women of a lower order. To him, Annabelle was fair game for seduction.

And you do not have designs? Or am I naïvely mis-reading your intentions toward me?

Denying a jab of guilt, Simon vigorously lathered his wet hair. He had been shocked when Annabelle had said that. He had not expected her to confront him so bluntly—or to compare him to Tremayne.

Yes, damn it, he wanted to bed her, too. But he would treat her far better than that scoundrel ever would.

Simon didn't view her as a quick amusement to be used and then abandoned. He wanted Annabelle to be his mistress—permanently. She was far too fascinating a woman for him to tire of her anytime soon. He planned to give her a house, fine clothing, servants, anything she desired in exchange for the pleasure of making love to her. And if their relationship bore fruit, he would pro-vide for their child—or children—because with Anna-belle he craved a long-term liaison.

Now it was just a matter of convincing her. She needed to be wooed—not snarled and snapped at as he'd done in the carriage. He had let jealousy get the better of him. That wouldn't happen again. However, such a strong, principled woman would not easily succumb to seduction. She might very well demand a wedding ring first.

Something deep and raw twisted in his gut. As much as he desired Annabelle, the notion of speaking his vows to her caused a tension akin to panic in Simon. Bachelorhood was far preferable to the daily drama of living with a woman. Diana's betrayal had cured him of ever wanting to commit himself to a marriage.

Simon dunked his head to rinse his hair, then sat up, his eyes shut against the water sluicing down his face. He blindly extended his hand. "Towel."

"Yes, my lord."

When nothing materialized, he squinted through drenched lashes to see Ludlow shuffling toward him from the other end of the chamber. The ancient retainer moved at his usual snail's pace. He had served Simon's father as valet and, before that, Simon's grandfather. Because Ludlow preferred employment over a pension, Simon had kept the man on despite his foibles.

Today, however, Simon suffered from a dearth of patience. He stepped out of the tub and stalked forward, dripping water all over the Turkish carpet. He snatched up the towel and used it to dry himself. Would that Annabelle were here to do the honors, using her soft hands to run the strip of linen over every inch of him, then kneeling before him to pay special attention to—

Ludlow gave a rusty chuckle. "'Tis that governess, eh?"

"What?" Realizing where the old man's rheumy eyes were looking, Simon turned his back and snatched up his trousers. "Who the devil has been linking her name with mine?"

"Pray be assured there is no gossip belowstairs, my lord. 'Tis only that I am experienced in such matters. Over the years, I have assisted the gentlemen of this family in covering up many an indiscretion."

Good God. Of all times for Ludlow to become verbose. "I'll keep that in mind. Now hand me my shirt."

Ludlow shuffled around for a bit and eventually gave over the garment. As Simon pulled it over his head and fastened the cuffs, the ancient retainer said, "Will you be wanting the blue or the brown coat?"

"Neither." Simon's voice halted Ludlow on his painstaking progress toward the wardrobe. "I'm going to my study now. Please have my tea brought there straightaway."

"As you wish, my lord."

With Ludlow's sluggish steps, that ought to take nigh on an hour. Simon was hungry and out of sorts right now—though the feeling had less to do with food than with his unsatisfied sexual needs.

He strode out into his bedchamber and then into the deserted corridor. Maybe he ought to go upstairs to see Annabelle. There had to be some way to get back into her good graces. The trouble was, he didn't dare send flowers or chocolates or, God forbid, *jewels* to the governess. That would only make her the subject of censorious gossip among the staff. No, he had to use more finesse than that.

But how? His nephew's constant presence precluded any real chance at flirtation, let alone seduction.

Oh, hell. Why was he letting the woman twist his gut into knots? He had plenty of other problems to occupy him, such as finding whoever had fired that gun. Unlike Annabelle, he didn't believe the villain had left the area. Simon had his suspicions, and he'd been keeping an eye on one person in particular. But until he found proof, he had to bide his time and do his best to protect Annabelle from harm.

So much for putting the woman out of his mind. He couldn't string two thoughts together without coming back to her. Which was why, when he turned the corner and spied her walking into a guest bedchamber, he wondered at first if she was the creation of a fevered fantasy.

He had only a quick glimpse of a dark-haired woman in an elegant blue gown before she vanished from sight. She looked like Annabelle—and yet she didn't. But who the devil else could she be?

Lengthening his strides, he made haste down the passageway. The carpet runner muffled his swift footsteps. There were no guests in the castle. So it *had* to be her.

What was she doing on this floor? The nursery was located in another wing of the castle.

Simon reached the room she had entered. The door was cracked open, and he gave it a slight push of his hand. Not seeing anyone, he slipped into the bedchamber and quietly shut the door behind him.

Empty.

The room was dim, the draperies drawn over the windows. There was only a canopied bed with green brocade hangings, a pair of chairs by the unlit fireplace, a dainty writing desk equipped with paper and quills. Had he mistaken the bedroom? No, it was this one, he was certain of it.

Maybe he had seen a ghost.

He irritably combed his fingers through his damp hair. More likely, this constant state of lust had thrust him over the edge into madness . . .

A sound came from the dressing room. The muted scrape of a footstep. His gaze riveted to the open doorway. Then he trod silently across the plush carpet.

He stopped there and stared.

Annabelle stood primping in front of a tall mirror in the dressing room. Her back to him, she wore a slim-fitting blue gown with a cream underskirt. She had discarded that ugly spinster's cap in favor of an upsweep of loose curls. He could see the swanlike curve of her neck as she gazed down at her bosom.

She was making some adjustments to the low-cut bodice. Then she smoothed her palms down over her hips, grasped the folds of her skirt, and lifted the hem of her gown. Underneath, she wore dark red dancing slippers that sparkled with crystal beads. She turned to and fro as if to regard them from different angles. Then she tilted up her chin again to study herself critically in the mirror.

Simon knew the instant she spotted his reflection in the looking glass. Her eyes widened and one of her hands went to her bosom. She uttered a small, breathless gasp.

For one long eloquent moment they stared at each other in the mirror. His heart thudded in his chest, pumping blood straight to his groin. He found it difficult to breathe, let alone move.

She whirled around to face him. "Lord Simon! I never thought . . . I only needed to use the long mirror . . . I'll leave now."

A pale pink blush tinted her skin, and her discomfiture charmed him. She was such a fascinating blend of innocent ingénue and mature woman.

"Don't leave," he said huskily. *"Don't."*

In a few swift steps, he closed the distance between them and pulled her into his arms. She placed her hands on the front of his shirt, yet made no attempt to push him away. As she looked up at him, her lips parted and her lashes lowered slightly over those expressive blue eyes. Simon recognized an invitation when he saw one and he took full advantage of it.

He brought his mouth down on hers. Subduing his own urgency, he kept the contact gentle at first, cupping her face in his hands and brushing his lips over hers in a series of small kisses designed to beguile her senses. How incredible to taste her at last when he had wanted to do this from the moment he'd seen her for the first time, emerging like a wood nymph from the forest below the castle. She remained motionless within his embrace, allowing his actions yet not fully participating.

He continued his persuasive assault, lightly stroking her hair and face and throat while running his tongue along the seam of her lips.

A little shiver coursed through her. On a soft moan, she dissolved against him, lifting herself up to slide her hands around his neck. That clear sign of surrender evoked in him a richness of emotion unlike anything he had ever known. Their kiss became deep and drowning as she awarded him full access to her mouth. Groaning with need, he sought out the feminine curves that had obsessed him for many weeks.

Her shapely body was a feast to his starving senses. Annabelle seemed just as eager to explore him, too, for she glided her fingers over his shoulders and chest as if to learn the texture of his skin and the shape of his muscles. When he moved his lips to her throat, she tilted her head back and closed her eyes. The swiftness of her breathing gave testament to her arousal.

God in heaven, she was perfection. Why had he waited in such torturous agony when she was so ready for his loving? Impatient to hone her desire, he cupped her bosom, his thumb rubbing over the tip of one breast. She rewarded him with another soft, needy moan. But the silken barrier of her gown only served to frustrate him. Desiring to caress warm, womanly flesh, he worked his hand inside the tightness of her bodice.

Something sharp jabbed into his finger.

Simon jerked his hand back. "What the devil—"

A spot of blood glistened on the tip of his little finger. He shook his hand to ease the sting.

Annabelle surveyed the tiny wound. "I see you found one of the pins in my gown." Her mouth forming a prim line, she gave him the stern look of a governess. "And I daresay you deserved it, my lord."

Frowning, she brought his finger to her mouth as if he were a child in need of a kiss to make it better. She must have realized the absurdity of her action because before her lips could touch him, she paused. They stared at each other, the air heavy with sexual awareness. Then she lowered her lashes. Instead of releasing his hand as he expected, she drew his finger into her mouth and gently sucked on it.

His knees threatened to buckle. God help him, where had she learned *that* suggestive move? It had to be an impulse born of her innate sensuality. Despite the passion fogging his brain, he knew she was not the sort of woman to give herself lightly. He would be the first man—the only man—to seduce Miss Annabelle Quinn. And when he was through, she would belong to him, body and soul.

Yet she was far too precious for him to take in a frenzy, no matter how much he craved his own release. A woman like her deserved to be flattered, enticed, worshipped.

Leaning his back against the wall, Simon settled her firmly against him. When he feathered his lips over the silken softness of her cheek, she turned her mouth invitingly toward him, and for a long while they nuzzled and caressed with increasing ardor. Nothing in his life had ever felt more right than being with Annabelle like this. He wanted it to last forever. She would feel that way, too, once they lay naked together, their bodies joined. He could no longer curb his impatience to bring about that moment. While he distracted her with kisses, his fingers made short work of the buttons down her back.

He pushed the sleeves down her shoulders, stroking her bare skin along the way. On a sharp intake of breath, she caught his hands. "You mustn't . . ."

"I need to touch you." He looked deeply into her eyes. "We belong together, my love. Surely you feel it, too?"

Her gaze softened. She sank her teeth into her lower lip and nodded, and this time allowed him to tug the dress down to her waist. By some miracle, she had not worn a corset, and the fullness of her bosom strained against the plain bleached cotton of her shift.

Once she agreed to be his mistress, he intended to garb her in the finest lace lingerie for his pleasure. Yet oddly he found this simple garment to be every bit as arousing.

His hand trembling, Simon brushed aside the loose shift to expose her to his view. He cradled her breast so that it lay warm and heavy in his palm, a perfect fit. "You are so very beautiful," he murmured, then bent to lave the tip with his tongue. The heady taste of her stoked the fire inside him. When she uttered a small sound of yearning, emotion crowded his throat, tenderness and desire and a fierce determination to brand her as his own.

Shuddering, she clung to his shoulders and looked at him almost in despair. "I shouldn't crave you so much."

He caught her face in his hands, using his thumbs to stroke her cheeks. "Yes, you should," he said. "You were made for my loving, Annabelle. We were made for each other."

Simon couldn't allow her to think any longer for fear she might succumb to maidenly doubts. Better he should keep her so enraptured that she would forget everything but him and the mutual ecstasy that lay in store for them.

He subjected her to another deep kiss while he worked the shift down to her hips so he could explore the satiny curves of her upper body. She was remarkably responsive, trembling and sighing as he ran his hand down the supple length of her back. Her fervent reaction drove him to the brink of madness. No longer able to resist, he pushed off her garments, letting them fall in a puddle on the floor. Then he touched the lush dampness between her legs.

Annabelle stiffened and clutched at his arms. He kissed her thoroughly, continuing to lightly caress her as he whispered of her beauty and how very much he wanted to make her happy. Every word poured straight from his heart. Simon could not remember any other woman he'd ever wanted to please so much.

She melted against him, and he looped his arm around her waist to hold her upright. If not for the wall behind him, he wouldn't have been able to stand up himself. She tucked her face into the crook of his neck while her hips moved in rhythm with his stroking. Her sweet mewling sounds of delight made his heart pound and his loins tighten to the point of agony.

Damn it, he wanted her beneath him in bed. *Right now.* He wanted to be inside Annabelle, to ride the tide of pleasure along with her, to join her in plunging over the edge. But before he could act on the impulse, she cried out, her body quivering with the force of her release.

A fierce triumph filled him even though he had not experienced the rapture with her. There would be ample time to seek his own pleasure. She was his now, forever and always.

Simon swept her up into his arms and bore her into the adjoining bedchamber. As he gently placed her on the bed, Annabelle offered no resistance, for she was limp and sated. Exactly as he himself intended to be in a moment.

He tore off his shirt, then worked at the buttons of his trousers. Like a goddess in repose, Annabelle lay on her side, naked save for the garters that held up her silk stockings. Her garnet shoes had fallen off while he'd carried her in here, and he found himself adoring even the shape of her feet.

His hungry stare traveled up the length of her legs and hips, to the lush feast of her breasts, and then to her face. A few curls had come loose, falling to her shoulders and giving her the look of a well-satisfied woman. Her gaze slumberous, she watched him as he opened the last button and freed himself.

Her eyes widened on his jutting arousal. With a gasp, she sat up abruptly, her hands clasped to her bare bosom in a vain attempt to cover herself. "No!"

Simon cursed himself for not anticipating her virginal reaction. Without pausing to shuck off his trousers, he sprang to the bed and pulled her into his arms, rubbing his hands soothingly over her back. "Shh, darling, don't be alarmed. You'll find even greater pleasure in this, I promise you."

She shook her head in a panic. "We can't . . . *I* can't."

"Listen, my love." He gently tilted her face to look at him. "This isn't merely an afternoon's romp. You mean far too much to me. I want you with me always."

Uncertainty softened her expression. "Always?"

"Yes. I'll be true to you for as long as you desire. You have my word on that."

"For as long as I . . . ?" She paused, her gaze searching his. "What exactly are you saying, my lord?"

"Simon," he corrected huskily, running his fingertip over her lips. "I won't have you addressing me so formally now that we'll be sharing a bed."

Talking was a waste of time when his heart's desire sat so tantalizingly close. Wanting to drown himself in her taste and scent, he leaned forward to kiss her, but Annabelle turned her head to the side so that his mouth grazed her ear.

She scooted backward, her arms still covering her breasts. "I want the truth, Simon. Are you suggesting I become . . . your mistress?"

Her big blue eyes were stark with accusation, and Simon realized through his lusty haze that she didn't appear exactly pleased by the prospect. Despite her lack of family, Annabelle had been raised to be a proper lady, and now that she could think clearly, she must be appalled by the notion of physical intimacy with a man who was not her husband.

He silently cursed his lack of finesse in allowing the question to arise. But now that it had, there was no side-stepping the answer.

"Yes, I do want you to be my mistress, Annabelle," he said in his most persuasive tone. "I promise to take care of you, to give you a fine house of your own, so you can lead the life of leisure that you deserve."

"And just when were you intending to ask me?" she said in a taut voice. "Apparently *after* you'd ruined me."

He clenched his jaw. Damn it, he couldn't deny that. Nor could he tell her a glib lie. "You know perfectly well I didn't plan to meet you like this today. It simply . . . happened. I was carried away by my feelings just as you were." In a desperate effort to renew her desires, he feathered his fingers over her bare breasts. "Please, my love, don't deny me."

She jerked herself away and scrambled off the mattress. "*No*. Never again. I must have been mad to let you touch me at all."

Gorgeously naked, she stormed into the dressing room.

Simon found himself alone on the canopied bed. *Never again?* She couldn't mean that. Not when he sat here in a state of rampant frustration. Then he realized he was in grave danger of losing more than just an afternoon of bliss with the woman who had tied him into knots. He might lose Annabelle forever.

The harsh reality of that clutched at his chest.

He sprang to his feet, intending to rush after her, but his trousers were sagging and he had to stop to button them. By the time he made it into the dressing room, Annabelle already had her shift on. She stepped into her gown and slipped her arms into the short sleeves.

He couldn't let her go. There had to be some way to get back into her good graces. Struggling to think, he raked his fingers through his hair. "Annabelle, I'm sorry. I've handled this badly—"

"Yes, you have. Did you ever stop to consider that you might get me with child?" She flashed a glower at him. "I know what it's like to be born a bastard. How could you expect me to inflict that pain on my own son or daughter?"

Her revelation startled him. "I only knew you were an orphan."

"Whatever the case, you regard me as beneath you." While reaching behind to fasten the gown, she gave him a look of stern reproach. "I don't know how you *ever* thought I'd agree to such a scheme. What a cozy arrangement you had planned, with me as your mistress and Lady Louisa as your wife."

"I'm not marrying Louisa. Where the devil did you come by such a notion?"

"It's plain to see. You're always flirting with her, visiting her, taking her for carriage rides."

Was Annabelle jealous? God, he hoped so. At least

that would prove she felt possessive of him. But he couldn't let her falsely believe he wanted to be involved with two women at once. Nothing could be more abhorrent to him.

Seeing her struggle with the buttons, Simon stepped behind her to lend his assistance. "Sweetheart, I've no interest in Louisa, I swear it. *She's* been chasing *me*. I can hardly be rude to her since her parents are old family friends. In fact, the day I saw you in the village, Lady Danville had talked me into taking Louisa out in the carriage."

Annabelle uttered a huff of disbelief. "That isn't the worst part. I'd like to know just what you were intending to tell Nicholas."

"Nicholas? What does he have to do with anything?"

"He's come to trust me, to love me like a mother. Yet if I were your mistress, I couldn't possibly remain his governess. It would be too scandalous. I'd have to move away from here and never see him again."

The catch in her voice affected Simon deeply. "I could bring him to visit you from time to time."

"And taint him with my notoriety? No! Meanwhile, he would feel abandoned by me—and that I could never bear." She glared over her shoulder at Simon. "But I don't suppose you stopped to think of the effect your selfish plan would have on him."

"Selfish." Rejecting the sting of guilt, Simon fastened the last button and then turned her around to face him. "By God, you'll find me a most generous man. I'll buy you whatever you like. A house, a carriage, jewels. You'll want for nothing."

"Nothing but my self-respect—and the little boy I've come to love like my own son."

Despite her forceful tone, her eyes held a watery

sheen. The realization that he'd driven her to tears shocked Simon to the core. He had wanted to give her happiness, not cause her pain. "Annabelle . . ."

She ignored his entreaty. Brushing past him, she snatched up her garnet slippers from the floor and walked out of the room without looking back.

Chapter 21

Just after luncheon the following afternoon, Annabelle was giving Nicholas an art lesson in the schoolroom when the sound of shuffling footsteps emanated from the outer corridor. A few moments later, Ludlow appeared in the doorway.

The stooped old retainer inched his way past the assortment of small tables and chairs. It was so odd to see him here in the nursery that Annabelle set down her pencil at once and went to greet him.

He handed a parcel to her. "For you, Miss Quinn."

Mystified, she took it. It was slightly larger than a book. The brown paper wrapping held no name or address. "Did this arrive by post?"

"Nay, but perchance you might guess the sender." Much to Annabelle's astonishment, Ludlow winked one rheumy blue eye at her.

As he turned around and retraced his steps, a blush suffused her entire body. Of course. Ludlow was Simon's personal manservant.

Lord Simon. She must not allow herself to think of

him in so familiar a fashion. He was her employer, nothing more.

But no matter how many times she'd repeated that to herself, Annabelle could not erase the memory of what had happened between them. Once she had succumbed to that fateful kiss, their relationship had altered forever. She had relived their intimate encounter a hundred times since leaving Simon in the guest bedchamber . . .

Nicholas trotted to her side, his eyes agog. "Is it your birthday, Miss Quinn?"

She gave him a distracted smile. "No, not until December. Perhaps this is from the school where I used to teach. I may have forgotten something there when I moved to Castle Kevern."

Nicholas accepted the explanation. "Aren't you going to open it?"

"Later. For now, I'm more anxious to see how your sketch is progressing."

She placed the parcel on the low bookcase nearest to her bedchamber, then went to view his drawing of horses in a pasture. She made some suggestions for improvement, adding shading in certain areas. All the while, her gaze kept straying to the parcel.

What lay inside it?

The light weight of the package gave a clue to its contents. *I'll buy you whatever you like. A house, a carriage, jewels.*

Well, it couldn't be a house or a carriage, so perhaps Simon had sent jewels as a bribe to entice her into yielding. The very notion was insulting to the extreme. How could he believe her so shallow, so greedy, so unprincipled that she would sell her body for a few precious stones?

In the midst of her anger, she felt the bone-deep ache of loss. When he had drawn her into his arms and kissed her for the first time, nothing could have prepared her for the intense pleasure of their closeness. A storm of desire had swept away her morals and reason. She had become a creature of sensuality, so susceptible to his persuasion that she had allowed him to disrobe her, to caress her in the most shockingly intimate manner. Now, in the cold light of day, she understood the origin of her weakness for him. She had lulled herself into believing he felt the same depth of emotion as she did. Because his whispered words had been a siren call to her lonely heart. *You are so very beautiful . . . We belong together, my love.*

But he didn't love her. Those tender phrases had been lies designed to deceive Annabelle into surrendering to him. She despised him for duping her—even as she yearned to experience the madness all over again.

No. She must never again succumb to temptation. It would mean the ruination of her. Gentlemen could carry on discreet affairs, but a woman in her reduced circumstances would suffer severe consequences. Annabelle would lose her position and no decent family would ever hire her again.

Dear God, she should have refused the parcel, sent it back with Ludlow. She really ought to take it downstairs unopened and leave it in Simon's study. Yet her intense curiosity persisted.

What had he given her? Surely there could be no harm in knowing.

When Elowen brought the tea tray, Annabelle used the opportunity to take the parcel into the privacy of her bedchamber. With trembling fingers, she untied the string. The paper fell away to reveal a pretty, enameled box. She slowly lifted the lid. Instead of jewels, a length of fine, cream-colored merino lay inside.

Unbidden, her fingers stroked the exquisitely soft fabric. It was the shawl she had admired in the village shop. Simon must have seen her holding it when he and Nicholas had come to take her back to the castle.

As she picked up the shawl, a card fell out of the folds. It was embossed with the gold Kevern seal. A single sentence was scrawled boldly across the front: *My love, I hope you can forgive me.*

In lieu of his name, he had signed a heavy black *S.*

Annabelle stared down at the card in her hand. Against her will, the dangerous allure of yearning filled her heart. *My love . . .*

How desperately she wanted to believe Simon loved her. But those were the same two words he'd spoken so ardently in the midst of her seduction. He hadn't meant them then, and he didn't mean them now. His sole purpose was to coax her into his bed. Because if he truly had deep, abiding feelings for her, he would not have dishonored her with his loathsome proposition.

A wild anger flared inside her. How dare he try to wheedle her with pretty gifts and false endearments! She would tell him so to his face, refuse him once and for all.

Snatching up the shawl, she left the bedchamber. She bade Elowen stay with Nicholas and then hurried downstairs to the study. But Simon wasn't there. The chair behind the mahogany desk was empty.

Of course, it was only mid-afternoon and he must still be digging at the Celtic site on the hillside. So much the better. She needed a brisk walk to clear her head. It would give her time to plan exactly what she would say to the scoundrel.

Annabelle hastened back out into the corridor. Upon reaching the landing overlooking the great hall, she glanced down and spied a couple standing in the shadows beneath the grand staircase. Their heads close together, they appeared to be deep in conversation. The woman had her hand on his arm in a distinctly intimate gesture. With a jolt, Annabelle recognized the two of them.

Mrs. Wickett and Mr. Bunting.

What was *he* doing here? For that matter, why were they whispering together?

In her agitated state, Annabelle didn't really care to find out. She had no wish to encounter either of them. But she could see the door to the courtyard and this was the quickest route to it.

She marched down the stairs. Out of the corner of her eye, she saw the housekeeper cast a furtive glance upward. The woman swiftly dropped her hand from the vicar's arm and took a step backward.

Pretending not to see them, Annabelle walked past a medieval suit of armor on display and headed toward the massive oak door. Her footsteps tapped sharply on the flagstones.

"Where are you going?" Mrs. Wickett called out.

Drat. Annabelle stopped and turned, feigning a look of surprise. "Oh, Mrs. Wickett, Mr. Bunting. I didn't see you there. If you'll excuse me, I'm going for a walk."

The vicar stepped out of the shadows. Clad in black except for his white clerical collar, he watched her with those foxlike features, his lips slightly curled. "Neglecting the young duke, are you?" he said. "I wonder what Lord Simon will have to say about that."

"I'll ask him. I was just going to visit Lord Simon on the hillside to check on his progress."

Bunting exchanged a glance with Mrs. Wickett. The two of them seemed to share a wordless communication.

"Then I shall accompany you," the vicar said. "I have been wanting to take a look at this much-vaunted Druid site."

Annabelle's fingers tightened around the shawl. Oh, for pity's sake! How was she to confront Simon with the vicar present? But she could hardly refuse the man's company when she'd already stated her destination.

Caught in a trap of her own making, she reluctantly led the way out into the courtyard with its merrily splashing dolphin fountain. The air was brisk, but she refused to put on the shawl, preferring to carry it over her arm lest Simon see her wearing it. The heat of her anger would have to keep her warm.

However, she didn't have the leisure to think about Simon, not with Mr. Bunting strolling beside her. They took the path that skirted the castle wall and for a few minutes there was only the scrape of their footsteps to fill the silence. It was apparent from his closed expression that he still resented her for ousting him as Nicolas's tutor. So did Mrs. Wickett, who had made her exalted opinion of the vicar quite clear.

After seeing them together, Annabelle wondered if there might be a secret romance between him and the widowed housekeeper. That would certainly explain Mrs. Wickett's resentment of Annabelle. The woman wouldn't appreciate having her lover banished from the castle.

Annabelle's wayward mind tried to picture those two sour, disagreeable people kissing with the same wild passion she and Simon had shared. But she succeeded only in stirring erotic memories of her own that were best kept buried.

As a distraction, she made a stab at polite conversation. "Have you an interest in the history of the ancient Celtic people, Mr. Bunting?"

"I've done some reading on the era," he said stiffly. "I know they had sacred groves of trees where their Druid priests practiced magic."

"There are four ancient oaks at the site. Though I can't imagine that such trees could survive for nearly two millennia."

"The Druids were reputed to be masters of spell-casting. Some might argue that they cast an enchantment over the place."

Annabelle laughed. "Surely *you* don't believe that."

"I am merely extrapolating from published works, Miss Quinn. For instance, Pliny the Elder described a ceremony in which the white-robed Druids climbed a sacred oak, cut down mistletoe, and then killed two white bulls. In that manner, the Druids gained the power to heal."

The spark of fervency in his dark eyes surprised her. She had read that selection herself, though with less enthusiasm for the animal sacrifice. "Mistletoe is said to be a natural healing agent. So perhaps their magic was really quite ordinary."

Bunting cast a disagreeable look at her. "That is hardly the only type of magic attributed to the Druids. It is written they were able to stop entire armies by uttering strong incantations. They even had influence over the weather."

"If that were true, then why are these powers not known to us today?"

"The Druids performed their rituals in secret. The spells were lost over the ages as the Celtic people were conquered."

"Thus we can conclude that the Druids' ability to stop armies must not have been very effective."

He narrowed his eyes to slits. "You are entirely too flippant, Miss Quinn. It would behoove you to develop a serious appreciation for British history since you are teaching His Grace of Kevern."

Annabelle had no wish to discuss Nicholas's schooling with this man. Besides, she was beginning to wonder at the cleric's interest in pagan priests. He appeared overly fascinated by their magical abilities. "Then do tell me more. You seem to be quite the expert on the Druids."

"I taught ancient history at Oxford, so I am well versed in Greek and Roman writings about the Celtic peoples." He slid a cunning glance in her direction. "You may be interested to learn, there is evidence the Druids were practitioners of human sacrifice. It is said they were able to read the future by observing the gushing of a man's blood from his body and the writhing of his limbs as he died."

Annabelle felt a twist of revulsion. The vicar must be deliberately trying to unsettle her. Or perhaps there was something more sinister to his knowledge of the Druids. Perhaps *he* was the one who had been secretly digging at the site.

The one who had fired the warning shot at her.

A chill tiptoed down her spine. They had reached the place where Nicholas had gone chasing downhill after the rabbit. Her heart beating faster, Annabelle felt a keen wish to reach Simon. Despite their estrangement, she would feel safer in his presence.

"The site is down this way," she said, pointing.

"Do lead on, Miss Quinn."

Annabelle had no intention of turning her back on the vicar. "Perhaps we should walk side by side. The way is difficult in places and I may need your assistance."

Clutching her skirts, she started down the slope with him. The humus was thick underfoot as the oaks and beeches shed their crimson and gold leaves. The scents of autumn decay masked even the ever-present brine of the sea. Brambles caught at her hem, and once she had to bend down to unhook herself.

As she straightened up, Bunting's voice startled her. "Has Lord Simon discovered any treasures?"

He was too close, and she edged away. "I don't know. He hasn't told me." The previous day, she had been too otherwise engaged with Simon even to think of asking. Nothing else had existed but the two of them, wrapped in bodily pleasure . . .

"Whatever he finds may contain a clue," Bunting muttered.

"A clue?"

"To the ancient ways of the Druids, of course. It would be most intriguing to discover more about how they performed their rituals."

His interest was too keen to be a coincidence, she thought uneasily. Did Simon know of it?

They passed the place where she'd almost been shot, but if Mr. Bunting had been the gunman, he showed no sign of recognizing the spot. His gaze was fixed downhill on the site now visible through the trees. A workman trundled a wheelbarrow full of dirt toward a heap at the edge of the clearing. Simon stood in a deep hole, only his head visible as he shoveled out more earth.

Uttering a low exclamation, the vicar hurried ahead of her, his shoes scuffing through the blanket of leaves. Annabelle breathed a little easier as she followed him.

Apparently he meant her no harm—at least not in front of witnesses.

Simon must have seen them coming, for he hoisted himself out of the hole and brushed the dirt from his shirt and trousers. Lifting his arm, he swiped his sleeve across his brow. He frowned at the vicar and then at her as she descended the final few yards to the site.

Annabelle's mouth went dry. The sight of him caused an involuntary pulse of desire deep inside her. His shirt was damp with sweat, the linen clinging in places to his muscled torso. With his black hair mussed, he looked more like a common laborer than the privileged son of a duke.

He glanced down at the shawl draped over her arm. His gaze searched her face again, and he took a step forward. Annabelle compressed her lips. How she wished they were alone so that she could tell him exactly how she felt about his attempt to buy her affections.

"This is quite a surprise," he said, frowning at both her and the vicar. "I hardly expected to see the two of you together."

"I came to the castle to deliver some religious tracts for the staff," Mr. Bunting said. "When I learned that Miss Quinn was on her way here, I thought to fulfill my curiosity." He peered into the hole. "Have you found anything yet, my lord?"

Simon coolly studied the man. "As it happens, yes. Have a look."

Annabelle turned her attention to the excavation. The vines had been cleared away and Simon had tunneled underneath the mound in the center of the clearing. Deep inside that hollowed-out place there was a large slab of stone rather like an altar. On it lay a jumbled pile of what looked like pale sticks.

"Are those . . . bones?" she asked in faint horror.

"Animal bones," Simon clarified.

"From sacrifices," Mr. Bunting said, a quiver of excitement in his voice. "That proves the Druids used this place for their holy rites."

"It would seem so. Though perhaps it's too soon to draw conclusions. I'm far from finished with the excavation."

Simon was watching the vicar closely, and Annabelle wondered if he had known of the man's interest in the site. In case he hadn't, she said, "Mr. Bunting is very knowledgeable about the ancient Celts, Lord Simon. On the walk here, he told me all manner of stories about the Druid priests. You may wish to consult him if you find anything else of significance."

Simon sent a scowl her way, and she had the distinct impression that he was warning her to stay out of the matter.

"Now there's a capital notion," the vicar said, rubbing his hands together. "As well you know, my lord, my background as a historian at Oxford eminently qualifies me for the task."

"Then you'll be interested to hear that I *have* found something else. I've just broken through to an underground chamber."

"Truly?" The vicar almost fell over in his haste to hunker down and peer again into the hole. "Where?"

Simon pointed deep into the hollowed-out opening. "In the back," he said. "It's hard to see without a lamp, but there appears to be an entrance to a small cave."

"A cave?" Annabelle asked in surprise.

"The area is honeycombed with them," Simon said. "Which is why I wouldn't get my hopes up that it's anything significant. It may be a natural occurrence that has nothing whatsoever to do with the Celts."

Annabelle sincerely hoped it was a burial chamber. That day in the library, when Simon had come to ask her to the Samhain ball, he had been so enthusiastic at the prospect of unearthing a trove of ancient artifacts . . .

But of course she didn't care a fig for his happiness. It was just that she wanted him to have something to occupy his time. Then he would be too busy to bother her with his unwanted attentions.

"We must fetch a lamp," the vicar declared. "There may be relics inside, perhaps even items the Druids used in casting their spells."

Simon shook his head. "It's too late in the day," he said. "I intend to start out fresh in the morning."

"But my lord—"

"Whatever is in there can wait," he said firmly. "Come, we'll head back to the castle together."

After dismissing the workman waiting by the wheelbarrow, Simon rejoined them and they climbed the hill to the path. He walked in the middle and spent the time grilling the vicar about his knowledge of the ancient Britons. Annabelle made no attempt to participate in the conversation. She was too busy battling a keen awareness of Simon.

Though she looked straight ahead, she could see him from the corner of her eye, and every glimpse brought a tidal wave of memories. How skillfully those hands had caressed her body. How expertly his lips had kissed her. How adroitly his words had fooled her into believing that he loved her.

Yet despite her rejection of him, the arrogant devil still believed he could charm her into his bed. She had to make it absolutely clear that he had no hope of ever doing so.

As they entered the courtyard, she said, "Lord Simon, if I might have a word with you in private."

He turned toward her, his expression cool. He glanced over his shoulder at Mr. Bunting, who had stopped to wait by the dolphin fountain a short distance away. "This is hardly the time," Simon said in a low voice.

Annabelle felt the scrutiny of the vicar's dark eyes. Nevertheless, she felt compelled to voice her grievance. The splashing of the fountain should mask a whispered conversation.

"I came to return this to you," she murmured, lifting her arm slightly to indicate the shawl. "I cannot accept it."

His jaw tightened. "Consider it a gift. To replace the one ruined by the crow."

"That isn't what your note implied. You wrote—"

"I *know* what I wrote," he growled under his breath. "I only spent the better part of half an hour debating how to word it so as not to offend you—though it seems that was an exercise in futility. Now, pray excuse me. I'll discuss the matter with you later."

Abruptly, he turned from her and rejoined the vicar. The two men walked into the castle, leaving Annabelle standing alone in the courtyard.

My love, I hope you can forgive me.

Simon had spent half an hour composing that simple message? Because he was anxious about her reaction? She imagined him sitting at a desk with pen in hand, attempting different versions, then crumpling them up and tossing them into the rubbish bin. And for a reason she didn't care to examine, a tender pang softened her heart.

Chapter 22

At the very same time the following afternoon, Annabelle held on to her straw bonnet as she carefully made her way down the rough-hewn steps to the beach.

The day was overcast and blustery, the sea choppy. A chilly wind whipped her skirts and threatened to entangle her legs. Despite the precariousness of descending the staircase cut into the cliff, she found herself marveling at the wild beauty of the scene. Dark clouds crouched on the horizon. White-capped waves crashed onto the sand and filled the rocky pools where she and Nicholas had come the day that someone had been watching them from the cliff. Someone with a gun.

Had that man been Mr. Bunting?

Annabelle shivered. She needn't worry about him since she'd seen no one on the path. The castle grounds had been deserted, too, as was the coast as far as the eye could see. Not even a fishing boat braved the rough waters.

Her mind dwelled on the purpose that had brought her here to the beach. Simon must have made a discovery at the site this morning. It had to be something spectacular

or he would not have asked to meet her away from the
castle.

His note had been waiting on her desk after she'd returned from a visit to the library with Nicholas. The
message had been written in Simon's distinctive, bold
penmanship: *I must speak to you. Come to the cave on
the beach at four. Pray tell no one. Simon*

Annabelle reached the bottom of the steps and gingerly picked a path through the jumble of enormous
rocks lying at the base of the cliff. It appeared as if a gi-
ant hand had tossed the boulders like so many marbles.
The waves sent out long fingers of foam that touched the
rocks.

Was the tide coming in? The water seemed closer than
she remembered from other visits to the beach. Perhaps
the turbulent winds were pushing the waves onshore. Simon surely would know the tide schedule. He wouldn't
arrange to meet her in this spot unless it was safe.

She reached the opening to the cave. The entry was a
foot or so higher than the beach and she had to clamber
over a pile of rocks. No doubt Simon knew the place
well from his boyhood. He had told her once that as a
child he'd roamed everywhere on the estate. She could
imagine him as a mischievous lad, tricking his governess, eluding his lessons, and stealing down here to the
beach to play.

Annabelle stepped into the dim interior. Never in her
life had she been inside a cave. It was surprisingly airy,
the walls and ceiling composed of well-worn rock, the
floor of moist sand. Several elongated pieces of stone
looked eerily like statues, and she fancied she had entered a sacred grotto. Venturing deeper into the cave,
she spied clumps of seaweed, a few scattered shells, and
even a little stream trickling through the piles of rock.

How peculiar to think that Castle Kevern stood directly above her. The servants would be going about their daily chores, ironing clothes, tending the fires, preparing dinner. Nicholas would be curled up in the window seat of his bedchamber, reading the new book he'd selected from the library. She hoped it wouldn't be too long before she rejoined him.

Darkness shrouded the far reaches of the cave, and Annabelle regretted not having a lamp to enable further exploration. She retreated to a place where she could see the opening and found a flat rock on which to sit and wait. The rhythmic roar of the waves out on the beach echoed hollowly in the cavern. The air was damp and chilly, but at least here she had protection from the wind.

She huddled inside her cloak. It must be past four o'clock by now. Where was Simon? Ever since visiting the site, she had been waiting on pins and needles to hear from him. When she'd attempted to return the shawl, he'd said that he would talk to her later.

But he hadn't. The previous evening, she had dawdled in the schoolroom, hoping he would come to visit. When she'd finally given up and gone to bed, it had been to dream of Simon. In the dark of night she had awakened, her body aching for him. Not even the knowledge that he wanted only to use her could hold sway over the weakness of her flesh.

Annabelle hugged her midsection. Passion had nothing to do with why she had come here to meet him, she sternly reminded herself. Rather, she wanted to relate her suspicions about the vicar. She had to make certain that Simon had arrived at the same conclusion as she had. Mr. Bunting must have left the spade they'd found hidden beneath the vines. He had to be the one who had been secretly digging there.

Which meant he was also the gunman.

She drew a shuddery breath. Dear heaven, what had Simon unearthed at the site this morning? Mr. Bunting must have been present to see it. Had the vicar said something to reveal himself as the culprit? Perhaps that was why Simon wanted to speak to her away from listening ears.

Then again, she might be wrong. Maybe he wished to meet her in private just so that he could hold her in his arms again. So he could ply her with kisses in an attempt to convince her to become his mistress.

It would be a futile effort. She would never relent. Her mind was made up.

Yet a wicked part of her hoped he would try.

She buried her face in her hands. But she could not shut out the needs that clamored inside herself. With his masterful touch, Simon had transported her to heaven. He had awakened her dormant desires, and she wanted him to satisfy the hunger in her again. God forgive her, she ached to learn the mystery of taking the act to its completion. For a few wicked moments, she allowed her imagination to run wild . . .

Icy water chilled her feet.

Annabelle opened her eyes and glanced down. Her hem rested in a puddle. Seawater had seeped into her shoes.

Gasping, she jumped up and looked toward the entrance. To her shock, waves were surging through the opening of the cave. The swells looked as high as her knees.

The tide *was* coming in. She had to leave at once. From the servants, she knew this cave filled completely during high tide. To remain here meant certain drowning.

Lifting her skirts, Annabelle sloshed through the

water. The wet sand sucked at her shoes and slowed her progress. Dear God, where was Simon? Why had he told her to meet him here at such a dangerous time? Had he merely made a mistake?

Devil take that man! Now her shoes would be ruined by the salt water. So would her gown, and out of vanity she had worn her favorite blue silk because she'd wanted to look her best. She certainly would give him a piece of her mind once she was on dry land again.

If she ever reached high ground.

Horror overtook her as she arrived at the entrance and saw the sea. Greenish-gray waves churned and boiled, splashing her with salty spume. The beach had disappeared completely; the boulders around the cave were already partially submerged. She could see in the distance the stairs that were cut into the cliff, but water covered the bottom steps.

Fear twisted her stomach. How was she to walk there? The sea had risen almost to her knees now, and the cave was situated a bit higher than the beach. Once she left this spot, she'd be submerged to her waist and unable to see anything beneath her.

While she hesitated, a large swell nearly knocked her off her feet. She braced a hand on the wall to steady herself. If the waves could do that to her right here, how much worse would it be on the trek to the stairs? She might be flung against the sharp rocks.

But she had no choice. She couldn't stay here to die.

Her muscles tense, she whispered a fervent prayer. Then she took a cautious step out of the cave.

"Annabelle!"

At first she thought the gusting wind had tricked her. Then the shout came again, an unearthly echo that emanated from behind her.

Behind?

Pivoting, she clutched at the slippery rock of the entrance to keep from falling. She strained to see into the dim interior. Much to her astonishment, she spied a ghostly figure with a lantern moving swiftly toward her from the depths of the cavern.

Simon.

With a joyful cry, she reversed course and splashed through the water to meet him halfway. Never in her life had she been happier to see anyone. A sob caught in her throat as she flung herself at him. She pressed her face to his chest and breathed in his scent, trying to convince herself she wasn't dreaming. He held her with one arm tight around her waist in a hug that was all too brief.

He drew back to grasp her hand. The light of the lantern revealed the intensity of his gaze on her. "We have to go," he said. "But you needn't be frightened anymore. We've ample time to get to safety."

"But we *don't,*" she said in confusion. "Simon, the water is already high out there, and maybe you know how to swim, but *I* certainly don't—"

"Then it's a good thing we aren't going that way. Come along."

He tugged on her hand as if to draw her deeper into the cave, but she resisted. "Where are you taking me?"

"There's more than one way out of here, my love. Where did you think I came from?"

Annabelle hadn't thought, she had been too agitated to reason things out. But of course he hadn't just been hiding back there to frighten her.

She clung tightly to his fingers and followed his lead.

The darkness thickened and the light of the lantern cast eerie shadows on the rock walls. The subterranean route progressed up a steady incline until there was no more water and the sound of the sea had diminished to a distant murmur. Simon limped a bit and she remembered him saying he had a scar on his leg. The dampness of the cave must have caused it to ache. At last, he drew her up a crude stairway hewn into the bedrock. He pushed open a door at the top and guided her into a tunnel.

She glanced around. "This looks like . . . the secret passageway! Are we in Castle Kevern?"

"Yes, thank God."

He stared fiercely at her; then he set down the lantern and pulled her to him again. Annabelle burrowed against him. It was sheer bliss to feel the heavy beat of his heart against her cheek and to let his heat seep into her cold body. There would be time enough later to consider the wisdom of allowing his embrace. For now, she needed him as much as she needed air to breathe.

As her fears ebbed, however, she remembered her annoyance.

She tilted her head back to look at him. "Why did you make me wait there so long?" she asked. "Didn't you *know* the tide would come in when you told me to meet you there?"

Simon placed his hands on her shoulders and set her back at arm's length. His expression was very grim in the lamplight. "Annabelle, listen to me. I did *not* write that note. I found it lying on your desk when I came to the nursery to speak to you."

"But it was *your* penmanship, Simon. I know it was."

"Then someone has learned to imitate it. Someone who intended for you to die in that cave."

Annabelle stared at him in horrified disbelief. "But who? Why?"

"I'd lay heavy odds on Percival Bunting."

Her blood ran cold. She recalled the bitter resentment

in the vicar's dark eyes whenever he looked at her. Slowly, she said, "I had the distinct feeling yesterday that he was the one on the hillside who'd shot at Nicholas and me."

"Then both of us came to the same conclusion. I knew from the outset that Bunting had an interest in Celtic history. I've been watching the knave for some time, but I lacked the proof to accuse him. Then when you brought him to the site yesterday and he went on about the Druids, I thought it was a brilliant opportunity to set him up. I let him think I was about to uncover a treasure trove."

"Then you didn't really find anything?" She actually felt disappointed for his sake. "Oh, Simon, I'm so sorry."

His mouth twisted wryly. "Don't be, the chamber never even existed. I invented that on the spot in the hopes that Bunting would return during the night to steal the artifacts. But the weather turned stormy and he didn't show up until morning."

"Do you mean to say you stayed up all night outside in the cold watching for him?"

"I took turns with the coachman." He chuckled at her appalled expression. "It's no different than sentry duty. I'm accustomed to it."

No wonder Simon hadn't come to visit her the previous evening. He'd been otherwise occupied. "What did the vicar say when there was no burial chamber?"

"I pretended to have made a mistake. I said my eyes unfortunately had deceived me. Bunting had a difficult time hiding his anger. He went stomping off at midmorning, and I didn't see him again." Simon's hands tightened on her shoulders. "But I swear, I never imagined he'd take out his fury on you."

Annabelle shuddered. "I can almost understand why he would want to warn me away from the site. But that's a far cry from luring me into the cave . . . to die."

"He's a madman, that's why," Simon said flatly. "He's resented you ever since you had him ousted from the schoolroom all those weeks ago."

She tried to imagine the vicar plotting murder. Had he come back to the castle to write that note? How had he left it on her desk without anyone seeing him?

Then she knew how. "He may have an accomplice, Simon. Yesterday I saw him speaking to Mrs. Wickett, and I had the distinct impression they were . . . intimate. Do you suppose he asked her to leave the message in the schoolroom?"

"I'll find out, I promise you that." He picked up the lantern, and though his expression was forbidding, his hand was gentle as he placed it against her back. "Your skirt is wet. You must be freezing. You're to go back to the nursery and warm yourself by the fire."

Annabelle walked with him through the narrow tunnel, which led upward into the cellars of the castle. "What will you do now?"

"What I should have done from the outset. I intend to have Bunting arrested for attempted murder."

Chapter 23

On the night of the Samhain ball, Annabelle perched on the edge of her narrow bed to don her dancing slippers. Picking one up, she admired it by the light of the candle. The crystals sparkled, and the satin lining glowed a rich garnet hue. It still touched her heart that Lady Milford had given her such an exquisite gift. She owed the woman so much that could never be repaid.

Since Lady Milford had asked for regular reports, Annabelle had dutifully written a long letter three days earlier describing Nicholas's progress in his studies. Then she had related all that had happened in regard to the Druid site, including the two malicious attempts on Annabelle's life. How gratified Lady Milford would be to learn that her instinctive dislike of Percival Bunting had not been mistaken!

The man now resided in a prison cell awaiting trial. According to Simon, Bunting had vehemently denied the charges of attempted murder, though he did admit to being the one who had been secretly digging at the site. In addition, Mrs. Wickett had confessed to having released the crow in the library in an effort to frighten Annabelle into leaving the castle. However, she'd claimed *not* to have left the note in the schoolroom. Nevertheless, the woman had been dismissed for aiding and abetting her lover. One of the upper maids had been promoted to housekeeper, just in time to direct preparations for to-night's ball.

All's well that ends well, Annabelle thought as she donned the heeled slippers. They felt as soft and supple as a cloud. The only other time she'd worn these shoes had been on the day she'd gone to one of the guest bed-chambers to check the ball gown she had sewn. The day that Simon had kissed her senseless and made her feel a bliss beyond belief. The memory glowed inside her like an eternal flame.

So perhaps not *all* had ended well, she amended. She would never know the joy of Simon's love. Such intimacy wouldn't happen between them ever again. It couldn't. She must never compromise her principles for a man who regarded her as unworthy of being his wife.

Having never been one to wallow in melancholy, Annabelle faced the reality of her situation. Gentlemen didn't marry women of her dubious background. They wed fine ladies with a blue-blooded ancestry. It was the way of high society and she could never change that. Yet as she checked her hair in the small mirror above the washstand, Annabelle couldn't deny a sense of excite-ment about the evening that lay ahead. Like a child with her nose pressed to the sweetshop window, she looked forward to enjoying a taste of Simon's dazzling world.

Leaving her bedchamber, she went to visit Nicholas. An oil lamp burned low on his bedside table. Since it was well past seven, he was already tucked into the four-poster bed with its blue-and-gold hangings. He sat propped against a mound of pillows with his nose in a book.

He glanced up and his green eyes widened. "Miss Quinn! You look like a princess!"

Laughing, she dipped a curtsy. "Why, thank you, Your Grace. That's very kind of you to say so." She walked closer and brushed back a lock of his flaxen hair, then bent down to give him a kiss on his brow. "Now, it's time to set your book aside. You mustn't stay up reading or you'll fall asleep during tomorrow's lessons."

Nicholas placed the book on the table. As he wriggled deeper under the covers, he said rather wistfully, "It must be fun to go to a party."

The longing on his face touched Annabelle's heart. She couldn't bear for him to feel left out of the festivities. It reminded her too much of her own childhood, when she had been forbidden to participate in celebrations with her fellow students. "Suppose I come back here at midnight and wake you up? I'll bring you a surprise from the ball."

For days, the kitchen had been a beehive of activity as sweets and other delicacies had been prepared for the midnight supper. It should be no trouble to find something special for him.

Nicholas's expression perked up. "What will you bring me?"

"If I were to tell you, it wouldn't be a surprise, now would it?"

"Will Uncle Simon come with you?"

Annabelle hesitated. It was a safe guess that Simon would spend the evening surrounded by his usual bevy of beauties. "He's the host of the ball, darling, so he'll be very busy tonight. However, I promise I'll do my best."

Nicholas seemed content with that, and after giving him a hug, Annabelle turned down the lamp and made her way downstairs. The murmur of many voices came from the great hall where the aristocratic guests were arriving. From the upstairs landing, she caught a glimpse of Simon's dark head as he greeted people in the receiving line. A steady stream of stylish gentlemen and ladies proceeded up the grand staircase. As they reached the upper floor, she joined the procession and kept her gaze averted so as not to attract anyone's notice.

Ludlow stood just inside the ballroom door and announced each arrival. The elderly man spied her, but Annabelle put a finger to her lips. Winking, he allowed her to slip into the party without fanfare.

The large room that appeared quite ordinary during the daytime now took her breath away with its splendor. Hundreds of candles glowed in the crystal chandeliers. The polished parquet floor shone from its new coat of beeswax. Large vases of asters and hothouse roses lent brilliant color to the scene. The finest decorations of all were the noble guests themselves, the gentlemen in tailored coats with white cravats, the ladies in elegant, low-cut gowns of every hue.

Annabelle knew that her own homemade garb could never quite meet the high style of these ladies who employed the finest dressmakers. Nevertheless, she felt confident in the sky blue silk with its cream underskirt. Simon had certainly admired it when he'd caught her trying it on.

You are so very beautiful.

A melting sensation curled inside her. Of course, when he'd said that, he had already peeled down her bodice and had been gazing at her bare breasts. So perhaps the compliment didn't quite count in regard to her gown. But the heated look in his eyes when he'd walked into the dressing room was something she wouldn't soon forget.

Would he dance with her tonight? Would he hold the governess in his arms in front of all his friends and neighbors?

It would be foolish to harbor any such expectation. He had issued the invitation to this ball when he'd hoped to make her his mistress. Out of a sense of chivalry, he had embraced her after her ordeal in the cave to offer her comfort. He had visited the nursery twice since then, but had paid more attention to Nicholas than to her.

More telling than anything else, Simon had made no further attempt to seduce her. Nor had he sent any more gifts beyond the shawl that she wore—and that was merely a replacement for the one ruined by the crow. She could only conclude that he had decided to abide by her refusal of him.

The too-brief romance between them had ended.

Refusing to succumb to misery, Annabelle accepted a glass of champagne from a silver tray offered by a footman. She strolled to the rows of gilt chairs at one end of the long room, where the matrons had gathered to gossip. Taking a seat at the rear, she struck up a conversation with an elderly lady who, upon finding out Annabelle was the governess, proceeded to regale her with complaints of a personal nature. By the time the musicians played the first tune, Annabelle knew every detail of the woman's lumbago, rheumatism, and megrims. However, the one-sided chat proved to be a boon when the lady's middle-aged son came to check on her and asked Annabelle to dance.

He was a tongue-tied, portly gentleman, yet she welcomed the chance to join the other guests on the dance floor. Annabelle knew the steps from her days at Mrs. Baxter's Academy, for she often had been required to assist the girls in their dance lessons. But never had she had the opportunity to participate herself in such a glittering assemblage. Even at the dinner party all those weeks ago, she had played the pianoforte in the corner while everyone else had danced.

Over the course of the evening, Annabelle partnered with several other gentlemen, and she derived a quiet enjoyment from the activity. She steadfastly refused to look for Simon. Nevertheless, she caught sight of him from time to time as he squired a succession of young ladies. She was standing alone at the edge of the throng when she spied him with Lady Louisa.

It was a waltz, and Simon had his hand at the girl's dainty waist as they whirled around the floor. Lady Louisa looked like an angel in her airy white gown, a diamond tiara glinting in her blond curls. Despite Annabelle's resolute gaiety, the sight was a dagger thrust to her heart.

He had claimed that Lady Louisa was merely a family friend. But it didn't appear that way to Annabelle. Or perhaps, she admitted to herself, she was merely jealous. *She* wanted to be the one in his arms.

"They make a lovely couple, don't they?" said a voice behind her.

She turned to find Lady Danville eyeing her with a superior smirk. "Who do you mean?" Annabelle said coolly.

"Don't pretend coyness, Miss Quinn. You know perfectly well that I am referring to Lord Simon and my daughter."

Annabelle had no intention of cowering before this woman. "I am never coy, my lady. I believe in speaking my mind."

Lady Danville pursed her lips. "Then I shall do likewise. You should know that Simon's mother and I planned for them to marry from the time Louisa was born."

"Indeed? How peculiar, then, that he has not yet offered for her."

Lady Danville's nostrils flared in her patrician face. "Why, you insolent chit. Are you implying he has no intention of doing so?"

"Certainly not. I cannot pretend to know his private thoughts. Nor can you. He will make his choice without any help from either of us."

"Perhaps you hope he will select *you* as his bride. Have you no shame in aspiring so very far above yourself?"

"I am as much a lady as any here. Perhaps even more so."

Turning away, Annabelle left the woman gaping like a fish out of water. The air suddenly felt too close and she craved escape. She'd had enough of these snooty aristocrats. She would join the staff at their festivities outside.

As was the custom on Samhain, the guests had brought their servants. The employees took turns serving at the ball so that all of them would have the opportunity to take part in the revelry outdoors.

But as Annabelle fetched her shawl and went outside, she realized she didn't quite belong there, either. She stopped near the raised portcullis and watched from a short distance away. The servants were enjoying a very different sort of party with a huge bonfire lit alongside the front drive and a fiddler playing a lively song.

The wild music had an energizing effect on the crowd. Women danced, their skirts thrown in the air, while men in animal masks playfully gave chase. She spied the stout figure of the cook in the thick of the action, along with several of the maids and footmen. From time to time, a couple broke away from the multitude to head into the darkness of the forest. Annabelle preferred not to imagine what amorous activities they had in mind.

"It's quite stimulating, isn't it?"

She gasped, for the man standing beside her seemed to have materialized out of nowhere. He was dressed casually with his cravat tied loosely in the manner of a common laborer. "Mr. Tremayne! What are you doing out here?"

"Lord Simon neglected to send me an invitation to the ball. So rather than miss all the fun, I thought I would come and observe the servants at their revels. They have quite the unfettered way of marking the feast of the dead."

"It's the final celebration before the dark time of year," she said. "At least that's how Samhain was described to me in the kitchen. But I don't understand why some of them are wearing masks."

"On this night, the veil between this world and the next is reputed to be thin. The costumes are meant to confuse any evil spirits that cross over from the netherworld in an attempt to lure us to an untimely death."

A shiver ran over her skin. "How do you know that?"

"From Percival Bunting, of course. The fellow talked of naught else but Druid nonsense in the vicarage. Which is why it's a good thing he's locked in a cell tonight. It means he can't observe the occasion in his usual manner."

Annabelle glanced sharply at the assistant curate. "His usual manner?"

The firelight cast harsh shadows on Mr. Tremayne's face so that it looked as though he wore an otherworldly mask. "Haven't you guessed? Bunting fancied himself a Druid priest. On feast days like this, he held secret rituals with other devotees like himself."

"Who? Do you mean people who live around here?"

"Walk with me and I'll tell you what I've found out."

Mr. Tremayne took hold of her arm and tried to urge her toward the shadows of the forest, but she balked. Something in his manner made her uneasy. Was this merely an excuse to press his attentions on her? Nothing could be more abhorrent.

"Whatever you have to say can be said right here," she stated.

The assistant curate frowned. "As you wish, then. I've found a diary hidden in the vicar's study. In it, Percival described participating in all manner of rituals, including blood sacrifices made to pagan gods."

Annabelle controlled another shudder. She would have thought such a tale preposterous of anyone else. But she knew firsthand the vicar's predilection for the Druids. "The diary would strengthen the case against him, especially since he's denied any wrongdoing. Have you told Lord Simon about it?"

"Actually, I brought the book with me. It's in the saddlebag of my mount. Come, we'll fetch it."

Grabbing her hand, Mr. Tremayne tugged her down the darkened drive. Annabelle attempted to dig her heels into the gravelly dirt. But it was downhill and hard to stop her momentum. She had a strong suspicion the diary was merely a ruse to get her alone with him. No wonder Simon had warned her to stay away from this man.

She tried in vain to jerk herself out of the assistant curate's tenacious grip. "I am *not* going anywhere with you, Mr. Tremayne. It's high time I returned to the ballroom."

"And I say it's high time you gave me a taste of what you're giving Lord Simon."

He yanked her close and tried to mash his lips to hers. Annabelle turned her head to the side just in time. At the same moment, she lifted her foot and thrust the heel of her slipper down hard on his instep.

He bit out a curse, his fingers loosening. As she broke free and backed away, he glowered at her. "Speak of the devil," he muttered.

With startling swiftness, he spun around and scuttled off into the darkness. Then her astonishment cleared as she realized Simon was striding down the drive. Anger radiated from his tall, broad-shouldered form.

He stopped beside her, his hands drawn into fists. "Was that Tremayne?"

"Yes, but there's no need to bluster. He's gone now."

"What did he do to you?"

"Nothing of consequence. Simon, he said he's found a diary that belongs to Mr. Bunting. Perhaps you can ask him about it tomorrow."

Simon frowned. "Never mind that. He had his hands on you, and you were struggling. The scoundrel deserves to be knocked in the dirt where he belongs."

"It's over now." Seeking to defuse his temper, Annabelle gently rubbed his fist, coaxing his fingers to relax. "Let's go back inside. Then you can tell me what brought you out here to mingle with the lower class."

He gave her a penetrating look as they started back toward the bonfires. "I could ask you the same thing."

"I needed air." He mustn't know that she found air in short supply right at the moment, too, for his very presence constricted her lungs and filled her with unwanted joy. "And unlike you, I belong out here."

"Bosh," he chided, turning his hand and lacing their fingers together. "If that were true, I wouldn't have come in search of you. Nor would I be asking you to join me for the supper dance."

All the magic returned to the evening. Her heart took flight on wings of foolish hope. Never had she dreamed Simon would single her out for the most coveted dance of all. A gentleman reserved it for the one lady he favored above all others because afterward, they would share supper together. Breathlessly, she said, "Lady Danville won't be very happy about that."

He chuckled. "She did try her best to arrange matters otherwise. But I informed her I'd already chosen my partner. *If* you'll accept me."

Oh, my. Annabelle realized she'd been very wrong to believe Simon had given up on romancing her. It was clear he still wanted to coax her into his bed. So much so that he would display his interest in her before all his guests.

Glancing away from the temptation he posed, she looked at the servants dancing around the bonfire and sternly reminded herself that she was one of them. "Perhaps, my lord, you *should* ask Lady Louisa. She's a dainty, blond blue-blood just like Nicholas's mother. I should think you'd be drawn to her."

"Good God, no! She's a mere child who's easily cowed by her dragon of a mother." With a gentle hand, Simon turned Annabelle's face back toward him. "And I certainly *don't* want someone who looks like Diana. In fact, if I were to describe my ideal woman, she would have chestnut brown hair, gorgeous blue eyes, and a most exasperating habit of rebuking me."

She was his ideal woman? Even as Annabelle reeled from his candor, he lifted her hand to his mouth and pressed a warm kiss to the back. "Please, Annabelle. You have my word that I won't press my attentions where they're not wanted. Besides, it's only a dance."

Only a dance. Nothing could be more tantalizing than to be held by him as they glided around the dance floor. How could she turn down this rare chance to be partnered by the man she loved? And she *did* love Simon with all her heart. Life without him was drab and colorless, devoid of warmth and excitement.

Desire warred with prudence. She shouldn't encourage him. Nothing permanent could ever come of their association. She should escape to her chamber and put these fairy-tale dreams behind her.

But not even Cinderella had left the ball before midnight.

"I would be happy to accept, my lord."

He released a long breath as if he'd been worried she might refuse. As they walked back into the courtyard, his hand at her back, he subjected her to another concentrated stare. "We've half an hour before the supper dance. I don't suppose you'd be interested in viewing the artifacts I've uncovered over the past few days, would you?"

She stopped in surprise. "Oh, Simon! Do you mean to say there was a treasure trove there, after all?"

He nodded. "I'd been digging in the wrong place. As soon as I switched course, there it was, a small chamber filled with a cache of ancient relics. I've transported everything to my study for safekeeping."

"I *do* want to see it—all of it. Right now."

He gave her that crooked smile, the one that always melted her. Tonight, however, it held an intriguing hint of mystery. "Then do come with me."

Chapter 24

Annabelle followed close behind Simon as he led her up a little-used staircase at the back of the castle. He held her hand and she relished the feel of his strong fingers laced with hers. The distant lilt of music lent a dreamlike quality to the gloomy passage. She felt the thrill of high spirits as if they had embarked upon a great adventure.

How shocked the noble guests would be if they were to learn that their host had gone off alone with the governess. She would face gossip and censure, the ruin of her good name. But the thought was only fleeting. Being with Simon meant far more to her than winning the approval of small-minded aristocrats.

Besides, this excursion would be their secret. No one need ever know.

They arrived at his closed study. Simon fished in an inner pocket of his coat for a key and unlocked the door. When he ushered her inside, there was a lamp already burning low on a nearby table.

"I was hoping you'd agree to come here," he said. "You seem to be as interested in the Celtic site as I am."

His gaze held a trace of uncertainty that she didn't quite understand. Did he fear she didn't share his zeal for antiquities? The thought touched her heart. "I'm not simply interested," she said. "I'm *fascinated* to see things that were made thousands of years ago. So where are they?"

"Straight ahead. You'll need some light."

He nodded at his desk in front of the night-darkened window. Hurrying forward, Annabelle saw that the broad mahogany surface held an array of shadowy objects. Simon brought over a lamp and turned up the wick. As the flickering flame illuminated the scene, her eyes widened in amazement.

There were so many items she didn't know where to look first: gold jewelry inlaid with precious stones, a pottery urn with faded images painted on it, a tiny stylized horse made of hammered silver, swords and small wooden statues and many other things whose purpose she couldn't readily identify.

Simon pointed to a long narrow object inlaid with bits of red and blue gemstones. "I believe the piece that Nicholas picked up was once a part of that scabbard. You can see where it broke off the hilt."

"Simon, this is astounding." She walked around the desk to view more of the items. Most had a sheen of dirt and an overall air of neglect. Others, like the scabbard, were damaged in some way. "It will take you months to clean and catalogue everything. I don't even know what some of these things are."

"Here's one that's simple enough." He handed her a shallow gold bowl that was beautifully engraved with horses and stags. "I believe it may be my favorite piece."

"The workmanship is marvelous—oh, there's a ring inside." Annabelle plucked out a dainty gold circlet with an inset gemstone. Carrying it closer to the lamp, she turned it to and fro, and the polished stone winked a deep midnight blue in the light. "How lovely! It looks like a sapphire. What do you think?"

He stood watching her, his mouth curved slightly in an enigmatic smile. "I think you should try it on."

His gaze held an intensity that bespoke his desire to kiss her. In her inmost depths, she felt a corresponding rise of passion for him. He must have brought her here in the hopes of charming her. And who was to stop them from indulging themselves? They were all alone. No one else need know . . .

But she had made up her mind. She must not encourage him. As tempting as he was, the life he had offered her held no honor.

Her heart sore, Annabelle lowered her gaze and slid the sapphire ring onto her finger. By its perfect fit, it had to have belonged to a woman. Unlike the other items, however, the ring had a timeless elegance that stirred a melancholy ache inside her. If only . . .

Needing to fill the silence, she murmured, "I wonder who owned this. Do you suppose it was a wedding ring?"

Simon stepped closer. He took her hand and examined it in the lamplight. "It was actually a betrothal ring."

She glanced up at his enigmatic expression. "How can you be sure?"

He smiled faintly at her. "Because it belonged to my grandmother."

Annabelle could only gape at him in uncomprehending shock. His words reverberated through her mind, but she couldn't fathom his purpose. *His grandmother?*

She shook her head. "I—I don't understand."

"It's the only piece on the desk that didn't come from the site. I placed it there for you to find." His voice lowered to a husky murmur. "Because I want you to wear it, Annabelle."

His thumb stroked lightly over the palm of her hand. He was gazing at her with a passionate intensity that thrilled her to the core. Yet an awful fear crept through her happiness. He had said nothing of love—or marriage. And that could mean only one thing.

Her eyes filling with tears, she tugged at the ring. But her hands were shaking too much to remove it. "If this is another bribe, Simon, I don't want it."

He took her fingers in his, stopping her frantic efforts. "Darling, it is *not* a bribe. Well, perhaps it is, but not in the way you're thinking. Please, will you just hear me out?"

Annabelle went still, her heart beating swiftly. His manner held a desperation that was utterly unlike his usual charm and finesse. And yet she didn't dare allow herself to hope. The pain would be too devastating if she was wrong. "Go on, then."

His fingers remained tight around hers. "I've done a lot of thinking these past few days," he said in a halting tone. "And I realize now why I made such a dishonorable offer to you. Even though you'd come to mean so much to me, I had to keep you at arm's length, just as I'd done with Nicholas." Grimacing, Simon glanced away for a moment, then looked squarely into her eyes. "You were right to call me a coward, Annabelle. I have been very much afraid to love again."

He looked so tortured that she felt a softening in her breast even though she wasn't yet ready to forgive him. "I'm not Diana," she murmured. "I would never betray you as she did."

"I know that, I think I've always known it. But because of her, I'd sworn never to open my heart again.

Yet here I stand, madly, hopelessly in love with you." On that breathtaking statement, he brought her hand to his lips. "I want you to be my wife, Annabelle. Will you do me the great honor of marrying me?"

A surfeit of emotions welled up into her throat. Never in her wildest dreams had she allowed herself to think that Simon harbored such deep feelings for her. She had feared that for him it was just a fleeting physical passion. Overcome by joy, she felt incapable of formulating words. So she slid her arms around his waist, pressed her face into the crook of his neck, and let her actions speak for her.

He held her tightly, brushing kisses over her hair. His hands moved over her back as if he never wanted to let her go. Then their lips met in a sweetly ardent kiss that was rife with mutual love.

Simon drew back slightly and touched his forehead to hers. "That does mean yes, doesn't it?"

The trace of worry in his voice burrowed into her heart. "It means yes, *yes,* a thousand times yes. Oh, Simon, I love you so much. Why else do you suppose I allowed you such liberties that day in the bedroom?"

A twinkle entered his eyes. "I thought you'd merely succumbed to my superior lovemaking skills."

"Well, I certainly can't deny that you have a way with your mouth and hands."

Smiling seductively, she traced her fingertip over his damp lips, and he smiled back as they gazed into each other's eyes. The richness of desire spread through her body, and what a blessing that she no longer had to resist it. The slow caress of his hands over her breasts and waist honed her passion for him, and she murmured, "There's no need to go back to the ball straightaway, is there?"

As she spoke, the clock on the fireplace mantel chimed the midnight hour. His hands stilled and he glanced sharply at the clock. "Yes, we *do* have to go, or we'll be late for our dance."

She moved her hips against him. "We could dance right here, just the two of us."

His lashes lowered slightly and he gave her a look that told her exactly how much he craved her. Then he clenched his jaw and firmly set her back from him. "As tempting you are, my love, I am determined to partner you in front of society. The supper will be the perfect time for us to announce our engagement."

He turned down the lamp, then caught her by the hand and led her out of the study, locking the door behind them.

As they started down the dim corridor, arm in arm, Annabelle tried to fathom why she disliked the notion of publicizing their betrothal. "Must we share the news tonight? Can we not keep it to ourselves for now?"

He cast a surprised look at her. "Why hide it? I want all the world to know that you'll be my bride."

"They'll know soon enough." To soothe him, she stroked her hand over his cheek. "Simon, you must remember I'm merely the governess. Even worse, I've no knowledge whatsoever of my family—I might be the baseborn daughter of a highwayman for all I know. And because the people in that ballroom judge everyone by their bloodline, there will be many who'll brand me a fortune hunter."

"Let them try," he said, his voice radiating resolve. "I'll set them straight."

"I don't doubt you'll defend me. Yet I don't wish to spoil this evening with gossip and ill feelings. It's far too special to us." Sensing that he was weakening, she added, "Besides, there's one person who ought to be the first to know."

A wry smile tilted his mouth. "Nicholas."

She nodded. "He was so despondent at missing the ball that I promised him I would awaken him at midnight with a treat. He asked if you would come with me. Will you?"

Simon took her into his arms and kissed her brow. "It shall be as you wish, my love. But we *will* dance first. I insist upon that part."

"Yes. Oh, yes."

In short order, they reached the ballroom to find the dancers assembled and waiting. She had been anxious that they would miss the opening bars, but Simon assured her that the musicians would not begin the supper dance until he arrived. A sharp buzz of conversation ensued as they walked to the dance floor. Many of the guests turned to stare, the ladies whispering behind their fans.

The rumor mill was already operating in high gear.

Annabelle held her head high as they took up their position for the waltz. Simon gathered her close. As she placed her hand on his shoulder, the sapphire on her finger sparkled in the candlelight. Would any of the guests observe that she now wore the ring? Would they ask each other if she'd had it on earlier in the evening?

Let them wonder. She would not enlighten them. Tonight was for her and Simon alone.

As the musicians began to play, he smiled at her and the world faded away. No longer did she notice the throng of onlookers or the other couples on the dance floor. Only the two of them existed, whirling around in perfect time to the music. For the first time, she felt free to flirt with him in the manner of ladies and gentlemen.

"It is far more pleasant to dance with you, my lord, than with the girls at the academy where I grew up."

"How comforting to know my skill compares favorably to that of adolescent girls."

She laughed. "I'd tell you more about how accomplished you are, but it would go to your head and then living with you would become quite impossible."

In the midst of their banter, his expression took on a potent quality. "I am most impatient to live with you, Annabelle. Do you know how much?"

The deeply passionate promise in his gray eyes stirred a flurry of anticipation in her. She felt it in every part of her body, a mad fervor to be his wife. Would he wait until their wedding night to seduce her? Oh, she hoped not. It was so unladylike, this hunger for him to whisk her away to his bedchamber and do all manner of wicked things to her.

At the end of the dance, he leaned close to whisper to her. "I'll fetch a plate. Go upstairs to the nursery and wait for me. We shouldn't be seen leaving together or your reputation may be tarnished."

Annabelle suspected her character was already in question with many of those present. And when they both went missing, wouldn't people put two and two together, anyway?

Yet his protectiveness made her feel cherished. As he headed to the supper room and she went toward the main door, Annabelle was too happy to pay heed to anyone who might be gazing askance at her. She was betrothed to the finest, most gallant man in all of England. A man who loved her enough to acknowledge his mistakes and correct them. A man who freely admitted his love for her. The reality of that still seemed like a wonderful dream.

She couldn't resist glancing down at the sapphire ring. How heavy it felt on her finger, yet how perfect. As a token of Simon's affection, it was more precious to her than the crown jewels. When she looked up again, the milling crowd parted and she found herself gazing straight at Lady Danville.

She was staring at Annabelle's hand, too.

Lady Danville raised her chin and gave Annabelle a look so malevolent it could have curdled milk. She said something to the stout matron beside her, who shook her head disapprovingly.

As much as she disliked Lady Danville, Annabelle actually felt sorry for the woman. It must be a bitter blow for her to see her plans for her daughter put to ruin by a mere governess.

But charity only went so far. Annabelle maintained a serene countenance until she left the ballroom. Then her buoyant spirits brought a smile to her lips as she proceeded through the dim corridors and up to the nursery.

The schoolroom was dark, and she lit a candle from the embers of the fire. Walking toward Nicholas's chamber, she decided it might be wise to warn the nursemaid that Simon would be coming.

She peeked into the smaller bedroom, but the cot was empty, the covers undisturbed. Where was Elowen?

Opening the opposite door, Annabelle saw Nicholas fast asleep in the big canopied bed. The fire on the hearth had burned down to glowing embers. The nursemaid didn't occupy the rocking chair in the corner. She wasn't in the bedchamber at all.

The woman must have stolen outside to the Samhain party.

Irked, Annabelle wondered if there was time to go and find her, but as she left the schoolroom, she met Simon coming up the stairs with a plate and two glasses of champagne. Annabelle told him what had happened. "I don't like for the duke to be here all alone," she said. "What if he has a nightmare and cries out?"

"He has nightmares?" Simon asked with a frown.

"No, but he might and I wouldn't want him to be frightened."

His eyes searched hers, and for a moment she thought he might lecture her on coddling Nicholas. Instead, he surprised her by asking, "Did that happen to you as a child?"

Biting her lip, she nodded. "I remember someone motherly when I was very young, a woman who rocked me to sleep and comforted me. But she died when I was not quite five. After that, I slept by myself in a little room off the kitchen."

He tenderly brushed back a stray curl. "My sweet Cinderella. If it makes you feel better, we'll send a maid up here when we leave."

She *did* feel better, but that was purely due to his presence. It felt good to share her troubles with him. Someday, they would be discussing their own children this way. The notion filled her with such hope and joy that she blinked back tears.

Upon entering the duke's chamber, Annabelle placed the candlestick on the bedside table. She settled onto the edge of the mattress and gently stroked Nicholas's cheek. He stirred a little and blinked at her. Then he sat up straight and rubbed his sleepy eyes.

"Miss Quinn! You came! And you brought Uncle Simon!"

Simon chuckled. "She brought more than that. Here is the midnight treat you were promised, Your Grace. But I warn you, it's for all of us to share."

Into the boy's lap he placed a large china plate heaped with a vast array of delicacies. There was so much Annabelle hardly knew what to try first. A slice of raspberry cake. Petite rolls of paper-thin ham stuffed with cheese. Bacon-wrapped oysters. A little pastry oozing with lobster salad. Sugared almonds that sparkled in the candlelight.

Nicholas went straight for the chocolate éclair. In between big bites, he asked, "Is it really midnight?"

"A bit later," Annabelle said, selecting a tiny lemon tart. "But close enough."

Simon handed the boy a folded handkerchief to wipe his mouth. "At the stroke of twelve, I was waiting for the fairy godmother to turn Miss Quinn into a pumpkin, but it never happened."

Finding that hilarious, Nicholas went into a fit of the giggles. "It's the *coach* that turns into a pumpkin. And Miss Quinn isn't Cinderella, anyway."

"Hmm. I daresay she isn't, at least not anymore."

Annabelle glanced over her shoulder at him and they shared a heart-melting smile. He had seated himself directly behind her, and she leaned back into the cradle of his chest while she nibbled on her tart. His hand rested casually at her waist, his thumb drawing lazy circles on her midsection. Rather than stir her desires, the arrangement made her feel warm and cozy, as if they were truly a family.

A family. All of her life she had felt alone. Even so, she had not really known what she was missing. It was *this,* a sense of belonging, of having people to love who would be a part of her life forever. The notion brought a lump to her throat.

Simon reached for the two glasses of champagne he'd placed on the bedside table, handing one to Annabelle.

"This celebration calls for a toast. To the most beautiful bride-to-be in England."

As Simon clinked glasses with her, and they smiled giddily at each other, Annabelle noticed that Nicholas was watching them in confusion, his forehead puckered.

She reached out to gather his small, sticky hand in hers. "Sweetheart, your uncle has asked me to marry him, and I have accepted. That means I'll soon be your aunt."

"Your aunt Annabelle," Simon clarified. "Or Aunt Cinderella, whichever name you prefer."

Nicholas's eyes widened as big as saucers. He looked from her to Simon and back again. "Does that mean you'll stay with us, Miss Quinn? You won't go away even when I'm at school?"

She drew him into her arms, treasuring the smallness of him and his little-boy scent. "No, I'm not going away. Not ever. I'll always be here waiting for you."

"But . . . won't you go to London all the time now? Like Mama and Papa used to do?"

The wistful note in his voice hurt her heart. No wonder he looked worried. His parents must have left him here in the care of servants for much of the time.

Before she could reassure him, Simon leaned over her to address the boy. "Absolutely not," he said firmly. "I vow that if we travel to the city we'll take you with us." He grasped the boy's hand and solemnly shook it. "There, that makes it official. And remember, a gentleman never breaks his promise."

Nicholas looked delighted now, beaming at them both. "But who will be my governess now? Will it still be you . . . Aunt Annabelle?"

"Yes, most certainly. I would not have it otherwise."

As she brushed a lock of hair from his brow, Nicholas

abruptly gave a big yawn. Simon bore away the plate from the boy's lap while Annabelle tucked him in. The instant Nicholas laid his head on the pillow, his eyes closed, and just like that, he fell fast asleep again.

Simon took the candle and they tiptoed out of the bedchamber, closing the door. As they walked through the shadowed schoolroom and went down the stairs, he wove his fingers through hers.

"You needn't feel obliged to remain his governess," he murmured. "We can hire someone else. You deserve to lead a life of leisure for once."

She shook her head. "I've no wish to spend my days paying calls and fretting over what to wear. And I certainly wouldn't be content if I was separated from Nicholas." The wonder of it all washed over her again. "Oh, Simon, he's going to be my nephew now, too. I couldn't be happier."

At the bottom of the stairs, Simon stopped to look at her. In the glow of the candle, the profound love in his expression made her heart beat faster. "Well, then," he said. "I'm agreeable under one condition."

"And what might that be?"

"You'll have to arrange time in your busy schedule for your husband."

Annabelle slid her arms around his neck and rubbed her cheek against his. "I have time right now."

His chuckle sounded strained. He took a deep breath as if to clear his head. "*Not* in the middle of a party when I'm the host. When we make love for the first time, Annabelle, I intend to spend all night at it."

"But I want you . . . please, my darling."

She whispered the words against his lips. Keen to convince him, she brushed kisses over his face while stroking his hair. The scent and taste of him fed the rich flow of desire throughout her body. How she adored this man, how she wanted to make him as happy as he made her. Without conscious thought, she undulated her hips against his, seeking the wild pleasure he had given her once before.

She sensed the resistance in him as he waged a battle against his own base urges. Then abruptly he muttered, "Oh, *hell*. Let's do it."

Chapter 25

Hand in hand, they made haste through a maze of dim passageways. Within moments, Simon pulled her into a shadowed bedchamber and turned to lock the door. She had a glimpse of a large four-poster bed and masculine furnishings. Then there was no time to think, for he took her into his arms and subjected her to a deep, blatantly sensual kiss.

She reveled in the stroke of his tongue, the slide of his hands over her body. Her fingers sought the hard contours of muscles that were so different from her own softness. By the time he drew back slightly to nuzzle her cheek, they were both panting and fevered. Driven by the desire to touch his bare flesh, Annabelle pushed the coat from his shoulders. Simon helped her, shrugging it off and letting it fall to the floor as they continued to kiss and caress.

He turned her around and swiftly undid the buttons down the back of her gown. Then he loosened the strings of her corset, bending to feather his lips along her exposed skin. The warmth of his breath along her spine sent delicious tingles throughout her body. When the

bodice hung loose, he paused, his fingers sliding partway inside to toy with the sides of her bare bosom.

"No pins this time?" he asked dryly.

Annabelle laughed a little at the memory, glancing
over her shoulder at him. "None. Now do touch me, lest
I die of impatience."

He obliged by reaching fully inside the corset to play
with her breasts. He weighed them in his palms and
lightly rubbed the tips, causing a delicious heat that fed
the hunger in her womb. She held her breath as he
slid one hand downward over her belly until he brushed
her privates. Much to her frustration, however, he stopped
short of delving inside where she wanted him.

A moan rose from deep within her. Caught in the grip
of a powerful yearning, she undulated her bottom against
the placket of his trousers. A tremor ran through him as if
he struggled to keep his passion in check. But she didn't
want him to hold back. She wanted him to immerse her in
mindless bliss, and this time, to join her in that irresistible joy.

Shimmying out of her gown and undergarments, Annabelle peeled down her stockings and stepped out of
her shoes. Simon stripped his shirt over his head and
gave her a magnificent view of a broad chest dusted with
dark hairs and the rippling muscles in his arms. Unable
to resist, she rubbed her cheek against the bare expanse
of his torso. His skin was hot and salty to her lips. All
the while, he worked at the buttons of his trousers, uttering a low curse when one refused to open.

"Allow me . . ." Annabelle reached down to finish the
task for him. As he shed the garment, she found herself
transfixed by the sight of his engorged manhood. What
little she knew of the act of lovemaking had come from
eavesdropping on the sometimes ribald chatter of the

servants. Simon was so large, though, it didn't seem possible that he could fit inside her. Yet the very thought of allowing him to try caused a deep pulse of longing in her.

She melted in his arms while they engaged in another heated bout of kissing. It seemed perfectly natural for them to stand naked together, his member nestled against the peak of her thighs. She and Simon were meant for each other, and her desire for him flourished and grew until it became almost impossible to bear.

She moved her hips in open invitation. Against his mouth, she murmured, "Please . . . I'm ready. Don't make me wait."

With a guttural groan, he swept her up in his arms and laid her down on the bed. It was then that she saw the long, puckered scar on his left thigh. She lightly ran her fingertips over it, realizing the pain he must have suffered. "Oh, Simon! You've never told me what happened."

"An unfortunate encounter with a Pashtun tribesman."

"Does it ache often?"

"At times." His eyes dark, he leaned down and brushed his lips over hers. "The best remedy is vigorous physical activity . . . like this."

He settled himself beside her, took her in his arms, and proceeded to show how much he wanted her. She could not get enough of him; every taste, every touch only made her want him more. With his hand, he traced her curves up over her hips to her breasts and then cupped her face. "You are truly a gift from heaven," he whispered.

He pressed her against the pillows and nuzzled her throat, his head moving down to commence a delightful exploration of her breasts. At the same time, his fingers strayed lower and he began to stroke her in the way that made her wild with passion. She gave herself up to the wanton sensations, her body straining to reach the tantalizing promise of rapture.

Just when she found the tension intolerable, he came over her and she felt the pressure of his entry. There was a brief moment of discomfort as her body adjusted to his. He held himself still, his rigid arms braced on either side of her, his breathing deep and fast. She sighed his name as a marvelous sense of fullness washed through her. How astonishing it was to be one with him. In all her life, she had not felt complete until this moment.

He cradled her face in his hands. "Annabelle," he whispered. "My love."

The swift beating of his heart against her breasts matched the wild rhythm of her own. Holding her gaze, he began to move in her, slowly at first and then faster. Each plunge of his hips drove her deeper into madness. Her lashes drifted shut as all of her awareness focused on the place where they were joined. Uttering throaty sounds of delight, she clung to him as her anchor. No longer could she form a coherent thought; there was only the dark intensity of ever-mounting pleasure. When the storm broke at last, she shuddered from a wave of white-hot ecstasy. She was dimly aware of Simon kissing her, whispering impassioned words of love. Then he gave one last powerful thrust and groaned in the throes of his own release.

In the aftermath, they lay closely entwined as their breathing slowed and their blood cooled. His face was buried in her hair, and the heavy weight of his body enhanced her sense of satisfaction. She felt as if the consummation of their love had been more binding than any vows spoken in church. Replete and happy, she could have drifted forever in the contentment of his arms.

He rolled onto his back and brought her with him so that she lay half sprawled over him. His lips touched her brow. Then they shared a smile that expressed their newfound knowledge of each other more deeply than words ever could.

"You have stars in your eyes," he said.

"Perhaps because I've learned something, my lord."

"And what might that be?"

"Now I know why the girls at the academy were warned against being alone with their suitors. Until I met you, I never understood just how tempting a man could be."

He chuckled. "When our daughters come of age, they will not be allowed within a mile of any lusty young men."

The notion of bearing his daughter or son filled Annabelle with joy. "Let us simply agree they will be well chaperoned. Else how will they ever become betrothed to the man of their dreams?"

Annabelle let her fingers drift over the solid muscles of his arm. As she caressed him, the sapphire on her finger glinted in the faint light.

Simon caught her hand and kissed it. "I never explained what this ring means, Annabelle. My grandmother was very special to me. She lived here at Castle Kevern, and it was to her that I went when I needed advice or a listening ear. Without her firm guidance, God only knows what sort of miscreant I might have become."

"What of your own mother?"

He shrugged. "My parents had eyes only for George, who was much better behaved than I—at least in front of them. I was the one who caused trouble, and he knew just what to whisper to make me explode with anger in their presence."

Simon spoke in a jesting tone, but Annabelle wasn't fooled. She could imagine him as a child, lashing out to hide the pain of rejection. "Oh, darling, they should not have shunned you. Parents are supposed to love all their children, not just the favored heir."

He looked away for a moment before returning his gaze to her. "Perhaps it made me the man that I am. I certainly would never have been so devoted to Grandmamma otherwise. I wanted you to have her ring because you remind me of her."

Annabelle gave him a look from under her eyelashes. "Are you quite *sure* I remind you of your grandmother?"

Simon laughed softly as he fondled her bare bottom. "Minx. I was referring to your strength of character. She was outspoken just like you. It was because of her that I developed an appreciation for sassy, impertinent women."

"What happened to her?" she asked quietly.

"She died while I was away in the military." He paused, his face pensive. "When I left, I broke off all ties with my family. But she always seemed to know where I was stationed. She would write to me from time to time, entreating me to come home and make amends with my brother. Then the letters stopped." A muscle worked in his jaw. "That played a part in why I'd decided to resign my commission. I returned to London, only to discover she'd died of old age the previous spring."

"George never wrote to inform you?"

He shook his head, his expression hard. "We never spoke after he stole Diana out from under my nose. I despised them both for a long time. But now . . . now it all seems like a wasted effort. George and I were often rivals, but we were comrades, too. Maybe if I hadn't been so stubborn, we might have mended fences. Then it was too late."

It was wrong to think ill of the dead, but Annabelle heartily disapproved of George and Diana. "You couldn't know they'd be killed in a tragic mishap—a carriage wreck, one of the servants told me."

"There was more to it than that." He gazed bleakly at her. "George was always a daredevil. He was racing his carriage against a few other friends. Diana was at his side when the vehicle lost a wheel, went into a ditch, and overturned. I've often thought, what if I had sought him out when I was in London? Could I have prevented him from doing something so damnably foolish?"

Shock and sadness enveloped Annabelle. Wanting to ease his pain, she lovingly stroked his face. "It wasn't your fault. It was an accident. But oh, how *could* they have taken such a chance when they had a young son who needed them?"

Simon closed his eyes briefly, turning his head to press a kiss into the palm of her hand. "Perhaps everything happens for a reason. You do realize, don't you, that if they hadn't died, I would never have met you?"

"Yes." As she softly said that, Annabelle reflected on the strange twists that life had taken in leading them both to this moment. Then, hoping to ease his mood, she added, "Of course, I am obliged to point out that you resisted hiring me from the start. You tried to send me away."

A faint grin lightened his face. "I sensed you were about to upset the well-oiled machinery of my life. And thank God you did. If not for you, I'd have remained a bitter old curmudgeon for the rest of my days."

"And I would have been a dry old maid who'd never know the joys of falling in love and finding a real home."

He brushed a tender kiss over her mouth. "I intend

to give you the family you never had, Annabelle. In the meantime, however, you'll have to be content with Nicholas and me."

Even as his words inundated her in happiness, she realized something and sat up with a gasp. "Nicholas! Oh, Simon, I forgot completely that Elowen abandoned him. He's all alone in the nursery."

"He'll be fine, my love." Simon feathered his fingers over her breasts, then with a look of regret, withdrew his hand. "Now, as tempting as you are, we mustn't linger. Tongues will be wagging already about our long absence."

As they arose from the bed, Annabelle placed her hand on his chest. "Will you mind so very much if I don't return to the ball? It's late, and I've no wish to parry gossip after what we've shared tonight."

A smile played at the corner of his mouth as he tucked a stray lock of hair behind her ear. "You do have the aura of a woman who has been thoroughly loved."

"And you look like a man who has been thoroughly satisfied. At least for the moment."

Annabelle stood on tiptoe and their lips met in a stirring promise for the future. She wanted nothing more than to lie with him again, but knew he had a duty to his guests. So she poured all of her love into the kiss, letting him know exactly how much she would miss him.

When at last they drew apart, Simon had that concentrated look in his eyes. "We shall be married as soon as I can make the arrangements."

She smiled sensually. "As you wish, my lord."

They helped each other dress, pausing for brief caresses and fleeting kisses, until the whole process took twice as long as it ought. Since there would be guests

spending the night, Simon checked the corridor to make
certain no one would see them leaving his chamber together. Then they walked through the deserted passageway to the stairway that led to the nursery.

He handed her the candle. "Dream of me?"

"Always, my love."

They kissed one last time. Weak-kneed, Annabelle
leaned against the stone wall as he strode away and vanished around a corner. The faint lilt of music drifted from
the ballroom downstairs. Supper would be over and people would be dancing again. If only she could have gone
with him. Already she felt bereft, lonely.

But she could only imagine how she must look with
half her hairpins gone and an expression of giddy happiness on her face. Better she should retreat to her chamber for now and not give the gossips more fodder. They
would be clucking enough already.

Climbing the stairs, she entered the schoolroom. It
looked as before, shadowed and serene. This had been
her domain for the past two months, and yet now, she
would be mistress of the castle as well. The reality of that
had not yet taken hold in her mind.

Annabelle went straight to check on Nicholas. He was
sound asleep in his bed, his breathing even, his pale
lashes fanned on his sweet face. She straightened his
covers. Simon was right, perhaps she did worry too much.
But she couldn't bear for anything to happen to the boy.
Like Simon, Nicholas had become very dear to her. They
were her family now and she was the luckiest woman in
the world.

After quietly closing the door, she checked across the
corridor to find Elowen's room still empty. Annabelle
had half a mind to go out and find the neglectful maid at
the Samhain revels, then decided it could wait until the

morning. At the moment she felt too happy to be giving anyone a stern lecture. Anyway, she'd be here now if Nicholas needed someone.

She wanted to snuggle in bed and bask in the memories of Simon's lovemaking. Never in her life had she imagined such joy could exist between a man and a woman. All of the poetry, the sonnets, the verses she had read over the years suddenly made sense to her. In those lines, love had not been exaggerated for literary effect as she'd always believed. If anything, the reality of it was more beautiful and exhilarating than mere words could ever express.

A smile on her face, Annabelle opened the door to her bedchamber and placed the candlestick on the washstand. She stood in front of the little mirror, wishing there was more light so that she could tell if her outward appearance had changed as much as she felt changed inside.

As she peered closer, something moved in the mirror. A distorted face appeared behind her. The visage of a devil.

Horror flashed through her. Even as she opened her mouth to scream, a hand clamped a smelly cloth over her mouth and nose.

Chapter 26

Shortly after entering the ballroom, Simon was astounded
to come face-to-face with the one person he had never
expected to see at the party. She had been on the original guest list, but had sent her regrets due to a prior
engagement.

Smiling, he kissed her on the cheek. "Clarissa! What
a delight to have you here."

Lady Milford looked agelessly slender and serene in a
gown of plum silk. A diamond aigrette decorated her upswept black hair. She had hardly changed since the days
when she had been a dear friend of his grandmother's.
"There you are, Simon. You're looking quite well."

If only she knew how invigorated he felt—and why.
"When did you arrive?" he asked. "Did I somehow miss
you? There was quite the crush of people in the receiving line."

"No, I fear I was hopelessly late. Supper was already
in progress."

"You traveled through the dark to join us?" he asked
in surprise. "As much as I welcome your company, I

would never have wished for you to take such a risk on these winding roads."

"My coachman is quite proficient. Besides, I needed to be here as swiftly as possible." On that enigmatic statement, she curled her gloved fingers into the crook of his elbow. "Do let us stroll to a quieter spot."

Intrigued, Simon guided her on a route that skirted the edge of the crowd. He nodded coolly to a few people, not wanting to encourage conversation with anyone else. It was clear that Lady Milford had something important on her mind—and that was fine with him because he had momentous news for her, too.

Simon could scarcely keep from grinning like a besotted fool. He had begun the evening uncertain if Annabelle could ever forgive him for his reprehensible plan to make her his mistress. But things had turned out even more spectacularly than he had dared to hope. She loved him, and never in his life had he been happier.

Lady Milford stopped by a night-darkened window, far from the throng of dancers at the other end of the chamber. "This will do," she said.

Simon noted the serious look on her face. "I must say you're being quite mysterious tonight," he said. "I hope you plan to enlighten me."

"First I must know, where is Miss Quinn?"

"Asleep in her bed, I presume."

"I had hoped she would still be here at the ball," Lady Milford said with a moue of regret. "However, perhaps it's for the best. It caused quite a stir when both of you vanished from the ball. And for nearly two hours!"

"Please be assured I did nothing to dishonor her." That was the absolute truth. He loved Annabelle with all his heart and soul, and their physical joining had been an expression of their mutual devotion. There was no force on earth that could stop him from marrying her.

At that moment, Simon spotted Ludlow's stooped figure shuffling toward them from across the room. The ancient retainer raised a gnarled hand in a beckoning wave as if he wanted to speak to Simon.

Good God. What if the old fellow had been up to the bedchamber and had seen the evidence of lovemaking? He might very well make a bawdy allusion to it in front of Lady Milford. It would confirm her suspicions when Simon was determined to guard Annabelle's privacy.

Lady Milford was already eyeing him sharply. "Tell me the truth, Simon. *Are* you dallying with her? I won't stand by while you heap shame on such a fine, decent woman."

"You've no cause for concern, I promise you." He placed his hands on her dainty shoulders. "In fact, I'll let you in on a secret. Tonight, Annabelle consented to be my wife. We're going to be married."

A misty light entered Lady Milford's violet eyes. Her mouth softened in a warm smile; then she leaned up on tiptoe and gave him a peck on the cheek. "Well! That is the *most* wonderful news! I can scarcely believe it."

"I've you to thank for sending Annabelle here—and for insisting that Nicholas needed a governess. He's blossomed under her care."

"And so have you, it would seem."

"To be honest, I don't know how I ever lived without her." Ludlow was almost upon them. Simon had no intention of having a conversation with him in front of Lady Milford. "Will you excuse me for a moment? I need a word with my manservant."

Lady Milford gave Simon a meditative look. "Actually, the matter that brought me here involves Miss

Quinn. I would much prefer to speak to both of you at the same time. Shall we do so in the morning?"

"If it pleases you, yes."

She glided away into the multitude of guests. Simon felt an intense curiosity. What *was* this issue involving Annabelle that had induced Lady Milford to drive through the night? He couldn't imagine.

Ludlow made a creaky bow. "Praise God I have found you at last, my lord."

"At last?"

"A messenger brought word more than an hour ago. It seems that Mr. Bunting has escaped from prison."

Annabelle awakened slowly to a groggy sense of dread. Her eyelids felt too heavy to lift and her head ached abominably. She wanted nothing more than to sink back into restful oblivion. Yet some inner imp prodded her to assess her surroundings.

She lay flat on her back on a cold, hard surface. Her right foot felt icy; she wore only one shoe. The scent of damp earth hung heavy in the air. Though she could not explain why, she had the impression of being trapped inside a tight enclosure.

A grave. I've been buried alive.

Alarm stabbed into her. With supreme effort, Annabelle opened her eyes. She was indeed underground. Directly above her loomed a dirt ceiling seamed with tree roots. She was close enough to discern every twist and turn in their thickness.

Gasping, she managed to push herself up onto one elbow. The world spun dizzily and she had to close her eyes again. When she opened them, it became clear why she was able to see at all.

Light emanated from beyond her feet. Something

black blocked the source of it. She blinked several times, then realized that a shadowed figure crouched before her. A creature wearing a devil's mask.

The memory of the face in the mirror flashed into her mind.

Terrified, she tried to scream. But in her weakened state, it sounded more like a squeak.

A laugh came from behind the mask. "Well, well, Miss Quinn. It's high time you awakened."

That voice.

As recognition struck, a cold tremor gripped her bones.

Holding a lantern, Simon raced up the nursery stairs two at a time. He assured himself the news posed no immediate danger. Bunting would not have escaped from prison and come straight here; he would have scuttled into hiding like the coward he was.

Yet Simon couldn't shake the premonition that Annabelle was in danger. Nor could he forget the loathing in the vicar's eyes whenever the man had looked at her.

He headed swiftly through the shadowed schoolroom. Though he'd never been in her bedchamber, Simon knew its location. The sight of her open door caused a lurch in his chest. But maybe she'd only wanted to be able to hear Nicholas if he called out in his sleep.

That brief hope died when Simon stepped into the chamber. The light of his lamp fell on her empty cot. The covers had not been disturbed.

Driven by alarm, he pivoted on his heel and strode across the schoolroom to the boy's chamber. Nicholas lay asleep in the big canopied bed. Annabelle was nowhere in sight.

Where was she? She would not have gone back to the ball.

Three quick steps took him to the tiny chamber where the nursemaid slept. It was empty as well.

Something sparkled on the floor: a single garnet shoe encrusted with crystal beads. It lay in front of the hidden entry to the tunnels.

Fingers trembling, Simon picked up the shoe and stuffed it into his pocket. Then he felt along the stone wall for the concealed latch. He pressed it and the door sprang open to a stygian darkness.

Annabelle would not have ventured into the tunnels merely on a lark. Especially not while missing a slipper. Someone had to have forced her through here.

Bunting.

Taking the lamp, Simon raced down the steep steps. As he neared the landing where the stairway split into two, he spied something that made his blood run cold. A woman lay there in a shadowed heap. It was obvious from the unnatural tilt of her head that she was dead.

His heart thundered in his chest. *No!*

He dropped to his knees, turned her over, and realized two things in swift succession. She was not Annabelle, but the missing nursemaid.

And she had been strangled.

"Scream all you like," he said. "No one can hear you out here."

Annabelle struggled to rise. But her head swam and her limbs felt shaky. She managed to wriggle into a sitting position while watching him. Something had been on the cloth that he'd put over her mouth when he'd captured her. Something that had made her swoon.

At least now, though, she knew his identity by his cultured voice.

"Why . . ." She paused to wet her dry lips. "Why are you wearing that silly mask?"

"In case we ran into anyone on the way here, I could pretend we were merely revelers from the Samhain party. But I don't suppose I need it anymore, now do I?"

He untied the strings behind his head. The devil's mask fell away to reveal a visage even more chilling for its mild-mannered appearance: Mr. Harold Tremayne.

She still felt too woozy to make sense of things. Yet instinct told her to try. The longer she kept him talking, the better her chance of regaining her strength and making her escape.

"Where am I?" she asked, her voice sounding feeble.

"Guess. You ought to recognize this place."

Annabelle glanced around. Revulsion filled her as she spied a pile of bones beside her. She was in the excavated hole at the Druid site. The hard surface beneath her was the stone altar.

She tried not to shiver. "How do you know I've been here before?"

"Percival Bunting told me. Besides, I've seen you here myself."

She knew at once what he meant. "It wasn't the vicar who shot at me. It was . . . *you*."

Tremayne smiled in the caricature of a gentleman. The lamplight behind him cast shadows that made his eyes look like the empty sockets of a skull. "I was watching you that day," he said. "And when the opportunity presented itself . . . I knew what I had to do."

Horror crept over her skin. He had to be mad. A raving lunatic. How was she to flee him? He blocked the entry to the hollowed-out area in which she sat. There was no one to save her but herself.

Time was her only weapon. Moment by moment, she felt more clear-headed. She prayed her physical strength would return as well.

He went on rather proudly, "I also sent the note luring you to the cave on the beach. It was quite simple to copy Lord Simon's penmanship from his correspondence with the vicar." Tremayne leaned over her feet to leer at her. "How eager you were to meet your lover."

The thought of Simon made her throat catch. Would she ever see him again? He believed Mr. Bunting had written that forged note with Mrs. Wickett as his accomplice. "Then you must have been very disappointed when Simon rescued me."

"Don't count on him coming for you again, not this time." Tremayne's tone took on a whining edge. "It wasn't supposed to happen this way, you know. It's all your fault for rebuffing me."

"Rebuffing you?"

"At the dinner party shortly after my arrival here. Right in the middle of our conversation, you turned your back on me and went straight to Lord Simon. You did the same thing when I was speaking to you as you played the pianoforte."

His resentment alarmed Annabelle. She had to relax him if she hoped to catch him off his guard. "I meant no slight, I assure you."

"Yes, you *did*. You snubbed me. You, a bastard-born *nothing*."

She stared at him. She'd told no one but Simon about her base birth. "I'm sorry, Mr. Tremayne. I can't imagine who has been gossiping about me."

His guttural laugh chilled her. "You think I obtained my knowledge from *gossip*? Nay, I have it from one in the innermost circle of royalty. You see, Miss Quinn, I am merely posing as a cleric. I was sent here to seduce you—to make certain you were ruined and never again found employment with any decent family."

The man was deranged. Nothing he said made any sense. "Sent here? By whom?"

"There is one at court who wants you out of the way . . . because of who your father was."

Stunned, Annabelle shook her head. "My father?"

Rather than enlighten her, Tremayne bared his teeth in a grimace. "I was paid a handsome fee to lure you into an indiscretion, but you wouldn't cooperate. So it became necessary to kill you instead."

He lifted his arm. In his hand gleamed a long knife.

After discovering the maid's body, Simon had raced through the tunnels. But he failed to find any further clue leading to Annabelle's location. Where would Bunting have taken her?

Simon fought off panic and forced himself to think. There were far too many possibilities—the cave on the beach, the countless rooms in the castle, the vast grounds outside. Worse, Bunting might have thrust her into a waiting vehicle and was now driving away. Simon needed help, and luckily, plenty of footmen and grooms had attended the Samhain festivities. A search party could comb the area much faster than one man.

As he made haste through the courtyard and then the open portcullis, Simon ran smack into a girl who was running in from beyond the castle walls. He recognized her as Livvy, one of the kitchen maids.

She had landed on her skinny behind, and as he helped

her up, Livvy babbled, "M'lord! They be out there! 'Ee mustn't go near!"

The terror in her voice struck him. *They* . . . Annabelle and Bunting? "Cease your gibbering and speak clearly."

"The piskies—they'll bewitch 'ee. I saw their light on the hillside!"

"Piskies! Good God!" Simon stepped aside to wave her past. "Go on with you."

But even as Livvy darted into the castle, comprehension swept away his scorn. A light on the hillside . . .

Suddenly he knew exactly where Bunting had taken Annabelle.

The lamplight gleamed on the sharp edge of the knife.

Willing her teeth not to chatter, Annabelle strove for the firm tone of a governess. "You're making a terrible mistake. You'll be sent to prison to hang."

Tremayne chuckled darkly. "Ah, but I'm too clever for that. You see, I arranged for Percival Bunting to escape from prison a few hours ago. When your bloody remains are found on that altar, Bunting will be held to blame and hunted down like a dog."

Dear God. Simon would have no reason to doubt the false story. He knew that Bunting had a keen interest in Druid sacrifices. In addition, Tremayne had claimed to have found a diary that added further damning evidence. Perhaps that too was a convenient forgery.

Eyeing the blade in his hand, Annabelle felt a clutch of terror. How could she fight him when she had no weapon of her own?

Out of desperation, she decided to play to his vanities. "I never realized how very clever you are," she said. "I do wish you would give me a second chance."

"You *are* beautiful," Tremayne said, almost regretfully. "It is truly a pity that you have to die."

In a crouch because of the low ceiling, he moved closer to her. Annabelle pretended to cower against the back wall. When he was near enough, she gathered all of her strength and kicked at him.

The tangle of her skirts blunted the blow. Yet she managed to graze his crotch with her heeled shoe and knock him off balance. Tremayne hissed out a curse as he fell sideways against the wall. A fine shower of dirt rained down on both of them.

Annabelle snatched up a hefty bone from the pile. She intended to hit him over the head and knock him out. But he recovered too swiftly.

With a feral growl, he lunged at her.

She had time only to grasp the long bone in both hands, using it as a shield to ward off his attack. She cried out as the hard strike splintered the bone and narrowly missed slicing her fingers.

His face twisted in a snarl, he drew back the knife again.

Annabelle brandished the broken bone like a spear. She would gouge out his eyes if necessary. But the blow never came. A dark figure dropped into the hole and seized Tremayne from behind.

Simon!

The lantern lit his grim features. He clamped his arm around Tremayne's throat in a chokehold. The knife thumped to the ground. Tremayne struggled, uttering strangled gasps, until he abruptly went limp.

As Simon dropped him, Annabelle stumbled out of the cavelike hole and threw herself at Simon. Shuddering, she slid her arms around his waist and clung tightly to his warmth. The swift beating of his heart made her fiercely glad to be alive.

She turned a glance at Tremayne's crumpled body. "Is he—"

"He's dead," Simon said flatly.

There was a coldness to his tone that she ached to heal. She cupped his cheek in her hand. "You did what needed to be done. He nearly killed me."

Simon drew a deep breath. "You're safe now, my love." As he pressed a kiss into her palm, his voice throbbed with emotion. "Praise God you're safe."

Chapter 27

Clarissa fought off a wave of weariness that had more to do with the weight of her secret than the lateness of the hour.

Yet it pleased her to watch Simon fuss over Annabelle. They were in his study, and he had settled Annabelle onto a chaise by the roaring fire. When he had brought her back to the castle, word of what had happened had spread quickly throughout the ball.

Clarissa had been about to retire for the night. But the time for explanations had come. Sick at heart, she knew that she alone had had prior knowledge that could have prevented the attack. If only she'd arrived sooner . . . but that had not been humanly possible.

Now, Simon brought Annabelle a glass of brandy, but she waved it away with a shudder. "Just tea, please. I don't want anything to cloud my senses. Mr. Tremayne put a smelly rag over my mouth, and I don't remember anything until I awakened on that altar."

"Ether," Clarissa said in distaste. "It is a drug taken by certain aristocrats at parties known as ether frolics.

In small amounts it can induce euphoria. Of course, a larger dosage will put one to sleep."

Simon's face tightened as he poured a cup of tea and added a lump of sugar. "Would to God I'd known that devil was lying in wait! I'd like to know how he learned about the secret passageways."

Annabelle took the cup from him. "He was very cunning, the sort who snoops at keyholes. I expect Mrs. Wickett somehow discovered the tunnels and told Mr. Bunting. Mr. Tremayne likely overheard them."

"In regard to Bunting, he will have to be tracked down and informed that he truly *is* a free man."

"You won't prosecute him for digging at the Celtic site, then?" Annabelle asked.

"In light of what's happened, no." Simon sat down beside her on the chaise and gently rubbed her hand. "Darling, you look exhausted. We needn't talk about all this right now. It can wait until morning."

They shared a tender smile; then she briefly laid her head on his shoulder. "I'm afraid I wouldn't be able to sleep. I keep remembering something odd that Mr. Tremayne said to me."

"What was that?"

"He said . . . that he'd been *sent* here to seduce me. By someone at court. It was only later that he decided to kill me instead."

Simon slipped his arm around her and pressed a kiss to her brow. "The ravings of a madman. He's best forgotten."

Watching them, Clarissa felt a bittersweet joy. How fondly she remembered her own youth when she had loved with such intensity. Now, it was marvelous to see her plan for Annabelle and Simon come to fruition. The bond between them was clearly powerful. But would it be strong enough to withstand what she was about to tell them?

Clarissa took a fortifying breath. "I know what Tremayne meant. It's the reason I came here. But first, Simon, I'll have that brandy."

Frowning, he handed the untouched glass to her. "I wondered why you arrived in the middle of the night."

"It was Annabelle's letter that brought me. When she wrote to me a few days ago that Mr. Bunting had made two attempts on her life, I feared at once that the wrong man had been arrested." Clarissa took a bracing sip of brandy. "But I am jumping ahead of myself. First, Annabelle, I must tell you something of my own background."

Annabelle gave her a perceptive look. "At the dinner party, Mr. Tremayne gossiped about you, my lady. He told me that you were once the mistress of a royal prince, a son of King George the Third."

"Yes." As always, Clarissa felt a trace of sadness at the loss of her one true love, but now was not the time for those memories. "I fear I must reveal a secret known only to certain members of the royal family. I myself discovered it only earlier this year in a deathbed confession from a servant. I don't know quite how to word this, my dear girl, except to say it straight out. You are not the child of some nameless commoner. Your father was the late Prince Edward, Duke of Kent, and the fourth son of King George."

Annabelle said nothing. She only stared with wide blue eyes. She shook her head slightly as if disbelieving her own ears.

Simon was not so silent. "The devil you say! The royals always look after their illegitimate children. How could he abandon her like that?"

"He didn't know she was alive," Clarissa said softly. "Let me explain the events. Prince Edward was wed in secret to a French lady—"

"The marriage was legitimate?" Simon broke in incredulously. "But that would mean—"

"Enough! You will allow me to speak without interruption." As he scowled and settled back to listen, she continued, "Mad King George sanctioned the union, but only days later, when he was declared unfit to rule any longer, the Privy Council revoked the approval. You see, the year was 1811 and a half-French child in line to the throne during the Napoleonic wars would have caused chaos. Then Annabelle's mother died in childbirth, as did her infant daughter—or so people thought." Clarissa leaned forward and addressed Annabelle. "I must add, I have never seen a man more grief-stricken than was Prince Edward. He would have welcomed a daughter, legitimate or otherwise."

Annabelle took a shuddery breath and closed her eyes, turning her face toward the fire.

Simon clenched his fists on his knees. "So what you're saying is that someone substituted a dead baby for Annabelle."

"Yes, that is precisely what happened," Clarissa said, sympathy welling in her as she watched Annabelle. What a shock this must be to the girl. "She was smuggled away and placed in the school in Yorkshire."

Simon sprang to his feet. "Who did this? Give me their names."

"Those responsible have since died. And I would not identify them to you, anyway."

"Well, clearly someone at court still knows about it. Who?"

"Do sit down, Simon, and allow me to finish."

Clarissa glared at him until he resumed his seat. She was glad to see him slide a protective arm around Annabelle, because he might very well resent what Clarissa had to say next, male pride being what it was.

"When I discovered what had happened all those years ago," Clarissa went on, "I could *not* leave a girl of royal blood to toil away at a rustic school. At the very least, Annabelle deserved to make a good marriage. So I arranged for her to come here to Castle Kevern. I did it in the hopes that the two of you would fall in love."

A disgruntled look came over Simon's face, but to his credit, it lasted for only a moment. Then he shook his head and laughed. "Well, at least *something* good has come out of all this intrigue and scheming."

Clarissa took another sip of her brandy. "I never meant to unleash mayhem with my actions. I thought no one would ever even know what I'd done. However, I have since learned that Mrs. Baxter at the academy had been sending regular reports about Annabelle to an address in London."

Annabelle spoke for the first time. "Mrs. Baxter *knew*?"

"No, my dear, she knew absolutely nothing except that she was paid a small sum in exchange for submitting a brief report now and then on your activities—and for making certain that you never left the school. When you *did* go, Mrs. Baxter immediately sent word to her contact, who then arranged for Tremayne to become the assistant curate here."

"I want the name of this contact," Simon demanded.

Clarissa gave him a stern look. "It is best that no one but I know. Do not ask me again. However, what Tremayne told Annabelle is true. He *was* sent here on orders to seduce her. He was to ruin her so that she would never again be hired by any decent family. Then there would be no possibility of her coming into contact with any of the nobility."

"But why?" Annabelle asked, shaking her head in bewilderment. "If the marriage of my . . . my parents wasn't valid, then what threat could I pose to the royal family? Did they think I would beg for money?"

"I suspect it has to do with the fact that you're the half sister of Crown Princess Victoria," Simon stated. "The *elder* half sister."

Annabelle uttered a small moan. She sat with both hands raised to her mouth.

"Indeed," Clarissa confirmed softly. "May I say, there were some anomalies in the Privy Council ruling all those years ago, and there may be a case to prove the validity of your parents' marriage in a court of law. That would make you, Annabelle, the true heir to the throne of England. It would mean that *you,* not Victoria, are the crown princess."

Annabelle said nothing. She sat as still as a statue. A statue with the same lovely blue eyes as seventeen-year-old Crown Princess Victoria.

Clarissa wondered what Annabelle was thinking. She had been raised in a hard life of servitude, and now she was being handed the ultimate prize on a golden platter. Would she seize the opportunity?

Simon looked dumbstruck as well. He surged to his feet and paced to the fireplace to watch Annabelle. The gravity of his features revealed his own dilemma. Her decision could alter their relationship irrevocably. He had planned to devote his life to the study of antiquities; the collection of Celtic artifacts on his desk was proof of that. Would he even *want* to be tied down as consort to a queen?

But the choice had to be made, so Clarissa addressed Annabelle. "Do you wish to pursue the matter of your right to the throne? You must think on that question, my dear. Perhaps in the morning you will give me your decision."

Annabelle looked starkly at her, then lifted her gaze to Simon and regarded him for one long, eloquent moment. She sprang to her feet and went straight to him, sliding her arms around his waist.

Then she returned her attention to Clarissa. "I need no time to consider, my lady. I assure you, I do *not* wish to be Queen of England."

A vast relief poured through Clarissa. She wanted justice to be done for Annabelle's sake. Yet she would have been loath to see such a fine woman become drawn into the spider's web of court intrigues.

Simon tilted up her chin. "Annabelle, are you sure? Think of what you're giving up. You would be rich beyond compare, monarch over millions of subjects. Even I would have to bow to you."

"No, *no,* a thousand times no! My only wish is to be your wife."

Chuckling, he wrapped her in his arms and pressed a kiss to her brow. "Giving up the throne to marry me, are you? Now there's the proof of true love."

They shared a smile of mutual adoration. Watching them, Clarissa felt misty-eyed. How well she had assessed them both as perfect for one another. Until this moment, she'd had no inkling that matchmaking could be so satisfying to the soul.

She set aside her brandy glass and rose from the chair. Despite the lateness of the hour, she now felt refreshed and content. Her purpose here was happily complete.

"What *is* this—" All of a sudden, Annabelle reached

inside Simon's coat and brought out a sparkly garnet slipper. "Oh! It's my missing shoe!"

"I picked it up in the nursery," Simon said with a slight frown. "It seemed important that I take it with me."

Clarissa smiled, for she understood his compulsion even if he did not. The shoes had been a gift to her a very long time ago from a wise old woman. "Do you have its match?" she asked.

"I slipped it off under the tea table." Annabelle went to fetch the shoe. Upon returning, she looked down at the pair in her hands and then at Clarissa. "These were to be a loan, my lady, remember? Perhaps it's time to return them to you."

"A most excellent notion," Clarissa said as she gave Annabelle a warm hug in exchange for the shoes. "Heaven willing, I shall find another deserving young lady who needs them."

As she left the study, Clarissa took one last satisfied look at the couple embracing by the fireplace. Yes, indeed, she had done well.

Epilogue

June 28, 1838

At the coronation ceremony for young Queen Victoria in Westminster Abbey, Annabelle sat in the gallery beside her husband. Ahead of them were rows of noblemen in ermine-collared robes, the ladies in elaborate court dress. Nicholas, the Duke of Kevern, stood at attention near the throne. The boy was so proud to be chosen to serve as a page.

Seated on the dais, the Queen accepted the golden orb from the Archbishop of Canterbury and then the two scepters, each presented with great pomp and circumstance. Annabelle could not take her eyes from Victoria. Her half sister. How incredible it still seemed.

There had been one brief meeting in secret the previous year, when Annabelle had signed a legal document renouncing all claim to the throne. Victoria had been cool and reserved. Yet as Annabelle had made a deep curtsy at her departure, Victoria's gaze had settled on the gentle rounding of Annabelle's belly. *When is your child due?* she had asked. They had chatted amiably for a few minutes, and, much to Annabelle's surprise, Victoria had stepped forward to give her a kiss on the cheek. There had been no communication since, but Annabelle hadn't expected any. They were strangers, after all, linked only by their royal blood.

Annabelle had her own family now.

She reached surreptitiously for Simon's hand. As his strong fingers closed around hers, he gave her a smile so full of love that her heart overflowed. No crown could ever be as glorious as the past year and a half had been. They had left nine-month-old Pippa in the nursery at Kevern House, the duke's London mansion. Simon did not yet know that their lively, precious daughter would soon be joined by a brother or sister. Tonight, Annabelle would tell him that wonderful secret.

On the dais, the great moment had arrived.

The Archbishop picked up the golden crown of Saint Edward and placed it on Victoria's dark hair. There was a moment of hushed silence as the Queen looked over the vast gathering of her subjects. Her head held high, she let her gaze make a slow sweep of the congregation.

Was it Annabelle's imagination, or did the Queen's eyes linger on her for just a moment?

Simon squeezed her hand. She looked at him, and from the glimmer in his warm gray eyes, she knew he'd noticed Victoria's glance, too.

Then everyone rose to their feet, Simon and Annabelle along with them. A great cry roared out in unison, "God save the Queen!"

In the festive aftermath, as the cheering died down, Simon leaned close to murmur in her ear, "No regrets, Cinderella?"

She gave him a serene smile. "None. You, my darling, are a far finer prize than any crown."

Don't miss Olivia Drake's spectacular
Heiress in London series

SCANDAL OF THE YEAR
NEVER TRUST A ROGUE
SEDUCING THE HEIRESS

And look for the next Cinderella Sisterhood novel

WHEN THE CLOCK STRIKES TWELVE
Coming soon from St. Martin's Paperbacks!